"She looks awfully stupid," said Sam. "Do you think she had her brain damaged in the Mind Wars?"

"Her brain's all right," Jonathan said confidently. "She's just acting stupid so we'll think we've made a mistake." He leaned over Vivian again. "This patch of time and space here is almost worn out. Time City is going to crumble away unless you tell us how to find Faber John so that he can renew the city. That isn't too much to ask, is it, V.S.?"

"I don't *know!*" Vivian screamed at him. "I don't know who you think I am, but I'm not *her!* I don't know you and you don't know me! I was being evacuated from London because of the War, and you can just take me back! You're a kidnapper!" Tears came streaming down her face. She scrabbled to get her handkerchief out of her bag. "And so are you!" she added to Sam.

Sam leaned forward and breathily inspected her face. "She's crying. She means it. You've got the wrong one by mistake."

Other Bullseye Books you will enjoy

Lucy Forever and Miss Rosetree, Shrinks by Susan Shreve
The Phantom Tollbooth by Norton Juster
Scruffy by Jack Stoneley
There's a Boy in the Girls' Bathroom by Louis Sachar
Witch Week by Diana Wynne Jones

A TALE OF
TIME CITY

DIANA WYNNE JONES

BULLSEYE BOOKS · ALFRED A. KNOPF
New York

DR. M. JERRY WEISS, Distinguished Service Professor of Communications at Jersey City State College, is the educational consultant for Bullseye Books. Currently chair of the International Reading Association President's Advisory Committee on Intellectual Freedom, he travels frequently to give workshops on the use of trade books in schools.

A BULLSEYE BOOK PUBLISHED BY ALFRED A. KNOPF, INC.
Copyright © 1987 by Diana Wynne Jones
Cover illustration copyright © 1989 by Richard Bober

Library of Congress Catalog Card Number: 86-33304
ISBN: 0-394-82030-4
RL: 5.6

Manufactured in the United States of America   0 1 2 3 4 5 6 7 8 9

T he train journey was horrible. There was a heat wave that September in 1939, and the railway authorities had fastened all the windows shut so that none of the children packed onto the train could fall out. There were several hundred of them, and nearly all of them screamed when they saw a cow. They were all being sent away from London from the bombing, and most of them had no idea where milk came from. Each child carried a square brown gas mask box. All of them had labels with their names and addresses on them, and the littlest ones (who cried and wet themselves rather often) had the labels tied around their necks with string.

Vivian, being one of the bigger ones, had her label tied to the string bag Mum had found to take the things that refused to fit into her suitcase. That meant that Vivian did not dare let go of the string bag. When your surname is Smith, you need to make very sure everyone knows just which Smith you are. Vivian had carefully written Cousin Marty's name and address on the back of the label, to show that she was not just being sent into the country, like most of the children, to be taken in by anyone who would have her. Cousin Marty, after a long delay, had promised to meet the train and have Vivian to stay with her until the danger of bombs was over. But Vivian had never met Cousin Marty, and she was terrified that they would somehow miss each other. So she hung on to the string bag until its handles were wet with sweat and the plaited pattern was stamped in red on her hands.

Half of the children never stayed still for a moment. Sometimes the carriage where Vivian sat filled with small boys in gray shorts, whose skinny legs were in thick gray socks and whose heads, each in a gray school cap, seemed too big for their bare, skinny necks. Sometimes a mob of little girls in dresses too long for them crowded in from the corridor. All of them screamed. There were always about three labels saying "Smith" on each fresh crowd. Vivian sat where she was and worried that Cousin Marty would meet the wrong Smith, or meet the wrong train, or that she herself would mistake someone else for Cousin Marty, or get adopted by someone who thought she had nowhere to go. She was afraid she would get out at the wrong station or find out that the train had taken her to Scotland instead of the West of England. Or she would get out, but Cousin Marty would not be there.

Mum had packed some sandwiches in the string bag, but none of the other evacuees seemed to have any food. Vivian did not quite like to eat when she was the only one, and there were too many children for her to share with. Nor did she dare take off her school coat and hat for fear they got lost. The floor of the train was soon littered with lost coats and caps—and some labels—and there was even a lost squashed gas mask. So Vivian sat and sweltered and worried. By the time the train chuffed its crowded hot fighting screaming crying laughing way into a station at last, it was early evening, and Vivian had thought of every single thing that could possibly go wrong except the one that actually did.

The name of the station was painted out to confuse the enemy, but porters undid the doors, letting in gusts of cool air and shouting in deep country voices, "All get out here! The train stops here!"

The screaming stopped. All the children were stunned to find they had arrived in a real new place. Hesitantly at first, then crowding one another's heels, they scrambled down.

Vivian was among the last to get off. Her suitcase stuck in the netting of the luggage rack, and she had to climb on the seat to get it down. With her gas mask giving her square, jumbling bangs and her hands full of suitcase and string bag, she went down onto the platform with a flump, shivering in the cool air. It was all strange. She could see yellow fields beyond the station buildings. The wind smelled of cow dung and chaff.

There was a long, muddled crowd of adults up at the other end of the platform. The porters and some people with official arm-bands were trying to line the children up in front of them and get them shared out to foster homes. Vivian heard shouts of "Mrs. Miller, you can take two. One for you, Mr. Parker. Oh, you're brother and sister, are you? Mr. Parker, can you take two?"

I'd better not get mixed up in that, Vivian thought. That was one worry she could avoid. She hung back in the middle of the platform, hoping Cousin Marty would realize. But none of the waiting crowd looked at her. "I'm not having all the dirty ones!" someone was saying, and this seemed to be taking everyone's attention. "Give me two clean and I'll take two dirty to make four. Otherwise I'm leaving."

Vivian began to suspect that her worry about Cousin Marty's not being there was going to be the right one. She pressed her lips against her teeth in order not to cry—or not to cry *yet*.

A hand reached around Vivian and spread out the label on the string bag. *"Ah!"* said someone. "Vivian Smith!"

Vivian whirled around. She found herself facing a lordly-look-ing dark boy in glasses. He was taller than she was and old enough to wear long trousers, which meant he must be at least a year older than she was. He smiled at her, which made his eyes under his glasses fold in a funny way along the eyelids. "Vivian Smith," he said, "you may not realize this, but I am your long-lost cousin."

Well, Vivian thought, I suppose Marty *is* a boy's name. "Are you sure?" she said. "Cousin Marty?"

"No, my name's Jonathan Walker," said the boy. "Jonathan *Lee* Walker."

The way he put in that "Lee" made it clear he was very proud of it for some reason. But Vivian knew there was something peculiar about this boy, something not as it should be that she could not pin down, and she was far too worried to wonder about his name. "It's a mistake!" she said frantically. "I was supposed to meet Cousin Marty!"

"Cousin Marty's waiting outside," Jonathan Lee Walker said soothingly. "Let me take your bag." He put out his hand. Vivian snatched the string bag out of his way, and he picked up her suitcase from the platform instead and marched away with it across the station.

Vivian hurried after him, with her gas mask banging at her back, to rescue her suitcase. He strode straight to the waiting room and opened the door. "Where are you going?" Vivian panted.

"Shortcut, my dear V.S.," he said, holding the door open with a soothing smile.

"Give me my suitcase!" Vivian said, grabbing for it. Now she was sure he was a robber. But as soon as she was through the door, Jonathan Lee Walker went galloping noisily across the bare boards of the little room toward the blank back wall.

"Bring us back, Sam!" he shouted, so that the room rang. Vivian decided he was mad and grabbed for her suitcase again. And suddenly everything turned silvery.

"Where is this?" Vivian said. They were crowding each other in a narrow silvery space like a very smooth telephone booth. Vivian turned desperately to get out again and knocked a piece of what seemed to be the telephone off the wall. Jonathan whirled around like lightning and slammed the piece back. Vivian felt her gas mask dig into him and hoped it hurt. There was nothing but a bare silvery wall behind her.

In front of Jonathan the smooth silvery surface slid away sideways. A small boy with longish, nearly red hair looked anxiously in at them. When he saw Vivian, his face relaxed into a fierce grin with two large teeth in it. "You got her!" he said, and he took what may have been an earphone out of his left ear. It was not much bigger than a pea, but it had a silvery wire connecting it to the side of the silver booth, so Vivian supposed it *was* an earphone. "This works," he said, coiling the wire into one rather plump hand. "I heard you easily."

"And I got her, Sam!" Jonathan answered jubilantly, stepping out of the silver booth. "I recognized her and I got her, right from under their noses!"

"Great!" said the small boy. He said to Vivian, "And now we're going to torture you until you tell us what we want to know!"

Vivian stood in the booth, clutching her string bag, staring at him with a mixture of dislike and amazement. Sam was the sort of small boy Mum called "rough"—the kind with a loud voice and heavy shoes whose shoelaces were always undone. Her eyes went to his shoes—such shoes!—puffy white footgear with red dots. Sure enough, one of the red and white ties of those shoes was trailing on the marble floor. Above that Sam seemed to be wearing pajamas. That was the only way Vivian could describe his baggy allover suit with its one red stripe from his right shoulder to his left ankle. The red clashed with his hair, to Vivian's mind, and she had never seen a boy so much in need of a haircut.

"I told you, Sam," Jonathan said, dumping Vivian's suitcase on a low table Vivian could dimly see behind Sam, "that it's no good thinking of torture. She probably knows enough to torture us instead. We're going to try gentle persuasion. Do please come out of the booth, V.S., and take a seat while I get out of this disguise."

Vivian took another look at the blank shiny back wall of the booth. Since there seemed no way out that way, she went forward. Sam backed away from her, looking just a mite scared, and that made her feel better, until the door of the booth slid shut behind her with a quiet hushing sound and cut out most of the light in the room beyond. It seemed to be night out there, which was probably what had given her the idea that Sam was running around in pajamas. What dim light there was came from some kind of streetlight shining through a peculiar-shaped window, but there was enough of it for Vivian to see she was in some kind of ultramodern office. There was a vast half circle of desk at the far end, surrounded by things that reminded Vivian of a telephone exchange. But the odd thing was that the desk, instead of being of steel or chromium, as she would have expected a modern desk to be, was made of beautifully carved wood that looked very old and gave off silky reflections in the low bluish light. Vivian looked at it doubtfully as she sat in an odd-shaped chair near the booth. And she nearly leaped straight up again when the chair moved around her, settling into the same shape that she was.

But Jonathan started tearing off his clothes then, right in front of her. Vivian sat stiffly in the form-fitting chair, wondering if she was mad, or if Jonathan was, or if she ought to look away, or what. He flung off his gray flannel jacket first. Then he undid his striped tie and threw that down. Then—Vivian's face turned half away sideways—he climbed out of his long gray flannel trousers. But it was all right. Underneath, Jonathan was wearing the same kind of suit as Sam, except that his had dark-colored diamonds down the legs and sleeves.

"Great Time!" he said as he dropped the trousers on top of the jacket. "These clothes are vile! They prickle me even through my suit. How do Twenty Century people bear it? Or these?" He plucked his glasses off his nose and pressed a knob on the belt that went around his suit. A flicker sprang into being across his eyes, shifting queerly in the blue light. The fold in his eyelids was much plainer to see like that. Vivian saw that Sam had the same fold. "A sight function is so much simpler," Jonathan said. He pulled the striped school cap off his head and let about a foot of plaited hair tumble out of it across his shoulder. "That's better!" he said as he hurled the cap down too, and rubbed his neck under the pigtail to loosen the tight hair there.

Vivian stared. Never had she seen a boy with such long hair!

In fact, she had a vague notion that boys were born with their hair short back and sides and that only girls had hair that grew long. But Jonathan had twice as much hair as she had. Perhaps he was Chinese and she had been spirited away to the Orient. But Sam was not Chinese. Whoever heard of a red-haired Chinaman?

"Who are you?" she said. "Where *is* this?"

Jonathan turned to her, looking very lordly and solemn—and not particularly Chinese. "We are Jonathan Lee Walker and Samuel Lee Donegal," he said. "We're both Lees. My father is the thousandth Sempitern. The Sempitern is the head of Time Council in Chronologue, in case you didn't have those in your day. And Sam's father is chief of Time Patrol. We feel this qualifies us to talk to you. Welcome back. You have just come through Sam's father's private time lock, and you are now once more in Time City."

A mistake has happened, Vivian thought miserably. And it seemed to be a mistake ten thousand times wilder than any of the mistakes she had imagined on the train. She pressed her lips together. I will *not* cry! she told herself. "I don't understand a word you're saying. What do you mean, Welcome back? Where *is* Time City?"

"Come, come now, V.S." Jonathan leaned one hand on the back of the peculiar chair, in the way Inquisitors did in the kinds of film Mum preferred Vivian not to see. "Time City is unique. It is built on a small patch of time and space that exists outside time and history. You know all about Time City, V.S."

"No, I don't," said Vivian.

"Yes, you do. Your husband built the city," Jonathan said, with his flicker-covered folded eyes staring eerily into Vivian's. "We want you to tell us how to wake Faber John, V.S. Or if he isn't sleeping under the city, tell us how to find him."

"I haven't *got* a husband!" Vivian said. "Oh, this is *mad*!"

Sam, who was breathing noisily and rustily on the other side of Vivian, said, "She looks awfully stupid. Do you think she had her brain damaged in the Mind Wars?"

Vivian sighed and looked rather desperately around the strange dark office. Was it really outside time? Or were they both mad? Both of them seemed to have it fixed in their heads that she was some other Vivian Smith. So how was she going to convince them that she was not?

"Her brain's all right," Jonathan said confidently. "She's just acting stupid so we'll think we've made a mistake." He leaned over Vivian again. "See here, V.S.," he said persuasively. "We're not asking for ourselves. It's for Time City. This patch of time and space here is almost worn out. The city is going to crumble away unless you tell us how to find Faber John so that he can renew the city. Or if you hate him too much, you could tell us where the polarities are and how to renew those. That isn't too much to ask, is it, V.S.?"

"Don't keep calling me Vee-Ess!" Vivian almost shrieked. "I'm not—"

"Yes, you are, V.S.," said Jonathan. "You were spotted coming up the First Unstable Era in a wave of chronons. We heard Chronologue discussing it. We *know* you are. So how do we wake Faber John, V.S.?"

"I don't *know*!" Vivian screamed at him. "I don't know who you think I am, but I'm not *her*! I don't know you and you don't know me! I was being evacuated from London to stay with Cousin Marty because of the War, and you can just take me back! You're a kidnapper!" Tears came streaming down her face. She scrabbled to get her handkerchief out of the string bag. "And so are you!" she added to Sam.

Sam leaned forward and breathily inspected her face. "She's crying. She means it. You got the wrong one by mistake."

"Of course I didn't!" Jonathan said scornfully. But when Vivian found her handkerchief and looked at him with her face mostly hidden in it, she could tell he was beginning to have doubts.

Vivian did her best to strengthen those doubts. "I've never

ever heard of Faber John, or Time City either," she said, trying
to stop herself from sobbing. "And you can *see* I'm too young
to have a husband. I won't be twelve until just after Christmas.
We're not in the Middle Ages, you know."

Sam nodded knowingly. "She is. She's just an ordinary Twenty
Century native," he pronounced.

"But I recognized her!" Jonathan said. He wandered uneasily
across the office. A sort of darkening to his flickering face told
Vivian that he was beginning to suspect that he had been a fool—
and he was the sort of boy who would do anything not to look a
fool. Vivian knew he would take her straight back to the station
and try to forget about her if she could convince him properly.

So she sniffed away what she hoped were the last of her tears
and said, "I know it says Vivian Smith on my label, but Smith's
a very common name. And Vivian's quite common, too. Look at
Vivien Leigh."

This misfired a little. Jonathan turned and stared at her. "How
do you know her?" he said suspiciously.

"I don't. I mean, she's a film star," Vivian explained.

She could see this meant nothing to Jonathan. He shrugged.
"We could go through her luggage," he suggested to Sam. "That
might prove something."

Vivian would have liked to go and sit on her suitcase and clutch
the string bag to her and refuse indignantly, but she said with
desperate bravery, "Do what you like. Only you're to take me
back to the station if you don't find anything."

"I might," said Jonathan. Vivian was fairly sure that meant
that he would. She tried not to mind too much when Jonathan
dragged the suitcase over into a beam of light from the odd-shaped
window, where he began briskly unpacking it. Sam attended to
the string bag. Vivian spread it out on her knee for him, because
that took her mind off Jonathan going into all her new winter
underwear, and wished Sam would not breathe so heavily. The
first thing Sam found was her sandwiches.

"Can I eat these?" he said.

"No," said Vivian. "I'm hungry."

"I'll give you half," Sam said, plainly thinking he was being generous.

Jonathan stood up, holding Vivian's new liberty bodice with suspenders attached to hold up her winter stockings. "Whatever do you use this for?" he asked, really puzzled by it.

Vivian's face went fiery hot. "Put that down!" she said.

"Corsets," Sam suggested with his mouth full.

There was a sort of buzzing from outside somewhere. Light came on and swifly grew bright from all the corners of the room. It showed Jonathan standing frozen by the window with the liberty bodice in one hand and Vivian's best jumper in the other. Vivian saw that the flicker over his eyes hardly showed in bright light and that the diamonds on his suit were dark purple. Sam was frozen too, with a third sandwich in his hand.

"Someone's coming!" Jonathan whispered. "They must have heard her yelling."

"They make regular rounds," Sam whispered back hoarsely.

"Then why didn't you *tell* me? Quick!" Jonathan whispered. He bundled everything back into the suitcase and shoved the lid down. Sam seized the string bag and a handful of Vivian's skirt with it and dragged. It was clear to Vivian that something frightening was about to happen. She let Sam tow her across the marble floor and around behind the huge carved desk.

"Hide!" he said. "Come *on!*"

There was a deep hollow inside the half circle of desk, so that a person's knees could swivel this way and that to reach the banks of switches. Sam pushed Vivian into it and dived in after her. Before Vivian had a chance even to sit up properly, Jonathan came scrambling into the space too, dragging the suitcase behind him. Vivian ended up half lying on her side with a clear view through the space at the bottom of the desk. She could see her last sandwich in its paper lying in the middle of the marble floor and the heap of Jonathan's gray flannel suit beside it.

Jonathan saw them too. *"Damn!"* he whispered, and he was off after them and back again while Vivian was still being shocked to hear him swear. "Don't make a sound!" he said to her breathlessly. "If they find us, they might even shoot you!"

Vivian looked from his face to Sam's, not sure if she believed this. They both had that tense look people have in films when gangsters are looking for them with guns. This made everything completely unreal to Vivian, like a film. She reached out and took her last sandwich from Jonathan before Sam's stretching hand quite got to it. She bit into it. It made her feel better to chew bread she had watched Mum butter and sardines she had helped Mum mash. It told her that real life was still there somewhere.

She was still eating when a door rumbled and the light grew stronger. Two sets of heavy, clacking boots marched into view across the gray-veined white floor. Vivian watched them under the desk, clumping hither and thither, as the people wearing them checked the room. Beside her, she could feel Jonathan beginning to shake and Sam puffing little tiny snorts in an effort to breathe quietly, but she could not believe in any of it, and she went on calmly eating her sandwich.

"Seems all right in here," the owner of one pair of boots said in a rumbling murmur.

"Funny, though," murmured the other. This one sounded like a woman. "I can smell fish—sardines. Can you smell sardines?"

Vivian stuffed the rest of the sandwich into her mouth and held both hands across it in order not to giggle. Jonathan's face was white, and the lordly look had somehow crumpled away from it entirely. Vivian saw that he had gone from being the inquisitor to being a scared boy in bad trouble. Sam was holding his breath. His face was going a steadily darker red, and his eyes were rolling at Vivian and the sandwich, quite horrified. She could tell they were both very frightened indeed, but she still wanted to laugh.

"No," said the rumbling man's voice. "Don't smell a thing."

"Then I'll blame you," said the woman, "if the chief gets attacked by a mad sardine tomorrow." They both laughed. Then the woman said, "Come on," and the boots clacked away.

The door rumbled. After a while the lights dimmed. As soon as they did, Sam let out his breath in a near roar and threw himself on his face, gasping. "I'm dying!" he panted.

"No, you're not," Jonathan said. His voice had gone shrill and quavering. "Shut up and sit up. We've got to think what to *do*!"

Vivian knew Jonathan's nerve had broken. It was time for her to be firm. "I'll tell you what to do," she said. "Open that silver booth again and put me in it and send me back to the station to meet Cousin Marty."

"No, we absolutely won't," Jonathan said. "We can't. If we use it again, that will make three times and the computer will register it. It always checks the odd numbers anyway, in case an agent goes out and gets lost. And they'll find out we've broken the law. They'll be on to us at once. We're right in the middle of Time Patrol Building here. Don't you understand?"

COUSIN VIVIAN 2

"No, I *don't* understand!" said Vivian. She could see well enough that the clacking boots had jolted both boys back to a sense of whatever passed for real life in this place. She thought, They were having an adventure up till then. Now it's not fun anymore. She was angry. "What's this law you've broken? What about *me*?"

"Twenty Century's part of an Unstable Era," Jonathan said. "It's against the law even to take a *thing* out of an Unstable Era, and taking a person out is much worse. Putting people back *in* after they've seen Time City is the worst crime you can commit."

"They'll send us out into history for it," Sam said in a shocked whisper, and shivered. Jonathan, Vivian noticed, shivered much harder. "What will they do to *her*?"

"Something even worse," Jonathan said, and his teeth chattered slightly.

"Well, you might have *thought*!" Vivian said. "What am I going to do now?"

Jonathan got to his knees. "I thought I did think!" he groaned as he crawled out from under the desk. He turned to face Vivian. His face looked pinched and frightened in the murky blue light. "I was quite sure you were— Look, can you give me your word of honor on the god Mao or Kennedy or Koran, or whatever you worship, that you really are just a plain person from Twenty Century and nothing to do with Faber John?"

"I give you my Bible oath," said Vivian. "But you ought to know when a person's real and telling the truth without it."

Jonathan, to her surprise, took this rather well. "I do know,"

he said. "I began to see something had gone wrong by the look
on your face when you saw my pigtail, but I still don't *understand* it! Let's get out of here and think what to do."

Crouching in the space behind the desk, they repacked Vivian's suitcase and tried to cram Jonathan's gray flannel clothes
into it too. Only the trousers went in. They had to stuff the jacket
into the string bag and the cap and tie into Vivian's gas mask
case. Sam took that. Jonathan carried the suitcase, and Vivian
hung on to the string bag. She felt that if she let go of it for an
instant, she might stop being Vivian Smith and turn into someone
else completely.

At the door of the office Sam produced a rattling bunch of—
not keys. They were little squares that might have been made of
plastic. He fitted one into a slot beside the door. "Pinched them
from my father," he explained in a loud, proud whisper. The
door slid aside, and then slid shut behind them when they were
through, just as if it had known. They stole along a number of
high corridors, where lights flicked on and off in the distance and
around corners as the two guards went on their rounds. Unnerving though this was, it gave Vivian enough light to see that the
building was all made of marble, with the same ultramodern look
as the office, except that there were carvings and sculptures up
where the walls met the ceiling, which did not look modern at
all. Vivian glimpsed angel faces in the dimness, winged lions,
and people who seemed to be half horses. It was like a dream.

I dreamt that I dwelt in marble halls! Vivian thought. Perhaps
I've fallen asleep on the train, and this is all a dream I'm having.
Though this was a comforting thought, she doubted it. *Nobody*
could have slept on that noisy train.

They tiptoed down a narrow marble stair that led to what was
obviously a grand entrance hall. This was much better lit. Vivian
could see big glass doors in the distance and a curving row of
silver booths like the one she had come through. There must have
been a hundred of them—with another hundred of them curving

around the opposite wall, although her view of those was partly blocked by a gigantic marble stairway. This was a true marvel. The stone steps were moving. The three of them had to hide under it while a lady guard walked slowly across the open space with her hand on some sort of gun at her belt, and Vivian could hear the moving steps softly rumbling above them. She wondered how on earth it worked.

The guard walked out of sight behind a large circular installation in the center of the hall. Jonathan and Sam led Vivian on a dash the other way, into the back of the building, where there were more corridors and, at last, a small back door. Sam stopped and fitted another card into a slot, and that door opened to let them out.

They went suddenly from ultramodern to very old. Outside, they were in a narrow lane of crooked little stone houses. There was a round blue light fixed to one of the houses in the distance which showed that the lane was cobbled, with a gutter down the middle. The air was fresh and cool. It made Vivian feel rather heady and giddy.

Sam and Jonathan plunged down toward the dark end of the lane. The cobbles dug into the underside of Vivian's feet as she trotted after them. There was a thick old archway there, black as night underneath, and after that they came into a blue-lit courtyard, where they went scuttling toward a building like a church.

"No, it's always left unlocked," Jonathan whispered to Sam as he bounded up the steps to the church place, with his pigtail flying. "And I left both doors to the Annuate unfastened just in case." Sure enough, the mighty door clicked and swung smoothly to let them in.

Quite a small church! Vivian thought in surprise. But it doesn't *smell* like a church!

It smelled warmer and more dusty than a church. It was harder to see than any place she had been in so far, because the blue streetlighting came in through high-up colored windows. Bars of misty blue-green light showed up leather-covered seats not quite like pews, and a splotch of dark violet light rested on a throne thing at one end with some kind of glittering canopy above it. A slant of orange-blue on a wall gave Vivian a glimpse of one of the most beautiful paintings she had ever seen.

"That's Faber John's Seat," Jonathan whispered, pointing to the throne as he led the way down an aisle. "This is the Chronologue, where the Time Council meets."

"We unlocked a door and listened to them," Sam said.

"That's how we heard about the crisis and the plans to intercept you—I mean, the real V.S.," Jonathan explained.

They moved to the right, and Vivian found herself facing a shining thing, misted with more violet light, that seemed to crown the end of a row of seats. It was like a winged sun, and it seemed to be studded with jewels.

"The Sempiternal Ensign," Jonathan whispered. "Solid gold. That's the Koh-i-noor diamond in the left wing, and the Star of Africa's in the right." He gave the thing a fond pat as they passed it.

This was too much for Vivian. I *must* be dreaming! she decided. I *know* both those diamonds are somewhere else.

"Given to Time City by the Icelandic Emperor in Seventy-two Century," Jonathan added as he undid a small heavy door. But Vivian felt too dreamlike to attend. She went dreamily down a long dark passage, through a door that creaked horribly, and out into a place like a huge mansion, where they hurried up what seemed endless dark wooden stairs. This dream keeps getting things wrong! Vivian thought as her legs began to ache. There ought to be an elevator or an escalator at least! She did not start thinking properly until she found herself sitting in another peculiar chair in a large room where all the furniture seemed to be empty frames, like a junglegym on a playground. Jonathan put a light on and leaned against the door. "Phew!" he said. "Safe so far. Now we have to think hard."

"I can't think," said Sam. "I'm hungry. She is too. She told me."

"My automat's on the blink again," Jonathan said. "What do you want if I can get it to work?"

"Forty-two Century butter-pie," Sam said, as if it was obvious.

Jonathan went to a thing on the wall facing Vivian that Vivian supposed must be a musical instrument. It had keys like a piano and pipes like a church organ, and it was decorated all over with gilt twiddles and garlands, which were a little worn and peeling, as if the instrument had seen better days. Jonathan pounded at the white keys. When nothing happened, he banged at the organ pipes. The thing began to chuff and grunt and to shake a little, at which Jonathan kicked it fiercely lower down. Finally, he took up what seemed to be an ordinary school ruler and pried at a long flap under the pipes.

"Well, it's done the butter-pies," he said, peering inside. "But the Twenty Century function seems to have broken. There's no pizza and no bubble gum. Do you mind food from other centuries?" he asked Vivian rather anxiously.

Vivian had never heard of pizza, though she thought it sounded Italian and not like the English food she was used to at all. She was past being surprised at anything by this time. "I could eat a *dinosaur!*" she said frankly.

"You almost have to," Jonathan said, carrying an armful of little white flowerpots over to the empty frame beside Vivian's chair. He dumped them into the air above it, and they stayed there, standing on nothing. "Butter-pie," Jonathan said, handing a pot with a stick poking out of it to Sam. "Otherwise it's done you algae soup, malty soy, two carob cornpones, and fish noodles."

Sam pulled the stick out of his pot with a yellow nubbly ice cream on the end of it. *"Yummy!"* he cried, and bit into it like an ogre.

"Er—which is which?" Vivian asked, looking at the strange marks on the other pots. "I can't read these words."

"Sorry," Jonathan said. "Those are universal symbols from Thirty-nine Century." He sorted out the pots for her and took a butter-pie for himself. The pots, Vivian found, were sort of stuck to the air. She had to give a little pull to get them loose. She discovered that you peeled back the lid, and if you needed a spoon or a fork, the lid shriveled itself into a spoon or fork shape. Algae soup was not at all pleasant, like salty pond water. But malty soy was nice if you dipped the cornpone in it. The fish noodles were—

"I'd rather eat Dad's fishing bait," Vivian said, putting that pot quickly down.

"I'll get you a butter-pie," Jonathan said.

"And another one for me," Sam put in.

The church organ received another banging, two more kicks, and a punch in the delivery flap, and Vivian and Sam received a pot with a stick each. Jonathan threw the empty pots into a frame beside the organ, where they vanished. "Now we *must* talk," he said, while Vivian dubiously lifted the nubbly lump out of its pot. "We've all broken the law, and we daren't be caught. It would have been all right if V.S. was really V.S., but she isn't, so we've got to think how to hide her."

Vivian was getting very tired of being called V.S. She would have objected if she had not at that moment bitten into the butter-pie. Wonderful tastes filled her mouth, everything buttery and creamy she had ever tasted, with just a hint of toffee, and twenty other even better tastes she had never met before, all of it icy cold. It was so marvelous that she simply said quietly, "You owe me an explanation. What were you trying to do?"

"Save Time City, of course," Sam said juicily out of the middle of his butter-pie. "We listened to the Chronologue. That's how we knew where you'd be."

"There's a passage between the Chronologue and here,"

Jonathan explained. "But it's been chained up ever since my father was elected Sempitern and I got curious about it. So Sam shorted it out for me and—anyway, we found it led to the Chronologue, and if we opened the door a crack, we could hear what they were all talking about. They were debating the crisis—"

"Only I couldn't understand a word," Sam said, as if this were rather clever of him. "It wasn't like the stories."

"It wasn't!" Jonathan said feelingly. "It was all about polarities and chronons and critical cycles, but I understood the part about Time City being nearly worn out. It's used one bit of space and time too often, you see, and they were trying to find a way to move it to another bit. The city's held in place by things called polarities, which are put out into history like anchors, but no one except Faber John ever understood how it was done. I heard Dr. Leonov admit that. So that was where V.S. comes in."

"Who *is* she?" said Vivian.

"The Time Lady," said Sam. "She's on the rampage."

"Yes, but we had to work that out," said Jonathan, "by putting the talk in the Chronologue together with what the stories say. Chronologue was being very scientific, talking about someone coming up through the First Unstable Era in a wave of temporons and chronons, causing wars and changes everywhere. But I guessed it had to be the Time Lady. The story says that Faber John and his wife quarreled about the way to rule Time City, and she tricked him into going down under the city and falling asleep there. They say he's still there, and as long as he sleeps, the city is safe. But if it's in danger, he'll wake up and come to our rescue. We're going by the stories. We know you—the Time Lady hates Faber John and the city because he saw how she'd tricked him at the last minute and threw her out into history. We think she's trying to get back and destroy the city now that it's nearly worn out."

"That's the bit I didn't understand," Sam said. He was cross-legged on the floor, licking the stick of his butter-pie.

"It *is* a bit puzzling," Jonathan said. Vivian could see he was very pleased with himself for working it out. "Chronologue seemed to be so sure that the Time Lady would be quite reasonable when they found her and explained about the crisis. I think the quarrel she had with Faber John must have been political in some way."

He looked questioningly at Vivian. Vivian caught the flicker of his flickering eyes and began to wonder if Jonathan really did believe she was just a normal person from the Twentieth Century after all. But at the moment she bit through into the middle of the butter-pie. And it was hot. Runny, syrupy hot.

"It's *goluptuous* when you get to the warm part, isn't it?" Sam said, watching her with keen attention. "You want to let it trickle into the cold."

Vivian did so and found Sam's advice was excellent. The two parts mixed were even better than the cold part alone. It sent her rather dreamy again. When Sam grinned at her, a wide, cheeky grin with two big teeth in the middle of it, she found herself thinking that Sam was not so bad after all. But she did her best to keep to the subject.

"I still don't understand what made you think the Time Lady was *me*," she said.

Jonathan started to say something. Then he changed his mind and said something else. "Because of the name, you see. Faber John's wife was called Vivian. Everyone knows that. And Faber really means Smith. So when I heard Chronologue say that you— she was on that evacuee train, I worked out that she must be posing as a girl called Vivian Smith."

"And we said V.S. when we talked about her so that nobody would guess our plan," Sam put in. "We started planning two days ago after they met the train and couldn't find her."

"Two days ago!" Vivian exclaimed. "But I was there *today*, and so were you!"

"Yes, but you can get to any time you want through a time lock," Jonathan said, waving that puzzle away in his most lordly

manner. "My father went there, and Sam's father, and so did the
Head Librarian and the High Scientist, but they all came back
saying she'd slipped through them somehow. That was when I
thought we had a chance of getting you—her—ourselves. Only
you're the wrong Vivian Smith for some reason—and I *still* can't
understand it! Sam, we've got to think what to do with her."

"Send her to the Stone Age," said Sam. "You wouldn't mind
that, would you?" he asked Vivian.

"Mind? I'd go crazy!" said Vivian. "There are spiders in caves.
Why can't you send me home?"

"I told you why we can't," Jonathan said. "Besides, it's an
Unstable Era and it's even more unsettled than usual at the moment. Suppose we put you back and that mucked up the whole
of history. They'd find out at once! Think of something, Sam!"

There was a long silence. Sam sat on the floor with his face in
his fists. Jonathan leaned against the wall, chewing the end of his
pigtail. Vivian licked the last of her butter-pie off its stick and,
for a while, could think of very little else except that she wished
she could have another one. But I *will* get home! she told herself,
sleepily twiddling the stick in her fingers. I *will*, whatever he
says!

"I know!" Sam said at last. "Pretend she's our cousin!"

Jonathan leaped away from the wall. "That's *it*!" he shouted.
"That's clever, Sam!"

"I *am* clever," said Sam. "You work out the details."

"And that's easy," said Jonathan. "Listen, V.S., you are Vivian
Sarah Lee. Your father is Sam's uncle and mine. Have you got
that?" He danced around the room, pointing at Vivian until she
nodded. "Good. You've been away from Time City since you
were six because your parents are Observers on station in Twenty
Century. That's all true. Got it? But they've sent you home because the era's getting more unsettled and there's a war on. This
is brilliant!" he said to Sam. "It will explain why she doesn't
know anything. And my mother's bound to ask her to live here

because Lee House is shut up—and we can even go on calling her V.S.!''

Sam rose from the floor and breathed heavily into Vivian's face. "She doesn't look like a Lee," he said critically. "Her eyes are wrong, and her hair curls."

"A lot of Lees don't have the eyefold," Jonathan said. "I don't think Cousin Vivian does. Her cheekbones are the right shape."

"Will you both stop staring and criticizing!" Vivian said. "There's nothing wrong with my face. The lady in the wool shop says I look almost like Shirley Temple."

"Who's he?" said Sam, and Jonathan said, "Who are you, V.S.?"

"What?" said Vivian.

"She's almost asleep," Sam said, leaning even closer to Vivian's face.

He was right. The long and worrying day, followed by the peculiar events of the last hour, were suddenly too much for Vivian. Or maybe it was the butter-pie. There began to be gaps in what she noticed. She heard Jonathan saying airily, "Oh, we can hide her in one of the archaic rooms. She'll be more at home there." At this Vivian noticed that Jonathan seemed to have bounced back from his scare in the ultramodern office and become once more the lordly, confident boy who met her at the station. This made her feel uneasy, but before she could work out why, they were telling her to get up and come along.

She almost forgot the precious string bag. She turned around for it and yelped. She found she had been sitting on nothing in a yellow framework, just like the flowerpots from the church organ. She tried to reach through it for the bag. But the nothing stopped her hand, and she had to grope underneath it before she could take hold of the string handles.

Next thing she noticed, they were going along a corridor. Then Jonathan was sliding a door aside and saying to Sam, "Mind you take those keys back *now*. And don't get caught doing it."

"I know what I'm doing," Sam retorted, and trotted off down the hallway with the trailing tie of his puffy shoe flapping on the carpets.

After that Vivian noticed she was in bed, a rather hard, scratchy bed, with blue streetlight coming in from somewhere. What a lot of Vivians! she thought sleepily. And then: I'll have another butter-pie before I go home tomorrow.

And after that Vivian noticed that it was daytime again and woke up. She turned over under a heavy, scratchy coverlet embroidered with lines of thin brown people and smelling of dust and knew at once where she was. She was in Time City, in the middle of a horrendous mistake. Oddly enough, although this was quite frightening, Vivian found it rather exciting, too. She had always wanted to have an adventure, the way people did in films. And here she was having one. She knew it was no dream. She sat up.

No wonder the bed felt hard. It was made of stone. It had four huge stone pillars like totem poles that held up an embroidered canopy overhead. Beyond, in the room, strong sunlight slanted onto Egyptian sort of carvings on the stone walls. Vivian knew it was quite late in the morning. She got out of the bed onto rush mats, where she was surprised to find that she had put on her nightclothes before she had gone to sleep. Her suitcase was open on the stone floor, and her clothes were scattered all over the room.

I wonder where the toilet is, and I do hope it's not invisible! she thought. A stone archway in the wall led to a tiled place. Vivian went through and found, to her relief, that the toilet and washbasin in there looked much like the ones she was used to, even though they were made of stone. But there were no taps, and she could not find out how the toilet flushed.

But at least I could *see* them, she said to herself as she hunted for her scattered clothes.

She was just putting on her second sock, which had somehow got right under the stone bed, and had only her shoes to find when the stone door grated open and Jonathan came in. He was carrying what looked like half a birdcage with dishes floating in the air beneath it.

"Oh good!" he said. "You were asleep when I looked in earlier. I brought you some breakfast, so you won't have to face my parents on an empty stomach." He was wearing bright green pajamas today and looking very spruce and confident.

Vivian had a feeling that he was going to rush her into something else unless she was careful. "You'll have to tell me a whole lot more," she said. "Or I can't face anyone."

"Well, you can't stay hiding here. Elio's bound to find you," Jonathan said, putting the birdcage down on a stone table. "What's your name?"

"Vivian Smi—" Vivian began, and then remembered that she was Jonathan's cousin. "Vivian Sarah Lee," she said. "You thought I'd forget, didn't you?"

"I wasn't sure," Jonathan said, setting out the dishes from under the birdcage. "Pull up that log over there and start eating. We have to catch my mother before she goes to work."

There was no butter-pie, to Vivian's regret, but there were syrupy pancakes that were almost as good and fruit juice that Vivian thought was even nicer than canned pineapple. Up to then, canned pineapple had been her favorite food. After that were slices of strange crumby bread that you ate with slices of cheese. "Why is everyone called Vivian?" she asked as she ate.

"The eldest Lee is always called Vivian," Jonathan said. "After the Time Lady. Her eldest daughter married the first Lee. We descend from Faber John himself. And we're the oldest family in Time City."

He was sitting on the stone bed looking lofty. Vivian could tell he was very proud of being a Lee. "How old is that?" she said.

"Thousands of years," said Jonathan. "Nobody knows quite how many."

"That's ridiculous!" said Vivian. "How can anyone think that Faber John and the Time Lady are still around after all that time?"

"I told you last night," Jonathan said, "that I'm going by the stories. I think the scientists have got it wrong—and even *they* can't account for the person coming uptime from Four Century to Twenty Century, bringing all the disturbance to history." He leaned forward earnestly. "I *know* that's the Time Lady, and I'm sure the stories are right and she's trying to destroy the city because she hates Faber John. The stories are almost the only history of Time City that we've got. The records are terribly hazy. You should hear my tutor swearing about how little we know!" He stood up impatiently. "Are you finished? Shall we go?"

Vivian was still eating cheese and crumby bread. "No," she said. "And listen here—I'm not going to be rushed and bullied all the time. You caught me on the hop yesterday, but that doesn't mean I'm feeble."

"I never thought you were feeble!" Jonathan protested. He hung about, standing on one foot and then on the other, until Vivian had put the last slice of cheese into her mouth. Then he rushed to the door. "Ready now?"

Vivian sighed. "No. I have to put my shoes on. And what about my luggage?"

Jonathan had forgotten about that. "You'd better bring it with you to show that you've traveled," he said. "That gas mask is a wonderfully realistic touch."

"It's not realistic," said Vivian. "It's *real*."

She found her shoes and packed her suitcase yet again, while Jonathan took his gray flannel disguise and hid it in a stone chest. "They'll be safe there until Sam can sneak them back to Patrol Costumes," he said. "Oh, and take that label off the string thing. It'll look pretty funny if I introduce you as V. S. Lee and you're waving a label saying 'V. Smith.' "

This was true, but Vivian felt a twinge of alarm as the label went into the stone chest too. It was as if she really had lost her name. How am I going to prove to Cousin Marty that I'm *me*? she wondered, putting on her school hat and her coat. "Now I *am* ready," she said.

The house was huge, with a sort of lived-in richness to it. The rugs along the passages had an ugly, valuable look, but they had worn places on them. The banisters of the many stairs they went down had been polished so much that the carvings on them had almost worn away. The stairs had dips in the middle from countless years of feet. People were hard at work putting another layer of polish on them. Jonathan took Vivian on a dodging, zigzag way down, using four different staircases, so that they never met any of these people face-to-face, and they came at last to the ground floor. Jonathan let out a sigh of relief. "Now we can let people see us," he said.

Vivian looked from the colored marble patterns on the floor to the wide oak stairway and then to a row of pointed windows—or maybe doors—on the other side. She could see a sloping town square out there with a fountain in the middle. "What is this house?" she said.

"The Annuate Palace," said Jonathan. "This way."

He took Vivian along the patterned marble floor to where the space stopped being a front hall and turned into a kind of room full of carved empty frames that were probably chairs. Just beyond an archway a lady was speaking into what was probably a telephone, though it looked rather as if she were gazing into a mirror and speaking into a magnifying glass. "I'll be along in five minutes," she said, glancing at Jonathan and Vivian, "and we'll sort it out then. Something seems to have come up here. Bye." She put the magnifying glass into a slot by the mirror and turned around, staring at Vivian.

Vivian suddenly felt truly uncomfortable. This lady had the same deeply anxious look that Mum had worn ever since war was declared. And though she looked nothing like Mum, since she had the same folded eyes as Jonathan with the same flicker in front of them, Vivian knew she was a real person with real worries, just like Mum. She might wear yellow and black pajamas and do her hair in a strange way, but it was not right to lie to her. And here was Jonathan smoothly telling her lies.

"You'll never guess, Mother!" he said. "This is Cousin Vivian—Vivian Lee! She's just got here from Twenty Century."

His mother put up a hand and clutched her jet-black hair. "Oh Great Time! Are the Lees back already then? I meant to air Lee House first!"

"No, she's on her own. Viv and Inga sent her back because World War II has just started," Jonathan explained.

And here am I standing here letting him lie! Vivian thought uncomfortably. But she had to join in the lying after that, because Jonathan's mother turned to her with a worried smile. "Of course! That war comes up about a third of the way through Twenty Century, doesn't it? Has it turned out worse than they expected?"

"Much worse," said Vivian. "London's been bombed quite a bit already. They think there's going to be gas attacks and an invasion soon." Though all this was quite true, it somehow amounted to a lie. Jonathan's mother turned pale. "They're sending all the children away from London," Vivian said, hoping that would make her feel better.

"You poor child! And my poor brother!" Jonathan's mother said. "Why does everything have to happen at once? Of course, you must stay here with us until your parents are recalled. And we'll find you some proper clothes. I suppose you've nothing but those awful things you've got on."

Vivian looked down at her coat and her best skirt rather indignantly, but she did not need to say anything. Jonathan's mother turned back to the telephone thing and pressed a knob in the wall beside it. "Elio," she said, "I need you at once. Can you come to the hall?" She said over her shoulder to Jonathan, "Will you take care of Vivian today, my love—show her around and so on? She's bound to feel very strange after five years in history. I've got a crisis on in Agelong. Someone's sent out the New Australian Grammar to Malaya nearly a century before it was invented, and I'm going to be all day sorting it out."

"I always have to do your dirty work!" Jonathan said, pretending to be annoyed. "You're never here at all!"

"I know, my love," his mother said, looking more worried than ever. "I'll try to get the day off tomorrow, I—"

But here a door slammed open across the room, and a tall, anguished-looking man came storming out in a swirl of gray robes. He was followed by a pale, respectful-looking man in sober fawn-colored pajamas. Jonathan's mother instantly turned more worried yet.

"What's this? What's going on?" said the storming man. "You can't take Elio away *now*! I need him." He glared at the pale man, who looked at the floor respectfully. He glared at Jonathan, who looked back as if he were used to it. Then he came right up to Vivian and glared at her. "What in Time's name is *this*?" he said. His pepper-colored hair was scraped into a knob on top of his head, and his eyes stared out of deep, hollow sockets, looking agonized. He was so alarming that Vivian backed away.

"It's little Vivian Lee, Ranjit," Jonathan's mother said in a guilty, soothing way. "Your niece. The Lees have had to send her home because Twenty Century seems to be getting quite dangerous, and she'll have to stay with us. Their house is shut up, remember? I wanted Elio to see about a room and some clothes for her."

"But she's too big!" the anguished man said, still glaring at Vivian. "This girl is not the right size!"

Vivian stood limply, looking at the floor like the pale man. It was almost a relief that he had realized she was not the right Vivian. Now she would not need to lie anymore. But she was very scared about what they would do to her now they knew.

"She was six when she went away, Father," Jonathan said. He did not seem in the least alarmed. "That was nearly six years ago. Think how much I've changed since then."

"So you have," said this alarming man, turning his glare on Jonathan as if he did not think the change was for the better. "I see," he said. "She grew." And to Vivian's great surprise, he turned to her again with his anguished face relaxed into a charming smile. The hint of anguish still there in his hollow eyes only seemed to make the smile more charming. He held out a long, knobby hand for Vivian to shake. "I believe that to be Twenty Century custom," he said. "How do you do, my dear?"

"Very well, thank you," Vivian managed to say. Relief seemed to have taken her voice away at first. No wonder Jonathan thought I'd better have breakfast before I met his father! she thought. I might have fainted without.

Jonathan's father turned around, saying, "I need Elio back in five minutes exactly," and went away in the same storming way that he had come, with his robes streaming, and banged the door behind him. Jonathan's mother took pale Elio aside and began telling him what she needed. She seemed quite flustered, but Elio nodded calmly. He had a little square thing in his hand and punched buttons on it respectfully as Jonathan's mother talked. It must have been a way of taking notes.

"What do I call them?" Vivian whispered urgently to Jonathan while his mother talked.

"Call who what?" said Jonathan.

"Your parents. Auntie *what*? Uncle *which*?" Vivian whispered.

"Oh I see!" Jonathan whispered. "Her name's Jenny Lee Walker. You'd better say Jenny. He's called Ranjit Walker. Most people call him Sempitern, but you're supposed to be a Lee, so you *could* call him Ranjit."

Ranjit, Vivian tried out to herself. Uncle Ranjit. It was no good. She just could not imagine herself calling that alarming man anything. Jenny was better. She could manage that, but she did wonder if Jonathan was very brave, or just mad, to think of deceiving either of them.

Jonathan's mother—*Jenny,* Vivian told herself—turned back to them smiling. "That's all seen to then!" she said. "Leave your coat and hat and your luggage here, Vivian dear, for Elio to see to, and run off and enjoy Time City with Jonathan. Or—" She looked worried again. "Do you need anything to eat?"

"No thanks," Vivian said, and once more found herself lying

by telling the truth. "I had—I had sandwiches to take on the train."

Then they were free to go back along the colored marble floor. Vivian went feeling rather shaky, but Jonathan walked with a bouncing, lordly stride, smiling broadly. "There! We got away with it!" he said. "I knew we would. This way." He swung toward the line of pointed windows. They clearly were doors. One in the middle flapped aside to let them out, as if it knew they were coming—or Vivian thought it was opening for them until she saw that two people, a man and a woman, were coming in from the square outside. Vivian stopped politely to let them come in first. But to her astonishment, Jonathan took no notice of them at all. He went on walking through the opening as if the two people did not exist. And to Vivian's utter horror, he walked straight through both of them, the man first and then the woman, as if they were made of smoke.

"How—who—how did you do that?" she gasped, as the man and woman walked past her through the hall, looking quite whole and undamaged. "Who—who are they?"

"Those? You don't want to take any notice of those," Jonathan said. "They're only time ghosts."

Vivian's still-shaky legs nearly folded under her. *"Ghosts!"* she squawked.

J onathan took Vivian's elbow and towed her down a bank of stone steps into the cobbled square outside. "Not really ghosts," he said. "Time ghosts—and you're supposed to know about them, so don't make such a noise! This square is called Time Close. All the important people live here. That's Lee House over there where you were supposed to have been born."

How can anyone get used to *ghosts*? Vivian thought, looking where Jonathan pointed. Lee House was the tallest building on the right-hand side of Time Close. It confused Vivian a little because it was built mostly of metal in a most modern-looking style, and yet she could see that it was very old from the gigantic flowering tree trained up the front of it. The tree had reached the straight metal roof and bent across it, and gone on to trail huge branches over the newer houses on either side. And these houses were built of mellow pink brick and weathered old wood in a way that ought to have been ancient. More confusing still, the Annuate Palace, when Vivian turned to look back at it, was simply a very large house built in a style she had never seen before.

"Then tell me about these ghosts, if I'm supposed to know," she said.

"Time ghosts," said Jonathan. "They happen because the city keeps using the same piece of space and time over and over again. If a person does the same thing often enough, they leave a mark in the air, like the ones you just saw. Habit ghosts, we call them. There's another kind called once-ghosts—I'll show you some of those latter. They get made—"

But the explanation was interrupted by Sam, who came shuffling gloomily away from the fountain in the middle of the Close.

He was in orange pajamas today, and his shoelaces were trailing off both feet. "I got caught. I got hit," he said, sighing gustily. His face was rather blotchy, as if he might have been crying. "I was tired," he said. "I took the keys back this morning instead."

"Oh *no!*" exclaimed Jonathan. His lordly air vanished, and he looked horrified. "I *told* you not to! You mean, they found out?"

"No, I covered up," Sam said. "My dad came in just as I was putting the keys back, and I pretended I was just taking them that moment for a joke. But he hit me and locked his study. We won't be able to get at them again."

"That's all right!" Jonathan said, much relieved. "We won't need the keys again. I got V.S. passed off as Cousin Vivian, so we're quite safe."

He was far too relieved to show any sympathy for Sam. Vivian felt she ought to make up for it by being sorry for Sam herself, but she was too worried on her own account. This meant there was no chance of forcing Jonathan to send her back to Cousin Marty by the way she had come. She would have to make them send her through another time lock—and soon. She knew she could not pretend to be Cousin Vivian for long. Someone was bound to find out.

Jonathan did not seem to be worrying about that at all. "Tie your shoes up," he said confidently to Sam. And when Sam had done so, with much heavy breathing and some cross muttering, Jonathan led the way through an archway in the lower corner of Time Close into a big empty square beyond. "This is Aeon Square," he said, waving a lordly hand.

There were huge buildings all around the square. But Vivian was a Londoner and used to tall buildings. What impressed her more was that, in the same confusing way as the buildings in Time Close, the ones which should have been ultramodern seemed to be the oldest there. There was a great turreted place that might have been a department store filling all the right-hand side of Aeon Square, and it was made entirely of glass—glass twisted and wrought into a hundred strange, futuristic shapes. But Vivian could see, even from this distance, that the glass was pitted and worn and obviously as old as the hills, while the nearer buildings with stone towers looked much newer.

"What do you think of it?" Jonathan said, clearly expecting her to marvel.

"It's not much bigger than Trafalgar Square without Nelson and the lions," Vivian said, refusing to be overawed. "But it's awfully clean." This was true. There was no soot or grime. The sunlight slanted on clear gray stone and sparkled green on the glass, or came dazzling off the golden roofs and domes that crowded up from behind the buildings at the end of the square. Vivian looked up into the soft blue and white sky as she followed Jonathan across the wide space and found no chimneys and no smoke. "Why is there no smoke?" she asked. "And don't you have pigeons?"

"No birds in Time City," Sam said, stumping along behind.

"And we don't use fossil fuels," Jonathan said, striding ahead. "We use energe functions instead. This is Faber John's Stone."

Right in the middle of the square, there was a big slab of bluish rock let into the whiter paving stones. It was very worn from being walked on. The golden letters that had once made up quite a long inscription had been almost wholly trodden away.

Sam stood and gazed at it. "The crack's got bigger," he announced.

Vivian could see the crack Sam meant. It was quite a short one, from one corner, stretching to the first golden letters of the inscription. FAB . . . they said. IOV . . . AET . . . IV and CONDI . . . on the next line. The rest was too worn away to read. "Is it Greek?" she asked.

"Latin," said Sam. "Measure the crack. Go on."

"In a second," said Jonathan. He explained to Vivian, "They say Faber John put this stone here when he founded the city. The words mean that Faber John founded the city to last the Four

Ages. My tutor raves at the way they've let it get trodden away. He thinks it should say why the city was made and whereabouts the polarities are out in history. The stories say that when Faber John's Stone breaks up, the city will break up too. All right," he said to Sam, who was bouncing impatiently about.

Jonathan put his foot, in a green, strappy sandal, carefully along the crack, with his green heel wedged into the corner. "It's grown quite a bit," he said. "It's nearly to the end of my toes now." He said to Vivian, "It was just a little tiny split for most of my life, but it started to grow about a month ago. I measure it every day on my way to school."

"The city's breaking up," Sam announced in a booming, gloomy voice. "I need comforting. I need a Forty-two Century butter-pie."

"Later," said Jonathan, and strode away across the square. "I want to show V.S. the time ghosts in Secular Square."

Sam stamped angrily and defiantly on the crack, which caused one of his shoelaces to trail again as he followed them.

Secular Square was behind Aeon Square and much smaller. It was crowded with stalls under red and white awnings, where people were buying and selling everything from fruit and meat to tourist trinkets. At first sight there were hundreds of people there. Then Vivian's flesh began to creep as she realized that half the people were walking through the other half. Music was playing merrily somewhere. Everyone was chattering and buying things, and nobody seemed in the least bothered that half the throng were ghosts who chattered and laughed without making a sound and paid for ghostly apples with unreal money. There was even a ghostly stall piled with ghostly oranges and tomatoes. It overlapped a real stall, but nobody seemed to mind. That stall was the only ghostly thing Vivian dared walk through.

"How do you *tell*?" she asked despairingly, as Jonathan and Sam walked through a crowd of laughing girls who looked as real as anyone else. "They all look quite solid to me!"

"You'll get to know," Jonathan said. "It's obvious really."

"But I can't go bumping into everyone until I do!" Vivian protested. She kept carefully behind Jonathan and Sam while she tried to see just what it was about the people they walked through. After a while she noticed that the people they *didn't* walk through were all the ones who were wearing the same kind of pajama suits as their own. Got it! Vivian thought. Pajamas are present-day fashion! She pointed excitedly to a group of people in gauzy dresses gathered around a trinket stall. "I know! Those are time ghosts."

Jonathan and Sam looked. "Tourists," said Sam.

"From Eighty-seven Century," said Jonathan.

As they said it, a gauze-robed girl bought a real white bag with TIME CITY on it in gold letters, and paid with a real silvery strip of money. Vivian felt a fool. A time ghost in a pink-striped crinoline walked through her, and she had suddenly had enough.

"This is giving me the creeps!" she said. "Go somewhere else or I shall scream!"

"Let's get butter-pies," said Sam.

"Later," said Jonathan. He led the way down a winding lane called Day Alley, explaining to Vivian, "I wanted you to see how old Time City is. There are ghosts in the market wearing clothes that must go back hundreds of years."

"I'm miserable," Sam proclaimed, plodding behind with his shoelace flapping. "Nobody ever gives me butter-pies when I need them."

"Shut up," said Jonathan. "Stop whining." This conversation happened so often after that that Vivian felt it ought to qualify as a time ghost. Meanwhile, they saw a round place with a golden dome called The Years, and then went over a bridge that was made of china, like a teacup, and painted with flowers in a way that reminded Vivian of a teacup even more. But the paint was worn and scratched and the bridge was chipped in places. It led to a park called Long Hours, where they saw the famous Pendulum Gardens. Vivian found them fascinating, but Sam stood glumly watching fountains fling water high against the sky and little islands of rock carrying daffodils, tulips, and irises slowly circle about in the spray.

"There's only nineteen islands left," he said. "Two more have come down."

"How is it done?" Vivian asked. "How do the flowers stay up?"

"Nobody knows," said Jonathan. "They say Faber John invented it. It's one of the oldest things in the city."

"That's why it's falling apart," Sam said dismally.

"Oh, do stop being so depressing!" Jonathan snapped at him.

"I can't," sighed Sam. "I'm in my wet-week mood. *You* weren't hit before breakfast."

Jonathan sighed too. "Let's go and have butter-pies," he said.

Sam's face lit up. His whole body changed. "Whoopee! *Charge!*" he shouted, and led the way back to Aeon Square at a gallop.

Jonathan and Vivian trotted after him, through narrow stone streets, through time ghosts, and past numbers of strangely dressed tourists. "He knows just how to get what he wants," Jonathan panted irritably.

That's the pot calling the kettle black, if I ever heard it! Vivian thought. "How old is he?" she asked.

"Eight!" Jonathan said in a short, disgusted puff of breath. "Sometimes I wish I wasn't stuck with him. But he's the only person anywhere near my age in Time Close."

Sam galloped straight to the glass building in Aeon Square and trotted along an arcade of glass pillars until he came to a place where tables were set out. He dived into a chair at a table with a view between two enormous greenish pillars and sat proudly waiting to be served. Vivian sat beside him, watching tourists walk through the square and cluster to look at Faber John's Stone in the middle. More tourists sat at the other tables or went in and out of the rich-looking shops under the arcade. Vivian had never seen so many peculiar clothes and strange hairstyles in her life. She heard strange languages too, jabbering all around her.

"Time City relies a lot on the tourist trade," Jonathan said.

"Where do they all come from?" Vivian asked.

"All the Fixed Eras," Sam said, quite cheerful now. "A hundred thousand years of them."

"There's a tour for every ten years of every century, except when there's a war on," Jonathan said. "The Time Consuls arrange them. Time Patrol checks everyone who wants to come, but almost anyone can come really."

"How much does a tour cost?" Vivian asked. But the waitress arrived to take their orders just then. She was a cheerful young lady in frilly pink pajamas who clearly knew Sam and Jonathan rather well.

"Hello, you two," she said. "How many butter-pies this morning?"

"Three, please," said Jonathan.

"Only three?" said the waitress. "One point five then. Numbers?"

"I'm not allowed a number," said Sam.

"I know about you," the waitress said. "I meant your friends."

"I'm paying," said Jonathan, and recited a string of numbers.

"Yes, but are you in credit?" said the waitress. "Show."

Jonathan pressed one of the buttons on his belt and held his hand out with a row of signs shining on his palm. The waitress looked, nodded, and pressed buttons on the pink matching belt around her pajamas.

"I must get Elio to give me more credit," Jonathan said when the waitress had gone. "I shall go broke paying for everything. Sam's not allowed any credit. When they gave him his first belt, he took it apart and altered the credit limit. Then he spent a fortune on butter-pies."

"A thousand units in two days," Sam said happily.

"How much is a unit?" Vivian asked.

"Um—about two of your pounds," said Jonathan.

Vivian gasped. "Weren't you sick?"

"All night," Sam said cheerfully. "It was worth it. I'm a butter-pie addict." His face lit up as he saw the waitress coming back. "Here they are! Yummy!"

While they ate and let the hot part trickle into the cold, Jonathan seemed to feel he had to go on showing Vivian Time City. He pointed to the gleaming white building across the square. Vivian was rather embarrassed to find that the tourists' heads were turning to look at it too. "There's Time Patrol, where we were last night," he said. "And there—" He pointed toward the end of the square, and tourist heads in strange hairstyles swung that way as well as Vivian's. "That building's Duration, where Sam and I go to school. I expect you'll be going there with us when half term's over." Then he pointed back along the arcade, and once more all the heads turned where he pointed. "That's Continuum behind us, where all the students are, with Perpetuum and Whilom Tower beyond that . . ."

Vivian was so embarrassed at the way the tourists were listening in that she stopped attending. Instead she thought: Half term! It's their half term, and they were bored with nothing to do. That's why they thought up this adventure with the Time Lady and saving Time City, to make life exciting. I can just hear them whispering together about V.S.! It's still not *real* to them!

". . . and opposite Agelong, where my mother works. Those twin domes—those are Erstwhile and Ongoing," Jonathan was saying. "Then there's Millennium at the end of—"

"I need another butter-pie," Sam interrupted.

Jonathan pressed another stud in his belt. A clock face appeared on the back of his hand. It said a quarter to twelve. "No time," he said. "We've got to show V.S. the Endless ghost."

"After that then," said Sam.

"No," said Jonathan. "It's my last credit."

"You count tomato seeds!" Sam said disgustedly as they got up to go.

"How does your belt work?" Vivian asked. "It seems like magic to me!"

She soon wished she had not asked. There were now crowds of tourists in the square. Jonathan said, "Energe functions," and dived vigorously this way and that among the people, shooting bits of explanation over his shoulder. Vivian followed as best she could, trying to understand, although almost the only parts of it she grasped were words like *and* and *the*. "And mine's made in Hundred-and-two Century, so it's got a low-weight function," Jonathan said. "Look." He pressed another stud and took off from beside Vivian in a long, floating leap. He landed, and at once took off in another, and another, floating this way and that among the groups of people.

"He's gone silly!" Sam said disgustedly. "Come on."

They dodged among the people, trying to keep Jonathan's green, swooping figure and flying pigtail in sight. It took them between buildings beyond the glass arcade. Vivian had a glimpse of the twin domes Jonathan must have been talking about on one side and, on the other, a most extraordinary place like a lopsided honeycomb that seemed to have stairs zigzagging dizzily all over it. Then they were at a grand flight of steps. Jonathan's green figure was bounding down them like a crazy kangaroo. They saw him bound right across the broad, crowded road below, where he dropped straight down at the top of a leap and landed with a bump, looking a little cross.

"Good. It's run down. He'll have to wait for it to recharge," said Sam. They ran across the road, where Jonathan was leaning against a stone wall. Below and beyond the wall was open countryside, with a river winding through it. Jonathan was watching a barge unloading at a wharf a long way below.

"The River Time," he said to Vivian, just as if nothing had happened and she and Sam were not hot and out of breath with trying to keep up. "This road is the Avenue of the Four Ages, and it leads to Endless Hill. Look."

A bit like the Mall, Vivian thought, or perhaps the Embankment, what with the river on one side. And Jonathan is a maddening boy! Worse than Sam!

There were arches over the avenue made of lacy metalwork, and in some way these arches were made to fly long streamers of light, like flags or scarves, in rainbow colors. It looked very festive, since it was full of crowds and clots of people all hastening toward the hill at the end. There the Avenue led into flights of steps up the round green hill, to the tower at the top. The tower looked old. Very, very old, Vivian thought, and dark, although she could see sky through the windows in it.

"That tower's called the Gnomon," said Jonathan. "It has Faber John's clock in it that only strikes once a day, at midday."

They began to follow the rest of the people toward Endless Hill, but, before they had gone very far, a tremendous bell began to toll. BONG. It buzzed the lacy arches and set the streamers of light fluttering. "Bother! Midday already!" Jonathan said, and started to run. They were still quite a way from the hill when the second stroke came. BONG. Again the streamers of light wavered. Arms in the crowd pointed. There came murmurs of "There it is!" from all sides.

Vivian saw a person in green clothes, distantly, on the lowest flight of steps up the hill. He was trying to climb them. He seemed in an awful hurry—she could feel that from here—and he ran and scrambled furiously. But something seemed to be stopping him. BONG! rang the great clock. The man in green staggered and pushed himself upward. BONG. Vivian could feel the effort it took the man. He was lifting his feet as if they were in lead boots. BONG. He was trying to pull himself up by the balustrade, and that was not working either.

"Is it very hard to climb those steps?" she whispered. BONG.

"No. You can run up them," said Jonathan. "But he's a time

ghost. A once-ghost. He tries to get up the stairs every day at twelve. Watch.''

BONG went the clock while Jonathan was speaking. With every stroke, the man in green seemed to find it more difficult to climb. But he did not give up. He labored upward while the clock struck seven, eight, and nine. By the tenth stroke he was on his hands and knees, crawling. He seemed quite exhausted, and he still had two turns of the steps to go before he reached the tower. As he crawled doggedly up the next-to-last flight, Vivian found she was holding her breath. BONG. Come on, come on! she said inside her head. It seemed the most important thing in the world that the man should reach the top.

And he did not do it. BONG came the twelfth stroke, and the green, crawling figure was simply not there anymore. "O-oh!" said Vivian, and the crowd all around her said, "O-oh!" too, in a long groan. "What a pity! What was he doing?" Vivian said.

"Nobody knows. He hasn't done it yet," Jonathan said. "He's a once-ghost, you see, and those happen when whatever they're doing is so important or so emotional that they leave a mark like the habit ghosts."

"What? From the future?" said Vivian.

"Yes, but it isn't really the future here," Jonathan explained. "I told you how Time City uses the same small piece of time over and over again. Past and future go around and around, so they're almost the same thing. What did you think of the End-less ghost?" he asked her eagerly. "Did he mean anything to you?"

The only thing Vivian could think of was Robin Hood because of the green clothes. "No," she said. "Should he?"

Jonathan looked a little disappointed. "Well, a fresh mind from an Unstable Era," he said. "You might have had a new idea. Let's have lunch before the tourists fill all the cafés."

"Butter-pies. You promised," said Sam.

"I said no," said Jonathan. "Ordinary food. It's cheaper."

"Slant-eyed meanie!" Sam muttered. But he took care to say it when Jonathan was pushing through the crowd some way ahead.

They went up steps between the houses. These steps were called The Decades, and there were ten steps between every landing, until they were quite high up near the golden dome of The Years. There was a place to buy food at the top, with a slant of lawn to eat it on under an old gray tower. They had sweet buns with meat in them, sitting in the sun, which was warm, but not too warm. I'm enjoying this! Vivian thought. I feel like a tourist on holiday! While they ate, Jonathan and Sam told her about other once-ghosts. There was a man who dived daily into the River Time, trying to rescue a drowning girl; the Time Patroller who got shot in the hall of Millennium; and the girl who was a Lee, and there-fore a long-ago ancestress of Sam's and Jonathan's, who threw her engagement ring angrily into the fountain in Century Place every day at sunset.

"She was awfully embarrassed about it later," Jonathan said, getting up. "She nearly left Time City, but she couldn't face living in history. Get moving, Sam. I want to show V.S. Faber John while the tourists are eating."

"You mean he's still *here*!" Vivian said.

"You'll see," said Sam, with his largest two-toothed grin.

The way to Faber John was at the bottom of the old tower, below the lawn. There was a dark doorway down there, with a lady in the dimness inside who demanded to see Jonathan's credit. When Jonathan pressed his belt stud and held out his hand, the glowing green numbers on his palm changed quite noticeably as the lady punched a machine in front of her. This was expensive. Vivian understood now why Jonathan had been so careful to buy a cheap lunch.

After that, they went down a flight of steps with a rope railing, down and down, under little balls of blue light fixed in the rocky ceiling, until they came to a muddy floor deep under Time City.

They could hear laughs and shrieks from a few tourists ahead of them, but those were nearly drowned by a noise of water pouring and dripping. Around a rocky corner, there was a notice. FABER JOHN'S WELL. A DRINK BRINGS HEALTH AND LUCK, it said, in letters almost too strange for Vivian to read. Beyond that, water came gushing from a groove in the roof and spilled into a small stone basin that was obviously made naturally from the water wearing the rock. A few coins glittered under its dark ripples.

"You don't need to pay," said Sam.

All the same, Vivian dropped a big round penny with "1934" on it into the strange little well. She felt she needed some luck to get her back home. Then she took one of a stack of jeweled goblets from one side and held it under the running water. The goblet was really only papery stuff, but it looked so real Vivian decided to keep it. The water tasted fresh and slightly rusty, both at once.

She followed Sam and Jonathan along the bends of the mud-floored passage, clutching her goblet, hoping it did mean luck. They went past cunningly lighted rock formations, like folded cloth and like angel's wings, and one beautiful one that was a dark, unmoving pool with a rock growing out of the middle of it that was just like two cupped hands, fingers and all. All the time there was the sound of water pouring and raining and gushing. At first Vivian thought it was the sound of Faber John's Well, but it grew steadily louder, until they entered a wider part of the passage with an iron railing down one side. Here it was warmer, and a little steamy, and the sound of water was a thunder with loud pattering in its midst.

"River Time rises here," Jonathan shouted, pointing to a deep crevice beyond the railing, where much of the thunder seemed to come from. They went around another corner and found the tourists they had heard before were just going on ahead. "Good," Jonathan said. "We've got it to ourselves. Look."

Beyond the rail and beyond the dark crevice, there was a smooth, oval cave many yards long in the wall. Water poured and dripped inside it. But lights had been placed to shine through the sheet of water into the cave. Vivian saw a shape inside. It was long and high, and it reminded her of— She had a sudden vivid memory of sharing a bed with Mum once, on holiday at Bognor Regis, before Dad could get there from work. In the morning she had woken up to find Mum lying on her side, facing away from her, but looking very near and large, so that Vivian saw Mum's rather thin back and shoulders like a cliff in front of her. What was inside the cave looked just like that. For a moment, Vivian could have sworn she was looking at part of a giant's back, with the giant's head hidden inside the rock to the left and the rest of him stretched out to the right under the City. There was a shoulder blade, and the knobby dent a person has down the middle of his back. But the shape was a shiny clay color. It looked like rock. Water pattered and poured on it perpetually, showing it must be hard as rock too.

"It *can't* be a person, can it?" she said. "He'd be huge if he stood up! It must be rock."

"We don't know," said Jonathan.

"But surely somebody's climbed in there and made sure!" Vivian said.

Jonathan took a quick look up and down the passage to make quite certain nobody else was there. Then he took hold of the iron handrail and twisted a length of it loose. People had done that often before—Vivian could tell by the easy way the bar came out. He handed her the long piece of iron. "Lean over and poke him," he said. "Go on."

The bar looked as if it would just about reach. Unsteadily, with her paper goblet in one hand and the bar in the other, Vivian leaned across the steamy, wet space and prodded the bar at the cave. And as soon as the end of it reached the sheet of pouring water, it refused to go any farther. Vivian shoved, as if the bar were a spear, and the railing bounced back again so hard that she almost overbalanced into the black gap where the river rose. Sam and Jonathan both caught hold of her by her shirt.

"Why? What's stopping it?" Vivian demanded.

Jonathan took the bar out of her fist and put it back in the railing. "It's some kind of force field, but nobody can discover what kind," he said. "Ongoing scientists have tried to find out for centuries. And it can't be there for nothing, can it? It does look as if that really is Faber John, doesn't it?"

"It does rather," Vivian agreed. She was surprised at how sober and awed this made her feel. She took a last amazed look at the giant's back under the constantly pouring water and followed the boys slowly around another corner. There was another long flight of stairs there, and then a way out, where a man checked them off on a screen.

Then they were blinking about at a wonderful view of the city. "There," said Jonathan. "Don't you think this place is worth saving?"

The mysterious stone giant had upset Vivian. "Yes, but what's that got to do with me?" she said snappily. "I don't want London to be bombed either."

"I'll have my next butter-pie now," said Sam.

Jonathan pressed a belt stud and flashed the clock face quickly to his wrist and away. "Later," he said. "I must show V.S. Millennium now. That's it, at the other end of the Avenue of the Four Ages. You mustn't miss seeing it. It's got all the greatest pictures in history in it."

He pointed. Millennium was vast, glittering with rows of windows and twisted glass spires and a gigantic blue glass dome. Vivian quailed. "Oh, no more buildings, please!" she said. "My mind's got indigestion!"

"Then perhaps we ought just to go quietly back to the Annuate," Jonathan suggested with great sympathy.

Vivian almost believed the sympathy for a second, until she saw Sam looking up at Jonathan with his mouth slightly open as if he had that moment caught on to something. "Great idea!" he said, much too heartily. "I don't need a butter-pie really."

That last touch overdid it, to Vivian's mind. She knew they were up to something. What is Jonathan planning *now*? she wondered, as she followed Sam's flapping shoelace down a cobbled alley. Another unreal adventure?

Jonathan checked his clock face several times on the way back through the city. Sam never mentioned butter-pies once. Back they trotted, across Aeon Square, through the archway and up Time Close, and Vivian followed, quite certain that they were up to something. Her legs were aching as she went up the steps to the glass doors of the Annuate.

I want some peace, she thought. I want to read a film magazine and listen to the radio. But I don't think there's such a thing as a radio in this place!

The hall of the Annuate was empty and quiet. Jonathan turned to Vivian with his most lordly, casual air. "There are some more once-ghosts I can show you if you like," he said. "Here in this very palace."

This is what we've come back here for! Vivian thought. "Then you'd better show me," she said. "Now you've dragged me all this way for them."

"Along here then," Jonathan said, and strode off, pigtail bouncing, the opposite way to the way he had taken her that morning. Sam went after him at a rolling trot. It's the way we came last night, Vivian thought, walking behind across the colored marble patterns of the floor. They went around a corner and, sure enough, Vivian remembered the long space with showcases against both walls. It had reminded her of a museum. Now she saw that it was indeed a sort of museum. And since she was rather sick of Jonathan hurrying her about, she purposely loitered, looking at the things in the cases. Each exhibit had a card written in neat, easy-to-read writing. SEVENTY-THREE-CENTURY AMERICAN GOLF CLUB, said the first. FORTY-FIVE-CENTURY IN-

DIAN WEDDING CHALICE, said another. But some of the exhibits were decidedly odd, like the HUNDRED-AND-FIVE-CENTURY GAS IRON and the THIRTY-THREE-CENTURY ICELANDIC DECORATORS' PAINT, while in the next showcase—Vivian found herself looking at her own luggage, labeled in the same neat writing: TWENTY-CENTURY REFUGEE EQUIPMENT (CASES OPEN TO SHOW CLOTHING AND PROTECTIVE MASK).

They *were* open, too. Her suitcase was artfully propped ajar, with that wretched liberty bodice arranged to show on top, and her gas mask was half out of its box. And there was her precious string bag spread open to show sandwich paper, magazine, gloves, and socks. Vivian stared at them in outrage. "The *cheek*!" she said. She was also rather scared, for how was she to get at her things when she went home? But it was worse than that somehow. It was as if someone had taken away the person she really was, so that she was forced to turn into somebody else. "But I won't!" Vivian said angrily. "I'm *me*!"

Sam and Jonathan came anxiously galloping back. Sam tugged at her arm. "You've got to come *now*!"

Vivian was too dismayed to care. She pointed to the showcase. "Look! Look at that! All my things!"

"Yes. Good old Elio's been busy as usual," Jonathan said. "Androids are like that. But the ghosts are due to walk any second now. Do come and look at them. Please!"

Vivian looked from him to Sam. Sam was staring at her anxiously. Jonathan was so urgent that he had gone white. He *is* high-strung! Vivian thought. She knew Mum would call Jonathan that. But it was plain to her that it meant a lot to both Jonathan and Sam that she should see these ghosts. "Oh, very well then," she said, and let Sam pull her down to the far end of the museum.

There was a dark old door there. It was the one Vivian remembered as creaking horribly the night before, but to her surprise, it was as locked as a door could be. A big, shiny chain, made of transparent stuff with wires embedded in it, was fastened across it from one metal box fixed to the doorframe by the hinges to another fixed to the doorframe by the handle. Cables led from both boxes into the floor. It looked as if anyone trying to open that door would get some kind of nasty shock.

Sam reached out a chubby hand, somewhat colored with butter-pie and mud from Faber John's cave, and deftly slid the metal box across from the doorframe onto the door just beneath the big iron handle. The cable stayed where it was, but the door still looked locked to anyone who did not look too closely. "I shorted it," Sam said proudly. "The first day of half term."

"And I asked him to," Jonathan said, checking his clock again. "It was my idea. When I was little, everyone had heard of these ghosts. They'd walked here every day for hundreds of years. So when my father was elected Sempitern six years ago, I wanted to see them. But my mother went and looked at them first, and when she had, she screamed and had the door chained up. I've been wanting to see them ever since, but I had to wait until Sam turned out to be a genius with energe functions." Sam beamed proudly. Jonathan checked his clock again. "About now," he said.

He turned the handle, and the door creaked slowly open. Beyond it was the dark stone passage that Vivian remembered walking up last night from the church place called the Chronologue. The open door let in enough light to show that the passage was quite empty.

"Wait," said Jonathan in a gasp, as if he were holding his breath.

Almost as he spoke, there were suddenly two people walking down the passage toward them. At first they were hard to see in the dark. All Vivian could tell was that they were wearing modern Time City pajamas and walking in the way people do when they are very excited about something. Then she saw that the taller one had dark diamonds down the sides of his suit. There was a flicker over its eyes and its hair was in a pigtail that trailed over one shoulder. The shorter one was a girl with light brown curly hair.

"Jiminy Cricket!" said Vivian. "It's *me*! And *you*!"

It was the oddest and most upsetting sight, to see herself as a ghost, looking almost but not quite like somebody else, with her face back to front from the face she knew in a mirror, breathlessly chattering without a sound to a boy she had met only the night before. It was worse still when the two ghosts swept unseeingly up to her. Vivian felt a jolt of sheer panic, such as she had never felt in her life before. They vanished almost where she was standing.

She stood wobbling for a moment, and her eyes felt queer and misty. Then her legs folded up, and she sat with a bump on the marble floor. "*Hundreds of years,* did you say?" she asked croakily.

Jonathan held out a hand to haul her up. "My legs did that too, when I first saw them," he said. "Sam ran away."

"Only six meters!" Sam protested. "I came back when they'd gone."

"I don't wonder your Mum screamed and had that passage locked!" Vivian said as she struggled to her feet. She hung on to the door until she felt steady. "She must have known it was you, even if you *were* only six!"

"She won't talk about it," said Jonathan. He was looking lordly and jubilant now. "*Now* do you see how I recognized you, V.S.? That was us last night. I wore that suit, and I took you that way on purpose."

Vivian still felt wobbly, but there was nothing wrong with her brain. "It was *not* last night!" she said. "Apart from the fact that I never said one word to you until we got to your room, I was not in those clothes. I was wearing this same skirt I have on now last night. That ghost had Time City clothes."

This made no difference to Jonathan at all. "Then it's some

time soon," he said airily. "And what we were doing is important. It *has* to be, or we wouldn't have made once-ghosts. So
what do you think we were doing, V.S.?"

He was back to being the Interrogator again. Bless me! Vivian
thought. He *still* thinks I'm the Time Lady! He just decided to
make me admit it in a different way after he got that fright
with those guards. Talk about bees in your bonnet! "If you
call me V.S. once again," she said, "I shall scream—I warn
you!"

Sam patted her arm. "You need a butter-pie," he said kindly.

Oddly enough, this nearly did make Vivian scream. She gave
a strange squawking laugh. "I'm going balmy!" she cried out.
"Why can't I get back to the War and have some peace for once?
Everything's mad here! None of this is *true*!"

Her voice was getting louder and louder. They stared at her.
Vivian opened her mouth to laugh at how foolish they looked
and decided that she would scream instead. She had her head
back to give a really loud, satisfying scream when she heard footsteps turning the corner into the museum. She shut her mouth.
Sam had the chain back in the right place in a flash. They all
hurried over to a museum case labeled FORTY-THREE-CENTURY
CHINESE HOME COMPUTER and stared at it intently until the person
arrived.

It was a friendly brown-faced lady called Petula, who was
looking for Vivian. "Madam Sempitern told me to look out for
you, dear," she said. "Would you like to come and see if everything in your room is the way you like it?"

"I'll come and show her," Jonathan said at once.

But Petula said, "No, go away, Jonathan, dear. You don't
own her." She took Vivian away upstairs, leaving Sam and
Jonathan looking like people who have been brought up short in
mid-adventure.

A while later Vivian was peacefully and happily installed in a
small, friendly room. Though none of the things in it were much

like things she knew, Petula had shown her how everything worked—for instance, if you wanted a mirror, you put your foot on a stud in the floor and a piece of wall reflected your face suddenly—and told her what everything was called. She had shown Vivian how to work the shower and where the switch was for music. Finally, she pressed a stud that made a wall unfold into a cupboard. Inside was a row of pajama suits mysteriously hanging on nothing and all miraculously Vivian's size.

"You can count on Elio for that," Petula said. "If you have any trouble with anything, put your hand across that blue square by the bed and one of us will come and sort you out."

When Petula had gone, Vivian took possession of the room by straightening out the paper goblet, which had become rather battered by then, and planting it on an empty-frame table by the wall. Then she lay on the bed, which was a flowered blanket draped over nothing, and listened to strange chiming music out of a thing called the deck which floated beside the bed. It was almost as good as listening to the radio. She thought she had better start thinking how to get the bees out of Jonathan's bonnet and make him help her get back to stay with Cousin Marty. In some strange way she knew that those two time ghosts she had seen would do that if she could think how. But she did not want to think of that ghost of herself walking beside the ghost of Jonathan, for hundreds of years before either of them were born. She went to sleep instead.

She woke because someone had come quietly in and laid out clothes for her. The sound of the door sliding shut made her sit up with a jerk. Now she found that she *did* want to think about the two time ghosts. I wonder what we were—I mean, what we *will be*—doing, she thought, with a great deal of interest. I can use them somehow. She almost had an idea how.

"Are you there, V.S.?" Jonathan's voice said out of the deck.

"No. I'm asleep," said Vivian. And the almost-idea was gone.

"Then wake up. Dinner's in half an hour," said Jonathan's

voice. "It'll be official, with guests, I warn you. It always is. Shall I come and get you?"

"Is it? Then perhaps you'd better," Vivian said.

This news made her very nervous. She managed to fumble her way into the silky white suit laid out for her. Its trousers were so baggy they were almost like a skirt, and she put both feet down the same leg twice before she got it right. When she stood up and put her arms into the baggy sleeves, the suit fastened itself down her back like magic and began to glow slightly. Blue flowers appeared, floating gently in spirals around her arms and legs. Vivian touched them, and they were as unreal as time ghosts. This was unnerving enough, but the most unnerving thing was the looseness of the suit itself if, like Vivian, you were used to the tight clothes and underclothes of 1939. She felt as if she had no clothes on at all, and that made her more nervous than ever.

When Jonathan arrived, all in white, with his hair newly plaited, he did not help her feel any better. "It'll be quite boring," he warned her on the way down the polished stairs. "The guests are Dr. Wilander—he's my tutor—and Librarian Enkian. They hate each other. There's a story that Wilander once threw a whole set of Shakespeare folios at Enkian. He's strong as an ox, so it could be true. They had another quarrel today, and my father invited them to soothe them down."

"I hope they'll all be too busy hating and soothing to notice me," Vivian said.

"Bound to be," said Jonathan.

But they were not. Jonathan's parents were waiting in the dining room, which was a round, vaulted room that put Vivian instantly in mind of a subway station, and the two guests were standing with them beside a pretend fire flickering in a real fireplace. Though all four were in solemn black, Vivian found it hard not to think of them as sheltering from an air raid. It gave her an instant feeling of danger. That feeling grew worse when

Jenny looked up and said, "Here she is," and Vivian realized they had all been talking about her.

Mr. Enkian, who had a yellow, triangular face and a way of sneering even when he talked about ordinary things, looked at Vivian and said, "What a pale little creature!"

Vivian's face at once contradicted him by growing red and hot. She felt like something the cat had brought in. Except I don't think there *are* any cats here! she thought rather desperately.

"Six years in smoke-polluted history isn't good for anyone," Jenny said, in her most worried-soothing way, as she led the way to the table.

Sempitern Walker shot her an anguished look over his shoulder. "She managed to grow, though," he said. He sounded as if he bore Vivian a grudge for it.

As for Dr. Wilander, he simply stared at Vivian. He was huge. He had a huge, hanging face like a bear's. Vivian took one look at him and found her eyes being met by shrewd little gray eyes gazing hard at her out of the bear's face. They terrified her. She knew she was being stared at and summed up by one of the cleverest people she had ever met. She was too frightened to move until Jonathan took hold of her shoulder and shoved her into a carved and polished empty-frame chair. Then it was a relief just to look at the table and find that it was not invisible, but made of some white stuff with patterns of white on it to imitate a tablecloth.

Dr. Wilander sat down opposite her, and the empty chair creaked. He spoke to her. His voice was a dull grunting, like a bear in a distant thicket. "So you're the youngest Lee, eh? Vivian Lee?"

"Yes," Vivian said, wishing she did not need to lie.

"Sent home because of the Second World War, eh?" grunted Dr. Wilander.

"Yes," Vivian agreed—with relief, because now she was back at least to lying by telling the truth.

"By which we understand," said Mr. Enkian, "that the notorious instability of Twenty Century must have escalated to a degree to cause concern to your parents. We hope you can give an account of it."

Help! thought Vivian. She looked desperately at Jonathan, but she could tell he was going to be no help. He was looking cool and well behaved, the picture of a boy trying not to be noticed.

"Don't be ridiculous, Enkian," grunted Dr. Wilander. "You can't expect an eleven-year-old child to judge degrees of instability."

"I *do* expect it from the child of two trained Observers," Mr. Enkian snapped. "She can answer questions at least."

Jonathan's father interrupted, realizing that his guests were starting to quarrel. "We all know the source of the trouble," he said, "and though extirpation is still a possibility, what most concerns us now is how the resulting temporonic unrest might be contained in a century of such low prognotic yield . . ."

He went on talking. Four ladies came in and set out a multitude of large and small dishes in front of everyone, and Sempitern Walker talked all the time they were doing it. It was very boring. Perhaps it was his job to be boring, Vivian thought, in which case he was very good at his job. He stared at the rounded end of the room as if something there worried him terribly and spoke in a droning voice of escalation waves and sociotemporal curves and paradigms of agon types and cultural manipulation of ideology and behavioral parameters and the Lee-Abdullah index, until a sort of heaviness fell on everyone.

Vivian tried to listen. She was sure that the more she knew about Time City, the easier it would be to get home. But she understood most of it rather less than she had understood Jonathan's explaining how his belt worked. She did dimly grasp that her own century seemed to be in an uproar and that when Sempitern Walker talked about the "source of the trouble," he *might* have meant the Time Lady. And she gathered that learned people in

Time City kept watch on the rest of history and tried to push it into behaving the way Time City wanted.

I think that's rather cheek! she thought.

The ladies finally gave everyone water and wine in matching tumblers made of thousands of jewellike bits of glass. Then they left, and everyone began to eat. Vivian's sense of danger returned. She knew she would make awful mistakes and everyone would realize she was not Cousin Vivian. She watched Jonathan and Jenny carefully and did what they did. And it was quite easy. The main difference in Time City manners was that you were allowed to pick up most of the food in your fingers and dip it into little bowls of bright-tasting sauce. The white surface of the table made any drips vanish like magic. Vivian was so relieved to find she could manage after all that she barely felt nervous when Mr. Enkian and Dr. Wilander began asking her questions.

"How do you feel to be back in civilization?" Mr. Enkian said. "It must be quite a change after a Twenty Century slum."

"We don't live in a slum!" Vivian said indignantly. "We live in Lewisham! It's respectable. A lot of people have cars there."

"Have you seen any slums?" grunted Dr. Wilander, looking up from his dishes. The ladies had given him twice as many without being asked. He probably needed them, Vivian thought, considering the size of him.

"Not really," she said. "Mum won't let me go down to Peckham Rye. It's very rough there. Policemen walk in pairs."

"But your parents go there, of course," asserted Mr. Enkian.

"No, they don't," said Vivian. "Nobody goes to slums if they can help it. But Mum goes through on a bus sometimes on her way to the West End."

"And your father?" growled Dr. Wilander.

"I don't know," Vivian said sadly. "I haven't seen him for ages. As soon as there was the threat of war, the Ministry moved him to a secret Government Establishment, and it's so hush-hush that he hardly gets home for weekends now. Mum says at least that means he won't be called up into the army to get killed."

"I call that a shrewd move on Lee's part," Mr. Enkian said. "It's not an Observer's job to get himself killed."

Sempitern Walker leaned forward with a look of puzzled agony. "I thought your parents had settled in a quarter called Islington?"

This gave Vivian a jolt. Her mind seemed to have played a strange trick on her. It had allowed her to tell one lie, by saying she was Vivian Lee, but otherwise it had settled for lying by telling the absolute truth about everything else. She had to think quickly. "Yes, but we moved," she said. "Mum wan't happy with my school there." That made another lie. And she hoped hard that nobody would ask her about Islington because she had never been there in her life.

"Tell us about your school," said Jenny.

Vivian heaved a sigh of relief and began to talk. She talked about school, clothes, buses, and the subway and how you sheltered there from bombs if you had no shelter of your own. She described the air raid shelter that made a hump in the middle of her own back lawn. Meanwhile, she dipped dry little dumplings and long crisp leaves into sauce and ate them as if she had been doing it all her life. She sipped wine—it tasted to her as if it had gone bad—and went on to films, where she was a true expert. Mickey Mouse, Snow White, Shirley Temple, and Bing Crosby took her through the time when the ladies brought more dishes, and she ate what was in those almost without noticing. Then she went on to jazz. But a grunted question from Dr. Wilander brought her back to the War. She told them about coupons, and the dark curtains she helped Mum make for blackout, and how there were tank traps on the roads and an antiaircraft emplacement up on the common. She described big silver barrage balloons over London. She told them Mr. Chamberlain was so good he was no good, and she imitated an air raid siren. It was such fun to be the center of attention like this that she even offered to sing them "Hang out your washing on the Siegfried Line." But they asked about gas attacks instead.

Vivian explained that this was the real threat. Then she went on to the way the Government was sending all the children out of London. She began describing the hot, noisy train and very nearly went on to say that she was being sent to Cousin Marty herself, but she stopped herself in time. "They all had labels," she said. "Just like luggage."

"This is a bit puzzling, my love," Jenny said. She looked at Dr. Wilander. "When *were* the evacuations in World War Two? Twenty Century's not my study."

"Always some months after war was declared," Dr. Wilander grunted. "That varies a bit, since it's an Unstable Era, but it's usually declared midway through 1939." His shrewd little eyes swiveled to Vivian. "When *was* this war declared?"

Vivian felt very uneasy because it looked as if someone had noticed something wrong in what she had been saying, but she answered with the truth. "Last Christmas, in 1938, of course."

She was amazed at the consternation this produced. Everyone stared at her and at one another. Jonathan, who had not said one word up to then or even looked at her, now gazed at her in obvious horror. Jenny looked quite as horrified. "It's moved right back!" she said. "Ranjit, it's gone critical! I think all the Observers should be recalled right away!"

"Our information seems to be wholly out of date," Mr. Enkian said disgustedly. "What is Time Patrol thinking of?"

"I'll find out," Sempitern Walker said, and he pressed a stud on his belt.

Dr. Wilander, popping crisp pancakes into his mouth by twos, said, "Not really so surprising. Three days ago there was a strong source of chronons in September 1939, and we know it's causing chaos. It's just surprising that the outbreak of war rolled backtime so fast. But"—his big jaw champed, and his little eyes once more rolled around to Vivian—"that Government of yours is pretty inefficient, don't you agree? Only just getting the kids out *now*."

"It's been phony war up to now," Vivian said apologetically.

"Still no excuse," grunted Dr. Wilander.

Pale Elio slipped into the room. Sempitern Walker whispered to him and sent him out again.

"At this rate," pronounced Mr. Enkian, "that century is going to be splitting the atom in the twenties, with all that follows."

"They've got to do it at some point, you fool," Dr. Wilander growled. "Life in the next Fixed Era depends on it."

"Not if they learn to do it during a war," Mr. Enkian snapped, "with a wave of chaos rolling uptime at them. There won't *be* the next Fixed Era then. The only bit of earth left will be Time City, and that's decaying fast!"

"Nonsense!" snarled Dr. Wilander.

"Gentlemen!" said Sempitern Walker loudly and boringly. "We are all agreed that there is a crisis both for Time City and for history, and we are all agreed that we will prevent it if we can. We will not sacrifice the art of the Seventies nor deprive the Hundreds of their expansion to the stars . . ."

He went on talking. Heaviness descended again. The ladies came to take away the second course and give everyone frothy little mountains of sweet stuff. Vivian had just dug a spoon into hers—it smelled as good as butter-pie—when the door crashed aside to let a wide sandy-haired man pounce into the room. Vivian jumped and dropped her spoon.

"What's this about an update on the moveback?" he said. He looked like Sam. He was so like Sam in fact that, while Vivian was bending under the table to get her spoon, she could not help taking a look at the man's feet to see if his shoelaces were trailing. But he was wearing smooth, shiny boots.

Everyone talked at once then. When Vivian sat up again, she found the sandy-haired man standing over her as if he meant to arrest her.

"Vivian, you remember Abdul Donegal—Sam's father—don't you?" Jenny said. "He's chief of Time Patrol now. Tell him what you told us."

Everything? Vivian wondered wildly. "You mean, about war breaking out last Christmas?"

Mr. Donegal pulled at his lip and stared at her as if she were a suspect. "You're telling me Twenty Century's gone critical then," he said. "When did you leave it?"

"Last n—yesterday about four o'clock, I think," Vivian said.

Sam's father pulled at his lip again and frowned. "And my next batch of Observer reports isn't due till tomorrow," he said. "Lucky you came. That means the start of that war's moved back ten months in two days. Bad. I'll get everyone on to Amber Emergency right away, and we'll do what we can to stop it sliding back any further." He gave Vivian a smile with two teeth in it just like Sam's and banged her on the shoulder. "Drop in and see us soon," he said. Then he seemed to be going.

"Er—Abdul," said Sempitern Walker.

"Look here, Donegal!" Mr. Enkian called out. His pointed yellow face was red and angry. "What do you mean by letting this moveback escape notice? If it hadn't been for this child, none of us would have known. Isn't that a little slack?"

Mr. Donegal whirled around and stared at him. "Slack?" he said. "Listen, Enkian, I'm handling an emergency in one of the most unstable centuries in history. I've just come from a flood of reports from the Eighties threatening World War Three two centuries early. I've patrollers out all over the era. What more can I do? It's been a week since the Lees' last report—maybe sending young Vivian was the best they could do—but I'll send a man to check now, if you'll let me get back to my job."

"All the same—" Mr. Enkian began.

"Abdul, won't you sit down and have some of this sweet?" Jenny interrupted quickly.

Mr. Donegal's eyes went to the frothy mounds rather in the way Sam looked at a butter-pie. Then he glanced at Mr. Enkian most unlovingly and rubbed at the stomach that sat roundly above his studded belt. "I'd better not, Jenny. My weight's up again. Besides, I've got to get back and contact the Lees, not to speak of having another try at catching that little lady." And before anyone could say anything else, he went out of the room with the same crash and pounce with which he had come.

"Do you think he has a chance of catching her?" Mr. Enkian said.

Dr. Wilander grunted into his sweet. "Change the subject," he growled. "Little pitchers."

Mr. Enkian looked at Vivian and Jonathan and then at Jenny.

"Dears, if you've finished your sweet, you can run along," Jenny said. "It's quite late and Jonathan looks tired."

Vivian saw that they were being got rid of, so that the grown-ups could talk about the Time Lady. Sempitern Walker made that quite clear by leaning back in his chair and fixing them with an agonized stare as they went out. "None of what we said is to go beyond this room," he said. "I put you both on your honor."

"Yes, Father," Jonathan said in a subdued mutter. It was no wonder Jenny thought Jonathan was tired, Vivian thought as they went across the hall. Jonathan was white, and his head hung.

"Is something the matter?" she asked.

But Jonathan refused to speak until they had reached his room. Then he flung himself into an empty-frame chair so hard that his ponytail bounded, and threatened to make an emotional scene. "*Curse* those two time ghosts!" he almost shrieked. "They made me quite *sure* you were the Time Lady! But you're not, are you? I could tell you were a real Twenty Century person with every word you said. *Mickey Mouse!*" he yelled. "And I'm stuck with you while she's still out there, messing history up!"

"Well, I told you," Vivian said. A great relief was growing in her. As soon as Jonathan mentioned the time ghosts, she knew how she was going to get home.

"I *hate* feeling a fool like this!" Jonathan snarled with his face in his fists and his pigtail draped over his arm.

Vivian took a long, happy breath. "I bet I know," she said, "how you can find the real Time Lady."

"No, you don't," Jonathan said flatly. "My father and Mr. Enkian and Sam's father went to that station in 1939, and she gave them all the slip. And me too, for that matter."

"Yes, but I know how she did it," Vivian said.

"Prove it," said Jonathan.

"All right," said Vivian. For lack of anywhere better, she sat on the empty-frame table. The nothing creaked a bit, but it held her up. "She was on that train, wasn't she? That was why you were all there."

"I don't know. All I overheard in the Chronologue was the place and the time. I worked the rest out from seeing our time ghosts," Jonathan said. "And I got it wrong," he added morbidly.

"Just listen," said Vivian. "Everyone else on that train went straight along to the exit to be shared out to homes. And they were all children on that train—I know that for a fact. So she must be quite small—small enough to pass herself off as an evacuee, mustn't she?"

Jonathan nodded. He had taken his face out of his fists and was trying not to look too hopeful. "All right. She puts her hand trustingly into a farmer's wife's hand, and off she goes. How do we find out which farmer's wife?"

"Easy," said Vivian. "We go and see Cousin Marty. She lives there. It's a small place, and she'll know everyone. She can tell us who took in which children, and we only have to go around the houses like detectives to find her."

Jonathan half sprang up. Then he flopped down again. "It's no good. She's time-traveling by now. Didn't you hear what Sam's father said about the war in the 1980s? That must mean she's got as far as that now.''

As far as Vivian knew, this might have been true. But if she let Jonathan think that, she would never get home. "Not if we go back to the precise moment on the station," she said persuasively. "We can catch her before she sets off."

Jonathan sprang up properly. "It might work!" Then he flopped down once more. "It's no good. We can't get near a private time lock after Sam got found with the keys."

"Can't we use an ordinary time lock? Say we're going to—to the Hundredth Century and change it secretly?" Vivian asked.

"Not a chance!" said Jonathan. "The public locks are all monitored. They don't let people our age anywhere near the Unstable Eras."

So this meant Vivian had to use the idea the time ghosts had given her. Though she had meant to lead up to it all along, it seemed very shaky now that she came to put it into words. "But what about our time ghosts?" she said. "We were coming from somewhere. And we had a look—I mean, we'd be all excited like that if we'd just found a secret time lock, wouldn't we?"

"You've got it!" Jonathan shouted. He leaped up, crashed out of his room, and went racing downward through the palace. Vivian flew after him to keep him excited. The little ghostly blue flowers circling around her white sleeves kept reminding her that she and Jonathan were in different clothes from the time ghosts. She was fairly sure they would not find a time lock. But she did not point this out in case Jonathan got depressed again.

Jonathan probably knew something was not quite right. He turned to her with a nervous smile as he moved the chain across to open the old door. "This is too easy. We can't be going to find anything." The door creaked open. Jonathan shut it securely behind them and turned on a light that Vivian had not known was there. The stone walls and floor stretched in front of them, very blank and empty. "You walk down there," Jonathan said. "And I'll tell you to stop when you get to the place where the ghosts start.''

Vivian paced slowly toward the door to the Chronologue at the other end. A few yards before she reached it, Jonathan called out, ''Stop! Can you see anything?''

Vivian looked at the stone floor, the arched stone ceiling, and the bare stone walls. They were all plain, except for a place in the left-hand wall where an old archway had been stopped up with smaller stones than the rest. ''There's a—'' she began, pointing. But she found herself speaking through the thump of sprinting feet, and Jonathan arrived before she could say another word.

''Let's see! Let's see!'' he said, shaking and wild with excitement. He put both hands to the smaller stones of the blocked arch and shoved. He pushed this way, and he pushed that. Nothing happened. ''I *know* it must open!'' Jonathan cried out, and he kicked the stones the way he kicked the church organ in his room. ''Ow!'' he said, hopping on one foot, holding the other in both hands. ''I forgot I was wearing sand—''

The wall of stones swung around, pivoting in the middle of the archway, to leave a narrow black opening on both sides. A dry, dusty smell came out. Jonathan let go of his foot and stared, so white with excitement that his face seemed all flicker from his sight function.

''We found it!'' he whispered.

''How do we know it's a time lock?'' Vivian said. Her plan had worked so easily that it scared her. And she felt very nervous of those yawning black slits.

''We go and look,'' Jonathan said. He pressed a stud on his belt, and it suddenly gave him a halo of light, as if he were yet another ghost. ''This only lasts about five minutes,'' he said, sounding quite as nervous as Vivian felt. ''We'll have to be quick.'' He started to edge his way into the nearest opening. The light from his belt showed that the back of the swiveled wall was made of something old and gray that was not stone. The stones were just a disguise.

He was halfway through when the door from the palace creaked. Sam's voice boomed down the passage. "What are you doing?"

I might have known! Vivian thought. There *had* to be a reason why those ghosts were in different clothes! "Hush!" she called. "It's a secret time lock."

Sam came down the passage at a rolling, pounding run and got to the archway just as Vivian was edging through after Jonathan. "Just at the right moment!" he said gleefully, in what was meant to be a whisper. "I have all the luck!"

"Shouldn't you be in bed?" Vivian whispered hopelessly as Sam squeezed through the slit on the opposite side of the wall.

"Of course not!" said Sam. "Hey! There are stairs going down!"

Jonathan was halfway around the turn of a spiral stair that was the only thing in the square stone space beyond the archway. Vivian and Sam followed the unearthly greenish glow from his belt, around and down, and around and down again. The stone steps were steep enough to give Sam trouble, and as they went lower, the steps got steeper still. Each one was a massive block of old stone. By the end Sam was sitting down, sliding from block to block. Vivian was holding on to the huge wedge-shaped stairs in the ceiling overhead and lowering herself gently, and even Jonathan was having to go carefully. The place felt awfully old. Oldness pressed quietly in on them from all around. It was a cold, nonhuman feeling.

Vivian thought of the giant stone shape of Faber John, sleeping under the city. Could he have made the bottom stairs long ago? she wondered. And ordinary-sized people built the top ones later?

"I'm down," Jonathan said softly.

They slid down the last huge step to join him in a small room built of the same enormous stones. Facing them was a plain sheet of slate, let into the wall like a door. It was glimmering faintly, with little flickers chasing across it. Beside it, one of the stones of the wall stuck out a short way. There was a hollow in the top of it, and a thing like a gray goose egg lay in the hollow. There was nothing else in the room at all.

"*Is* it a time lock?" Vivian said.

"I don't know. I've never seen anything like it before," Jonathan said.

"No controls," said Sam. "No chronograph, no way to set it, no activator, no emergency phone—it's been dismantled, or it's not a time lock."

"It doesn't look as if there ever *were* any of those things," Jonathan said. "But that flicker looks active. Do you think this is a control?" He put his hand to the gray goose egg in the hollow and jumped a bit when it turned out to be quite easy to pick up. He weighed the thing dubiously in his hand. "It's heavy," he said. "And it feels active, too. But it's smooth. There aren't any control studs or finger grips anywhere. Look."

He held the egg out, and they all bent over it in the green light from his belt. It might have been a real egg. There were no joins in it. Sam began to breathe even more loudly than usual. "It's weird!" he said. "Where were you trying to get to?"

"The station when Jonathan kidnapped me," Vivian said.

The moment she spoke, the glimmer of the slate blazed into yellow daylight, the color of a hot day late in the afternoon. They all blinked, and sniffed smells of chaff and cow manure and coal smoke. When the dazzle went off, they stared along the platform of a railway station. It was full of children at the far end, a mass of scraggy legs and necks and old suitcases mixed with square brown gas mask cases, with school hats and caps bobbing above. Nearer to them, beside the train with all its doors standing open, a hot-faced, distraught girl was just turning to look at a lanky boy in glasses.

The sight did not give Vivian any jolt of fear, the way seeing the time ghosts had, but it was not pleasant either. She had no idea her nose was that shape from the side. And the hot coat made her backside bulge. "Don't we look awful!" she said, looking at the disguised Jonathan instead. "I know what was wrong with you—I couldn't *think* at the time! You should have been carrying a gas mask. It's illegal not to. I knew something was odd."

"We can't go through now," Jonathan said. "We'd look even odder."

"My dad would spot us," Sam whispered, pointing.

Vivian searched among the crowd of adults waiting up by the station exit. The first one she recognized was Sempitern Walker, looking thoroughly peculiar in plus fours and a tweed cap. Mr. Enkian was standing beside him in a raincoat and snap-brim fedora, looking even odder. Sam's father was one of the men wearing armbands. He was efficiently dividing the evacuees up into twos and fours, and somehow he looked far more convincing.

"I can't think how she escaped, with your father doing that," Jonathan said to Sam.

Vivian, to tell the truth, wondered too. "But she did—" she began.

At that moment the lanky disguised Jonathan picked the hot Vivian's suitcase up off the platform. Vivian's earlier self dived for it, and both of them started to turn around to face the small stone room. Sam, Jonathan, and Vivian, with one accord, all backed away toward the stairs in order not to be seen. It was a silly, instinctive thing to do. The marvel was that it worked. As soon as they moved, the station disappeared and left them only the green glow of Jonathan's belt to see by. The slate was solidly there again, still glimmering faintly.

"How did that happen?" said Sam.

"I've no idea," said Jonathan. He rolled the smooth gray egg from hand to hand before he put it back in the hollow. "But the point is that it *does* work. Let's go and get our Twenty Century clothes. Then we can go through."

Sam's voice rose in a roar of protest, filling the little room. "It's not *fair*! I haven't *got* any clothes! You have to wait for me to get some. I'm not going to be left behind this time! It's not *fair*!"

Vivian said nothing. She hoped Jonathan would tell Sam to get lost. But Jonathan—after a moment when he obviously wanted to—said fair-mindedly, "Well, can you snitch some clothes in time for us to go first thing after breakfast tomorrow?"

"Yes!" Sam danced about, hugging himself. "Whoopee! I've never time-traveled! Whoopee!" He scrambled for the stairs. "I'll go and get around the Costumes Patroller now!" he called. "I won't need to snitch them. She gave me yours to play dress-up in."

As Vivian and Jonathan climbed the stairs after him, Jonathan said consolingly, "It only *feels* like a long wait. But now we know that the lock works, we can go back to that precise moment anytime we want." Vivian thought he was trying to console himself as much as her.

Here the light from Jonathan's belt turned dim purple and faded out. There was a strange noise from up in front. "I'm not frightened," Sam called down. "I just can't see."

"Neither can we," Jonathan called back, in a voice that was too carefully calm. It was not just dark. It was a thick blackness that made you feel the world had gone away. "You'll have to go by touch."

They fumbled their way slowly up the steep stone blocks. In that dark it was hard to believe they were climbing at all. And Vivian suddenly had the horrors. She was certain that a spider was going to drop off the roof and down her neck any second. She hated spiders. She had not noticed any spider webs on the way down, but then, of course, she had not been looking. She shut her eyes and kept her neck scrunched down. She wanted to scream.

"Bring a flashlight next time," Sam said, in a wavery, wanting-to-scream voice.

"Yes. Do," said Vivian. "Are—are there many spiders in Time City?"

"Only in Erstwhile Science Museum," Jonathan said from below. He sounded properly calm now. "I've found what to do. Think of something quite different. I'm doing timefield equations in my head."

"I'll do Roman script spelling," Sam called, suddenly cheerful again.

Vivian tried the seven-times table, but she had always had difficulty with that one, and besides, school things seemed very far away from a hole in the floor in Time City. She was forced to think of something nearer at hand. Tomorrow, she thought, she would be back in her own century staying with Cousin Marty. Except, if you went by those time ghosts, Sam shouldn't have been there. There were only herself and Jonathan, and they were coming *back,* not going. Perhaps that meant that Sam would not be able to get any clothes, or catch measles or something. But even if Sam didn't come too, that still did not explain why Vivian had to come back, or look so excited doing it.

The stairs were becoming shallower. They must be getting near the top.

"Eff, Eh, Bee, Ee, Are." Sam's voice came down. "Jay, Oh, Aitch—I can *see!*"

By the next step Vivian could see, too, enormous stones in a very dim light that must be coming through from the passage in the palace. She stood up and galloped the rest of the way, with Jonathan jostling her behind and Sam's shoelace flipping the stones in front of her face. In seconds, they were squeezing through the gaps beside the pivoting false wall and into light that seemed so bright that their eyes watered. Jonathan had to switch off his eye flicker in order to scrub his eyes with his rather smudged white sleeve. Then he swung the false door carefully shut again so that it looked once more like an archway that was walled up.

"Oof!" Sam said as they went along the passage. "That was exciting!"

Almost *too* exciting! Vivian thought, but she did not say anything because now she had started thinking about those puzzling time ghosts, she could not stop. What *could* be going to happen? she wondered while Jonathan slid the chain back to the right place on the door and while he was telling Sam to turn up at nine the next morning or they would go without him. Perhaps Sam turns up too late, Vivian thought, but she was not really sure. Sam went trotting off. Vivian went on wondering until Jonathan interrupted her thoughts at the top of the polished stairs.

"V.S., I'm sorry," he said awkwardly. "I really am. It was stupid of me to keep on believing you were the Time Lady. I know you're not now. And I know I've got you into a mess. You can go home if you like, when we've found the real Time Lady."

That was pretty surprising from a proud boy like Jonathan, Vivian thought. "Thanks," she said. "But won't people wonder if Cousin Vivian just disappears?"

"We'll get around that somehow," Jonathan said confidently. "Good night."

"Good night," Vivian said, but she said it rather absentmindedly because now she was thinking, If even Jonathan thinks I can go home, why *did*—I mean, why *will* I—be coming back?

This was still a complete mystery to her next morning when she got up. After thinking about it all over again, she decided that, as a precaution, she ought to wear the same clothes as her ghost. So when I *do* come back for whatever reason, she thought, that will be got over with and I can go home straight after that.

She unfolded the wall cupboard and looked at the row of suits hanging so strangely on nothing. And she had not the foggiest idea which of them her ghost had been wearing. She remembered the diamonds on Jonathan's suit, but all she knew about her own was that it was colored, and not the white one with the ghostly blue flowers.

"Bother!" she said.

The only thing to do seemed to be to shut her eyes and pull

out the suit she touched first. If it's the right one, it's going to be right however I choose it, she decided. And not, if not. Her hand met a suit. She opened her eyes and discovered it was electric yellow and violet, in zebralike stripes that moved this way and that of their own accord.

"I don't think this is right," she said. "I'd have remembered *this*." Still, it was chosen, so she put it on fatalistically. As soon as the suit sealed itself up the back, it became even more memorable. Big scarlet hearts lit up on her knees, her elbows, and her front.

Vivian was so busy looking down at them dubiously that she ran into Petula in the corridor outside. "Oh, you're up!" said Petula. "I was just coming to wake you. Elio *will* be pleased you're wearing that suit. He liked the colors ever so. Androids don't have much color sense, you know."

"It's very bright," Vivian said truthfully.

Petula took her downstairs and showed her to a room she called the matutinal. Jonathan was there, eating pancakes in a blaze of light from a swirly window. He had clearly been thinking the same way as Vivian, because he was wearing the suit with diamonds.

"I'll give Sam until five-to," he said. "Then we'll go."

Vivian could tell that he was regretting his fair-mindedness of last night. "Yes, but is this the right suit?" she said.

Jonathan glanced at it. "I can't remember, but it's bound to be wrong if Sam comes too. Unless something's happened to Sam," he added hopefully.

Sam's name was hardly out of his mouth when the door slid aside and Sam came in, hauling a birdcage carrier with a big white bundle floating under it. "I'm here," he announced. "She gave me all the right clothes."

"Speak of the devil!" Vivian said.

Jenny followed Sam into the room. "Meaning me?" she said, laughing. "What have you got there, Sam?"

"Dressing-up clothes," Sam said guiltily.

"Oh. I wondered if you'd brought the picnic," Jenny said. "Jonathan, Vivian, since it's the last day of half term, Ramona and I have decided to take the day off and show Vivian the country. We've checked the weather, and it's going to be a lovely hot day, so we thought we'd go down the river with a picnic."

It was lucky Jenny had her back to Sam. He went purple with dismay. Vivian had to push a big smile onto her face in order not to look as bad as Sam did. Jonathan's face went rather fixed, but he answered smoothly, "Good idea! When do you want to start?"

"Will about eleven do?" Jenny asked. "I've a load of things to see to here first."

Sam held his breath in order not to sigh with relief.

"We'll meet you in the hall at eleven then," Jonathan promised. As soon as Jenny had gone, he surged to his feet. "Pick up a pancake and bring it with you, V.S. We've got to get going."

Vivian picked up a pancake, but she sat down to eat it. Jonathan's mother is being really kind, she thought. I know it's because she thinks I'm her niece; but if I don't turn up for the picnic, she'll have wasted a day off work, and she'll worry where I am. And then it'll all come out, and Jonathan and Sam will be in really bad trouble. Oh bother! This must be the reason why my ghost was coming back!

"Come on," said Sam.

"Listen," said Vivian. "We can get to the right precise moment on the station, can't we?"

"Yes," Jonathan said impatiently. "All the same—"

"So can't we get back to the right precise moment too?" said Vivian. "How *do* we get back?"

Jonathan and Sam stared at each other. "Yes, how *do* we get back? You never thought of that!" Sam said accusingly.

"I, er—" said Jonathan. "Well, we know we did get back, so it must be going to be all right."

"Yes, when you and her go off on your own," said Sam. "What about me? Find out. Ask Elio. He knows everything."

"All right," Jonathan agreed. "But I'll have to be awfully cunning about asking him. If he gets a hint of what we're doing, he'll tell. It would be his duty. Androids are like that."

Sam rubbed his behind nervously. "Be cunning," he said. "Very cunning. But find out or *I'll* tell."

Jonathan made an impatient noise and rushed to the door. It opened as he got there, and he nearly bumped into Elio coming in. "I was just coming to look for you!" he said.

Speak of the devil again! Vivian thought, taking three more pancakes and carefully pouring syrup over them. She was not going to let Jonathan rush her off to the Twentieth Century without breakfast first.

"You see, Elio, I've been reading this book," Jonathan began cunningly.

Elio advanced in his soft, respectful way. He walked around Jonathan and then around Sam. He came over to the table. Vivian looked up from her first bite of pancake to find Elio standing beside her and smiling all over his pale face. "Ah, Miss Vivian," he said. "Petula told me you were wearing that suit. I'm so glad you like it. Those are my favorite colors."

"Very pretty," Vivian said, with her mouth full. "Thanks for choosing it."

"Thank *you*," Elio said, with a little bow. He switched himself from Vivian to Jonathan. "You mentioned a book, Master Jonathan?"

Vivian had time to eat a hearty breakfast while Jonathan exercised his cunning. He gave a long, long description of the book. Elio stood with his head bent, listening attentively, and did not move for nearly ten minutes.

"It sounds a rather confused plot," he said at length. "What is the title?"

"I've forgotten," Jonathan said hurriedly. "But the point is— well, it's not important what happens in the end. It was the time locks they kept using that I wanted to ask you about. They sounded too simple to be true. The book says they were just a sheet of energized greenstone and no controls, no chronometers—nothing!''

"Ah," said Elio. "I see it was a very old book. Those are the most primitive kind of time locks there were. They were discontinued many centuries ago because agents were always losing the controls."

"The controls?" Jonathan said, trying not to sound too eager.

"An egg-shaped device, which nobody understands," said Elio, "since they are all reputed to have been made by Faber John himself. The power source and chronometer, together with spatial directionals of great accuracy, are all contained within it. Thus, in order to open the lock back into Time City from history, the agent had to take the device with him. In the hurly-burly out there, it was fatally easy to drop, mislay, or be robbed of this control. It happened so frequently that there were eventually very few left. They were, you must understand, irreplaceable. If you wish to examine one of the remaining few, you will find it on display in Erstwhile Science."

"We'll go and see it now," Jonathan said, with a meaning look at Vivian, who had started to eat melon. "Er—how did the egg things work?"

"Upon mental orders from the agent," said Elio. "As I said, they were somewhat mysterious, but I believe that they obeyed commands of the voice or thoughts properly directed. Does that explain your difficulty?"

"I hope so," said Jonathan. "I mean, yes—thanks, Elio."

"Then I must go," said Elio. He bowed to them and went to the door. "Please try to remember the title of that book," he said, pausing in the doorway. "I do not like to hear of something I do not know."

"I'll think hard," Jonathan promised. As soon as the door closed behind Elio, he rounded on Vivian. "Come on, V.S.! Stop stuffing your face and get your Twenty Century clothes."

Pushing me about! Vivian thought. "When I've eaten my fruit," she said. "I've never had this huge, juicy kind before. Anyway, now you know, all you've got to do is tell that egg thing to get us back just before eleven. It doesn't matter *when* we go."

"Yes, but I'm going to need a butter-pie if I have to wait much longer," Sam said plaintively.

Jonathan was well prepared this time. He had found a square box on a strap, which looked almost like a gas mask case, to carry the egg-shaped control in. From this box he took a slender tube of oil and oiled the big old-fashioned hinges of the chained door to stop it from creaking. This might be only an adventure to him, Vivian thought, as they all tiptoed down the stone passage, carrying their clothes, but he was being quite serious about it.

Jonathan had a powerful little flashlight in his box too. At the blocked archway, he shone it over the stones until he found the white mark his sandal had made the night before. Then he kicked the same place. The false door pivoted smoothly around, and they squeezed through the gaps. With the stronger light it was much easier to go down the stairs. When they reached the stone room at the bottom, Jonathan propped the flashlight on the stairs to give them light while they changed into Twenty Century clothes.

Sam's excited breathing filled the room as he unwrapped his bundle. Vivian was silent with dismay as she unfolded hers. Petula or someone had put her clothes through the cleaner that washed the Time City pajamas, and it had not suited them at all. Her coat was two sizes too small, and her school hat was ruined. She decided to leave them behind and wear just her skirt with the top of the pajama suit as a blouse. Her skirt *seemed* the right size, but it felt strange and tight when she put it on, and it felt worse when she had rolled up the legs of her pajamas under it and fastened them with the garters from her socks. Then the top of her pajamas shone out luridly in the flashlight beam. Vivian realized that nobody in 1939 was likely to wear purple and yellow stripes that moved about all the time. She was forced to ram her arms into her navy blue knitted cardigan, which had shrunk almost as badly as her coat, and then use all her strength to get it buttoned up. She felt terrible.

Sam was in trouble too. The Time Patrol lady had given him gray shorts with red suspenders, and he got tangled in the suspenders. For his feet he had heavy lace-up boots with nails in the soles, and these gave him even more trouble. So, while Jonathan, dressed in gray flannel and glasses, jittered impatiently about with the egg in his hand, Vivian did her best to sort Sam out. She got the suspenders straight. She knelt down and laced the boots, and tied each one in a double bow, knowing what Sam was like. But nothing would persuade Sam's hair to stay hidden under his striped school cap. Vivian had to find a rubber band from her shrunken coat pocket and fasten his hair in a knob on top of his head, like Sempitern Walker's.

"I feel hideous!" he complained.

"You look it," said Jonathan. "Are you ready *now*?" He held the gray egg up. "The station at the moment I found V.S.," he said.

Hot afternoon daylight streamed from the slab of slate and was interrupted by a big billow of yellow smoke, which blew into their faces, smelling like fish. Sam coughed. "It's different!" he said hoarsely, and the smoke cleared.

Maybe, Vivian thought, they had come a moment or so later. The train was chuffing slowly out of the station, sending fogs of the yellow smoke rolling along the platform. It was hard to tell just what the difference was, but it did seem that the figures of herself and Jonathan were a long way farther up the platform toward the exit, as if Vivian had just climbed out of quite a different carriage. The crowd of evacuees was milling about beyond them, and it seemed a much thinner crowd than Vivian remembered. Sam's father, when she glimpsed him murkily through the smoke, was not having nearly so much sorting out to do.

"Get going while the smoke's there to hide us!" Jonathan said, hurriedly stuffing the egg into his box.

Sam walked forward, and Vivian followed. Smoke surrounded them. The nails in Sam's boots chinked on the platform. Vivian looked around in time to see Jonathan coming out of nowhere behind them. Oh dear! she thought. Now he's the only one with a gas mask. I hope we don't meet an Air Raid Warden!

"Where do we go now?" Jonathan whispered.

Vivian had not given as much thought to details as Jonathan. She had to think quickly. If they went up to the exit, they would run into Sam's father and Jonathan's. She turned the other way. "There must be a way out this way," she said.

They passed some milk churns. The smoke cleared as the train left, and they came out into hot yellow sunlight at the very end of the platform, where it sloped down to the grass beside the railway lines. There was a convenient little white gate in the wire fence labeled GWR PRIVATE. They went through it, private or not, and came onto a road, where sparse groups of children with gas masks and luggage were already walking away with the people who were giving them homes.

"You'll want a nice cup of tea," they heard one say. "And you can have the room my Will had before he was called up."

"I brung me teddy," one of the children announced. "Ain't he loverly?"

Jonathan looked back to the station building. "Shall we go and look for your cousin Marty?" he said. "She must be quite worried by now. Or would it be safer to wait here till she comes by?"

"I don't know what she looks like," Vivian confessed. "I'm not even sure that she's a she. All I know is the address on the other side of my label: M. Bradley, Fifty-two Gladstone Road. We'll have to go to the house and wait for her to get back. Or him."

"You might have said so *before*!" Jonathan said, exasperated. "I could have brought a street map."

"It's the country. It won't be big," Vivian said soothingly.

They set off after the crowd of evacuees and hosts, down the sort of street there always is near a station.

"Horrible houses," Sam said, chinking sturdily along.

"Hideous," Jonathan agreed.

"I'm not responsible," Vivian said huffily. But she felt she was rather. The red-brick rows made a dismal contrast with the buildings of Time City. And by the end of that street it became clear to her that, though this town was small compared with London or Time City, it was still big enough to get lost in. They turned into another street and another. The crowd in front of them dwindled away down other streets, and none of the roads were called Gladstone Road. In the end, Jonathan stopped the last group of evacuees before they could dwindle away too, and politely asked the grownups with them where Gladstone Road was.

He was given rather confusing directions, and they set off again. Before long they found themselves in the center of what was obviously a thoroughly sleepy town. There was nothing much in sight except some ancient ruins over the road and a garage with one rusty gas pump and TYPHOO TEA painted on the house that belonged to it. There was a man in overalls pottering about the pump. Vivian timidly crossed the road and asked him the way.

His directions were much clearer, but it was a long distance. They walked and walked, right to the other end of the town. It was still very hot. Vivian's mixture of clothes felt more and more uncomfortable. Sam's bootlaces came undone in spite of the double bows, and he stumbled over them. Jonathan had sweat dripping out from under his glasses. He became more and more snappish and kept staring around as if he expected someone to ambush him from behind a streetlight or a mailbox.

"You might have explained properly that you had no idea where you were going!" he said angrily, while Vivian was kneeling in the road tying Sam's boots.

"And we could have brought something to drink. I'm boiling!" Sam complained.

"So am I. At least you've got bare knees," Jonathan said.

"But these boots are like lead footmuffs," said Sam. "Can't I take them off?"

"No. That's not respectable for these days," Vivian said. "There. That's *double*-double bows, and if they come undone again, I'll—I'll eat my socks!"

"Oh, let's get on with this wild-goose chase!" Jonathan said. "I don't believe there's a Gladstone Road or a Cousin Marty anywhere in the *century*!"

Vivian took a moment to haul up her socks. Without her garters they fell down every other step. She was not sure she believed in Cousin Marty any longer either. Ever since those slight but definite differences at the station, she had felt very uneasy. History had changed here. It could mean that nothing she knew was true anymore.

She was quite surprised when they came to Gladstone Road around the next corner. It could have been the road outside the station. There were the same red houses, yellow privet hedges, and silver railings, but since it was on the other side of the town, they could see green country rearing up beyond the roofs. There was a hump of hill with trees on it and, almost behind that, another taller hill, covered in grass, with some kind of tower at the top.

Number fifty-two was halfway along. They hovered uncertainly outside its spiked silver gate. "Let me knock," Vivian whispered. "If she's back, I'll ask for a drink of water and then get talking." But she still hovered. This town was so much bigger than she had expected that it did not seem likely any longer that Cousin Marty would know anything about the other evacuees. Jonathan was right to call it a wild-goose chase. And I still have to go away again and come back for some reason, she thought. It all seemed more impossible the longer she stood there.

"Bother you!" said Sam. He boldly opened the gate and climbed the path to the front door, where he seized the door knocker and battered away with it.

Someone snatched the door open. A thin, withered lady stood there with her arms folded, looking grimly at Sam. She had warts on her face. Her hair was done up in a brown turban and the rest of her in a brown dress. "What do you want?" she said. "I thought it was the other one come back, or I wouldn't have opened the door."

"Water!" groaned Sam, like someone dying in the desert.

Jonathan pushed him aside. "Mrs. Bradley?" he asked smoothly.

"*Miss* Bradley," the lady contradicted him. "Miss Martha Bradley is my name, my boy, and I don't—"

"Quite so," said Jonathan. "And you were supposed to be having Vivian Smith to stay with you—"

"Don't talk to me about that!" Miss Bradley said angrily.

"I only wanted to inquire—" Jonathan began, still trying to be smooth.

But Miss Bradley interrupted him with a gush of angry talk. "I know there's a war on," she said, "and I know we all have to do our bit. So when my Cousin Joan writes to me from London after never a word for all these years, I *don't* tell her the things I had a mind to tell her, though I know she only remembers me when she wants something. I said I'd have the child. Mind you, in the ordinary way nothing would possess me to have a shoddy little Cockney in my house—"

"Shoddy little Cockney!" Vivian exclaimed, staring at the lady with indignation mixed with strong horror. Surely she could not be Cousin Marty! But Mum's name was Joan, so it looked as if she must be.

"That's what I said," Miss Bradley agreed. "They all have head lice. And worse. I was prepared for that. But I nearly dropped when I found he was a boy. Then he cheeks me to my face—"

"Excuse me," Jonathan interrupted. "Did you say a boy?"

"I did," said Miss Bradley, refolding her arms more grimly still. "I don't have boys in my house. You may have nice manners, but you don't step over my doormat, my boy—you or the other one. My cousin Joan played a dirty trick on me, with her nice letter, all Cousin Marty this, Cousin Marty that. She never mentioned that Vivian is a boy's name, too. I'm going to write and give her a piece of my mind about that!''

So this *was* Cousin Marty! And it sounded as if there had been another mix-up worse than any of the wildest worries Vivian had had on the train. She nudged Jonathan to suggest they come away. There did not seem much point in finding out any more. But Jonathan stood where he was.

''Your story fascinates me strangely,'' he said. ''So you met a boy named Vivian Smith at the station just now?''

''What else could I do?'' Cousin Marty demanded. ''He went up to Mrs. Upton and then to Lady Sturge and asked them if they were there to meet someone called Smith. Then he came up to me and waved his label at me! I was standing right beside them. I couldn't very well deny my own flesh and blood in front of Lady Sturge, could I? So I took him in charge and brought him back here. And we were hardly through the front gate before he cheeked me and went off again. If you're looking for him, my boy, he's not here!''

''Do you know where he went?'' Jonathan asked.

''Up the Tor, for some reason,'' Cousin Marty said. ''I said, 'And where do you think you're going?' And he said, 'I'm going up the Tor. And since you've made it so clear you don't want me, I probably won't come back.' The cheek! Then he says, 'I'll find someone else more like a human being,' he says, and off he goes. I wish I'd never bothered to get in some meat paste for his tea now!''

''Ah,'' said Jonathan. ''Then perhaps you'd be kind enough to direct us to this Tor?''

''So you *are* a friend of his!'' Cousin Marty said. This clearly damned all three of them black in her eyes. ''Everyone knows the Tor!'' But probably to make sure that they went, she stepped down from her stance in the doorway and pointed above the roofs of the houses. ''That's the Tor. The green hill behind with the tower on top.''

"*Thank* you, Miss Bradley," Jonathan said unctuously. He was very excited. He turned around and bundled Vivian and Sam down the path to the gate so fast that Sam's sliding boots struck sparks from the gravel. "Go on, go *on*!" he whispered.

"If you find him, tell him from me he's not coming back here!" Cousin Marty shouted after them. "He can go to the Mayor and get himself allocated to someone else!" She waited to make sure they were out of the gate and the gate was shut. Then she went indoors and shut her front door with a slam.

Jonathan set off at a fast walk toward the green hills. Sam chanked behind miserably. "She never gave me any water," he said. "I don't like it in history."

"You won't die," said Jonathan, striding along. "If you ask me," he said to Vivian, "you're well out of that. I did you a favor the other night. She must be one of the most horrible women in history!"

Vivian agreed with him. "Shoddy little Cockney!" she muttered to herself. The thought of having to stay with Cousin Marty made her back crawl. She would just have to make the time lock take her back to Lewisham instead. Mum would understand when she heard what Cousin Marty was like. "Why are we going after this boy?" she asked.

"Don't you see?" Jonathan said excitedly. "*That's* how she gave everyone the slip! She knew they were looking for a girl, so she disguised herself as a boy and asked people if they'd come to meet someone called Smith. Ten to one, someone would say yes, with a common name like that, and then she could go off with them under Sam's father's nose. It was pretty clever! And thanks to you, we've got a chance of catching her that Chronologue never dreamed of!"

"But what if this is just an ordinary boy who happens to be called Vivian?" Vivian objected.

"We have to check up on him. You can see that," Jonathan said confidently. He clearly had not the least doubt that they were on the track of the Time Lady at last. His confidence seemed to blaze them a trail to the Tor. At the end of the next street, where there did not seem any way to go, he led the way without hesitation onto a grassy footpath. This took them along under the nearer hill with trees, between hedges loaded with hawthorn berries and some ripe-looking blackberries.

Even Sam revived here. He ate all the ripe blackberries he could reach. "This part of history's better," he announced.

At the end of the path, they climbed a stile into a field. Now the Tor was directly in front of them. It was a strangely regular round hill, quite high and steep and covered with grass. The tower on top was like the tower of a church without any church to go with it.

"It looks like Endless Hill," said Sam.

"With the Gnomon on top," said Jonathan. "It does. How peculiar! No steps up it, though—just a path."

They climbed another stile and went steeply up a second field. There were cows in this field. Sam shot them a sideways look and tried to walk behind Vivian. "This bit of history's not so good," he said.

Vivian had never been near any cows before, and she was quite as scared as Sam. They were unexpectedly big. They stared and they chewed, like gangsters in films. She tried to walk on the other side of Jonathan. But Jonathan shot the cows a look too, and began to walk twice as fast.

"We want to be in time to catch her," he said.

They all walked as fast as they could. Maybe it was the cows. Or maybe it was some other reason. A feeling grew on them that they had to get to the top of the Tor as fast as possible. The tower was out of sight now. All they could see was a sheer grassy slope with a mud path zigzagging up it. But they all wanted to get to the tower, more and more urgently. Jonathan took the first part of the path at a run, with his box bouncing on his back. Then, to save time, he took to scrambling straight up the grassy slope, sliding and panting and pulling himself up with his hands.

Vivian and Sam clambered and panted and slid behind. One of Sam's boots came untied with the effort. Vivian supposed that she should be eating her socks at that, but she was far too busy trying not to slip on the short grass or put her hands on the flat thistles that had cunningly disguised themselves as grass.

Sam gradually got left behind, being smaller and burdened with boots. Vivian climbed furiously and kept just under the soles of Jonathan's shoes. That was all she ever seemed to see of him, climb as she would, until he slowed down over the last grassy bulge. Vivian thought her chest was going to burst by then.

"My legs ache," Jonathan said. "Let's rest."

They were clinging to the bulge, panting, when someone came up the hill beside them, running as fast as if the slope were level ground. Vivian saw long legs and caught a glimpse of an old squashed hat on the head above them as the man raced past them. He shouted something as he passed. Then he ran on and disappeared over the bulge of the hill.

"What did he say?" asked Jonathan.

"It sounded like 'Hurry'!" said Vivian. "Come on!"

Somehow neither of them had any doubt that it was urgent. They went up over the bulge in a floundering run, into sudden wide blue sky at the top of the hill. The space was quite small and flat. The tower was only some yards away, and it was indeed a church tower without a church. There were two open church-like archways in it at the bottom. Vivian could see sky right through it for a second, before Jonathan blocked her view by springing upright and sprinting for the tower.

"*Stop that!*" he yelled. His cap fell off and his pigtail flailed as he ran.

Vivian pelted after him. She had just a glimpse of something going on inside the tower, low down on the floor, and she knew that was what the man with the hat had been shouting about. Jonathan flung himself through the archway. Vivian hurtled after him. Over his shoulder, she saw a small figure in gray flannel crouched over a hole in the tower floor, and a mound of broken stone and loose earth beside that with a spade stuck in it. The boy looked up as they came. He was fair. His thin face glared like a cornered animal's. Then his thin hands dived for the earthy hole in front of him, found something, wrenched at it, and pulled it free. It looked like a rusty iron box.

Jonathan pounced for it and tried to drag it out of the boy's hands. But the boy was up, quick as a flash, and running out through the opposite archway with the box under his arm. Jonathan stumbled forward. Vivian dodged around him, past a clear sight of Jonathan's glasses falling into the hole and Jonathan's stumbling foot coming down on top of the glasses, and raced after the boy.

"Sam!" she shrieked. "Stop him!"

The boy was running down the other side of the hill, his thin legs flying under his gray shorts. Sam came around the tower, with his face crimson and both sets of bootlaces flapping loose, and pounded across the hill to cut the boy off.

Sam should have caught the boy and Vivian would have arrived an instant later to help. But the boy was no longer there. By the time Vivian converged with Sam, there was only bare green slope where there had just before been a boy running away. One of Sam's bootlaces whipped itself around his ankles, and he fell on his face, breathing like someone sawing wood.

"I may be dying!" he gasped.

"But where did he *go*?" Vivian said, quite bewildered. She looked around. There was no sign the boy had ever been there. Nor was there any sign of the man who had run past them shouting, and that was quite as puzzling now that she thought about it. The only other person in sight was Jonathan, coming slowly and fumblingly down the hill.

Jonathan looked white and wretched. "Why did I have to shout?" he said. "He hadn't seen us. I could have got there in time to save that polarity, if I'd only held my tongue!"

"What do you mean?" said Vivian.

"That thing he stole," Jonathan said. "It was one of Faber John's polarities—the things that keep Time City in place. I *know* it was. I can feel. And now he's stolen it and gone time-traveling with it, messing up history for ten centuries to come, and it's all my *fault*!"

Vivian would have liked to say that this was nonsense. There was not a scrap of proof of what Jonathan said. But there was no doubt that the boy *had* stolen something from the tower. And she could feel that something important had gone from the Tor. It was suddenly a much duller place. Mist was forming down near the bottom of the hill, and though the evening light was red on the low land all around, it was a melancholy and final sort of light. From somewhere in the distance an air raid siren began to howl. Vivian shivered and took hold of Sam to pull him up. "Let's go back to Time City," she said.

But Jonathan said at the same moment, "We've *got* to go after him!" He was carrying the egg control in the box on his shoulder, and the egg obeyed him instantly.

It was suddenly afternoon again. Sam was now lying on his face in a road. The air felt different, heavier and more dusty. But the houses lining the road were not very different from the ones Vivian had known all her life. Apart from one or two new yellow ones, they were the sort of houses that lined the main roads out of London and had probably been built about the time she was born. But they had been cared for since with bright white paint to a smartness Vivian had never seen in houses before. The only obviously future thing was a giant silver building standing smoking quietly out near the horizon.

"I think we've moved about a hundred years," she said. Somehow she was rather more awed to be in 2039 than she had been to be in Time City.

"Yes, but I've lost those stupid glasses," Jonathan said. "Is the boy here?"

"There," said Sam, waving his boots about in an effort to get untangled.

The boy was walking away from them up the road with the box still under his arm. His clothes had changed. He was now in wide trousers that were either too long or too short, depending whether you thought they were shorts or not, and his jacket had immense gathered sleeves. As Vivian looked and Jonathan peered at him, the boy sensed they were there. He jerked and looked over his shoulder. The thin face stared angrily back at them. Then he was gone again.

"I can't see him," said Jonathan.

Sam struggled to his knees. "Gone again," he said. "He's probably got one of those egg things too."

A roaring, which they had been hearing without truly noticing, came suddenly louder out of the distance and swept up to them, where it settled to a dull drumming. Before Jonathan could suggest following the boy again, they were surrounded by six things a bit like motorcycles. Six men in wide-sleeved uniforms sat on the cycles, looking jeering and grim.

"North Circular Vigilante Group Seven," one of them announced. "What are you folk doing going around dressed like that?"

Vivian uncomfortably realized that nearly all the buttons on her cardigan had burst off and that one of her pajama legs had fallen down from its garter under her skirt.

Another of the six men produced a board with a form clipped to it. "Unseemly clothing," he said, leaning back in his saddle and ticking off squares in the form. "Disturbing the peace. Littering." He looked at Sam's cap, which had fallen off beside him. "Failure to wash," he said, looking from the blackberry stains around Sam's mouth to Vivian's muddy hands. "Not from around here, are they? That makes unauthorized travel. Vagrancy, too."

"This is going to earn them a right good whipping!" one of

the other men said, obviously liking the idea very much. "Twelve strokes each already."

"Jonathan!" said Vivian.

"Truancy from school—that's obvious," said the man with the form. "Lying down in a public road. Think they've stolen anything?"

"Use that egg, you fool!" Sam bellowed, rolling around in the road and grabbing Vivian's ankle as he tried to get up.

"Abusive language," said the man, ticking another square.

"Eighteen strokes," said another man, even more pleased.

"Time lock," Jonathan said desperately. "Time City! *Time lock!* Oh, why won't it—"

The egg worked at last, in a slow, heavy, swirling way. They seemed to be dragged away backward a long, long distance, and then to hang there. Vivian had time to think that only the accident that she had grabbed Jonathan for balance when Sam took hold of her ankle had caused the egg to take all three of them. Then she had time to wonder if the egg was working at all. And at last they were in pitchy darkness. Jonathan, after furious fumbling, found the flashlight in his pocket and switched it on. The light seemed weak and yellow after the open street, but it showed the massive stones and the glimmering slate of the time lock. They all sighed with relief.

"That was frightening," Sam said, still on the floor. "What went wrong?"

"The egg wouldn't work at all at first," Jonathan said. "Maybe it's too old and worn out. Or maybe we asked it to do too much." He put it carefully back in its hollow. "Now I don't know what to do," he said dejectedly.

"What time is it?" asked Vivian.

Jonathan fumbled again and found the clock stud on his belt. He stared at the green-glowing dial on his hand. "Twelve forty-two. No, that *can't* be right! I don't know. I've no idea what time we've come back to!"

"That picnic!" said Sam. He wrenched off his tangled boots and began tearing off the rest of his disguise. The other two pulled off their things in an equal hurry.

Vivian was so alarmed at what Jenny might be thinking that she was ready first. Mum hated to be kept waiting. Jenny was probably the same. Vivian rushed in front up the staircase and was first out into the passage. All she could think of was the uproar there was bound to be if it was really nearly one o'clock. She left Jonathan to swing the false door back and ran up the passage. She barged through the chained door.

It was lucky that Jonathan had oiled the door. Elio was standing only a few yards away, straightening an exhibit in one of the showcases. He had not seen Vivian. She had made barely a sound coming through the door. She had the presence of mind to catch hold of the chain before it could rattle as the door swung, and ease the door shut behind her. Then she stood in front of it, wondering what to do. If she stayed there, she could stop Sam and Jonathan from barging through behind her. But Elio was bound to wonder if he saw her. And if he realized what they were doing, he would tell. Jonathan had said so.

Elio started to turn around.

V ivian took three giant tiptoe strides until she was more or less level with Elio. "Er, hello," she said.

Elio finished turning around with astonishing speed. "Hello, miss. You walk very quietly. I failed to hear you approach."

"You were busy with your museum," Vivian said. "That's why you didn't hear me."

"True," said Elio. He looked back at the display case in a dissatisfied way. It was labeled SEVENTY-THREE-CENTURY MOUN-TAIN BOOTS (MARS), and Vivian supposed that you could just tell that the things inside *were* boots. "Would you say these were shown to advantage?" he asked. "They tell me I have very little artistic sense."

"I think," Vivian said, "that they may be the kind of things that never look right. We had bathroom curtains like that." Out of the corner of her eye she saw the chained door move. Sam's face came around it and vanished again in a hurry. "By the way, do you know the time?" she said.

Elio turned to her contritely. Luckily the door was shut by then. "Of course, you have no belt yet. I will get you one for tomorrow, miss, I promise." He pressed one stud out of several dozen on his own belt, and a clock face lit up on his wrist. It looked much more complicated than Jonathan's. "Ten forty-six and ten seconds," he said.

Thank goodness! Vivian thought. We're in time for the picnic after all! At least, she realized, they *would* be, if only Sam and Jonathan could get out of the passage without Elio seeing them. The only thing to do seemed to keep Elio distracted somehow. She smiled at him. "Er—" she said, "I've heard people call you an android, Mr. Elio. What is an android please?"

"It means that I am a manufactured human being," Elio said.

"What? Made in a factory!" Vivian exclaimed, truly surprised.

"Not quite a factory. It was more like a highly equipped laboratory," said Elio. "I was assembled from human protoplasm by scientists working at a bench."

All the Frankenstein films she had seen flooded into Vivian's mind. She gave Elio a wary look. He looked like an ordinary person, only rather smaller and paler than most. Nevertheless, she would have gone away quickly if she had had any choice. But she seemed to have got him talking. So she moved gently down the gallery toward the hall. "Did it hurt at all?" she asked.

"I was not conscious for much of the process," said Elio. He took a step along the gallery with Vivian. But he turned back almost at once and frowned at his showcase. "Perhaps I should move the boots a half turn to the right."

"If you do that, the red bits at the top won't show," Vivian said. She took another step down the gallery.

"You have a point," Elio said, still staring at the boots.

It was maddening. He seemed to be stuck in front of them. "What did they make you *for*?" Vivian asked rather desperately. "An experiment?"

"No, for efficiency," Elio said. "I am stronger and faster than a born-human. I live longer, and I need less sleep. My bones do not break so easily." He turned toward her. Vivian thought he might be moving at last. She sidled a few more steps toward the hall. Elio took a step in the same direction. "And of course, my brain is the best part of me," he said. "I have twice the intelligence of a born-human and five times the memory. Thus, I am acutely observant. But—" To Vivian's exasperation, he turned back to the showcase. He frowned. "This does not make up for the finer points of human taste," he said. "What if I turned the boots completely around?"

In the passage, Sam and Jonathan were clearly getting impatient. Vivian had a glimpse of the door shutting hurriedly again and of Jonathan's pigtail caught dangling over the chain. "But *I* have taste," she said. "The boots look very nice. Do you eat the same things as born-humans, Mr. Elio?"

"I live mostly on liquids," said Elio, "though I am partial to fruit."

"And," said Vivian. "And." She walked on a few steps. This time Elio came with her. "And—" She racked her brains for more things to ask. "And were you the only one they made, or were there more of you?"

"They made about a hundred," Elio said, walking slowly beside her. "It was a very costly process, and no more could be afforded."

"Where are all the others?" Vivian asked. Now they were really walking toward the hall, but awfully slowly.

"They were sent out," said Elio, "to help colonize the stars eventually. This is what we were designed for. I am from Hundred-and-five Century, you see, when mankind spreads throughout the galaxy and mostly departs from Earth. But I was ordered by Time City, as a rarity of history. Time City collects one of every rarity, this being a policy begun by Faber John."

"You must be awfully lonely," Vivian said. She was beginning to feel mean, pretending to be so interested in Elio. "Don't you miss all the other androids?"

"Not at all," said Elio. "The only time I met another android, I became extremely irritated with the creature. I confess I wished to hit it in the face. It is the one occasion on which I have felt those strong emotions that you born-humans seem to feel all the time."

"Don't you feel *any*thing?" Vivian said. By now they were walking briskly and they were nearly at the corner into the hall. "Don't you even feel happy?"

"No, but neither do I feel sad," Elio said. "Amusement I do feel, and much contentment. The alarms and fusses of generations of born-humans keep me entertained all the time."

They turned the corner into the hall, onto sunlight lying in patterns on the patterned marble. Vivian sighed with relief. But she was finding Elio much more interesting than she expected. "How long have you been in Time City?"

"A hundred years come next New Year," Elio said.

"But you don't look anything like that old!" Vivian exclaimed.

"I told you—" Elio began. But he was interrupted by Sempitern Walker, rushing down the stairs in a long blue robe.

"Elio! For great Chronos' sake!" Sempitern Walker called out. "Will you stop messing with that museum of yours for a minute! I've a session of Privy Chronologue in five minutes, and you haven't given me my notes for it yet!"

"They are all ready in the study, sir," Elio said, "if you will come with me." But before he went away with the Sempitern, he said to Vivian, "I told you I was designed for endurance as well as efficiency." This caused Jonathan's father to give Vivian a look as if she was the last straw and hurry Elio away. Vivian was left perversely wishing she could have talked to Elio for much longer.

Jonathan and Sam shot around the corner, looking hot, tired, and relieved. "Whoo!" said Sam.

"I thought we were going to be stuck in that passage all day!" Jonathan said. "What's the time?"

"Just before eleven," said Vivian. "Isn't that lucky?"

They agreed that it was. "I need a drink," said Sam. "That warty woman never gave me anything."

Jonathan took them to the matutinal, where there was a gadget on the wall that gave out cups of fruit juice. Sam drank three. Vivian and Jonathan each had two. They were sucking up the last drops when Jenny hurried in. "I thought you said you'd be in the hall," she said. "Hurry up. Ramona's waiting."

Vivian never had a chance to ask who Ramona was. She turned out to be Sam's mother. She was paler and wider and sleepier-looking than her sister Jenny. She was carrying two birdcages like the one Sam had left hidden in the time lock, with interesting-shaped foods floating under them. She smiled at Vivian. "You don't look much like either of your parents, my love," she said. Vivian hurriedly remembered that she was supposed to be Cousin Vivian and wondered what to say. "You were the image of our brother Viv when I saw you last," Ramona said. "Funny how children change."

"BURP!" said Sam. It was the natural result of drinking three cups of fruit juice without pausing to breathe, but it luckily turned everyone's attention off Vivian and onto Sam.

"What *has* he done to his hair?" said Jenny.

Sam's hand and everyone's eyes went to the top of his head, where his hair still stood in a tuft with Vivian's rubber band around it. "I want to look like my uncle Ranjit," he said. "It suits me."

"No, it doesn't. Take it down," said Ramona, and added without looking, "and tie up your shoes."

"Mothers ought to be sent out into history," said Sam. His own time in history had put him in a very bad mood. He stumped in the rear, muttering crossly to himself, while they crossed Time Close into Aeon Square and took a shortcut past the great glass building down some steps to the Avenue of the Four Ages.

Ramona led the way across the avenue to one of the archways in the wall. "We thought we'd take a boat," she said.

Sam cheered up at once. He raced ahead, through the archway and down the dizzily long flight of steps to the wharf. When the others got to the steps, he was already sitting in a red thing floating on the river beside the wharf. There was a line of the things, all different colors. Vivian supposed they were boats, but they looked more like cars to her. That put her in mind of a strange fact about Time City. "You don't have cars here!" she said.

Jonathan was clearly thinking about something else. "We don't need them," he said vaguely.

They went down and settled into the comfortable squashy seats aboard the boat Sam had chosen. "Red's my favorite color," he told Vivian.

The boat spoke, in a rattling voice from under the floor. "Where to, passengers?" it said. It made Vivian jump.

"All-day hire. Main locks first," said Jenny. "And trans-mogue for us."

Transmoguing seemed to mean that the roof suddenly vanished, which made Vivian jump again. Cool winds blew in her hair as the boat made a wide half circle out into the middle of the river and set off, with the faintest of rattling sounds, away from Time City. Vivian soon began to enjoy herself as much as Sam. The day was warm, though nothing like as hot as that day in 1939, and the sky was blue. The flat lands sliding past were green with new crops. There were houses at intervals in the fields— all kinds, from thatched cottages to one built mostly of shimmering nothingness—and orchards, orchards, orchards, loaded with white and pink blossoms.

"It's spring here!" Vivian exclaimed.

"Yes, we keep the seasons," Jenny said. "It must seem strange to you. Wasn't it autumn when you left Twenty Century?"

Vivian nodded, thinking of the blackberries still staining Sam's face from the lane by the Tor. She saw a machine in the distance, rushing across a field spraying out a white cloud of something. She turned to Jonathan to say that Time City *did* have cars of a sort, but Jonathan had his head together with Sam's. Sam, after five minutes of bouncing about showing how much he was enjoying himself, was busy taking Jonathan's belt to pieces to put the clock function right, and seemed to have forgotten he was on a boat at all.

"What's wrong with it?" asked Jenny.

"A faulty consistor connection," Jonathan answered glibly.

It seemed amazing to Vivian that neither of the mothers put the stains around Sam's mouth together with the fact that Jonathan's belt was showing the wrong time and realized where they had just been. But they didn't. Ramona said placidly and rather proudly, "Sam can mend that easily."

Meanwhile, the boat surged steadily around bend after bend of Time River, missing other boats as if it could see them. They passed, and missed, other boats like their own, small barges, rafts where people were fishing, and a huge pleasure boat full of tourists, who all waved. After that came a boat huger still, making waves that piled up along both banks. It was a great barge as high as a house and nearly as long as a football field, with men in strange hats on top, who waved too.

"There goes meat from Forty-two Century," said Ramona.

"All that!" said Vivian. "Who pays for it?"

"We all do," said Jenny. "Time City trades in exchange— only what we trade is knowledge, Vivian. There are records in Perpetuum, Erstwhile, Agelong, and suchlike of most things the human race has ever known or done. Students come to study here. And anything anyone in history wants to know, we can tell them for a fee—provided it's something from *before* the date they ask, of course."

"Oh, we stretch a point sometimes, Jenny," Ramona said. "My department gives weather forecasts, remember?"

Jenny laughed. "Yes, and Ongoing Science quite often gives hints to make sure science goes the right way. But we do have to be careful about sending history wrong."

"We can't have all of it going unstable," agreed Ramona.

The voyage lasted nearly an hour. Jenny and Ramona pointed out interesting farms or said things like, "You get an even better view of the city from here," as new domes and towers came into sight at new bends of the river. Vivian saw Endless Hill from all sorts of different angles. It *was* like the Tor. The only difference was that the Gnomon Tower was not at all like a church. It was more like an old, old lighthouse.

About the time Sam finished Jonathan's belt and Jonathan buckled it back on, Jenny and Ramona turned and pointed the way the boat was going. "We're nearly down at the locks now. Can you see the land's ending?"

About a field away, the green country just stopped. The blue sky came right down to the ground there. "Ooh!" said Vivian. "That looks a bit creepy!"

"No, it's not," said Jonathan. "It's safe. The thing I *hate* about history is the way the ground goes on and on. If I had to live in history, that would send me mad in the first week."

Vivian thought of the way Jonathan had become so uncomfortable while they were looking for Cousin Marty's house. This must have been the reason.

"Don't be silly, Jonathan," said Jenny. "No one's going to send *you* out into history!"

Shortly, the boat turned a corner and nuzzled into a side channel of the river. There were high stone walls on either side. The boat drew into a wharf behind a line of others. "You still wish to retain me?" it asked in its rattling voice.

"Yes. I said All-day hire," Jenny said, as they stood up to get off. "I wish they'd make those things a bit more trusting," she said to Ramona, while they were climbing steps up the side of the wharf.

"It may be faulty," Ramona suggested. But when they looked back, the boat's roof was back in place with the word HIRED shining in big letters along the roof. "It was just making sure we hadn't changed our minds," Ramona said.

At the top of the steps, they came to a kind of stone platform, right at the very end of the land. There was a long row of silvery booths at the back of the platform, in a line against the sky. Their doors were sliding open and shut as people came through in all sorts of costumes. Some of them looked businesslike, but most of them stopped and stared around excitedly and pointed to the strange dress of the others. After that, they went and showed long golden tickets at a kiosk in the center of the platform, where they were given maps and a crackling sheet of information and directed to the other side of the platform, where a man stood at a gate checking tickets. The platform rang with excited exclamations and happy laughter, and the few people going the other way, mostly in Time City pajamas, had to push their way through the slow throng in order to get to the booths.

Jenny and Ramona led the way to the railing by the gate, where they leaned and looked down at a huge tourist boat waiting to take people to the city. Colorful people were going down the long ramp and taking their seats aboard. There was another boat waiting across the river, where there was the same sort of platform and another row of booths. In between, stretching right across the river, were six really massive time locks, standing high against the sky above the platforms. As they watched, another big barge came slowly nudging through the third lock along, against the strong brown current of the River Time.

"Where does the river go to?" Vivian asked.

"It runs out through the locks into different rivers at various times," Jenny said.

The tourist boat across the river was full. It clanged a bell and set out in a swirl of brown water on its journey to the city. Music was playing on board it, and people were opening bottles. It looked very festive.

"I'm thirsty," said Sam. *"Thirsty!"* he added loudly. And when nobody noticed, he went on saying it.

"What happens," Vivian asked, "if a tourist meets his own grandchildren and hates them and decides not to get married? Wouldn't that change history?"

"There's a whole branch of Time Patrol checking to make sure that won't happen," said Ramona. "Hush, Sam."

"But quite a lot of people come here specially to meet their ancestors or their descendants," Jenny said. "We have conference rooms in Millennium where they can get together."

"I do think," Ramona said, "that Viv and Inga should have told Vivian more about Time City. It's not fair to the child!"

She meant this to be covered up by the noise from all around and by Sam's shouts of "Thirsty!" But Sam's voice dropped to a mutter just then, and Vivian heard her clearly. She was forced to invent some reason for her ignorance.

"They didn't trust me not to say something at school," she said. "That *would* spoil history, wouldn't it? Does it matter much?"

"Yes, it does," Ramona said, looking very uncomfortable. "If your general knowledge isn't good enough when you come to the Leavers' Tests at school, you'll be sent away to live in history even though you *are* a Lee."

"Nobody stays in Time City by right, Vivian," Jenny explained. "We all have to earn our place. And there's a lot of competition from the students. Most of the young people studying in Continuum are hoping for jobs in the city when they finish."

Jonathan swung away from the rail and stalked off. Vivian could see he was upset by this. But the next moment he was back. "I say! Look at all these!"

They turned around to find the platform full of frantic people all coming from nowhere. A few did seem to be coming up the steps from the wharf, and one or two came swarming over the edge of the platform; but most of them were just there out of nowhere. They all went rushing toward the line of time locks. There, some of them vanished into silvery doors or open silvery spaces, but most of them beat at the booths in a panic as if they were trying to get the doors open. This looked very odd when the door they were beating on happened to be open already. They were coming across the platform in waves, and later waves were running through earlier ones. The platform was suddenly a melting, rushing tumble of running figures and waving arms. They were in all sorts of clothes, but the greatest number were in Time City pajamas.

"Time ghosts," said Sam.

"I'd heard about these, but I'd no idea there were so many," Ramona said, as the running crowd grew thicker yet.

The man standing by the gate to check tickets said, "There's been more of them every day this month. They start around midday and tail off around two in the afternoon. We've no idea what's causing them."

"Don't they frighten the tourists?" Jenny asked.

The man shrugged. "A bit. But what can anyone do?"

Certainly some of the real people coming out of the silver booths cringed rather when they found a crowd of ghosts rushing straight at them. But when they discovered they could walk through them, most of them laughed and seemed to decide that this was one of the sights they had come to see. The kiosk had a loudspeaker going now, muddled a bit by the loudspeaker from the kiosk on the platform across the river, where more frantic time ghosts were also rushing at the time locks.

"Visit-it-itors, please-ease pay no attent-ention to-to the persons appar-ently runn-unning to-toward the ti-time lo-locks. They-ey are a Ti-time City-ity phenom-enomenon know-own as Ti-time gho-ghosts and qui-quite harm-arm-less."

A number of the real tourists looked as if they had half a mind to go straight home again until they heard this message. Only one person took no notice of the ghosts at all. He stepped out of a booth and strode forward as if the platform was empty. But he was a time ghost too, Vivian realized. She was beginning to be able to tell. He was wearing old-fashioned-looking clothes, and he had a slight blurring around the edges of him. But the odd thing was that she thought she had seen this particular ghost before somewhere. She tried to follow him as he strode through the crowd of running ghosts and among surprised, slower-moving tourists, but he vanished in the way time ghosts did.

"Let's go," said Jenny. "I really hate time ghosts."

They were all glad to go. The waves of silently rushing figures made them all uncomfortable. It was hard not to feel panicked at the way the ghosts were so desperately beating on the time booths, even when you knew they were not real. They went down the steps to the boat again.

"The Lagoon," said Jenny. "We'll tell you when to moor."

The Lagoon was a bend of the river that the river had left behind. It had turned into a long, curved lake with a narrow channel for boats at either end. A filter in the channels kept the water a pure clean green so that people could swim.

"You can swim first or eat first," said Jenny, when the boat drew into a grassy bank. "But if you eat first, you must wait at least an hour before swimming."

"Eat first," they all said. They were ravenous. The time they had spent in 1939 had stretched the morning nearly four hours longer than it should have been. It was as if they had missed lunch. They made up for it now, sitting under flowering bushes on airy rugs that Ramona had brought. They wolfed down long loaves with savory fillings and round buns with cheesy centers, and they crunched apples. There were butter-pies after that, to Sam's loud delight. Then there was an hour to pass. The ladies spent it stretched on a rug in the shade of the bush, talking in low voices.

"Abdul's really worried," Vivian heard Ramona say. "The outbreak of that war has gone back a whole year now, to September 1938. They seem to be inventing weapons they shouldn't have had till the end of the century."

"I wish they'd recall the Observers!" Jenny said. "Viv could be killed. Don't tell me Observers haven't been killed before this! Remember that poor girl who was covering the Reconquest of America."

"Viv's all right," said Ramona. "His report was one of the ones that came this morning. The new developments seem to have taken him by surprise. I'm afraid Abdul will keep him out there for a while, because he sent straight back to Viv for an explanation. At least Vivian's safe."

Sam fell asleep on his face in the grass.

Jonathan wandered off around the lake, jerking his head at Vivian to come along. When Vivian grudgingly followed him, she found him sitting on a fallen tree, looking white and scared. "We've *got* to think what to do," he said. "If it really was one of the polarities that boy stole, Time City isn't balanced anymore and nor is history."

"Do you think he *was* the Time Lady in disguise?" Vivian said.

"I don't know," said Jonathan. "I don't know who he is or what's going on, but he time-traveled after he took that box, so he *has* to be a threat to Time City whoever he is."

"I think we should tell someone," said Vivian. "It's serious."

"But we *can't*!" Jonathan said. "Think. The only way we could have known about that boy and that box is by illegal time travel to an Unstable Era. And if we tell them how we happened to find out through your Cousin Wartface, it'll come out that you're illegal too. We can't tell. We have to do something ourselves."

"Would it really be so bad—what they'd do to us if they found out?" Vivian asked.

"I don't know what they'd do to you. It could be very bad," Jonathan said. "But I know what they'd do to me. They'd send me out into history, into a really boring Fixed Era, and I'd have to stay there. And I can't face that!" He was shaking at the mere idea. "I've *always* been afraid I wouldn't qualify to stay when it came to the Leavers' Tests. I worked and worked at school, and I made a fuss about being a Lee so that I could have Dr. Wilander for my tutor because he's the best there is. And I stuck with him, though he scares me stiff most of the time—because I *know* I'd go batty in a week somewhere where the land just goes on and on and on!"

Vivian knew this was a real confession of Jonathan's true feelings. It was the kind of thing nobody ever said except as a last resort. "But if that really was a polarity," she said, "someone who can do something ought to know. Couldn't you drop hints to your father?"

"No," said Jonathan. "He'd wonder how I knew."

"Then drop hints to someone else," said Vivian.

They wandered along the lake, arguing about it, for the rest of the hour. Jonathan thought of a hundred different reasons why hinting was impossible. But Vivian thought of her own Mum and Dad out in history that seemed to have been sent wrong and bad by that beastly thief of a boy, and argued grimly on. In the end, she won. When Jenny appeared on the lakeside, waving what seemed to be a swimsuit and shouting, "Are you going in, you two?" Jonathan set off toward her saying, "All right. You win. I'll drop Mother a hint."

"Wait a sec!" Vivian called after him. "I can't swim. Does it matter?"

Jonathan stopped as if she had shot him. "Oh no! My cousin Vivian could swim like a fish. She was always ducking me. Mother and Ramona are bound to remember she could."

"Couldn't I have forgotten how?" Vivian suggested.

"Swimming's not a thing people forget. It's like walking or something," Jonathan said. "Look, let me give Mother that hint now I've got all nerved up to do it. Then we'll think what to do."

When they got back to the boat and the picnic, Jonathan looked casually at the sky and remarked, "I've had an idea, Mother, about all that upset in Twenty Century. Suppose someone there had stolen a Time City polarity—wouldn't that send history critical around it?"

Jenny just laughed and threw a swimsuit over his head. "Shut up and get into that. You and your ideas, Jonathan!" The swimsuit was large, because it covered your whole body and had heaters in it to keep you warm when the water was cold, and it muffled the rest of Jonathan's hint completely. All anyone heard of his reply was "Oh but—" When he had fought his way free, he had stopped trying.

It was quite easy to disguise the fact that Vivian could not swim, because Jenny and Ramona were busy teaching Sam and Sam was making a great noise objecting. Jonathan and Vivian just went farther down the shore and put some bushes between themselves and Sam's roars and splashes. There Jonathan did his best to teach Vivian to swim, too. She splashed about bravely with Jonathan's hand under her chin, and sank every time he took his hand away. She drank pints of lake. And all the time she knew perfectly well that Jonathan was secretly very glad that Jenny had only laughed at his hint. So, every time she came spluttering out of the water, she pawed the water out of her own eyes and looked into Jonathan's, which were strangely naked and folded-looking without his sight function. "You *will* try hinting again, won't you?" she said.

"Oh all *right*!" Jonathan said at last. "If I'd known what a nag you were, I'd have left you with Cousin Wartface. The two of you would have got on wonderfully!"

He kept his word. When they came back to the Annuate Palace, tired and sun-soaked and feeling very jolly, Jonathan honorably made another attempt to drop a hint during dinner. The guests that night were the High Scientist Dr. Leonov from Ongoing, a lesser scientist from Erstwhile, and a World Premier and her husband from 8210. Jonathan waited for a pause in the stately talk and said loudly, "I have a theory that Twenty Century is being disturbed because someone there has stolen one of Faber John's polarities. Does anyone think that's possible?"

The Premier said, "Do you people really believe in those legends here?"

Jenny looked very embarrassed. The Premier turned to Dr. Leonov for an answer, but Leonov did not deign to reply. He left it to the lesser scientist, who said, quite kindly, "Well, no, lad. The forces that interact with history to hold Time City in place are not really of a kind that anyone could steal. And Faber John's only a myth, you know.''

"But suppose the polarity was quite small and buried in the ground or something,'' Jonathan said bravely. "Someone could *steal* it.''

Sempitern Walker gave him an anguished glare. "Stop talking nonsense, Jonathan. That idiotic notion was disproved in your grandfather's day.''

Jonathan stuck his chin in his chest to hide how red his face was and gave up. Vivian could hardly blame him. She knew it had taken a lot of courage for Jonathan to hint at all. And that night in her room she tried to have a serious think about what they ought to do now. She felt she ought to help Jonathan put the mess right before she went home, but the only idea that came into her head was the thought of Mum sitting in Lewisham with bombs dropping and history going wronger and wronger around her.

P etula woke Vivian early the next day. She was carrying a
studded belt, like Jonathan's but pale and stiff and new.
"Elio sent you this," she said. "It's school today, so get moving. But do us all a favor, and don't wear that yellow and purple
horror that Elio likes so much. I can't bear to think of them setting eyes on it in Duration."

Vivian chose a plain blue suit and buckled the stiff belt around
it. She went downstairs, fingering the studs, wondering which
was which and not quite daring to experiment. There seemed to
be a lot of activity in the palace. She could hear feet hammering
up and down the other staircases and voices calling out.

"What's going on?" she asked Jonathan when she met him in
the hall.

But Jonathan only said, "Hints are no good. Nobody takes any
notice. I was awake half the night trying to think what to—"

He had to jump to one side. Sempitern Walker came bursting
out of a door by the stairs and went flying past them down the
hall. He was wearing a stiff red robe and a gold embroidered
cloak, but the robe was undone and streaming on both sides of
him. Vivian saw a suit of white underclothes underneath and a
lot of thin, hairy leg. She stared after him as he dashed away,
unable to believe her eyes.

"Gold bands!" Sempitern Walker roared. "Where in Time's
name are my *gold bands*?"

Elio came racing out of the door too, carrying a red silk hat.
Jenny rushed out after him with a huge gold necklace like a
Mayor's chain. After her, Petula came running, followed by the
ladies who served at dinner and five other people Vivian had not

seen before, and behind them pelted the men who polished the stairs. They were all carrying bundles of robe, or hats, or golden boots, or different sorts of gold chain, and Petula was waving a pair of wide gold ribbons. Vivian watched, fascinated, as they all tore after Sempitern Walker and managed to corner him at the end of the hall.

"No, you stupid android!" Sempitern Walker shouted out of the midst of them. "The other hat! And I said the *gold* bands, you stupid woman! *Find* them, can't you! The ceremony's starting in twenty minutes!" He came bursting out of the crowd and sped toward Jonathan and Vivian again.

This is marvelous! Vivian thought, as the others all turned themselves hastily around and raced after the Sempitern. Sempitern Walker swung himself nimbly around on the end of the banisters and went flying up the stairs two at a time. "And I have to have the carnelian studs!" he bellowed. "Can't anyone find anything in this place?"

A giggle began to rise up Vivian's throat as everyone else went streaming up the stairs after him. "You're all useless!" she heard him shout. "Gold bands!" They all went running around the railed landing overhead, tripping over mats and getting in one another's way. Vivian nearly laughed outright. This is as good as a film! she thought, turning to see what Jonathan thought of it.

Jonathan swung haughtily away. "This happens every time there's a ceremony," he said wearily. "Come on. We'd better get breakfast."

The giggle was sitting right behind Vivian's teeth, fighting to get out. She swallowed it down. "Do you have ceremonies very often?" she asked, trying to stop her voice from shaking.

"About every two days," Jonathan said dourly.

They had breakfast to the din of running feet, shouting, and one or two metallic crashes, as if someone had thrown a gold chain downstairs. Jonathan pretended not to notice. Vivian understood perfectly that he would be very hurt if she laughed, but the giggle would keep rising up her throat whenever the running feet and the roars came close to the matutinal. This made it hard for her to follow what Jonathan was saying.

"We ought to go after that boy and get the box back," he said. "If he was doing a hundred years with every time jump, he'll be in the middle of a Fixed Era by now and probably sending that crazy too. We should be able to find him if that time egg works. But I didn't like the way it nearly didn't bring us back. We don't want to get stranded in history."

The Sempitern's feet pounded past the matutinal, followed by the feet of everyone else. Vivian struggled with the rising giggle again. "Do you think he might be trying to steal all the polarities?" she asked, trying to think sensibly. "Couldn't we go to them first and ask the people in those places to keep guard on them? How many of them are there?"

"I don't know," Jonathan said, almost groaning. "I don't know where or when they are. I'm not even sure now that it *was* a polarity he stole."

It was clear that what the scientist said last night had shaken Jonathan's faith badly. And he certainly had jumped to that conclusion, Vivian thought. There was no proof. On the other hand— Here Sempitern Walker's feet thumped across the ceiling of the matutinal, and she had to swallow the giggle again. "Do cheer up," she said. "Think of our time ghosts. You can tell we did— *do* do something."

"That's true!" Jonathan said, brightening a little.

Soon after this, the palace suddenly became quiet. Jonathan pressed the clock stud on his belt and said that they ought to be going. Vivian got up and followed him, feeling very nervous. Jonathan did not seem to be taking anything to school with him, not even a pen. This made Vivian feel odd and incomplete. She thought she had got used to the naked feeling of wearing Time City pajamas, but she felt naked all over again without any books or even a pencil box.

The hall and the stairs were littered with silken cloaks, various hats, shoes and several gold chains. Elio was soberly backing down the stairs, picking everything up. Vivian could not see his face clearly, but she could have sworn that Elio was smiling.

Sam was definitely smiling when they met him by the fountain in Time Close, his widest smile with two teeth in it. "Your father ran," he said. "Like a rocket. He picked up his robes, and he sprinted. Was it a big fuss?"

"About average," Jonathan said haughtily. "Get moving. It's due to rain in ten minutes."

Vivian looked up at the sky as they came through the archway into Aeon Square. White clouds were billowing up, with gray ones following, but it did not look very much like rain. "Are you sure it's going to rain?"

"Yes, because we're getting this year's weather from 3589," said Jonathan. "They never pick a drought year because of the crops. You can get a forecast from your belt."

"Which stud?" said Vivian.

They went across Aeon Square showing Vivian how her belt worked. The weather stud lit up a shining green list along her forearm. *5:00–8:40 FAIR TEMP 14–17°C; 8:40–10:27 RAIN, Thunder c. 9:07; 10:28–15:58 SUN TEMP 13–19°C. . . .*

"See how efficient Elio is," Jonathan said. "He's got you one you can read. Mine's all in universal symbols."

"How many units credit did he give you?" said Sam. "No— *that* stud, stupid!"

Vivian put her finger on that stud, and the palm of her hand lit up. *VSL/90234/7C TC Units 100.00,* she read, rather awed. Two hundred pounds? Surely not!

"Lucky blister!" said Sam. "Two hundred butter-pies!"

"You've got a low-weight function, too," Jonathan said. "And that one's the pen function. What's your time function—clock-face or digital?"

Vivian was so fascinated by her belt that she did not notice straight away that the ceremony that had caused all the fuss at the palace was taking place on the other side of Aeon Square. A line of figures all in red, looking tiny below the huge buildings, was pacing slowly down the square. Jonathan's father was walking near the head of them, behind someone carrying a silver battle-ax thing, pacing in the most grave, stately, and important way. You wouldn't believe, to look at him, that he's spent the last half hour rushing about and yelling! Vivian thought.

"Who are the ones with him?" she asked.

"Annuate Guard," said Sam.

"A lot of old folk retired from Time Patrol," Jonathan said. He pointed to the other end of the square. "And the blue lot look to be the Librarians. Hurry up. Everyone's going into Duration."

The blue line was pacing toward the red one, robes billowing, tall blue hats on their heads, led by two who seemed to be carrying a gigantic old book open on a cushion. Behind them, where Jonathan was really pointing, much smaller figures were streaming along the end of the square from right and left and going in through the high open door of Duration. The sight made even Sam hurry. But he stopped again at Faber John's Stone. By this time the two processions of the ceremony were close enough for Vivian to recognize Mr. Enkian under the tall blue hat just behind the two Librarians with the book, looking very sour and self-important. The two lines were obviously going to meet just beside Faber John's Stone.

"Hey! Look at that crack today!" Jonathan exclaimed.

The crack had grown right down from the corner of the slab, through the golden letters FAB, and on into the bald part. There it forked into three new cracks, zigzagging faintly out into the middle of the stone. There was no need for Jonathan to measure it to see that it had grown.

"Great Time! I hope it *doesn't* mean what they say!" he said.

The two processions had met by then. "Sempitern greets Perpetuum in the name of the Chronologue," Jonathan's father intoned from quite near. A few drops of rain came down.

"Perhaps Faber John's woken up enough to wriggle his toes,"

Vivian suggested, not very seriously. "They'd about reach here from that cave."

Sam's face bunched up, and he stamped defiantly on the branching crack. His shoelace burst undone. Jonathan took his arm and dragged him off. "Careful! You could make it worse!"

"By the power vested in me, through me Perpetuum greets Chronologue and Sempitern," Mr. Enkian was now intoning. "These, my Librarians—"

His voice was suddenly drowned in a skirling of pipe music. Vivian looked up to find the ceremony dissolving into confusion. A long-legged man in a tall, floppy hat was dancing figures of eight around the Sempitern and the old man carrying the ax, playing on a set of bagpipes as he pranced. Just as Vivian looked, he cavorted in among the Annuate Guard, leaping and bounding and throwing out his long legs like a lunatic. The elderly people in red uniforms scattered out of his way, except for one old lady, who drew her ceremonial sword and shakily tried to bar the dancer's way. But the leaping man danced clean through the sword and pranced on, quite unharmed and still skirling away at his bagpipes.

Vivian realized that the lunatic must be a time ghost. Oddly enough, nobody in the ceremony seemed to think he was. When he pranced in among the Librarians, the blue-robed people scattered too. "Will you stop that, whoever you are!" Mr. Enkian shouted.

The man whirled and did a neat high kick toward the cushion with the huge old book on it. Vivian could see that the long leg and the pointed shoe never touched the cushion or the book, but the two Librarians were fooled and tried to snatch the cushion out of the way. The book slid to the ground in a flurry of stiff pages.

"Doomsday Book!" Mr. Enkian shouted. He and the two Librarians pounced for the book, horrified, and the dancing man sprang capering across their groping backs. Next moment, he was cavorting straight toward Vivian, Sam, and Jonathan.

"Arrest him!" Sempitern Walker commanded the Guards. They shouted back that the lunatic was only a time ghost. But most of the shouting was drowned in the deafening sound of the bagpipes. Vivian had an instant's glimpse of the lunatic's pale, intense face as she backed out of its way, before the figure whirled around and pranced onto Faber John's Stone.

The slab broke into a hundred pieces beneath the madly dancing pointed feet. The pieces broke again, and those pieces broke too, milling away to pale gravel in seconds. By this time, the dancing man had become oddly hard to see and the din from the bagpipes sounded muffled. Then he faded away entirely, and there was silence mixed with a growing patter of rain. Faber John's Stone was whole again, except for the forked crack, and turning black and wet.

"Confound it!" Mr. Enkian said angrily, trying to shield Doomsday Book with a fold of his robe. "We'd better begin again."

Jonathan, Sam, and Vivian ran through the rain, leaving the ceremony reorganizing itself in the downpour. "That was a funny kind of ghost!" Jonathan panted. "I wonder if it *was* one."

Sam had no doubt about it. As soon as they dashed in through the door of Duration, he began shouting, "We've seen a new kind of time ghost! Everyone, I've seen a new time ghost!" His voice could be heard booming this all morning. Vivian heard it oftener than she would have liked because, to her shame, she was put in the same class as Sam. The class she should have been in was, as far as she could tell, learning things that even her teachers in London had never heard of.

"I'm sure you'll soon catch up," the Head Teacher said. "All you Lees are quick. But I can't move you up until you know universal symbols."

Sam's class was learning universal symbols. Vivian sat in an empty-frame chair that was rather too small in front of an empty-frame desk a trifle too low and tried to form strange signs on a white square that was not really paper. The rest of the class were using green pencils, but as Vivian was older, she was allowed to use the pen function on her new belt. When you pressed the stud, a green light sprang up between your fingers. It felt like a pen. It wrote in green, and it was easy to use. Unfortunately, the stud for it was next to the stud for low-weight function. Vivian kept pressing the wrong one by mistake and soaring gently out of her empty-frame chair.

"Be quiet, Sam. Tie up your shoes," the teacher said every time Vivian caused a disturbance by doing this. He was right in a way. Every other disturbance was caused by Sam telling people about the time ghost. But it made Vivian ashamed. By the end of the morning, when the teacher collected their work by pressing a button, whereupon what they had written vanished from the white squares and appeared lined up in an empty frame on his desk, Vivian was feeling very low.

Lunch cheered her up. They went to a long room surrounded by automats—like the one in Jonathan's room that needed kicking, except that these did not need to be kicked so often. The automats allowed each child four things. They seemed to know if you tried to cheat by going to more than one. Even Sam could not get them to give him more than four butter-pies. Then you sat at the long tables to eat the four things.

Vivian was new, and she was a Lee. This made everyone very interested in her. A crowd gathered around her. By now Vivian was so used to pretending she was Cousin Vivian Lee that she almost forgot that she was not. She told them she had just come from Twenty Century, from World War II. This caused even more interest and a bigger crowd still. Most of the children had never been in history, and they wanted to know how it felt.

As she answered their questions, Vivian looked around the room and was quite surprised that there were no more children than this in Time City. True, it was a big school. But all the children in it, from tiny ones far smaller than Sam to nearly grown-up ones a head taller than Jonathan, were all fitted into this one long room for lunch. When she asked, they told her that Duration was the only school in the city. More than half the children came in every day by boat or hovercraft from farms in the countryside. This was very strange to Vivian after the crowded schools of London. She told them about those. And they were astonished to think that one teacher could teach over thirty children at once.

"How *can* he hold thirty sets of brain rhythms in his head at once?" someone asked. "Now tell about the War. Is it quiet like the Mind Wars or noisy like the New Zealand Takeover?"

"Do they run up and down the streets fighting?" someone else wanted to know.

Vivian tried to explain that when two *countries* fought each other, they did not usually do it in the streets unless the army from one country invaded the other. Then she had to explain what *invading* was.

"You mean, as if all the tourists came screaming up the River Time to kill people in the city?" a small girl asked, rather upset.

While Vivian was trying to decide if it *was* like that, Jonathan pushed through the crowd and said loudly in her ear, "Message for you. It's on your belt."

"Where? How?" said Vivian.

"Press that stud there," everyone said helpfully.

Vivian did so, and green writing appeared on the table in front of her. *"Hakon Wilander's compts to V. S. Lee. Come for special tuition with J. L. Walker 1300 sharp."* Under that was a second message: *"Duration affirms assignment, F. T. Danario, Head Teacher."* "Is it true?" she asked Jonathan. "Not a joke?" She just could not imagine anyone so large and so learned as Dr. Wilander even remembering she existed, let alone wanting to teach her.

Jonathan pressed a stud on his belt. Another message appeared beside Vivian's: *"H. Wilander to J. Walker. Stupid child V. Lee not answering belt. Bring her with you 1300."*

"He sounds angry," someone said.

"He mostly is," said Jonathan. At which a number of people remarked fervently that they would rather have Bilious Enkian for a tutor. Vivian gathered from what they said that everyone went to a special tutor as soon as they were ten years old. Dr. Wilander was considered one of the worst. "Yes, but we've got to go or we really will get eaten," Jonathan said.

They left Duration at 12:36 by Vivian's belt clock. Jonathan was still thinking about the dancing time ghost. "You know, that was all wrong for a real time ghost," he said as they pushed through a glass door at the side of Duration. "They don't make a sound usually. I bet it was one of the students having a joke."

"What—even Faber John's Stone breaking up like that?" said Vivian.

"Some centuries can do wonders with holograms," Jonathan answered. Since Vivian had never heard of holograms, she was none the wiser. "If I see any students I know, I'll ask," Jonathan said.

Outside, as Vivian's belt had predicted, the rain was over. Sun was sparkling on wet grass between the tall block of Duration and the airy arched building that was Continuum. Since the grass was still damp, the students who had come out to sit in the sun were mostly perched on the various statues that stood about on the grass. The air rumbled with their lazy talk. They all looked alarmingly grown up to Vivian.

"I greet you, Jonathan," called a young man in a black velvet smock, who was sitting on one of the knees of a statue like a large Buddha with a lion's head.

The girl in a gauzy robe who was sitting on the statue's other knee smiled and said, "Hello, young Jonathan."

Jonathan stopped. "Hello," he said. "Do either of you know about that time ghost that interrupted the ceremony this morning?"

"We wish we did!" they both said together.

This attracted the attention of a row of students sitting along a statue of a sleeping man nearby. "So do we!" they all called out.

A young man in a little white kilt who was sitting on the statue's head said, "I'm offering a year's beer money to that joker if he can come up with tri-dees of the whole caper. I want to see the look on Enkian's face!"

"Close up," said the girl in gauze.

"No reward is high enough," said the man in the kilt.

"Enkian's raging about, offering to expel the one that did it," explained the young man in black velvet. "So of course, he's not going to find out."

"Which means we're *all* dying of frustration," added the girl in gauze. "*You* don't know anything, do you, Jonathan?"

"I'll reward you, too," said the man in the kilt.

"Sorry, no," Jonathan said. "I was hoping *you* did."

He started to walk on, but the young man in the kilt called him back. "Seriously," he said, laughing. "If you can give me an eyewitness account, I'll do anything you want in return."

Jonathan laughed too. "Later," he said. "We have to get to Dr. Wilander." They went on, up some steps and into a long arched corridor. "It was obviously somebody having a joke with a hologram," he said to Vivian. "This is Continuum, by the way. We have to go right through and into Perpetuum—that's the main library. Wilander lives in a den right at the top. They say he only comes out to quarrel with Enkian."

Perpetuum was huge, and very strangely shaped. The open entry facing them beyond Continuum was made of granite blocks, and it had five sides. Of course, Vivian thought, if you imagined an ordinary doorway with a pointed arch at the top, that would have five sides too, but the sides making the point would be shorter. In this entry, all five sides were the same length, and it looked lopsided. Above and beyond it, she could see the same five-sided shape repeated over and over again, in a vast honeycomb, all combined together into a huge half-toppled-looking five-sided building. There were old, eroded letters carved along the upper-most side of the portal, picked out faintly in gold:

MONUMENTS MORE LASTING THAN BRASS

"That means books," Jonathan said. "Press your low-weight stud. There are thousands of stairs."

There were indeed thousands of stairs. Shallow and made of granite, they climbed left, then right, then left again, past more five-sided entries labeled DANTEUM, SHAKESPEAREUM, ORPHEUM, and other names that meant nothing to Vivian. At each archway, other flights of steps led off in four different directions. It was like climbing a maze. Jonathan told Vivian that the sharp electric smell that hung around each five-sided archway was the smell of the millions of book cubes stored in each section. It seemed that there were not many real books in Perpetuum. But shortly, even with their low-weight functions turned on, they did not have breath for talking and just climbed. By the time they reached an arch-way called CONFUCIUM, Vivian had realized that Time City was appearing around them at all sorts of strange angles. At CONFU-CIUM she saw the Gnomon Tower in the distance sticking out sideways from under her feet and tried not to look. The stairs felt as if they were right way up, even if they were not.

Finally, at an entry named HERODOTIUM, Time City came the right way up but slanting, quite a long way beneath them. Jonathan turned into HERODOTIUM, to Vivian's relief. It was rather dark inside and smelled strongly of wood. The five-sided corridor was carved from the same kind of silky wood as Sam's father's desk. Vivian glimpsed grass shapes and people shapes as Jonathan hurried her along.

"They say Faber John got the man who carved Solomon's Temple to do this," he told her breathlessly. Vivian did not think he was joking. He was too much out of breath. "Turn off your low-weight function. It'll need to recharge."

At the very end of the corridor a flight of wooden steps led to the last five-sided portal. SELDOM END, Vivian read, as Jonathan knocked on the silky wooden door.

The door sprang open on light that was warm and orange because of the wood. "You're nearly a minute late," growled Dr. Wilander.

He was sitting at a wooden desk under the window in the sloping roof of the room. All the straight walls were filled with shelves of real books. Thousands of little square things that were probably book cubes were clamped to the ceiling. Piles of papers and books filled most of the floor. Dr. Wilander was smoking a pipe and wearing a shaggy brown jacket that made him look more like a bear than ever. He looked completely comfortable, like a bear resting in its den after a feast of honey.

"You sit there," he grunted at Vivian, pointing his pipe at a small real-wood table. "What do you see in front of you?"

"Er—" said Vivian, wondering what he wanted her to say. "This looks like a chart. And there's a list and a piece of paper covered in shiny stuff and a sheet for writing on. And a table underneath, of course. Do you want me to say the chair, too?"

Jonathan snorted as he sat at a small table in front of Dr. Wilander's desk, and stuffed the end of his pigtail into his mouth.

"That will do," Dr. Wilander growled. "I intend to give you a crash course in history and universal symbols, my girl. You're a Lee. Yet your aunt and your teacher tell me you're completely ignorant. It won't do. The chart is a map of history from the start of man to the Depopulation of Earth. Learn it. The list is a glossary of universal symbols, and the paper is one of the very first pieces of writing in those symbols. That is why it is covered in energized plastic: it is extremely valuable. Make me a translation of that writing. In short, use your brain for once in your life. I'll test you on both things when I've done with Jonathan."

It was clear that everyone thought that the real Vivian Lee was very bright indeed. Vivian had no choice but to sit down and try to be brainy too. She picked up the chart. It was almost circular—horseshoe-shaped really—so that the end on the left marked "Stone Age" nearly met the end on the right marked "Depopulation." Along it were lines marked in thousands of years. The parts that were white except for the lines were marked "Fixed Era." The parts colored gray were labeled "Unstable Era." Very few other things were marked in the gray parts, but the curved stretches of white were a mass of writing and dates. Vivian's eyes scudded over them in horror. World War IV . . . Conquest of Australia . . . Mind Wars . . . Icelandic Empire Begins . . . The Waigongi Atrocity . . . Primacy of Easter Island Ends . . . Revolt of Canada . . . Fuegan Economic Unity . . . The Sinking of the Holy Fleet . . . The Demise of Europe . . . And these were only some of the things in large print! Vivian gave the chart another desperate stare and turned to the valuable paper. It looked easier.

Meanwhile, Dr. Wilander was growling questions at Jonathan, and Jonathan was answering after long pauses filled with a faint crunching noise. The crunching was Jonathan chewing his pigtail, which he did whenever he was stuck. It must end up quite wet! Vivian thought, as she got down to translating. This was nothing like as easy as she had hoped. Universal symbols did not exactly stand for letters, nor for whole words either. You had to fit the things the symbols *might* stand for together, and then try to make sense of them. Vivian's brain began to complain that it had never worked so hard in its life. Every so often it went on strike, and she had to wait for it to start working again, while she watched Dr. Wilander plucking down book cubes, slapping open real books, and growling at Jonathan.

"Don't be a fool, boy!" she heard him growl. "You're like everyone else in Time City. You think the only real history is outside in time. Nobody bothers to keep a record of what goes on in the city, but of course, it's got a history, just like everywhere else."

Dr. Wilander had obviously said this many times before. Jonathan bit his pigtail in order not to yawn. Vivian went back to her symbols. When her brain gave out next, Dr. Wilander was grunting, "Time Lady, Time Lady! That's just what I'm complaining of. All we've got in this city is legends like that instead of history. It's a disgrace. You can hardly find out something that happened a hundred years ago, let alone whether creatures like your Time Lady really existed or not.''

"But *someone* was coming up through Twenty Century, making a wave of chaos, weren't they?" Jonathan said, twisting the damp end of his pigtail. He was so obviously trying to pump Dr. Wilander about the boy on the Tor that Vivian turned off her pen and held the chart in front of her face in order to listen.

"Undoubtedly," grunted Dr. Wilander. "Keep to the subject. What came out of the Second Unstable Era?"

"A great deal more science," said Jonathan. "How would a person like that time-travel?"

"How should I know?" Dr. Wilander snarled. "Now put that together with what you know of the Icelandic Empire and see if you can explain its decline."

"They relied on the science too much," said Jonathan. "But what would someone be time-traveling through Twenty Century *for*?"

"To get out of a vile era as quickly as possible, I should think," Dr. Wilander said. "Tell me how they relied on science too much."

Jonathan's teeth clamped around the end of his pigtail again. He was getting nowhere with Dr. Wilander. Vivian sighed and turned her pen on. It seemed only a short time later that Dr. Wilander was barking at her, "Well? Have you learned that chart yet, or haven't you?"

"I, er, no," Vivian said.

"And why not?"

"There's so *much*!" Vivian said piteously. "History was *short* in the twentieth—I mean, Twenty Century!"

"Because history was incomplete then," Dr. Wilander growled. "That's no excuse."

"And I don't understand it. Why is it round?" Vivian pleaded.

"As everyone in Time City knows, except you apparently," said Dr. Wilander, "it is because historical time is circular. The beginning is the end. Time used by Man goes around and around—in a small circle here in the city, in a very large one out in history. Possibly the whole universe does also. What were your parents thinking of, not telling you that at least? So you haven't learned any history. Haven't you done any translating either?"

"I've done some," Vivian admitted.

"Let's hear it then." Dr. Wilander leaned back and lit his pipe with a tap of one huge finger on its bowl, as if he expected to be listening for the next hour or so.

Vivian looked miserably at her few lines of crossed-out and rewritten green writing. "One large blacksmith threw four coffins about," she read.

Jonathan hurriedly stuffed a doubled-up lump of pigtail into his mouth. "Oh, did he?" Dr. Wilander said placidly. "To show off his strength, I suppose. Carry on."

"So that they turned into four very old women," Vivian read. "One got rusty for smoothing clothes. Two became white in moderately cheap jewelry. Three of them turned yellow and got expensive, and another four were dense and low in the tables—"

"So now there were ten coffins," Dr. Wilander said. "Or maybe ten strange elderly ladies. Some of these were doing the laundry while the rest pranced about in cheap necklaces. I suppose the yellow ones caught jaundice at the sight, while the stupid ones crawled under the furniture in order not to look. Is there any more of this lively narrative?"

"A bit," said Vivian. "Four more were full of electricity, but they were insulated with policemen, so that the town could learn philosophy for at least a year."

"Four more old women and an unspecified number of police," Dr. Wilander remarked. "The blacksmith makes at least fifteen. I hope he paid the police for wrapping themselves around the electrical old ladies. It sounds painful. Or are you implying that the police were electrocuted, thus supplying the townsfolk with a valuable moral lesson?''

"I don't know," Vivian said hopelessly.

"But just what," asked Dr. Wilander, "do you think your multitudes of old women were really doing?''

"I've no idea," Vivian confessed.

"People don't usually write nonsense," Dr. Wilander remarked, still placidly puffing at his pipe. "Pass the paper to Jonathan. Perhaps he can tell us what all these people were up to.''

Jonathan took the paper out of Vivian's hand. He looked at it and stuffed another lump of pigtail into his mouth. Tears trickled from under the flicker of his eye function.

"Jonathan considers it to be a tragedy," Dr. Wilander growled sadly. "The police were killed by high-voltage crones. Here. I'll read it.'' He plucked the paper out of Jonathan's shaking fist and read, "The great Faber John made four containers or caskets and hid each of them in one of the Four Ages of the World." He turned to Vivian. "*Faber* does indeed mean 'smith,' and the symbol is the same; but your old ladies came about because you took no notice of the double age symbol, which always means 'time' or 'an Age of the World' if it's female. To continue." He read, "The casket made of iron, he concealed in the Age of Iron. The second, which was of silver, he hid in the Silver Age, and the third, which was pure gold, in the Age of Gold. The fourth container was of lead and hidden in the same manner. He filled these four caskets with the greater part of his power and appointed to each one a special guardian. In this way he ensured that Time City would endure throughout a whole Platonic Year. . . . There,'' he said to Vivian. "That makes perfect sense to me *and* supplies Jonathan with another of the legends he likes so much.''

Jonathan unstuffed his mouth and asked seriously, "Do you think what it says is true?''

"The writer thought so,'' Dr. Wilander grunted. "He or she

believed it enough to put the paper in the time safe up here many thousands of years ago. The containers of power it talks about are, of course, what we nowadays call polarities.''

''And what's a Platonic Year?'' Jonathan asked.

''The time it takes for the stars to work their way back to the pattern from which they started,'' said Dr. Wilander. ''This is sometimes calculated to be two hundred and fifty-eight centuries, which, if Vivian would look at that chart for a moment, instead of letting her eyes slide off it, she will find to be almost exactly the length of human history. Vivian, you will learn that chart for me by tomorrow. And since that paper is too valuable to take away, you will take this copy instead and make me a proper translation of all of it, also by tomorrow. Jonathan will do me a detailed essay on the Icelandic Empire.''

Vivian left the warm wood-smelling room feeling as wet and chewed as the end of Jonathan's pigtail.

''I think he's a monster!'' she said as they started down the thousand stairs.

GUARDIAN

GUARDIAN 9

They walked back across Aeon Square. "Would you call Twenty Century part of the Age of Iron?" Jonathan asked thoughtfully.

"Certainly not!" Vivian said indignantly. "We use aluminum and plastic and chromium. The Iron Age was when they lived in huts!"

"I was only—" Jonathan began. But he was interrupted by the skirling of bagpipes from the center of the square. There was a lot of surging and pointing among the crowd of tourists gathered there around Faber John's Stone. They had glimpses of the ghost capering among them. "The student doing that is going to get caught if he's not careful," Jonathan said. "It must take quite a big projector."

"You mean a hollow gramophone is a kind of film?" Vivian asked with new interest. Films she knew all about.

"Hologram. Yes," said Jonathan. "You use laser beams to make an image you can see all around. About the time of the Mind Wars people get really good at it. I bet that student comes from then."

"What are laser beams?" Vivian asked.

"A special kind of beam," Jonathan said in his most lordly manner. Vivian suspected that this was because he had very little more idea than she had.

The ghost had vanished by the time they got to the center of the square. They skirted the crowd and went toward Time Close. Sam was waiting for them under the archway. "Are we going to go after the boy who stole the polarity?" he demanded.

"When I've decided the best way to go about it," Jonathan

said, using his lordly manner again. This told Vivian that Jonathan had no more idea how to go after the boy than he had about laser beams. "I told you we don't want to get stranded in history," he said. "You know that egg didn't work properly after we time-traveled with it."

"I'll come and eat butter-pies in your room while you think," Sam offered.

"No, you won't," Jonathan said. "I've got to do an essay for Wilander."

Sam turned his widest two-toothed smile toward Vivian. "Then I'll come to your room and show you how your automat works," he said.

"Not now—anyway, I know how it works," Vivian said. She felt suddenly overwhelmed with work. "I've a chart and universal symbols and a translation— I shall be up all *night,* I think!"

"Round-eyed blister and slit-eyed swot!" Sam said. "I hate school days. Everyone gets boring!" He went stumping disgustedly away, flapping two sets of shoelaces on the cobbles.

"Now he'll do something to get back at us," Jonathan said. "He usually does."

Vivian did not much care. She was far more frightened of Dr. Wilander making fun of her again. She hurried to her room and tried to force her unwilling brain to work. It would not. She spent an hour staring at the chart and the symbols, and the only thing she learned was that a pen function was not like a real pen in the most important way there was. You could not chew it. She was forced to get up and try to remember what Petula had shown her you did to work the neat little automat on her wall. Sam would have found it deeply disappointing. It did not do butter-pies. It gave Vivian two seaweed chews and a cherry brandysnap twist, all of which were thoroughly nourishing and good for the teeth, and did nothing for Vivian's overtaxed brain at all.

"Oh bother!" she said. She turned on some music that called itself Antarctic Bedlam-style, fixed her teeth grimly in a seaweed chew, and tried again.

By dinnertime she had translated the part of the valuable paper that Dr. Wilander had read out—which was cheating really, because she remembered what it said. Then she had to stop and change into the crisp white pajamas Petula had laid out for her. They gave her ghostly red roses in her hair and on one shoulder. Vivian turned to the mirror and admired them before she went down to see who tonight's guests were.

Mr. Enkian was one of them. The others were all high-ups from Continuum or Perpetuum who had been offended by the student's joke. After one look at their faces, Vivian knew that Sempitern Walker was going to have to be very boring indeed. And she was right. Mr. Enkian started as soon as they were sitting at the table.

"Sempitern, I will not have our traditional ceremonies mocked, particularly in this time of crisis, when everyone should be standing solidly behind Time City. They poked fun not only at me— and yourself of course—but also at Faber John's Stone. And as if this was not enough, Doomsday Book fell in a puddle!"

Sempitern Walker fixed his eyes anxiously on a far corner and talked drearily for five minutes about "youthful high spirits" and "not condone it in the least but should endeavor to take a lenient quasi-parental line."

Mr. Enkian waited for him to stop and said, "I shall put forward a motion in Chronologue. My colleagues here will vote for it. In future we shall ban all students from Sixty-seven Century or any other era with disruptive technology."

Which meant that Sempitern Walker had to fix his gaze on another corner and drone on again about "a balanced mix of students from all feasible eras." Vivian watched him while he talked and willed him to jump up from the table and run about shouting the way he had that morning. It would be so much more interesting. And she was sure it would shut Mr. Enkian up in seconds.

"We don't take students from Unstable Eras," Mr. Enkian snapped. "If we already ban everyone from Fifty-eight to Sixty-five Century, we can quite easily extend the ban to cover Fifty-six Century as well. That's where the culprit came from—I'm positive of that.''

"But if we did that," Sempitern Walker said, crumbling the food in his dish and looking as if he had a toothache, "we run the risk of attempting to exclude some student whom history states to have studied here. This would initiate instability in that era.''

"Please," Vivian asked, while Mr. Enkian was opening his mouth to reply, "please, *why* don't you have people from Unstable Eras?" As soon as she said it, she realized how very brave Jonathan had been to interrupt the talk the night before. Mr. Enkian glared at her. Sempitern Walker turned his toothache look on her. Vivian felt her face going hot.

But Sempitern Walker seemed to think her question was perfectly reasonable. "We don't let them in for a number of reasons," he said. "The most important one is that we need the Unstable Eras to stay just as they are in order to keep the Fixed Eras steady. We can't have a man from, say, Sixty Century knowing he could come to Time City and find out about his future. We rely on his era—the Third Unstable Era—to have the wars and make the inventions that lead to the Icelandic Empire in the next Fixed Era. If this man from Sixty Century knew this, either he might sit back and not do anything, thinking the future was fixed anyway, or—which is probably worse—he might get annoyed and do something quite different. And the trouble with Unstable Eras is that quite small things can change the course of history in them. Is that clear?''

Vivian nodded, trying to look as clever as the real Cousin Vivian. From the way Mr. Enkian was glowering, she suspected that Sempitern Walker was quite glad she had interrupted. "And what happens when an Unstable Era goes critical?" she asked, before Mr. Enkian could say anything.

Sempitern Walker's toothache look subsided to the usual look of mere anguish. "That," he said, "happens when enough changes happen to the history of that era to change the Fixed Eras before and after them—as in Twenty Century at the moment. The change rolls forward first, as you might expect. We're now having trouble in Twenty-three Century because several inventions that ought to have been made then have been made already in 1940. But the instability is beginning to roll backward, too. Time Patrol is having to work very hard to make sure the Roman Empire—"

Mr. Enkian sprang to his feet with his pointed yellow face twisted. "Oh, this is *too* much!" he shouted.

"Now *really*, Mr. Enkian!" Jenny said, sounding crosser than Vivian had ever heard her.

"No," said Mr. Enkian. "I meant. That." He pointed to the rounded end wall of the room. "Excrescence," he said. He was so angry that he was having trouble speaking.

Everyone's head switched that way. The students' time ghost was there. Jonathan swallowed what he was eating and crammed his pigtail into his mouth. Vivian slammed both hands across her face so that no one should see her laughing. It was such nerve of the students! The tall, crazy-looking man with his high, floppy hat was standing against the half circle of wall, obviously projected there like a film, leering at them like a slightly anxious court jester. Vivian felt she knew his long, lunatic face quite well by now.

"Go away," Mr. Enkian said, still pointing.

The court jester's answer was to spread its hands out toward him pleadingly. Its leer became a mad grin.

Jonathan's parents exchanged looks. Sempitern Walker cleared his throat and stood up. "That will do now," he said. "Turn your apparatus off, please."

The court jester's grin faded. It looked almost as agonized as the Sempitern. Its mouth opened as if it were about to speak.

"I said, Remove this vision, please, at once," said Sempitern Walker. "Or you will find yourself up before Chronologue for contempt."

The ghost's mouth closed. It looked resigned. It bowed its head to the Sempitern and backed away through the wall, leaving everyone with a faint afterimage, like sun dazzle, of its strange, lanky shape.

"Quite a realistic holo," someone said.

"At least this time they left out those awful bagpipes!" said somebody else. And everyone began talking about the false ghost, or soothing Mr. Enkian, who seemed to think the thing was a personal insult to himself. Vivian said nothing for the rest of the meal. Now that she had had a clear and detailed look at the apparition, she knew why she thought she knew its face. It was the same face, under the same floppy hat, that she had seen coming through one of the time locks up the River Time, ignoring the panic-stricken rush of the other time ghosts running the other way. She was trying to think where she had seen it before that.

"I don't think that *was* a hollow phone," she said to Jonathan afterward.

"Yes, but Fifty-six Century holography is wildly realistic," he answered, and went off to write his essay.

"*Or* a hollow giraffe either!" Vivian muttered as she crawled back to her own tasks. The translation came out as nonsense twice. At this point Vivian's brain gave out and began arguing at her. There was no *point* in flogging it like this, it told her. She was going home to Mum before long, and the best thing she could do was to think of ways of getting there. Not at the moment! her brain added hastily. One more thought would kill it. But it was her duty to sit there at least feeling restfully homesick, instead of going on to learn that awful chart.

She picked up the chart a little guiltily. It was perfectly true, as her brain pointed out, that she had hardly spared a moment being homesick, except just a little at night, for the last two days. That was because of the two time ghosts in the passage. She knew she could not go home until she had been somewhere else with Jonathan, and then come back to Time City again. And as soon as she realized this, she also realized that she was unlikely to get to wherever it was and back and then home without seeing Dr. Wilander again. And Dr. Wilander was going to make tears of laughter run down Jonathan's face at her expense, unless she did better than last time.

That was enough to set Vivian bending over the history chart in earnest. She fell asleep that night murmuring, "First Unstable Era A.D. 300 to 2199. Second Unstable Era 3800 to 3950. Third Unstable Era 5700 to 6580. Fourth Unstable Era—oh, isn't history *long*!" And when she woke in the morning, her head was still swimming with things she almost knew.

As she went downstairs that morning, Sempitern Walker came flying down past her in a rustling plum-colored cloak. "Elio!" he shouted. "Elio!" Vivian hurried down after him, certain there was going to be another ceremony and another fuss. But it did not look like it. Elio was waiting in the hall with Sam's father. "Oh, you got him. Good!" said the Sempitern, swooping down on the pair of them. "Any news of that holo projector yet?"

"Time Patrol is working on it, sir," said Elio.

"Among about a million other things. That projector must have its own power pack. It's not drawing any from the city," Mr. Donegal said, and he nodded at Vivian. "Hello there."

To Vivian's surprise, Sempitern Walked nodded at her too and said, "Good morning," before he swept Mr. Donegal and Elio off to his study, leaving Vivian rather disappointed that there was no more rushing about than that. She was still hoping and listening when she and Jonathan had to set off to Duration.

Sam was waiting by the fountain in Time Close as usual. "I'm not speaking to either of you," he announced. "You went off without me."

"Well, we had work to do from Dr. Wilander," Jonathan said.

"I don't mean that, stupid!" said Sam. "I mean you went without me wherever your two time ghosts were coming back from. You're green mean obscenes, both of you!"

"No, we didn't," said Vivian.

"Stupid yourself!" Jonathan said, stalking ahead to the archway into Aeon Square. "We haven't been there yet."

"Then you will soon," Sam said, pounding after him in a patter of shoelace. "What's the difference? I know you're going to."

"I'd go without you this moment if I'd the least idea of what we were doing!" Jonathan said angrily over his shoulder.

"And you have no right to blame us for something we haven't done yet!" Vivian added, also over her shoulder.

The court jester apparition was leaning against the brick wall under the archway. The long, mad-looking face turned toward them as they came through. Jonathan nearly ran into Vivian, because they had both been looking the other way until the last minute. They stumbled to a stop and stared. Somehow, in the dimness under the arch, the false ghost seemed both harder to see and a great deal more solid. He towered over them both. And he seemed to be watching them earnestly.

"Well, I *do* blame you!" Sam said, stumping into the archway after them. He stopped when he saw the apparition. His voice went to a heavy whisper. "It looks awfully real!"

Jonathan swallowed. "But he's not," he said. "If you tried to touch him, your hand would hit the wall."

The court jester's mouth spread into a long, long smile. "Come try me," he said. His voice was distant and indistinct, like a man speaking in another room. And he held out a long, shadowy arm, almost in Jonathan's face. Jonathan ducked away back from it hurriedly.

That left Vivian out in front. She pulled in a deep breath. "I'll try," she said, and went forward toward the outstretched arm with her own arm and hand held stiffly out like a sleepwalker. And her hand met something. As it did, it gave Vivian a jolt of the sort of fear you feel on finding yourself face-to-face with a large, fierce dog. Not that the ghost was fierce. She just had the feeling that it hated to be touched. The arm she met was not exactly solid, but it was not nothing either. It was coldish, and the cloth of the sleeve was rough. And though her hand did not sink into that arm, she knew that the flesh and the cloth over it were made of something that was spread thinner than normal. "I can feel you," she said, and found she was whispering. "You're not a hollow gramophone, are you?"

"No. I am real," the ghost said in its strange, muffled voice. "You may all touch and believe." Its smile died away, and it looked sad; but it stood patiently holding its arm out while first Jonathan, then Sam, came and put their fingers on the rough cloth of its sleeve. Sam prodded a bit, and the ghost endured it patiently. Sam backed away, looking awed. Jonathan cleared his throat, but even so, his voice came out choky.

"It's . . . sort of solid."

The ghost took its arm away, and for a moment they all stared at one another, as if everyone including the ghost needed to recover from the experience.

"What do you want?" Jonathan said at length.

"To make my trouble known," said the ghost. The dejected thread of its voice seemed to wind about the archway and come to them from several directions at once. Probably, Vivian thought, its voice was spread as thin as the rest of it. "I have tried to make folk in the city hear me," it said, "but I have little substance here without my Casket, and they take me for a ghost."

"Well, you can't blame people for thinking that when you go galloping about playing the bagpipes in the middle of a ceremony," Jonathan said.

The ghost shook its head, with a sad, puzzled smile. "Did I do that? My memory is not good. I did not remember until last night that it was you I should be speaking to. Then I came and tried, but a powerful man dismissed me in the name of the Chronologue, and I had no choice but to depart."

"You mean you wanted *us*?" Jonathan said incredulously.

"What are you," said Sam, "if you're not a ghost really?"

"Myself," said the ghost. "I am the one who was set to guard the Iron Casket, and I failed. You saw how I failed. You saw the Casket dug up and stolen from its place."

"Oh!" they all said, and Vivian thought, Of course! This was the man with long legs who had run past them so easily up the Tor, shouting at them to hurry. He had looked a lot more solid then. She looked down at his almost-solid foot standing on the cobblestones. She recognized those pointed shoes now. From the look of Sam and Jonathan, they knew him too.

"But why did you go and vanish?" Sam said. "You just let the boy get on and steal it!"

The Guardian of the Iron Casket spread his big pale hands helplessly. "I did what I could. When I saw the theft begin, I ran to the early days of the Age of Iron, and from there I ran back to the late days, pulling the threads of history as I came. In the first ages of Time City this should have summoned powerful help from the folk of the city, but the allotted span of the city is ending, and it made my power to summon weak. Only you two answered the summons." This made Sam and Jonathan give each other self-conscious looks. "So then"—the Guardian's thin voice muttered on—"I surrounded the thief in the threads of history and wrapped them around any who would help in the Age of Iron to drag them together. And all who came was one girl, and the three of you arrived too late." The long face looked desperately sad.

"And why did you come here?" Vivian asked.

"I did not know what else to do," the Guardian admitted. "When the Iron Casket leaves its hiding place, the Age of Iron ends, and I must return to the city. So here I came to Time City, hoping that my Casket had been restored to its place in the Gnomon. But it is not there. It has been stolen."

"We know. We didn't do any good at all," Jonathan said. He was so worried that he almost looked like Sempitern Walker.

"Look, is Time City really coming to an end? Isn't there *any-thing* we can do?"

The Guardian gazed at him sadly. "It is moving into its last days. The Great Year is nearly ended, yes. But if the Guardians of the other three Caskets could be warned, and the Silver, the Gold, and the Lead brought to the Gnomon safe from the thief, then the first days might come again."

"Then we'll do—" Jonathan began, but Vivian interrupted him eagerly.

"Who *is* that thief?" she said. "The Time Lady?"

The Guardian's long pale face turned to her in a look of utter reproach. He shook his head, slowly and sadly, and faded away while he did it, into the wall of the archway. They were left looking at rows of narrow red bricks with an afterimage of a sad, long-legged shape against them. Vivian could have kicked herself. She felt hot and cold and weak in the legs, the way you do when you have said something perfectly dreadful. She wished she had *known* that it was a dreadful thing to say. Meanwhile, Jonathan was crunching his pigtail between his teeth and still looking as anguished as his father, and Sam seemed to be holding his breath. He let it out in a sort of roar.

"Don't just stand there! *Do* something!"

"Yes, but we'll have to think *how* to first," Jonathan said. He began to walk out through Aeon Square, frowning and chewing his pigtail. Vivian went after him. She could tell by the flapping of shoelace that Sam was just behind. "If that really was the Guardian of the Iron Casket and not another student joke," Jonathan said.

"No, it was too sad," Vivian said. "And too real."

"Then things aren't the way we thought," said Jonathan.

"And that boy's not got anything to do with the Time Lady," Sam said. "So get on and think. It's your sort of idea we need now."

Jonathan turned and snapped, "I *am* thinking! But my mind

needs to adjust first. Besides, do *you* know where the other Caskets are? Have *you* any way of knowing which bit of thousands of years of history is the Golden Age? Or the Age of Lead? No, I thought you hadn't. So shut up!"

He marched on across the square with Vivian, followed by heavy breathing and expressive flapping of shoelaces. But of course, they all had to gather around Faber John's Stone in the middle. Jonathan stared down at a whole new spiderweb of cracks spreading out from the new cracks of yesterday.

"I think Time City really *is* in its last days," he said miserably. "What do we do? How can we find those other Guardians?"

"I have a bit of an idea," Vivian said hesitantly. Jonathan whirled around on her, and Sam jerked his chin up to stare at her. She felt rather a fool. "Well, if the Twentieth Century *is* part of the Age of Iron," she said, "and I suppose it *must* be if the Iron Casket was stolen from it, then it's part of an Unstable Era, isn't it? Don't you think the other three ages may be Unstable Eras too?" She squatted down and spread Dr. Wilander's horseshoe-shaped chart out on the fractured stone. She knew it quite appallingly well by now, the long white stretches and the shorter gray ones. And, as she remembered, the gray blocks were very evenly spaced through history, as if they had been made that way on purpose. It was the first time in her life that she had found learning anything even remotely useful. "Look," she said.

Jonathan unclenched his teeth from his pigtail and knelt down to look. "But there are seven, no, eight other Unstable Eras."

"Six of them are little ones—only a hundred years or so," Vivian said.

"Only three long ones," Sam said, breathing windily across them. He was lying on his stomach with his chin almost on the chart.

"And those are all about thirty centuries apart," Jonathan said. "I never realized before." He put his finger on the Third Unstable Era, 5700 to 6580. "Then this *could* be the Silver Age, if

that comes next after the Age of Iron. And''—his finger moved
around to the last long gray block—''this could be either the Age
of Lead or the Age of Gold. But that means the fourth Age has
to be one of the short ones. Anyway, it's worth looking at the
Third *and* the Ninth Unstable Era—what is it? Ninety-two Century to One Hundred—''

They were interrupted by a loud bell ringing from Duration.
The last few children were running hard across the bottom of
Aeon Square.

''Oh great Time!'' Jonathan said. ''I've never, ever been this
late!''

They scrambled up. Vivian scooped up the chart and folded it
as they raced over the flagstones. They were going to be late.
The bell had stopped long before they got to Duration.

''You've got it, V.S.!'' Jonathan panted as they ran. ''But
we're going to need help finding out which Age is which. Let's
pump Wilander.''

School was not so bad for Vivian that morning, even though
she arrived late. Probably it was because she knew what to expect
now. She spent quite a lot of time using her pen function to draw
long-legged men in tall, squashy hats and thinking about the poor
sad Guardian of the Iron Casket. She wondered what a person
who was not quite real spent his time doing in the city. Fading
in and out, looking for help, she supposed. So it hadn't been a
student joke after all. . . .

Then she thought about what the Guardian had said. It sounded
as if he couldn't tackle the thief himself. Perhaps he was too
ghostly, now that Time City was coming to the end of its days.
So he had caused a wave of chaos in the Twentieth Century and
the history before it, trying to get help, and all that must have
happened was that Sam's father and Time Patrol wasted their
time hunting him.

We ought to tell them about the thief! Vivian thought uneasily.
The Guardian seemed to think that the thief was going to go on

and steal all the Caskets—or polarities, or whatever. And that could be right. Why steal only one, if you could time-travel the way that boy could? He was probably traveling toward the Silver Age at this very moment. But as Jonathan had pointed out, if he and Vivian and Sam told anyone about it, they would be in trouble. And no one listened to Jonathan's hints. Almost the only thing they *could* do was to do what the Guardian wanted and go and warn the other Guardians themselves. They could do that if the time egg worked properly. But they had to know where to go first. Jonathan was right. They would have to get Dr. Wilander to tell them this afternoon.

She expected that Jonathan would want to rush off early to Dr. Wilander. So she was very surprised not to see him at all during the lunch break. At twelve thirty-five by her belt clock, there was still no sign of him. Vivian waited a few more minutes and then tore herself away from the eager crowd who wanted to hear more about the War. Very nervously, she set out for Perpetuum on her own.

Jonathan was in the grassy space with the statues outside Continuum. He was leaning against a vast statue of a woman without any arms, talking eagerly to one of the students. It was the young man who had offered beer money for a film of the Guardian interrupting the ceremony. Vivian remembered the short white kilt and the young man's brawny legs beneath it. The young man had one of those brawny legs comfortably hooked over the great foot of the statue as he talked to Jonathan, and the rest of him was sprawled on the grass. From that position, he saw Vivian before Jonathan did and gave her a friendly wave.

"Oh, is it that late already?" Jonathan said. "Leon, this is my cousin V.S. Meet Leon Hardy, V.S. He's from One Hundred and Two Century."

Leon Hardy rose gracefully to his feet. "Pleased to meet you, Vee," he said, and smiled, two rows of white teeth in a brown face. Vivian was rather taken aback by him. He was so like a film star.

"Isn't One Hundred and something an Unstable Era?" she said doubtfully.

"Just after the end of the Ninth," Leon told her. "The last Fixed Era before the Depopulation—but that's not for centuries after my time. My time is busy repairing the mess left by the Demise of Europe. It's a very exciting time, full of new technology, and I came here to learn all the science I could."

"We'd better go," Jonathan said.

"Or Wilander will throw you down all the stairs in Perpetuum," Leon said, laughing. "I heard he threatened to do that to Enkian once. Right, young Jonathan. Payment for the eyewitness account coming up. Expect to hear from me in a couple of days or so."

So that's what they were talking about! Vivian thought. She walked beside Jonathan down the arched corridor of Continuum, wondering why it was that people you could admire perfectly well as film stars were the people you didn't quite like in real life. "What did he mean about payment?" she asked.

"Tell you later," said Jonathan.

Vivian looked and saw that Jonathan was walking with his most bouncing and lordly stride. Oh no! she thought. He's got one of those ideas of his again! I hope he isn't going to kidnap someone else now!

CEREMONIES

T hey ran up most of the many stairs of Perpetuum. It seemed to be one of those days when you are late for everything. Even with the low-weight functions of their belts to help, Vivian and Jonathan threw themselves into Seldom End almost five minutes late. Dr. Wilander sat lighting his pipe. All he did was stare at them through the smoke, but neither of them dared move or speak until he grunted, "I see you don't intend to waste any more time making feeble excuses, at least. Sit down. Vivian, how is your translation?"

"The second part is peculiar," Vivian admitted.

"Then get on and make sense of it while I tear a few pieces off your cousin," Dr. Wilander growled.

Vivian did her best, while she listened to the clicking of book cubes and Jonathan's teeth crunching hair. It was very peaceful in the odd-shaped wooden-smelling room—too peaceful. As Vivian's breath came back, she slowly realized that Jonathan was asking almost no questions at all. Those he did ask had nothing to do with Unstable Eras. Vivian had a nagging feeling that something was wrong. She had no idea why Jonathan had decided not to fish for information about the Four Ages, but she thought she had better try fishing herself—if she dared, that was.

"Er—" she said.

Dr. Wilander turned his great head to look at her. "Yes?"

Faced with those clever little eyes looking at her through the smoke, Vivian lost her nerve. "I don't know if this symbol means 'comic' or 'old,' " she said.

"Try 'antic'—that means both," Dr. Wilander grunted, and turned back to Jonathan.

Vivian sighed and made an attempt to chew her pen function. Her teeth clacked together on nothing. Come *on*! she told herself. Ask! Be cunning or you'll never get home to Mum. But it was no good. She was too frightened of Dr. Wilander to say anything, until Dr. Wilander swung his bulk around in her direction.

"Now let's have the further adventures of the blacksmith and the madly multiplying old ladies," he said.

"Before you do," Vivian said. Saying it, she felt the same jolt of fear she had felt as she touched the Guardian's nearly solid arm, but she made herself go on. "Before I read it, please could you tell me about the Unstable Eras. How you tell which they are, I mean. And all about them." There, it was out. Vivian was shaking, and Jonathan was staring at what he was writing, disowning her. But she knew it was important.

"Trying to put off the evil hour, are you?" Dr. Wilander grunted. But he puffed placidly at his pipe and considered what to say. "Having just come from one yourself, I suppose you would be puzzled," he remarked. "You can't tell they're unstable at all when you're living in them. You can only tell from outside, here in Time City. And it isn't only that nobody *in* an Unstable Era knows what's going to happen in their future—*nobody* knows. It can differ from day to day." He laid his pipe on his desk and clasped his fat, hairy hands around one of his huge knees. "But let's not take the era you came from. That's a terrible muddle, particularly just now. Let's take the one closer to hand. Let's look at Time City."

"Time City!" Vivian exclaimed.

Jonathan was so astonished that he gave up disowning Vivian and swung his chair around to join in. "But Time City isn't unstable!" he said.

"One point proved," grunted Dr. Wilander. "You don't know it is because you're living in it. Of course it's unstable, boy! If you could get right outside time as well as history, you'd find the city had a past and future as changeable as Twenty Century. What do you think is the real reason we have records of every single year of history and almost none of the city itself? Because those records wouldn't stay accurate, of course. And do *you* know what's going to happen in the city tomorrow? No. And nor do I."

"But we *do* know!" Jonathan protested. "We know the weather and what ceremonies are due—"

"Ceremonies!" Dr. Wilander snarled. "They were probably invented to make people *feel* they knew what would happen tomorrow. That's all the use I've ever seen in them. Or maybe they had a meaning once. Oh, I grant you that Time City is the most uneventful and stable-*seeming* of Unstable Eras, but that's all it is. We might hope for a bit of a crisis perhaps when it comes to an end—and since it's almost worked around to its own beginning again now, that won't be long—but my guess is that it'll just peter out in some ceremony or other. With that fool Enkian complaining somebody put him too low down the order. Gah!"

"Did you say it's come around to its own beginning?" Vivian asked.

"I did. Pass me that chart," said Dr. Wilander. And when Vivian had handed the chart to him, he showed her what he meant, running his big, square-ended finger around the horseshoe from the left, where it was marked "Stone Age," and up to the right, where it said "Depopulation of Earth." "The city has lasted the whole length of history, until now," he said. His big finger stopped in the blank space between the beginning and the end of history. "Here. It's moving into the gap at this moment, where it almost certainly began. When it gets to the middle of this gap"—his finger tapped the very top of the chart—"it will probably break up. People are trying to think of ways to prevent that, of course. The trouble is we don't know what will happen. Maybe nothing will. Or maybe it will go critical like this Twenty Century you came from."

Jonathan shot Vivian a scared look. "Oh," she said. This was not exactly what she had meant to find out, but it was worth knowing all the same. "If it goes critical, does it take the whole of history with it?"

"That's one of the many things we don't know," said Dr. Wilander. "There's no point in looking scared, boy. There's nothing you can do. And that's enough of that. Translation now. Skip the first bit—you'll have remembered that—and read out the rest."

Vivian sighed, because the first bit was the only part that made sense, and began, " 'The first Time Patrol officer—' "

"Guardian," said Dr. Wilander. "It makes a change from old ladies, I suppose. Guardian is the word."

" 'Guardian,' " Vivian read obediently, " 'in the Iron Age is upon a hill, and he is a long man with an antic'—is that right?— 'weather and boring shorts—' "

"Antic nature and drab clothing," said Dr. Wilander.

" 'Which suits him in the first place,' " said Vivian. It suddenly dawned on her that she was reading a description of the very Guardian they had met this morning. She wished she could have made more sense of it. Perhaps, if it was nonsense enough, Dr. Wilander might tear the paper out of her hands and read it himself. But that was not to be.

"No, *no*!" said Dr. Wilander. " 'As befits the guardian of an early Age.' Go on."

Vivian was forced to go on, in fits and starts, with corrections every other word from Dr. Wilander, and try to make sense of it as she went. Jonathan was not even pretending to do the work Dr. Wilander had set him. She could see his eyes wide behind their flicker, looking at her past his pigtail, waiting for the next word. And to her relief, he was having the sense to write it down on a spare sheet of writing stuff as she stumbled on. He read it out to her afterward as they went slowly down the stairs, with Time City appearing slanted this way and that around them and once almost over their heads.

"This is it," he said. " 'And the second Guardian is in a sea that is dry and is all in silver which befits an Age where men create and kill in marvelous ways' (I wonder why). 'The third Guardian is young and strong and in every way a man of the Golden Age. He is clothed all in green, for he lives in a forest that covers a town that was once great. And the fourth Guardian goes secretly, lest any should guess where the Casket of Lead lies, for that is the most precious Casket of all.' Oh, for Time's sake, V.S.! You are a fool! Why didn't you say what this was about?"

Vivian fixed her eyes on the glitter of Millennium, lying sideways down a green horizon. "I couldn't make head or tail of it," she said. "I'd no idea it was telling how to find the Caskets."

"It is, but it's not telling *enough*," Jonathan said discontentedly. "Knowing the Iron Casket was on a hill doesn't mean much unless you know anyway. And there are about ten seas that have been dry at one time or another. As for towns that were once great, I can think of forty straight off, starting with Troy and ending with Minneapolis. Still, if I give Leon Hardy this, he might make something of it."

"Why? What have you gone and told him?" Vivian said.

"Nothing really. I was very cunning," Jonathan said. "But he offered me anything I wanted in return for telling about the Guardian dancing through the ceremony, so I asked him to look in records for legends about the Caskets. Students can look in all sorts of sections of Perpetuum without anyone wondering what they're doing, and I thought he just might come up with where and when the polarities are hidden."

Vivian felt very dismayed. Leon Hardy might be nice enough really, but he was quite old, old enough not to bother about things that seemed important to people her age and Jonathan's. "I hope you told him not to tell anyone."

"He understands that," Jonathan said airily, plunging down another flight of stairs, which brought the Dome of The Years wheeling right way up. The twin domes of Science now blocked the view of Millennium. "And I got him to concentrate on the Ninth Unstable Era anyway, because he's from near then himself and knows a lot about it to start with. You see, I had a really good idea this morning in Duration. I think we ought to go and warn the Guardian of the last Casket *first,* so that he can be ready long before the thief gets there, and perhaps get him to help us find the other two. But we need to find out where he is before we can do that. You can see that, can't you?"

It did make sense, Vivian agreed. But she still felt uneasy. She had to remind herself that their two time ghosts in the passage showed that she and Jonathan were certainly going to do something like this, and quite safely and happily, it seemed. Then she reminded herself that Jonathan had managed to snatch her off the station in 1939 very cleverly, without being found out. This was such a comforting thought that Vivian quite forgot that the whole kidnapping had been a mistake anyway.

She came into the Annuate Palace with Jonathan to find that there was going to be another ceremony. The hall was littered with golden hats and jeweled shoes. Feet were hammering, and voices shouting somewhere overhead. Jonathan took one look and quietly disappeared. Vivian never even noticed him go because a crowd of people came rushing downstairs just then, with Sempitern Walker leading the rush.

"Not *that* golden hat!" Sempitern Walker roared. "I need the Amporic Miter, you fool! And where the devil has someone put the Amporic Cope?"

He turned and sped along the hall toward the matutinal, with everyone else pelting after him. Elio ran after the crowd, waving a frail golden vestlike thing. Jenny came mincing down the stairs last of all. She was obviously part of the ceremony too, because she was half dressed for it in a blue and lilac gown that held her knees together and flared out at her feet, and she was looking more than usually worried.

"Oh, Vivian!" she said. "Be kind and helpful and find him the Amporic Miter. It must be *somewhere*! I have to get dressed too. This is one of the really big ceremonies, and we really daren't be late."

"What does it look like?" Vivian asked.

"Like a sort of golden drainpipe," Jenny said over her shoulder as she minced back up the stairs.

Vivian threw herself into the search with a will. It was much more fun than worrying about the Caskets and their Guardians, and it gave her a wonderful opportunity to hunt about in parts of the palace where she had not yet been. Every so often, as she hunted, the crowd of people rushed past, with Petula in front, waving something furry, and Elio behind, waving the golden vest. Sometimes they were close behind the Sempitern. Sometimes the Sempitern was pelting about on his own, roaring for the Miter, or the Esemplastic Staff or the ermine buskins. Each time he appeared, a giggle rose into Vivian's throat, and she had to dodge through the nearest door to laugh.

That was how she found the Amporic Miter in the end. The last room she dodged into turned out to be a bathroom. At least Vivian gathered it was a bathroom from the wet prints of the Sempitern's feet on the cork floor, but she had never, in her part of the Twentieth Century, come across anything like the huge glass bath that stood halfway to the ceiling full of green water bubbling like a caldron. Her eye caught something like a golden drainpipe on the other side of the glass bath, and she thought at first that it *was* just a golden drainpipe. Luckily she was so amazed by the bath that she walked all around it. And there was the hat, lying on the damp floor.

Vivian picked it up and joined in the chase, waving the hat and shouting to Sempitern Walker that she had found it. But he just scudded on in front and took no notice at all. After they had all raced up to the attics and then down once more, and seemed about to set off to the attics again, Vivian had the giggles so badly that she had no breath left at all. So she did the obvious thing and waited in the hall until they all came tearing down again.

Sempitern Walker appeared first, speeding downstairs toward her, with one ermine buskin flapping off his leg and the other in his hand. "Where is that Amporic Miter?" he roared.

Vivian took a deep breath to stop herself laughing. *"Here!"* she shrieked, and held on to the rest of the breath to keep the giggle down. But it did no good. As she jammed the hat into the Sempitern's free hand, the laugh came out. She more or less hooted in his face. Then she had to bend over with tears running down her cheeks. "Oh, oh, oh!" she said. "You are so *funny!*"

Sempitern Walker stood completely still and gave her his most anguished look ever. While he stood there, staring, Petula raced down the stairs and handed him the Esemplastic Staff. Elio burst through the other people straggling downstairs after her and flung the golden vest thing around his shoulders.

"The Amporic Cope, sir," he said. He was the only one not out of breath.

Sempitern Walker turned his anguished stare on Elio. Then he gave the rest of the stragglers a deeply hurt look all around and stalked off to his study with his buskin flapping. Everyone soberly followed him, carrying their pieces of regalia. Vivian was left feeling exactly the same as when she had said the wrong thing to the Guardian that morning.

"You shouldn't have laughed, miss," Elio explained seriously before he followed the others. "Not to his face, that is. The Sempitern, like all born-humans, needs excitement, and his work is very boring. I usually take care to mislay at least one garment before every ceremony."

Vivian felt more like crying than laughing. "Will he forgive me?"

"I do not know," said Elio. "No one has dared to laugh at him before."

Vivian went and sat in the matutinal, feeling ashamed, until the palace quieted down. Then she went into the hall. Just as she expected, Jonathan was coming carelessly downstairs, looking as if it were the merest accident that he had happened to reappear the moment the fuss was over.

"Let's go and see the ceremony," Vivian said to him. She felt she owed it to Sempitern Walker.

"Do you want to?" Jonathan said, much surprised. "It'll be horribly boring." But he obligingly went with her to Aeon Square, where they packed in among rows of tourists near the glass arcade. They were in time to watch a smart squad of Time Patrollers march out of the Patrol Building and take up a position near Faber John's Stone. People in red robes, and white, and blue filed out of other buildings and archways and stood in position too. Then came processions. Vivian saw Jenny, now wrapped in a wide mauve cloak, among a whole lot of people all walking with small steps because of the tight robe underneath. She saw Mr. Enkian marching importantly at the head of a line of blue-robed Librarians. There was a group of students in dusty green gowns. Everybody seemed to be taking part. Even Dr. Wilander was there, bulking in a shabby purple robe. Vivian saw why he spent so much of his time sitting in Seldom End. He walked with quite a limp.

She watched Jonathan's father pace slowly past, stately and golden, with the tall, pipe-shaped hat towering on his head. "What is this ceremony about?" she asked.

"No idea," said Jonathan.

"Then you should know," said a severe man next to them. He was an obvious tourist in respectable blue and yellow check drapes. He folded his information sheet over and held it in front of Jonathan. "It's the first of the Four Ceremonies of the Founding of the City. It's very old—it goes right back to the beginning, and it's said to mark the first moments when Time City was separated from history. You should be proud to witness it, my boy.

We've come specially to see it." He took back the information sheet and said anxiously, "And it *says* the forecast rain will hold off until the ceremony's over. I hope it's right."

So the city really had arrived back to the time when it was founded, Vivian thought. She felt unexpectedly anxious. Another procession was winding its way in from Secular Square. This one seemed to be of ordinary people, all dressed in sober pale pajamas, each with a chain of some kind hung around his or her neck. The sun twinkled on the chains and flashed on the buckles and shiny boots of the Time Patrollers. Jonathan's father flared gold in the midst of all the bright-colored robes. There seemed no sign of the rain the tourist had talked about, but it was coming, hanging over the ceremony, just like the end of things seemed to be hanging over Time City. What will happen to all these people, Vivian thought, if Time City just collapses?

Jonathan must have been thinking the same thing. "I don't want all this to go!" he said.

"It won't. We're going to do something about it," Vivian said. "The Guardian called us in."

But the ceremony did go on rather. Sam found them and stood for five minutes with them, watching, after which he yawned loudly and went away. Vivian felt it would be a bit rude to go away too, after what the tourist had said. So she kept herself amused by pressing the studs of her belt. Time function—they had already been watching for more than an hour—pen function, weather report—rain due in two minutes—low-weight function— at which the severe tourist gave her a very reproving look—and finally credit function. Her palm lit up. 00.00. Vivian stared at it. She pressed the stud again and yet again to bring the numbers back. It still said 00.00.

"Jonathan! What's wrong? This said one hundred yesterday morning, and I haven't *spent* anything yet!"

"Ask Elio. It must have a fault," Jonathan said. "And just look over there!"

Vivian looked where Jonathan nodded. All the important people had formed themselves into a new procession, with Mr. Enkian stalking proudly at its head. Dr. Leonov, the High Scientist, was walking behind Mr. Enkian beside the huge purple bulk of Dr. Wilander. And the poor crazy Iron Guardian had joined the procession too. His floppy hat was bobbing and his face was very serious and he was imitating Mr. Enkian's important walk exactly. Probably he thought that was the right way to walk. Dr. Leonov glanced at him once, doubtfully, and then seemed to decide he was a time ghost or another student joke. Dr. Wilander must have decided the same, because he took no notice of the Guardian at all and simply limped grimly on with his eyes fixed on Mr. Enkian's strutting back. Quite a number of people had seen. A wave of amused murmuring swept down that side of the square. But Mr. Enkian was far too wrapped up in his own importance to notice.

Then the rain came down in white sheets. Vivian was glad of the excuse to go. The severe tourist and his wife raised a small blue and yellow tent above their heads and stayed to watch, but Vivian and Jonathan ran for Time Close, with umbrellas of all possible shapes and sizes going up around them. Elio had been watching the ceremony too. They met him under the archway, while they were pushing through the crowd of damp people sheltering there. By this time, rain was battering on the cobbles of Time Close and gargling in every groove of the buildings. The three of them dashed for the Annuate Palace together.

There, as they stood dripping on the patterned marble floor, Vivian seized the chance to tell Elio about the credit on her belt. Elio asked to look at it. Vivian took off the heavy wet leather and passed it over. Elio's straight pale hair dripped on it as he ran the belt between his fingers. He looked annoyed with himself.

"I weighed the odds," he said, "and decided against having a rain-shield function on any of our belts. My calculation was that we would be outside in only two percent of the year's rainfall.

What I forgot is that two percent is as wet as any other rain. No, this belt is in perfect working order. The fault must be in the city computer." He passed Vivian the belt back. "I will check the computer tomorrow," he said. "Just now I shall be busy. The Sempitern is going to be very wet and very cross when he comes in."

But Vivian discovered what was wrong with her belt next morning, long before Elio did. It was a moist, blue, after-rain morning. She and Jonathan set off for school and found that Sam was not waiting at the fountain as usual. Vivian thought she saw him lurking under the archway. But Jonathan said quickly, "No, that'll be Leon. I asked him to meet me there if he'd found out anything. You go over and ask about Sam—it's that house there— while I talk to Leon." And he went racing off to the archway, pigtail flying, obviously very excited.

Hm, Vivian thought as she went toward the rosy brick house Jonathan had pointed out. I think Jonathan doesn't want me to know what he says to Leon Hardy. I wonder why!

She stood and looked at the front door of the Donegals' house. There was no knocker and no bell. But there must have been some other device. While Vivian was standing there wondering what to do, the door opened and Sam's father came out, pulling the pajama top of his uniform down through his belt, obviously ready to leave for work.

"Morning," he said. "I waited for you. It's no good calling for Sam. He won't get to Duration today. He's had another but-ter-pie orgy and made himself sick as a suicide, I'm afraid."

As soon as Sam's father said that, Vivian knew what had gone wrong with her belt. "Oh," she said. "Thank you." And she turned to go back to the archway. But Mr. Donegal shut his front door and stepped out beside her in the most friendly possible way. This made Vivian feel very awkward. For one thing, she was very angry with Sam. For another, she wanted to hear what Leon Hardy was telling Jonathan. And on top of all this, she found she was rather shy of Sam's father. He had a fierce, active feel about him, which she had not met in the other people of Time City. She was sure this was the feeling you got from someone with a lot of power, who gave orders and got obeyed, and that was alarming in itself. But she remembered that Mr. Donegal was supposed to be her uncle and did her best to give him a niecelike smile. "I thought Sam didn't have any credit," she said.

"He hasn't. He went into Patrol Building during the ceremony last night and tinkered with my computer outlet," said Mr. Donegal. "Got it to give him a credit strop from someone else's account—cunning little devil!" He sounded stern, but Vivian could tell he was secretly rather proud of Sam. "He won't say whose account it was. Can't get it out of him."

But *I* know! Vivian thought. Just because he was annoyed that Jonathan and I are going to go off without him, and we haven't even *gone* yet! She was angrier than ever with Sam. But she did not say anything to Mr. Donegal, because she wanted to be revenged on Sam for herself. "How many did he eat?" she asked.

"A hundred units' worth, would you believe that!" Mr. Donegal said.

Vivian did believe it. It was the final proof. She would have liked to tell Jonathan, who was standing under the archway talking to Leon Hardy. But, frustratingly, both of them looked around, saw Vivian and Mr. Donegal walking across Time Close, and set off out into Aeon Square, talking hard all the time.

"I was wanting to speak to you," Mr. Donegal said, "about Twenty Century."

"Yes?" Vivian said nervously.

"It's gone critical all right," said Mr. Donegal. "World War One is affected now. It's run right back into a thing called the Boer War. War Two starts in 1937 at the moment. It's getting pretty nasty out there. I won't lie to you, but I don't want you to worry either."

But I *do*! Vivian thought as they went into the shadow of the archway. She forgot about Sam, and about Jonathan and Leon Hardy. All she could think was, What about Mum and Dad?

They came out into the brightness of Aeon Square, where Jonathan and Leon were small shapes out beyond Faber John's Stone. "Your mother and father are quite safe," Mr. Donegal said. It was just as if he could read Vivian's thoughts, except that he was talking about the wrong mother and father. "Observers are given plenty of protection, and Time Patrol keeps going in and checking. I won't deny that I was a little annoyed with your father for being so slow to report the deterioration, but that doesn't mean I'm neglecting him or Inga. I'm putting a Zero Hour request to Chronologue to recall all the Observers from that era. I thought you'd want to know that. Chronologue will do it, but they'll be a bit slow because of all these Foundation Ceremonies. It couldn't have happened at a worse time for us! But not to worry. You'll have your father and mother safe back in Time City in three or four days at the most."

"Th-thanks," Vivian managed to say.

They walked on toward Faber John's Stone. Mr. Donegal went on talking. Vivian dimly heard him say that Time Patrol had still not caught the cause of all the trouble, and she rather thought he went on to say that the Second and Third Unstable Eras were in a mess too, but she did not attend to any of it. When at last he patted her cheerily on the shoulder and went off to Patrol Building at a rolling trot just like Sam's, Vivian's legs were almost refusing to move her. Jonathan was at the doorway of Duration by then. Vivian saw Leon wave to him and stride off along the bottom of the square, past a line of children hurrying toward Duration. With a great effort, she managed to cross the rest of the square at a weak run. She was almost too alarmed to think straight.

In three or four days the Lees would be back, and the real Cousin Vivian would be with them. Somehow, she had never really thought of that happening. And that was quite stupid of her. Jenny had talked about Observers' being recalled days ago.

I've been living, Vivian panted to herself, in—what does Mum call it?—a fool's paradise. That's what I've been—a fool in paradise. How *daft*!

She was glad of school to take her mind off it, even though the morning's lessons did not seem so lively without Sam making a noise every few minutes. But at least universal symbols were something to think about beside the Lees. She almost looked forward to Dr. Wilander that afternoon because he made it really very difficult to think of anything else at all.

Then, halfway through the morning, the message stud flashed on Vivian's belt. She was quite pleased with herself for noticing, considering what was on her mind. She pressed the stud, and the empty space of her desk shone with the words: *"Hakon Wilander to V. Lee. Sorry forgot beastly ceremony this afternoon. See you tomorrow instead."*

Oh bother! Vivian thought. Now I've got a whole afternoon with nothing to do but worry!

But as soon as she went into the lunchroom, Jonathan grabbed her arm. "Get some food and come back to the palace," he whispered. "Leon's going to meet us in Hundred and One Century."

Vivian looked at him and realized he was wearing the suit with diamonds. She looked down at herself. Her suit was a brownish orange with small white stripes, which had not shown up very well in the darkness of the passage. But she recognized it now as the suit her ghost had been wearing. And Sam had made himself ill.

This is it! she thought excitedly. I have to go and come back. Then, with any luck, I can leave before the real Vivian Lee gets here!

J onathan rushed straight off, but Vivian treated herself to four butter-pies before she left. Her only regret was that she might not have time to get her revenge on Sam. Otherwise, she walked across Aeon Square, eating the last butter-pie, full of pleasant thoughts. By tonight, she could be home. She saw herself telling Mum how awful Cousin Marty was, and she saw Mum being very understanding and letting her stay in Lewisham in spite of the bombs. She saw Dad coming home for the weekend and being really surprised. This wonderful daydream was enough to set her making little skips as she crossed the square. And when she got to Time Close, where there was no one about to see, she did a silly dance around the fountain, waving the stick of her butter-pie.

"What kept you?" said Jonathan. He was waiting by the chained door with the diamond-shaped pockets of his suit bulging. Vivian could see he was in a fever of impatience.

"Sorry," she said, not really meaning it. The best thing about time travel, as Vivian had seen almost straight away, was that you could waste hours on the way and still arrive at the exact right time. "*Why* do we have to meet Leon Hardy in One Hundred and One?"

Jonathan hurried her down the passage. "He knows all about the Dark Nineties," he said. "He says we'll need protective equipment to go then, and he's going to get us some from the nearest Fixed Century he can get to. But of course, he has to leave by an official time lock down the river, so he can't get to an Unstable Era himself. So he's going as close as he can. He's being awfully kind."

Jonathan stopped and gave the secret door an expert kick. It swung smoothly around. They squeezed in and pressed the light studs on their belts. The spiral stair did not seem either so endless or so frightening by now.

"And why are we going to the Dark Nineties?" Vivian asked as they scrambled down.

"It's one of the long Unstable Eras," Jonathan called up. "So it must be either the Age of Lead or the Age of Gold. I thought we'd find the Guardian and tell him to bring his polarity back to Time City before the thief gets it, like the Iron Guardian said."

This seemed a good idea to Vivian. In fact, she thought as she slithered off the last step into the little room, where the slate still flickered and their Twentieth Century clothes lay where they had thrown them off, that she had told Jonathan they should do this a long time ago.

Jonathan picked the egg-shaped control off its stone and installed it carefully in one of his pockets. His pockets chinked.

"What else have you brought?" Vivian asked.

"Metal detector, map, compass, flashlight, emergency rations," Jonathan said. "I'm going to do this properly. Now be quiet while I focus my mind on Leon." He concentrated. Nothing happened. "Leon Hardy," he said loudly. Still, nothing happened. "Oh *no*!" Jonathan almost screamed. "The control's run out!"

"It can't have," said Vivian. "We were coming back—I mean, our time ghosts were."

Jonathan took the egg out of his pocket again and held it in front of his face. "Leon Hardy," he told it loudly and slowly. "The first year of One Hundred and One Century."

That did the trick. The slate cleared into light that was so dim that they hardly realized that the egg had worked at first. A cold wind blew in at them, smelling strongly of sawdust and wet grass. Jonathan switched his belt light off and walked cautiously forward. As Vivian switched hers off and fumbled after him, she heard a blackbird sing, loud and clear, from somewhere near.

Funny that there are still blackbirds! she thought, looking around
for Leon Hardy. If this *is* right at the other end of history, of
course. It felt just like any dark morning anywhere.

Leon Hardy was there, sitting on a fallen tree just behind them.
As Vivian's eyes adjusted, she saw him get up, shivering and
rubbing his arms. That little kilt he wore did not look very warm.
"You made it!" he said, in a low, cautious voice. "I was beginning to wonder if you'd get here before the people came to work.
I've got the stuff. I've been sitting over it half the night. Let me
help you get it on."

There was a heap of what looked like tree bark beside his feet.
Leon picked up a piece of it, and it proved to be the top half of
a sort of suit of armor. There was too little light to see more than
that it was dullish, with wrinkled places at the elbows and shoulders where it was supposed to bend.

"Do we really need that?" Jonathan said.

"I'll say you will!" said Leon. "There are gangs of wild men
and wild dogs and Time knows what-all back there in the Nineties. We still have trouble with them in this era." He helped them
fasten themselves into the armor, rather hurriedly, as if there were
not much time. It was made of some tough, bendy stuff Vivian
had never met before, and it was far heavier than she had thought
it would be. The lower part was only for the front of their legs.
Vivian was glad. She did not think she could have walked otherwise. The light was growing brighter all the time, and she began to wonder what color the armor was. It looked almost as if
it might be red.

As the light grew brighter, Jonathan became more and more
uneasy. Vivian knew that it was his fear of the wide-open spaces
of history. But Leon belonged to history, and he seemed more
and more uneasy too. Vivian caught his uneasiness when he said,
trying to joke, "Jonathan tells me there are a couple of time
ghosts of you back in the Annuate, so it looks as if both of you
come back, armor or not. He tells me you know London."

"That's right," said Vivian. She had caught the uneasiness,

too, and kept trying to see all around her. They seemed to be in a large timberyard. Felled trees lay everywhere. The place where they were was hidden from the main part of the yard by a pile of sawn planks.

"Well, London is where that Casket is," Leon said, calling her attention back. "That's certain, and I'm certain that you'll find it's the Gold. But the records I looked at mentioned three places, and I've no idea which of them it's going to be in. Does Buck House mean anything to you?"

"Buckingham Palace?" Vivian said.

"And the second place is Spauls," Leon said hurriedly. "Does that mean anything?"

"Saint Paul's?" Vivian said dubiously.

"And there's Laununsun—that's the third," said Leon.

It was nearly daylight now. Leon was bending over Vivian with his face close to hers. She felt the uneasiness stronger than ever. He seemed far too interested in knowing. "Laununsun, Laununsun," she said, looking away from Leon while she tried to think. There were deep ruts in the grass where trees had been dragged. A dark lump beside the pile of sawn planks was resolving into a patient-looking horse that must have done the dragging. "Laununsun," said Vivian. "Oh I *see!*" Lord Nelson! That's Nelson's Column in Trafalgar Square."

Leon smiled flashingly at her and turned to help Jonathan do up the buckles on his legs. "So you've got your three places," he said to him. "Have you any further thoughts on where the Lead Casket might be? My research hasn't come up with a clue."

Jonathan *has* told him a lot! Vivian thought, more uneasy than ever. By now she could see that Jonathan's armor was red. As she looked down at her own, she heard a man singing somewhere behind the pile of planks.

Leon jumped rather and looked around furtively. Then he hurried to the horse standing so patiently beside the planks, unhitched it from the plank it was tied to, and brought it over, clopping in huge strides on huge, round feet. "Up you get," he said. "Quickly."

They looked up at it in dismay. It was bright brown, and it was gigantic, bigger than the biggest carthorse Vivian had ever seen. It must have been a new breed.

"Get your helmets on and get up," Leon said impatiently. "The workforce is arriving."

Jonathan picked up the heavy spiked helmet. It looked almost the color of blood in the new pink light. "But that creature won't fit into our time lock," he said. "It's only a tiny room."

"But you told me you'd got one of the old controls," Leon said. "You can go straight to the Nineties from here with one of those. Or do you want the foreman to arrive and find us stealing a horse? Horse stealing's a serious crime in this era."

There were now quite a few voices ringing out from behind the pile of planks. Some were calling good mornings, but one at least was swearing angrily. "Where's that brown logging horse?" Vivian heard among the swearwords. "Anyone seen my damned horse?"

Vivian and Jonathan crammed the helmets on their heads. Leon led the horse alongside a felled tree, and somehow, largely because the man behind the planks was shouting more and more angrily, Jonathan and Vivian managed to scramble first onto the tree and then onto the horse's wide, slippery back. There was no saddle, and the horse was so huge that there was no way Vivian could get a grip with her legs. She had to hang on to Jonathan's shell-like armor, while Jonathan grabbed the horse's mane with one hand and fumbled the egg control out with the other. Luckily the horse seemed as placid as a table—a very high table, Vivian thought, staring down at Leon's face a long way below. Leon was smiling up at them in a way that looked very relieved indeed.

"Buck House in London, year 9500," Jonathan said.

And they were there. Or Vivian supposed they must be. It was broad daylight, slanting green through a thick summer forest. Instead of Leon standing there in the pink light, there were trees everywhere, ancient, enormous trees with moss on them and rows of large earlike fungus growing down their trunks. The smell was the mushroom smell of deep woodland, and the sounds—the rustles and creaks, the distant squawks and flaps—were the sounds of the forest that stretched for miles. Jonathan felt those miles and shifted uneasily. Vivian did for an instant wonder what Leon was saying at that moment to the man looking for his horse, but Jonathan's movement drew her attention to a cloud of midges circling them and the horse. And their armor was indeed red. It shone bright as blood against the crowding green of the trees.

"Does this mean London's all overgrown with trees now?" she said.

"That's right. They were cutting those trees down in the next era, where we've just been," Jonathan said, rather muffled in his helmet.

The horse had pricked its ears at suddenly finding itself in a forest. Their voices must have given it the idea that it had to get somewhere. It began to walk forward over the uneven ground. Its back swayed under them like a warm, hairy boat on a sea. Vivian felt herself slipping. She grabbed at Jonathan's scarlet shoulders. Whereupon they both started tipping slowly sideways across the horse's vast right side.

"Oh help!" she said.

"Let go! Press your low-weight stud!" Jonathan said desperately.

Vivian clawed her hand under the tough armor and somehow found the stud. She was suddenly about the weight she would have been without armor. By flinging an arm across the horse, she managed to work herself upright, and Jonathan managed to do the same. But the strange floating effect of the belts meant that they were now sliding slowly backward toward the horse's tail. Jonathan had to seize the horse's mane, and Vivian had to seize his shoulders again. That seemed to anchor them. For the horse, quite unconcerned by all the scrambling about on its back, went on pacing slowly forward through the trees.

"We have to stop and look at the map and use the metal detector," Jonathan said. "How do you get a horse to stop?"

"Pull the reins," said Vivian.

"It hasn't got any reins. There's only a strap thing around its face."

"Stop!" shouted Vivian. *"Whoa!"* And when that made no difference to the horse, she racked her brains and shouted, *"Arrêtez-vous!"* in case the horse spoke French. But it might have been deaf for all the effect that had. Trees continued to slide by, and the great hooves continued to crunch dead leaves and lichen. Jonathan tried the method that worked on his automat. He hit the horse on its vast brown shoulder and banged at it with his heels. The only result of that was that the horse went slightly faster.

"Look!" he said despairingly.

Up to then Vivian had not really believed that this forest might be London, or that they might be riding through the remains of Buckingham Palace. But Jonathan was pointing to where a tree had fallen sideways, tearing up a big circle of roots and earth. In the gap under the circle, she saw an old greenish piece of stone wall.

"It could be *there*!" Jonathan said. *"Stop,* you stupid time-bound brute!"

But the horse marched steadily on, and trees slid steadily by, until they came out into more open ground, where its hooves smashed brambles and trudged upon briars. Soon after that, Vivian noticed that they were going up a small round hill. If that *was* Buckingham Palace, she thought, then this hill must be that ornamental roundabout in the road outside.

Halfway up the hill, the horse trampled sideways a little. They had a glimpse of an animal in the grass almost under its hooves, springing up and dashing away, snarling over its shoulder as it ran. It was yellowish. It gave Vivian the same jolting fright that she had felt when she touched the Iron Guardian.

"Wild dog, I think," Jonathan said, sounding as shaken as Vivian felt.

The horse tramped on peacefully, over the rise and down the other side. Vivian saw the Mall stretching ahead. There was somehow no doubt about it, though it had shrunk to a long lane of wet green grass hemmed closely in by mighty old trees. It was too straight to be anything but the Mall. The horse descended into it quite speedily, and as soon as it reached the grass, it stopped and started to eat. Jonathan only just saved himself from sliding off down its head.

"Now what?" he said.

"We could get off," Vivian suggested.

"But then it would just walk away and we'd never get on again."

They did not seem to have much choice but to sit there and wait for the horse to finish its meal. They sat, and the cloud of midges that had accompanied them ever since they arrived worked their way under the armor and bit. Vivian began to think that they would be better off without the horse. She was just going to say so, when Jonathan stiffened suddenly in front of her.

"Look," he said. "Over to the left."

Vivian looked and stiffened too. There were people there in the trees. Whoever they were, they were keeping quite still and wearing dull greenish rags of clothes, so that Vivian only had glimpses whenever one of them moved. When one did, it was to shift a nasty-looking homemade spear in a skinny arm. When the next moved, it was to adjust a sheeny knife in his mouth, and that gave her a sight of a savage, bearded face.

"They're probably after the horse," Jonathan said with a slight wobble in his voice. "To eat."

They sat there, high on the horse, conspicuous in their shining red armor, feeling quite helpless. They could only hope that the horse would decide to finish its meal before the people plucked up courage to attack. But the horse went on peacefully tearing up mouthfuls of grass.

"Oh, *move*, horse, please!" Vivian whispered.

And the horse suddenly did. It raised its head. Its ears pricked and then swiveled forward like two gear sticks in a car. Then it uttered a shattering whinny and set off down the green Mall in a bone-destroying trot. Jonathan and Vivian bounced and slid and clung. Vivian bit her tongue painfully. Trees rushed by. The only good thing she could see was that they were leaving the lurking people behind fast.

The horse broke into what might have been a canter. "What's it *doing*?" Jonathan gasped.

The answer came when they could see the gray broken remnants of Admiralty Arch among the trees ahead. Another horse, which had been hiding behind the left-hand lump of arch, swerved out into the Mall and came galloping straight toward them. The rider on its back wore the same kind of armor as they did, except that his was black streaked with green for camouflage. He was carrying a long, heavy-looking spear under his right arm, and this was pointed straight at them.

"Stop, stop!" they both shrieked. *"Friends!"*

The rider took no more notice of them than the horse did. He thundered down on them, with clods flying out behind, while their own horse cantered trustingly to meet the other one. Jonathan scrambled himself around and gave Vivian a frantic push. They both sailed sideways off the horse and went tumbling and wafting to the ground. The low-weight function meant that it did not hurt a bit. Everything seemed to be in slow motion from then on. Vivian saw their own horse lumber to a stop, looking puzzled, and the rider shoot pounding past. She had time to think, Oh, why does Jonathan *always* end up making a mess of things! while she was landing and trying to climb to her feet again.

Beyond her, Jonathan was struggling to get his helmet off his eyes. The piece of armor on Vivian's right leg had gone around to the back of her knee, like a splint. As she fell down again, she saw the rider pulling his horse up in a long gouge of brown earth. While she was trying to work the armor back around her leg, he swung his horse around and came galloping back. His spear was pointing downward now, straight at Jonathan. Then the rider was between her and Jonathan. She heard a crunching bang. Above the trampling legs of the horse, she saw the spear sweep in a vicious half circle, coming toward her. Vivian threw herself backward. She had one sight of the rider's face, a blank, unpleasant pale face, with slitted eyes and no pity in it. Whoever he is, he's not the Guardian, she thought. Then the spear crashed against her helmet, and she was not sure of very much for a while after that.

It was probably only a minute or so. When she sat up, the rider had gone, and so had their own horse. Jonathan was half sitting in a bush at the side of the Mall, spread out like a blood eagle, staring at her with eyes that were wide and queerly blurred under the flicker of his eye function. The front of his armor was crushed in, into a big dent. It was so much the color of blood that Vivian could not tell whether he was bleeding there. But she knew it was blood that ran out of the corner of Jonathan's mouth when he spoke to her.

"I think he's killed me," he said in a quiet, matter-of-fact way. "My chest's all broken." The blood running from the corner of his mouth was a much more purple color than his armor.

Vivian wrenched the piece of armor off her leg and crawled toward him unbelievingly. It can't have happened! she thought. The two time ghosts meant that we came *back*! Then she thought, This is an Unstable Era. Anything can happen. And she realized that, just like Sam and Jonathan when they kidnapped her, she had been treating everything that happened as an adventure. And it had suddenly turned very serious indeed.

Two large black crows came planing down out of the trees and settled in the bush above Jonathan's head, where they sat looking down at him expectantly. They peck out the eyes first! Vivian thought. She did not dare touch Jonathan. She did not know what to do. Without stopping to think anymore, she tipped back her face and screamed, "Help, help, *help*!"

"All right. I'm coming," somebody said irritably, pushing through the undergrowth beyond Jonathan. At the sound, the crows wheeled up from the bush to a branch overhead. "And stop shouting," the woman added sharply. "There are bandits all over this forest." She came wrenching through the brambles onto the clear grass, leaving a lump of her greenish handwoven skirt on one, and knelt down in front of Jonathan. "I came as quick as I could," she said. "But I didn't want him to see me. Oh, good grief, this looks a mess!"

"It doesn't hurt as much as you'd think," Jonathan remarked in the same calm, matter-of-fact way as before.

"Just as well," said the woman. She had fair hair twisted into a bun, and she would have been beautiful, Vivian thought, if she had not been so weathered-looking and so worried. The look on the brown, lined face reminded Vivian of Jenny or of Mum, and it grew more worried still when the woman put the flat of her hand on the dent in Jonathan's chest. "He did really mean to kill you, didn't he?" she murmured. "Let's see what we can do." She took a deep breath.

The dent billowed and noisily straightened itself out. *Clap-boing*. Jonathan gave a great sigh of relief and put up a hand to wipe the blood from his mouth.

"Hold still," said the woman. "That's the ribs and the breastbone, but there's still your collarbone to mend, not to speak of all the torn muscles."

She kept her hand on his chest. Jonathan stayed as he was, with his hand up. After a while, his face turned a better shape and color, though his eyes were still blurred-looking. "That feels all right now," he said.

"It is," said the woman, and took her hand away. "But go steady for a time. The bones and flesh are healed, but the shock is still with you." She took Jonathan's arm and helped him to his feet. The crows left their branches at that and flapped disgustedly away along the Mall.

"How did you do that?" Vivian asked, feeling rather dizzy.

The woman gave her a harassed smile. She lifted Vivian's helmet off and put her hand to the bruise on the side of Vivian's head. "Hm. I think that's sound," she murmured. "There could have been a fracture, but I don't think there is."

A headache, which, up to then, Vivian had not noticed, was suddenly gone. "How do you do it?" she said.

"How do I?" the woman said distractedly. "I suppose because we're far on in history here. Things get learned in the course of time. Where were you two trying to go?"

"Nelson's Col—er, Laununsun," Vivian said.

"Then take off that silly armor and I'll go with you," the woman said.

"But—" Jonathan began.

"But me no buts," the woman said in her irritable way. "It sticks out like a sore thumb. If anyone sees it, they'll think you're going to try to kill them, and they'll try to kill you first. That's the way of life here. Whoever gave you the stuff made a bad mistake."

Feeling rather ashamed of themselves, they unstrapped the armor and threw it into the bushes. Vivian felt soaringly light for a second, and then very heavy. "I think my belt's run out," she said.

"Only the low-weight function," said Jonathan. "So has mine. Turn it off and let it recharge."

"*Will* you come on!" the woman said impatiently. She was listening and watching the bushes as if she could hear someone coming.

They hastened with her along the rest of the Mall and between the trees growing on the stumps of Admiralty Arch. Beyond that, the forest opened out into a large, squarish meadow a little smaller than Vivian remembered Trafalgar Square. There were no buildings to show her that this *was* Trafalgar Square. The meadow was surrounded by tall trees. It sloped gently upward, rippling with gray-headed grass and a few flowers.

The woman sighed and looked a little less harassed. "Safer here," she said. "The bandits don't usually come out into the open. But walk carefully. And stamp. There are snakes."

The ground was very uneven under the grass. Occasionally an old square stone turned under their feet. They picked their way after the woman, stamping as they went, and there were various rustlings that could have been snakes or could simply have been wind in the grass. Vivian found this scary enough. But she could tell from the way Jonathan's head turned from side to side that he was scared of the wide-open space and probably about the bandits too. She found she was admiring his courage. He may have started it just as an adventure, she thought, but he really is trying to carry it through.

Toward the middle of the field, the woman stopped and pointed to a high clump of bushes, wild roses mostly and hawthorns. "There it is," she said. "You won't get right up to it. The Watcher keeps a good guard up." She sat down on a straight-edged bank that may have been part of a fallen column and turned her back on the bushes.

"You're not coming?" Jonathan said to her.

She shook her head dourly and wrapped her homemade cloak around her shoulders. "He takes no notice of me. I don't know why I come here," she said. She sighed. "I suppose because it's peaceful. You go on. He might take account of you."

Jonathan and Vivian stamped their way up to the bushes. They were growing above them, on some kind of raised place. And it *was* the stump of Nelson's Column, Vivian realized. They stumbled against steep stone steps under the grass, and Jonathan saved himself by catching hold of a mound that, even covered with earth and grass, had the shape of a large stone lion. They got up. And stumbled again. Somehow they could not get up the last of the stone ledges. After two more tries, they saw that they were not going to be able to get right up to the bushes.

"Is anyone there?" Vivian called.

The twined-together briars above them shook a little. A few rose petals blew down. Vivian felt a jolt of fear, fear of a kind she was beginning to recognize. She looked up to find an extremely large young man standing on the ledge in front of the bushes with his arms folded, looking down at them consideringly. He made her think of a farmer's boy. He had a lumpish, weather-beaten face. The fairish hair under his jaunty green hat badly needed combing. He was chewing a straw. He looked very strong and very solid. There was none of the unreal look of the poor, sad Iron Guardian about him, but he *was* wearing a billowy green shirt and tight green trousers.

" 'He is clothed all in green, for he lives in a forest that covers a town that was once great,' " Jonathan said. "Are you the Guardian of the Golden Casket?"

The young man shifted the straw to the other side of his mouth. "They call me the Watcher of the Gold," he said. He had a raw, rather booming voice. "And if that's what you mean, then yes, I am. Who are you?"

"We're from Time City—" Jonathan began.

"Then you're too early," the young man interrupted. "I know my business. When the city comes to rest in the gap between the beginning and the end of time, that's when I bring the Gold to the city, and not before. Don't worry. I'll be there."

"But it's nearly got to the gap now," Vivian said.

"And someone's trying to steal the Caskets, we're fairly sure," Jonathan said. "He got the Iron Casket. We saw him take it. We came to warn you—"

"Kind of you," the young man said, shifting the straw back

to the left-hand corner of his mouth. "But I know all about him, thanks. He's been lurking around here and Spauls and Buck House for two weeks now. He knows the Gold's in one of those places, but he doesn't know which. So I'm staying right here in this patch of time with him. He's not getting a chance to come near the Gold."

"But he's got the Iron—couldn't that help him against you?" Vivian asked.

The Watcher shrugged. "Only maybe. Gold's stronger than Iron ever was."

"From what Mr. Donegal said this morning, I think he's nearly got to the Silver by now," Vivian said. "I didn't listen properly, but if he steals that too, couldn't that be too strong for you?"

"It *might*," the Watcher conceded, wrinkling up his plowman's face. "But he's left it too late. You said yourself the city's nearly in the middle of the gap. When it is, I bring the Gold and it unites with the Lead, and Lead and Gold together are stronger by three than the other two. No, no need to worry. It'll be all right."

"Listen," Jonathan said. "The city's in a bad way. It may be going to break up. Faber John's Stone has cracked all over since the Iron Casket was stolen. I think you ought to take the Gold to the city *now,* to be on the safe side. Or we could take it for you, if you like."

The Watcher spat out his straw and laughed. "And unbalance the whole of time? No, thanks. The Gold goes where I go, and we both stay here until the proper moment. When midday strikes on the tower clock on the last day, I'll be there. But thanks for the warning."

He turned away as if he were going back among the briars. Jonathan said hurriedly, "Then please—tell us which Unstable Era the Lead Casket's hidden in. Tell us where the Silver Casket is. We ought to warn those Guardians too."

The Watcher gave him a wary look over his shoulder. "Uh-

uh," he said. "I don't fall for that one. If you know how to find me, you know where Silver is. As for Hidden Lead, if you're honest about coming from Time City, you can work out where it is for yourself. If you're not, you don't find out from me!" He unfolded his arms and stretched, in a lazy way, like people do who know they are very strong. Then he was gone. The bushes quivered a little, but it could have been through heat haze. The Watcher had not walked away into them. Vivian thought he had just ceased to be in that particular piece of time. She had a feeling he had not gone far—perhaps only a week or so back to keep watch on the lurking thief—but he was definitely not where they were.

"He seemed very sure of himself," she said.

Jonathan leaned on the lion-shaped mound. Under his flickering eye function, his eyes were smudged, and his face had a queer blueness to it. "I don't think he had much brain," he said. "If the thief's clever, he could trick him easily. We *have* to find the Lead Casket. If that's the strongest, it's *got* to be kept safe!"

Vivian did not like the way Jonathan looked. The woman had warned him to go easy. "Let's find her first, and then perhaps eat something," she suggested.

Jonathan agreed, rather limply. They went back to the place where the woman had been sitting, but she was not there. They thought at first that she had gone away entirely. Then they saw the huge shape of the horse Leon had stolen for them, browsing down in the corner of the meadow. The woman was stumping after it with one side of her dress held up, trying to coax it to come to her. They sat on the ledge that might have been a fallen column and watched her. It seemed safe enough to do that while the woman was behaving so peacefully. She got almost up to the horse, but the horse cunningly moved on just as they thought she had it. This happened over and over again. They got out the squares of nourishing food that Jonathan had brought and ate them while they watched. At first they carefully saved some for the woman. But after a while, the horse edged away into the forest, and the woman followed it.

"That horse is just like the Watcher," Jonathan said. "It's obstinate as—as Sam and won't listen to people, and it probably thinks it's as clever as Wilander. But she'll catch it in the end, I know she will. Do you think everyone in the Golden Age is as gifted as she is?" He did not sound as gloomy as he had before. The food had done him good.

They sat until it was clear that the woman was not coming back. Then they shared out the food they had saved her. "We never said thank you," Vivian said guiltily. "And I think she saved your life. Hadn't we better get back to Time City?" Long tree shadows were slanting over the meadow by then.

"I suppose so." Jonathan stood up and fetched the egg control out of his purse. "I hope this works from here. I'm not going back down that glade and facing that bandit again, not for anything! Here goes. Time City, just after we left."

The egg worked, but it worked even more slowly and erratically than it had when they made it take them back before. Jonathan and Vivian were pulled, and hung, and pulled, and hung again. Strange sights flickered in front of them: rows of mud huts, a town burning in great rolls of smoke, a frozen river, then crowds of people dancing and waving flags. Once, Vivian clearly saw a big red London bus, but it was not the shape of the buses she knew. Finally, when they were getting quite frightened, they were in a stony-smelling darkness lit by a faint flicker from the slab of slate.

"Thank goodness!" said Vivian.

"You knew we'd get back," Jonathan said. He sounded very depressed. He got out his flashlight and began to climb the stairs. "This is all wrong," he said as they went. "It's not how we looked to be feeling as the time ghosts. You could tell from those we were really excited, and I feel miserable as sin, don't you? We haven't done a scrap of good. He wouldn't even say where the Lead Casket was. It's enough to make you think Time City's gone critical like Twenty Century!''

''Except that the Twentieth Century went critical because someone stole the Iron Casket,'' Vivian called up.

At that, with a sort of *snap,* the truth hit both of them.

V ivian said, "Time City's an Unstable Era!"

Jonathan answered, "The longest one there is!"

Then they both said together, "Then the Lead Casket must be *here*!"

They climbed the rest of the stairs without noticing them. At the top, the false wall had closed itself. They swung it around and squeezed past, one on each side. Jonathan turned off his flashlight, and they hurried up the passage, talking eagerly the whole way.

"That's what he meant about Gold uniting with Lead," Vivian said.

"I bet it's in the Gnomon Tower somewhere!" Jonathan said. "That fits in with the clock striking midday. What a relief! We can make sure it's safe."

"We can tell someone it's here without giving away how we know," Vivian said.

"Yes, and get them to put a proper guard on it," said Jonathan. "We don't want old grannies from the Annuate Guard. We want real Time Patrollers who know what they're doing."

"Let's tell Sam's father," said Vivian.

"Let's. He might take it seriously—not like scientists talking about polarities," Jonathan agreed.

"That means the same thing," Vivian said. "Where do you think the Lead Guardian is? He must be in the city. We ought to warn him too."

"He'll be hard to find. The old paper said he kept secret," Jonathan said. Here, halfway along the passage, he looked down and discovered he was still holding the control egg. "Oh blast!" he said. "I forgot to put this back!"

"Agents were always losing them," said Vivian. "This is how." They both laughed about it.

Jonathan said, "I'll keep it for now. We'd better get to the Gnomon before we do anything else."

Vivian said, "It sounds as if *all* the Caskets are supposed to come back to the Gnomon when the city gets to the end of time. And the Iron one won't."

"I know," Jonathan said. "As soon as we've made sure of the Lead Casket, we'll go after the Silver and make the egg get us there before the thief." He swung the chained door open, saying, "And let's hope that Guardian's a bit more reasonable than the Gold."

Leon Hardy was waiting outside. He had a thing in his hand with a shiny snout and a blue bulb halfway along. He was pointing it at them as pitilessly as the rider's spear. Vivian knew it was a gun as quickly as Jonathan did. They stopped dead and stared at him. Leon laughed in their faces, with his handsome white teeth bared in a most unpleasant way. "I knew he wouldn't kill you," he said. "Not after you told me about those time ghosts. I led you up the forest path in red armor beautifully, didn't I? How did you like my hologram Iron Guardian? Convinced you, didn't he, Jonathan? Hand over that Gold Casket and I won't shoot you."

"We haven't got it," said Vivian. "The Watcher wouldn't let us near it."

"Don't lie to me," Leon said, moving the gun menacingly a fraction, from Jonathan to Vivian.

"We're not," Jonathan said. His face had gone bluish again, and he looked like death. "I swear! What do you want it for?"

"Because it's the most powerful thing in the world after the Lead Casket," Leon said, "and it's clear nobody's going to find that. The people who sent me here to look after the Time City end of things told me a bit much for their own good—just like you did, Jonathan, my boy! It must be my frank, open face that does it!'' He laughed, in another flash of white teeth. Then his face went straight and pitiless. ''Where's that Gold Casket?''

''We haven't got it!'' they both said.

Vivian added, ''Guides' Honor!'' She had a slow, sick feeling because she knew Leon was going to shoot them whatever they said. He was working himself up to it, because they knew too much about him. It seemed queer that it was going to happen here, in the sunlit marble gallery, with Elio's museum cases lined up on either side. He's going to break a lot of glass! she thought.

''Very well then,'' Leon said, not believing them. ''Both of you turn out your pockets. And hand over that time egg first. I can use one of those.''

Vivian numbly pulled her pocket inside out and held out the piece of seaweed chew that was in it. Jonathan looked at the egg in his hand and, in a dazed sort of way, held that out, too. There seemed nothing else to do.

There was a scutter of shoelaces from the end of the gallery. Sam's voice boomed along it. *''You rats! You DID go without me!''*

Leon jumped—they all jumped—and Leon swung around. As soon as he moved, there was another movement, so fast that it was blurred, from among the museum cases behind him. Someone leaped from crouching there and hurled himself on Leon. The next moment, Elio's left arm was across Leon's throat in a strangling grip, and Elio's right hand was crunched around Leon's hand with the gun in it. Elio's face looked calmly over Leon's shoulder, beside Leon's furious, frightened one. ''Will one of you please remove the gun from his hand?'' he asked politely.

Jonathan looked about to faint, so Vivian did it. While she worked the weapon carefully loose from Leon's white, crushed fingers, Sam came up and stared. ''What's going on?'' he said. He had not yet got over the butter-pies. His face was quite yellow. There was not much to choose between Sam and Jonathan at that moment, Vivian thought, and ridiculously, as the gun came loose, she thought of a way to teach Sam a lesson.

But that was for later. "What do I do with this?" she said, pointing the gun uncertainly at Leon in a way that made Leon give a choking sound and shut his eyes.

Elio swung Leon around sideways in order to unwrap his arm from Leon's neck and take the gun away from her. He dug it into Leon's back. "Keep very still!" he warned him. "Who is this man?" he said to Vivian. "Why is he doing this?"

"Leon Hardy. He's a student," Jonathan said, in a faint, wretched voice. "I—I went and told him far too much."

Leon grinned slightly at that. Elio noticed. "Then we had better get him out of the way at once," he said. "I take it that none of you wishes the Sempitern or Patrol Chief Donegal to be made aware of these events?"

"No!" they all said together, and Sam said it even more devoutly than Leon.

Leon, in fact, looked quite happy. He must have thought that Elio was going to let him go. But his face changed when Elio politely asked Vivian to open the chained door. When Elio bundled him through into the passage, he braced his feet and said, "What's this?" Then he tried to dive back through the door again. But Elio kept hold of his wrist and dug the gun into him and pushed him on down the passage as if he had not noticed Leon move. He stopped in front of the blocked-up archway. "Will you open this, please?" he said to Vivian. "A kick on the third stone from the left three courses up will do it."

Vivian kicked the stone, and the false wall pivoted around. The sight of the two dark openings was too much for Leon. "What are you going to do?" he cried out. "Take me underground and shoot me?" And as Elio pushed him toward the nearest opening, he yelled, "No, no, *no!*" and braced his feet again.

Elio took no notice. He simply forced the yelling, kicking Leon through the slit and followed him in. Vivian had not realized how strong Elio was. Leon was taller than Elio, with brawny muscles rippling out all over him, but Elio handled him as if he was the same size as Sam. In the midst of the struggle, he somehow found time to switch on a very strong light from his belt. Then he dragged and bundled the yelling Leon down the spiral stairs.

As Vivian followed the light downward, with Sam behind her and Jonathan behind Sam, they could hear Leon bracing his feet on the walls and trying to hang on to the ceiling, but the light kept moving remorselessly downward. "Let me go! Don't shoot me! I'll do anything you want!" Leon yelled.

"Then tell me who the people were who sent you to Time City," Elio's voice said calmly.

There was a short silence. "I can't do that," Leon's voice said pathetically. "He's learned things—from the Mind Wars. My brain won't let me." And a moment later he screamed, "It's true! I *can't*! I swear!"

"But you have a secret time lock." Elio's voice rang up. "Where is that?"

"I can't tell you that either!" Leon's voice yelled. "Let me *go*!"

"Maybe I believe you." Elio's voice came up. "But I do not believe you are from Hundred-and-one Century as your dress suggests."

"No, no—I'm from Sixty-six Century," Leon babbled. It was clear he was glad to tell the things he could tell. "I was a student in Helsinki, studying history and holographics. There, I've told you all about myself. You needn't take me down here to shoot— Why! That's their secret time lock!"

They had obviously reached the bottom. Vivian slid hurriedly down and around the huge old stairs and sat on the last one, with Sam and Jonathan staring over her shoulders. Elio had let Leon go, and Leon was backed against the wall. The lurid light glittered on the gun and shone smoothly off the egg-shaped control Elio had in his other hand. It was like the one Jonathan was still holding, except that it looked a little smaller and seemed to be a reddish color.

"This is indeed a time lock," Elio agreed. The flickering slate vanished, and a strong smell of manure blew in their faces. It seemed to be a rather primitive place beyond the slate. They could see a stack of old wooden barrels beside a patchily plastered wall, some washing blowing on a line, and a carefully trained creeper overhead with unripe grapes dangling from it. A goat wandered into view and peered through the opening at Elio curiously. "You have a choice," Elio said to Leon. "You can go through this lock or you can be shot. Which do you choose?"

Leon gestured rather hopelessly toward the goat. "Where is that place?" he said. "*When* is it?"

"It is Fifteen Century," Elio said. "The location is a farmyard near a small place in Italy called Vinci."

"But that's primitive!" Leon protested. "And it's an Unstable Era! And I *hate* goats! You can't mean you're going to strand me *there*!"

"Then you would rather be shot," Elio said, and trained the gun very precisely on Leon's heart.

"No, no! I'm going through now!" Leon said. He jumped hurriedly into the farmyard, where he landed with a squelsh. They had a last sight of the goat, turning to stare at him, before Elio used his control egg again and the wall turned back into flickering slate.

Elio turned away, looking satisfied. "That disposes of him," he said, "most tidily. Forgive me that I allow him to threaten you for so long. He had the gun hidden in his clothing while he approached the door, and when I saw he had it, I could not readily see how to attack him without causing him to shoot you. It was fortunate that Master Samuel interrupted."

A proud grin spread over Sam's face. "But why did you send him to that farm?" he said.

"Because," said Elio, "an amusing thought struck me as soon

as you told me his name." He stuck the gun in his belt and gestured politely to the stairs. They all found themselves obediently getting up and climbing the steps. Elio followed them. "I instantly recalled," he said, "a certain Italian from Fifteen Century, named Leonardo da Vinci. That man was always considered to have ideas far ahead of his own time, and it occurred to me that this must be the reason for it. Master Leon may well feel a little out of place where he has gone, but I assure you he will make his mark there. I knew he was a genius the moment I viewed the hologram he termed the Iron Guardian."

"What else do you know about?" Jonathan said, weary and subdued, from up in front.

Elio seemed not to have heard. He did not say anything else until they had all squeezed past the false wall into the passage. Then, as he swung the door shut, he said, "I believe we must talk. Will you all please come to my room?"

They followed him obediently, out of the passage and into the gallery. There Elio opened a door between two of the display cases and led them into the back parts of the palace where Vivian had never been. She felt rather as if she were at school, being taken to the Headmaster in disgrace. Jonathan and Sam trudged after her, obviously feeling much the same. Elio opened a door and ushered them in.

It was a large room on the ground floor, looking out onto a narrow strip of garden behind the Chronologue. Elio must have had it for the whole hundred years he had been in Time City. The furniture in it was a wild mixture of styles and colors, and on top of every bit of furniture there were things. Vivian stared at a pink empty-frame desk with a statue of Frankenstein's monster on it. Then her eyes shifted to a thing like a cake stand, loaded with clutter. The thing on the top shelf was a golden hat full of padlocks and marbles. Next shelf down was a jar labeled MOON DUST (TITAN). Her eyes went to a model spaceship hanging from the ceiling and then to a screen on the wall showing a cartoon film without the sound. She looked again and saw the film was *Snow White*.

"Oh! Can you get that here?" she cried out.

"Certainly, miss," Elio said, going over to his automat. It was a vast object, with three times more pipes and gold paint than Jonathan's. "Time City has copies of every film that was ever made. You need merely request Whilom Tower to relay you whichever one you want."

Vivian began to feel like Sam at the prospect of a butter-pie orgy. "Oh, I *love* films!" she said.

"I, too," Elio said. "I have a special preference for cartoons and horror films, but you must allow me also to introduce you to the chariot race episode from a film called *Ben Hur*. That ranks high with me." He came away from the automat and politely passed her a frothy, fruity drink. He handed Jonathan another. "This is a stimulant," he said. "I judge you need it. Please sit down." He turned to Sam. "I am not sure what to prescribe for you."

"Nothing, thanks," Sam said hastily. His face was still an unhealthy yellow.

They found seats by clearing dolls and motor tires and paintings off some of the empty frames and padded sofas. Jonathan found a set of false teeth just where he was going to sit down. He gave them a long, dubious look before he collapsed into the opposite corner of the sofa. "How long have you known about that time lock?" he said.

"For four days now," said Elio. "To be exact, from the time Miss Vivian came through a door I thought was chained up and tried to distract my attention from her companions."

"Oh!" said Vivian, hanging her head over her drink. "You were fooling me!"

"I felt some guilt at doing so," Elio admitted. "But I wished to know the facts. I therefore waited until that afternoon and refreshed my memory of the time ghosts that so much distressed

Madam Sempitern some years before. I recognized them for Master Jonathan and Miss Vivian, and I noticed that Miss Vivian's clothing was not that in which I had seen her emerge from the door. I concluded from this that the two of you would be doing something of great import at some future date, and that it was impossible to prevent you, since I clearly had not. I then went down the passage and discovered the false door and the time lock below. And I do not think that the control provided for it is fully functional, Master Jonathan.''

Jonathan looked at the egg he still had in his hand. ''No, it doesn't get you back properly. But how do you know *that*?''

Elio brought his own control from his pocket and held it out. It was slightly smaller, with the sheeny redness to it that Vivian had noticed before, and it had various hollows on its surface to make places for a person's fingers. ''I think,'' he said, ''that yours is a very much older model than this. As was natural, I made a couple of experimental journeys through the lock, using the control you have there. It malfunctioned slightly on my first trip. I went to Twenty Century, where I was somewhat aghast to find napalm and rocketry already in use in 1939. This should not have been so. It proved to me that the era had gone critical, and I made haste to get out of it. But I found myself simply advanced in time. It was most embarrassing. I was in Twenty-four Century in the middle of a ladies' nude bathing party—''

Vivian could not help laughing. Even Jonathan's anxious face relaxed into a grin. ''What happened?'' he said.

Vivian was interested to see that androids could blush, just like ordinary people. ''The ladies objected, and the control then returned me home,'' Elio said primly. ''Considering that, it was perhaps foolish of me to make another trip the following day. But I wished to know if the Second Unstable Era had gone critical too. It had not, perhaps because it is so short, though it remains barbaric. I then once more attempted to return to Time

City, but the control instead switched me to the Third Unstable Era—''

"We know that's the Silver Age for certain now," Jonathan muttered to Vivian.

"—which is in a state of great upheaval," Elio said, "and close to going critical too. And I had such difficulty returning from there that I very nearly became alarmed. I could, of course, have called on Time Patrol for aid, but I would then have been liable for prosecution for trespassing in a banned era. So I redoubled my commands to the control, and I was quite glad when it at length responded and brought me back to the lock." He looked blandly at the three of them. "I then made investigations in Time City," he said.

"What do you mean?" Jonathan said uneasily.

"I mean that I looked at Observers' reports from the era you just now termed the Silver Age," Elio said. Jonathan tried to nod wisely to cover up his relief that this was all Elio meant. "There is very little evidence for the disorder I noticed in minutes myself," Elio said. "Either the disorder is very new or the reports are wrong. Something strange is going on either way." He sauntered away to the window, tossing the red control egg in his hand, and from there, just as Jonathan and Sam were grinning at one another, sure that no one knew about their adventure in 1939, Elio sprang his bombshell. "I also checked the lock entries," he said. "There is no record of Miss Vivian Lee entering Time City. That was very careless of you."

They stared at him. Sam's yellowness increased, and so did Jonathan's paleness. Vivian thought she probably looked a mixture of the two. "What are you going to do?" she said hopelessly.

"I have done it," said Elio. "I inserted an entry for the morning you arrived."

They went on staring at him. On the wall screen the wicked queen was changing into a witch, which might or might not have

been a fitting thing to happen. "Why—why did you do that?"
Jonathan said at last.

Elio glanced at the screen too. "I was breaking the law by
time-traveling in secret," he said. "One more transgression seemed
unimportant. After that I confess I transgressed again. I forged
an official request from the Sempitern to Erstwhile Science to
have this newer control delivered to the palace." He tossed the
red egg up again. "My mind was in turmoil, you see," he said.
"I had, of course, recognized Miss Vivian as one of the time
ghosts as soon as I first saw her. Matching her with my memories
of Miss Vivian Lee, I became sure that she was not the Sempitern's
niece. But her presence here was important enough to have cre-
ated a time ghost many centuries ago and I was anxious to know
why." He looked at them gravely. "I have told you that I do not
like to discover facts of which I have been unaware. I am then
compelled to find out."

"And you did," Jonathan said glumly. "What did you do—
keep watch every afternoon until we went?"

"*I* did," said Sam. "And I saw her skipping around the fountain, but I had to go away and be ill then, so I missed going with
them."

"Ah. Then you did not happen to see where Leon Hardy came
from?" Elio said.

"Nope," said Sam.

"A pity," Elio said. "For I think there must be more than one
secret time lock in Time Close. All I know is that Master Hardy
did not come from Aeon Square, as one might expect, if he had
used a lock up the river or in the Patrol Building. The officials at
Erstwhile Science refused to release this control egg unless I fetched
it myself this afternoon. That is how I know. I was coming back
with it when I saw Master Jonathan and then Miss Vivian go
ahead of me through the archway. This made me hurry. I was
the next person to go through the arch, yet when I came into
Time Close, Master Hardy was already there ahead of me, walk-

ing toward the palace from the other side of the Close. I thought at the time that he might have been sitting by the fountain, waiting—"

"He wasn't," said Sam. "The first time I saw him was by the door to the ghost passage."

"He went ahead of me there," Elio said, "and I conjectured he intended to meet Miss Vivian and Master Jonathan as they returned. I confess to concealing myself in order to hear what was said. If I had known he had a gun—"

"Thanks about that," Jonathan said awkwardly. "He was going to shoot us."

There was a silence. Elio tossed the egg from hand to hand. Snow White on the screen bit into the witch's apple. The silence stretched from awkward, to meaningful, to unbearable.

"There are still many things I do not know," Elio pointed out at last. "It would relieve my mind if you were frank—though I shall find out some other way if you do not tell me."

"Tell him," said Sam. "I want to know too."

Vivian looked at Jonathan. Jonathan made an effort to look lordly, but it did not come to much. He nodded. And they told Elio. Elio stopped tossing the red egg and stood still with his face absolutely expressionless, drinking everything in with an efficiency Vivian found quite frightening. She wondered how she had ever thought she could deceive him, particularly when he began to ask questions. Each of Elio's questions pounced on something they had not told him and brought that up to the light, so that they went on and on telling him things. Meanwhile, Snow White and the Prince rode away together. The screen flickered a moment and then began another cartoon film, one about rabbits, which Vivian did not know.

Elio's last question pounced on something they had not even noticed. He said, "How did Master Hardy discover the whereabouts of the Golden Casket?"

"From the records," said Jonathan. "Why?"

"He lied," said Elio. "It is something even I do not know. I have looked in the records, in Perpetuum, Continuum, and Erstwhile, and then in Millennium and Whilom Tower and all the other places I could think of, over many years. I found much written of polarities, and some old accounts that tell of Caskets, but nowhere is there any mention of their hiding places. Yet Master Hardy found out in half a day. It is clear he had some other source of information, which he used to get you to fetch him the Golden Casket—or, if that failed, to get Miss Vivian to identify Laununsun for him.''

''And he used that hologram to get me interested,'' Jonathan said mournfully. ''It was so real, too! I suppose we can't believe a word it said.''

''Ah, no, the being you spoke to was real,'' Elio said. He was frowning slightly, with most of his huge mind on something else. ''When the hologram appeared a second time, I took care to go out and walk through it, and it had no solidity at all. Even Sixty-six Century art cannot make an image solid. This simply proves that Master Hardy's employers must have taken him to the First Unstable Era, perhaps to interview the real Guardian. But that is a side issue. The main thing that perturbs me is that I did not guess that the Lead Casket is in Time City—though now you point it out, I naturally see how the Caskets work. I should have seen before. It makes me feel very unintelligent.''

''I feel stupid then,'' Sam said. ''How *do* they work?''

''Like magnets on the face of a clock, naturally,'' Elio said. ''I will find a chart of history and show you.'' He sped about the room, searching, upending sofas, opening cupboards, and lifting huge piles of clutter. Finally, he lay flat on his face and looked under all the furniture. The chart was rolled up under the automat. He pulled it out and spread it open on the floor.

Vivian saw the horseshoe of known time, very familiar by now, with Stone Age near the beginning on the left and Depopulation at the end on the right. Elio put his finger on the gap at the top, right in the middle of it.

''Time City starts here,'' he said. ''Like the hour hand of a clock at midday. And, like the hand of a clock, it moves from right to left, in the opposite direction to history. It has to do this in order not to mingle with normal time. But it needs something to push it around the circle. So it is provided with a powerful motor. That is the Lead Casket. But the Lead Casket, like all motors, needs fuel on which to move, for it is highly unnatural to go backward through time. So the other Caskets are placed regularly around history to catch the city as it comes and fling it onward. The Gold comes first—a little before three o'clock, as it were—and that is the most powerful because the city has not long been moving and there is much temporal inertia to overcome. It attracts the Lead and flings it onward to Silver—placed around six-thirty—which in turn flings it on to Iron. Iron is weakest, for it is obvious to me now that the city was intended to slow down and stop when it gets back to the end of time, at midday again.''

"Why is that?" Jonathan said indignantly. "I thought it went on forever!"

"I conjecture that the Caskets need to be recharged and placed out again," Elio said. "Or maybe the small area of time that contains the city has to be replaced by a fresh area. Those are both things that I stupidly do not know yet. However, what *is* clear to me is that the whole system is in danger now that the Iron Casket has been stolen. We must think what to do about it."

They sat staring at him, trying to absorb the picture of Time City stopped like a broken clock, unable to start again. All those people and buildings! Vivian thought. What happens to Jonathan and Sam and Elio and Jenny? And she remembered the frantic time ghosts beating at the locks down the river. They were trying to get away! she thought, and it was too late because the city had broken down! That made it certain that the city was indeed going to break down. And there was nothing they could do about it.

"The city is an Unstable Era," Elio pointed out, seeing their faces. "Our future is not fixed. So it follows that there is something we can do. First, we must locate the Lead Casket and ensure its safety. We must also discover how it works. There are scientists and historicans here who can do that, or I can do it myself. But I should need to examine one of the other Caskets to find out how they interact. The only one that seems within our reach is the Silver.''

Jonathan scrambled to his feet. "Let's go at once. If we get there before the thief does—"

Elio shook his head. "Master Jonathan," he said, "you are not fit. You have been at death's door, and I should not have kept you talking. We can go at any moment and still arrive before the thief. And there are two days before the city reaches its beginnings. Much can be done in two days. You must go to bed.''

Now Elio pointed it out, Jonathan clearly felt fainter than ever. He clutched at the back of a sofa. "But—"

"But nothing," said Vivian. "You look awful."

"But I've still got this," Jonathan said, holding up the egg. "I ought to put it back.''

"That would be most unwise," Elio said. "Were someone else to find that lock and use it, the thing might malfunction more seriously yet and strand that person in history. Let us put it where it will do no harm.'' He took the egg from Jonathan's fingers and buried it in the golden hat on the cake stand, among the marbles and the padlocks. "There—we will keep it for use in an emergency," he said. Then he took Jonathan's arm and marched him from the room, much more gently than he had marched Leon to the time lock but quite as irresistibly. "We will see you to bed," he said, "and I will inform Madam Sempitern that you have a slight fever.''

Jonathan protested all the way to his room. Sam followed, protesting too. "I'm coming too, when you get the Silver! You've no right to leave me behind!''

"You shall go," Elio promised. "But first give me time to prepare. The Silver Age is at least as dangerous as the Gold.''

If Elio hoped to put Sam off by saying that, he made a mistake. Sam insisted he was not afraid, and went on insisting while Vivian was helping Elio bundle Jonathan into his bed. A look of great relief came over Jonathan as soon as he was lying floating under his cover. "Great Time! This feels good!" he said. "I feel as if I've been on the go for a week!"

"A night's sleep will restore you," Elio said, and he left to tell Jenny that Jonathan had a fever.

Sam, to Vivian's secret delight, doubled up in the empty-frame chair. "I feel awful too," he complained. "My stomach's all green obscene."

"Serves you right," Jonathan said, turning over with his back to them both. "Go away to bed and leave me in peace."

Sam sighed and got up. Now for it! Vivian thought. "Oh, Sam," she said sweetly, "before you go, can you work Jonathan's automat for me? I want a butter-pie, and I don't know how to get one."

Sam saw nothing peculiar in this. He trudged to the automat and banged away at its pipes and kicked its brass twiddles, until the flap finally came up to show the usual flowerpot with the stick in it. "There you are," he said.

"Don't you want one?" Vivian asked, picking up the flowerpot.

Sam, to her great pleasure, actually shuddered. "Not till tomorrow," he said.

"Then," said Vivian, "you are going to eat this one. Now. As a punishment for stealing all my money." She grabbed Sam by the back of his head before he could move and forced the butter-pie against his mouth. Sam bawled and kicked and struggled. But he was smaller than Vivian, and she held on to him almost as easily as Elio had held Leon. Every time he yelled, she got butter-pie into his mouth. If he shut his mouth, she stuffed it down his neck. Jonathan rolled over under his cover and laughed till his eyes ran.

"That's made me feel better!" he said, when Vivian decided

Sam had had about one hundred credits' worth and let go of him at last.

"It's made me feel worse," Sam said glumly. "I think you've put me off butter-pies for life."

Vivian was glad to see from this that she had got Sam's character right. Sam knew a fair punishment when he met one. He was not going to try for another revenge.

THE GNOMON

V ivian went to her own room feeling almost as exhausted as
Jonathan. That was the real disadvantage of time travel.
She and Jonathan had come back only five minutes or so after
they left Time City, but in between they had spent half a day in
the Age of Gold and had some frightening experiences there. And
there were still hours of the day left in the city. Vivian let her
door slide shut, very thankful that Dr. Wilander had not been
able to set her any more brain-damaging tasks.

Elio's voice spoke out of the bedside deck. "Miss Vivian, I
have ordered a selection of my favorite films to be relayed to
your room. Just press the white button on your deck, and the first
one will start to play."

"Thanks, Elio. You're an angel," Vivian said.

"My pleasure," said Elio's voice.

Vivian sat on the floating cover of her bed. It made a great
difference to have someone as efficient as Elio helping them. All
the same, she had a suspicion that Elio was thinking of it all as
an adventure, just the way she had herself. She knew it was serious now. She could still see Jonathan half sitting in that bush if
she closed her eyes. And there was another serious thought: If
Time City broke down entirely, it could damage the rest of history horribly. In which case, what would become of Mum and
Dad? I *have* to stay here now, Vivian thought, and do my best
to put it right. Nobody else here cares about history except me.

Then she pressed the white button and forgot her worries. She
had a film orgy. She saw films that were made before she was
born and films that would not be made until long after her life-
time was over. She would have forgotten to go down to supper
if Petula had not come along to remind her. As it was, she forgot

that Jonathan would not be there. She went down with her head in the clouds and came out of them with a bump when she found that the only other people there were Jenny and Sempitern Walker. They seemed rather tired too, after the Founding Ceremony that afternoon.

"I looked in on Jonathan, but he was asleep," Jenny said anxiously. "Did he seem very ill to you?"

Vivian found that she had perfected the art of lying by telling the truth. She did not even have to think. "He was quite bad to begin with, but he got better soon after that," she said sedately. "He felt a lot better as soon as he was in bed. He laughed."

"Oh good. Then he can't be too bad," Jenny said.

Sempitern Walker did not speak to Vivian, but he kept shooting her strange, anguished looks. Oh dear! Vivian thought. He's not forgiven me for laughing at him yesterday. She sat and listened to the two of them talking. It seemed that the Iron Guardian had joined in the procession again. Poor thing! Vivian thought. It doesn't know what to do with itself without its Casket! This time, however, Mr. Enkian had seen it. He was so angry that he had refused even to come to dinner and let himself be soothed.

"I feel quite grateful to whichever student it was," said Jenny. "Enkian in that mood is dreadfully hard work."

But it wasn't a student! Vivian thought. Leon Hardy was in long-ago Italy long before the ceremony stopped, so he couldn't have been working his gramophone. That proves Elio's right. It *is* the real Guardian.

"I always hope," Sempitern Walker said wistfully, "that someday Wilander will break Enkian's neck. It's a long, thin neck, perfect for breaking. I'd break it myself if I had the strength." And he shot Vivian another anguished glare. Vivian looked hurriedly down at her plate in order not to laugh.

Toward the end of dinner, Jenny said, "By the way, Vivian, did Jonathan tell you there's no school tomorrow morning or the day after?"

"He forgot," said Vivian. "Why isn't there?"

"It's so the children can come and watch the ceremonies," Jenny explained. "Everybody comes to the last ones. Time City simply grinds to a halt for these two days." This turn of phrase gave Vivian an uncomfortable jolt. Nor did she feel much better when Jenny added, "But Dr. Wilander asked me to tell you to come to him in the afternoons as usual."

Vivian realized that they would have the whole morning in which to look for the Lead Casket in the Gnomon Tower. She got up early the next day and went to Jonathan's room to see if he was well enough to come with her. Jonathan was not there. Nor was he downstairs in the matutinal or anywhere else Vivian looked. She could not understand it at first. Then the palace began to resound with running footsteps and shouting.

"Oh no!" Vivian exclaimed. "He *has* started early!"

"He has indeed, miss," Elio said, rushing past with a heavy pleated coat. "The ceremony does not begin until ten-thirty."

Jonathan must have an instinct! Vivian thought, watching Elio race away along the hall. Elio was not running anything like as fast as she now knew he could. He was humoring the Sempitern. But she had no doubt that if Sempitern Walker did seem likely to be late, Elio would start moving with blurred speed and get the Sempitern there in time.

She turned to go back to the matutinal and almost ran into Sempitern Walker charging the other way. He was wearing nothing but pale green underwear and a red scarf. His hair had come out of its topknot and was hanging down over one ear. Vivian found herself starting to laugh. She tried to dodge around him in order to go away quickly, but Sempitern Walker reeled backward as if she had almost knocked him down and pointed at her accusingly.

"You," he said. "Find me my Semiotic Slippers—quickly!"

"What—what do they look like?" Vivian quavered, biting the insides of her cheeks.

"Black with twisted toes and platinum embroidery," said the

Sempitern. "They must be upstairs somewhere. They're not down here anywhere. Hurry up, girl!" He rushed past her and raced away up the stairs in a patter of long bare feet.

Vivian clattered up the stairs after him with her hand over her mouth, trying to keep her eyes off the streaming red scarf and the flying hairy legs. This must be his revenge on me for laughing! she thought. I shall *die* trying not to giggle!

At the top of the stairs, the Sempitern swung around. "Don't *follow* me!" he shouted unreasonably. "You go that way. I'll look along here," he said, and went bounding away along the railed landing. Halfway along, he swung around again and saw that Vivian was still standing there with both hands helplessly over her mouth. "What are you *doing*?" he bawled. "You're all useless, useless! I shall be late!" And he went into a dance of rage and frustration.

The sight of the Sempitern in his green underwear leaping and jumping and waving his arms was too much for Vivian. She doubled up over the banisters, screaming.

"This is no time to be seasick!" the Sempitern yelled.

Vivian managed to raise her head. The Sempitern's yells had enabled the palace helpers to find him. Petula was tiptoeing from one end of the landing with a bundle of embroidered robe, and the others were creeping up from the other end, hoping to trap the Sempitern between them and get him into the things they were carrying. But the Sempitern continued to caper about, his topknot flying like Jonathan's pigtail, waving his arms at Vivian. "Hunt the Slippers!" he bawled at her.

Vivian went on laughing, but she was laughing with amazement now. Good heavens! she thought. He *knows* he's funny, and he *wants* me to laugh! "Only if you haven't hidden them yourself!" she screamed back at him.

"I never hide things. It happens quite naturally," the Sempitern roared. He avoided Petula with a leap like a ballet dancer's, just as Petula seemed sure to catch him, and sprinted away around the landing. "Slippers!" his voice shouted in the distance. "Where has that fool Elio put my Caucasian coat?"

Vivian wiped her eyes and sniffed and tottered after everyone as they tore after the Sempitern. The slippers were halfway up the next flight of stairs, where the Sempitern must have known they were. Vivian picked them up and joined in the pursuit. I think everyone's taken him far too seriously up to now, she thought as she pelted up the stairs. Maybe he took *himself* seriously, until I started to laugh and he discovered he liked it!

Whatever the reason, Sempitern Walker excelled himself that morning. He careered along corridors, plunged down stairs two at a time, threw golden hats into baths and shoes at people. He shouted. He danced. And whenever they seemed to have him cornered, he escaped all the hands reaching to give him vestments and trousers as if they belonged to so many time ghosts and sped off in a new direction, bawling for different garments. Vivian became weak with laughing. Jenny kept turning up to join in the chase, in various stages of getting dressed herself, and after a while she caught Vivian's laughter. She had to stagger away with her hands over her face. One of Petula's younger helpers was soon as bad as Vivian, and they lost one of the men who polished the floors halfway, when he had to sit on the back stairs and guffaw. By the end, nearly everyone was in fits of laughter. There were even lines around the ends of Elio's mouth when he caught Sempitern Walker in the hall and firmly put him into the pleated coat.

It was nearly time for the ceremony by then. Outside in the Close, the Annuate Guard was lining up in scarlet and gold, and Sam was on the steps of the palace, looking in through the glass doors and grinning all over a face that was once more pink and healthy. Sempitern Walker stood still and let Elio clip the red scarf to his headdress. He climbed meekly into the pleated trousers Jenny passed him and let everyone pass him the various staffs and chains that went with the clothes. Last of all, he held up each foot in turn so that Vivian could put the Semiotic Slippers on them. When she stood up, he gave her an unusually anguished glare. She was fairly sure that this was the Sempitern's way of winking.

Elio brushed the stiff coat into order and sent Sempitern Walker safely out to meet the Annuate Guard, with Jenny beside him. Then he turned to Vivian. "We have all suffered a good deal of amusement," he said. "Will you investigate the Gnomon, miss, while I explore the other possibilities?"

"Yes, I was going to," Vivian said. "But I can't find Jonathan."

Elio nodded toward the stairs. Jonathan was coming down them, looking cool and lordly and as healthy as Sam. "Let's get going," Jonathan said.

Jonathan, Vivian thought, did not take the right attitude to his father. In fact, now she considered it, she had scarcely even seen them speak to each other. As she and Sam and Jonathan followed the last of the Annuate Guard across the Close, she tried to put things right. "Why do you always vanish when your father's getting ready for a ceremony?" she said. "You shouldn't. It's so funny! I *ache* from laughing!"

"I'm not going to stand and watch my father making an ass of himself," Jonathan answered haughtily. "I'm a Lee, after all."

"He's a very *good* ass!" Vivian protested. But she saw from Jonathan's face that he would not forgive her if she said any more. So she gave up.

They made their way toward the Gnomon through an increasing throng of people. What Jenny had told Vivian seemed to be true. Though there were tourists there in thousands, more than half the throng was in Time City pajamas. When they got to the Avenue of the Four Ages, the crowd was thicker still and the Avenue itself was roped off, with Time Patrollers standing by the ropes. The zigzag stairs up Endless Hill were roped off too, and guards in colored uniforms lined the ropes the whole way up.

"Bother!" said Jonathan. "I'd forgotten the ceremony was here today. We'll have to go around the back."

They worked their way out again, the opposite way all the other people were going. Vivian looked back regretfully. A band was playing. The Avenue looked very splendid with the streamers of light fluttering from the arches in wonderful combinations of color. Children in the crowd had flags and long sticks that played musical chimes. This ceremony looked fun.

"It is," said Sam. "Never mind. We can see it next year."

But *I* can't! Vivian thought, just as Jonathan said, "There may not *be* a next year unless we can find that Casket." This made Vivian think, Jonathan's the only person in the city who isn't like Sam. Sam thinks it's all right deep down. I know Sam's little, but even Elio thinks everything will be all right. And everybody else is carrying on just as usual, even though they must know there's a crisis—as if Time City is going to go on forever. I suppose there's not much else most of them can do. But you'd think *some* of them would be worried!

It took them quite a while of pushing and squeezing to work their way around to the back of Endless Hill. There all the alleyways were empty, and Jonathan took them quickly to a tall gilded iron gate, which opened onto a long flight of stairs. The gate was kept shut, he said, so that people would not realize there was another way into the Gnomon, but it was not forbidden.

The stairs went straight up among the ornamental bushes planted all over Endless Hill. Jonathan took them at a run. Vivian switched on her low-weight function, but even so, she was puffing by the time they reached the tower. She had already run up and down more stairs than she cared to think that morning.

"No entry today," said the Annuate Guard at the small door opposite the end of the stairs. "The procession's due here soon." There were twelve doors into the tower, and there was an Annuate Guard standing to attention in front of all the doors Vivian could see. She began to feel that if the Lead Casket *was* in the Gnomon, it was probably quite safe anyway.

Jonathan managed to look piteous. "But we have to get in! Dr. Wilander's giving us a test on the Gnomon this afternoon. He told us to come here."

"Dr. Wilander, eh?" the Guard said respectfully. "He's not someone I want to fall foul of. I'll see if we can stretch a point." She opened the door and put her head inside to speak to someone there. After a while, two heads looked out at them around the next door along. They belonged to two Patrollers who knew Sam well. They let them all inside.

The round room at the bottom of the tower was empty except for a spiral pillar in the middle. The empty spaces between the twelve doors were painted to look like flowering trees half hiding views of Time City. They could tell at a glance that nothing could be hidden here. The floor was one huge round slab of stone. If the Casket's under that, we'll never find it! Vivian thought.

Sam's voice boomed through the room. "He wants us to see the whole tower."

"All right, son," a Patroller said. "That can be arranged."

They were given a guided tour. The way up the tower was by the spiral pillar in the middle. The Patroller put his foot on one of the ridges that wound around the pillar and began to travel up and around the pillar. When his head was near the painted ceiling, there was room for Sam to put his foot on a ridge and travel upward too. Vivian followed Sam, and Jonathan followed her. They were carried up and around miraculously, through the ceiling—where there had not seemed anyplace to get through—and up into somewhere that was full of light. Vivian had to shut her eyes. She opened them in time to see that they were spiraling upward inside what seemed to be a glass pillar. Up they went, into a part where the light was so confusingly split and reflected that she could not tell what was doing it, and after a time they spiraled out into the Time Pagoda at the very top of the Gnomon. Vivian, a little giddily, stared out through lacy arches at Time City spread about her. She could see the jets of the Pendulum Gardens rising and falling behind the Dome of The Years, and the graceful finger of Whilom Tower in front of strange, lopsided Perpetuum. There was even a glimpse of the sloping golden roof of the Chronologue in the distance and a gray roof in front that must be the Annuate Palace. Beyond, the green country stretched away to its sudden end in the sky.

From the next archway around there was a marvelous view of the Avenue of the Four Ages, down to Millennium, and the procession of the ceremony halfway along it. The thing that took up most of the pagoda behind was the huge bell of the Midday Clock. They could see that there was no Casket hidden in the bell. It was made of something transparent, right down to its giant clapper, and the sun flashed blindingly off it in the southern arch.

"Best not to spend too long up here," the Patroller warned them. "You'd go deaf when it strikes. It breaks your eardrums."

Jonathan checked the lacy stone all around the pagoda, but it was too open to hide anything. A tourist had tried to hide the stick from a butter-pie in one of the larger openings, and the Patroller found it at once. He sternly removed it before he led the way down a staircase that spiraled outside the tower. It was a cunning staircase, with a high outer wall, only open to the sky. You could not tell it was there from the ground. It was a long way down, because the next floor took up half the height of the tower.

"The works of the clock," the Patroller announced proudly, as he turned off the stairs and in through a tall thin doorway.

The works were all made of glass and they were all moving. Vivian stared around in amazement at shining cogs slowly turning to connect with transparent ratchets and glass rods and springs— hundreds and hundreds of them, each brightly and gently moving and each connecting somehow to the giant glass pillar in the middle, which was slowly, slowly turning too. We came up that pillar! she thought, dazzled by the rainbow twinkles and stunned by the clear greenish depths of the glass. But there was nowhere for anything to be hidden because you could see through everything. Even the walls between the long, thin windows were made of something half transparent. The light shone through them almost the color of a butter-pie. Anything made of lead would have shown up like an ink blot.

The flicker over Jonathan's eyes had thickened to protect him from the light, but Vivian could see his eyes screwed up in disappointment as they turned to follow the Patroller again. The Patroller did not want them to stay for long here either, because the Midday Clock could deafen you in this part too.

"Faber John wanted to show people it wasn't hidden here," Sam whispered breathily.

"Hush!" Vivian whispered back, although the space was filled with faint chiming tinkles from the moving glass and the Patroller probably could not hear.

The outside staircase went onto the ground, but there were stairs inside the wall to the next floor, because the tower was thicker near its base. It must have been a sort of lookout place at one time, because the room below had wide windows all around, but now it was done up as a small museum and was really rather dull. The only unusual thing was the glass pillar in the middle, gently turning, turning all the time. But the Lead Casket might easily have been put in as a museum exhibit. They rushed eagerly to the nearest display case.

"This is one of the first-ever automats," the Patroller said, stopping at a machine by the doorway. "Still in working order, too! Do any of you fancy a butter-pie?"

Sam shuddered.

"Er—no thanks," Jonathan said. "We—er—we're supposed to be working." He switched on his pen function. As they went around the cases, he pretended to be very busy taking notes on a rather bent note sheet he fished out of his pocket.

Vivian went around ahead of him and saw quite quickly that there was nothing at all like a Casket here either. Most of the things had once belonged to Faber John. There was a hat rather like Sempitern Walker's Amporic Miter, only it was for a much bigger head—and it was on its side so that Vivian could see nothing was hidden in it—and a very large, frayed glove; a star-shaped gold medal; a page of notes in universal symbols; documents; and nothing interesting at all. Vivian loitered over to the glass pillar and waited for Jonathan to give up.

There were four niches in the pillar, about level with Vivian's eyes. She saw each niche in turn, as the pillar slowly revolved and the boys slowly investigated each case. She walked around the pillar and looked at the niches again. They were all different. She could see they had been molded specially to fit four things that were not the same size and shape. One was flat and square and quite large. The Iron Casket! Vivian thought. The two niches on either side of that were both oval, one small and one big. I bet those are for the Silver and the Lead! she thought. But she had no way of telling which was which. The fourth space, on the side of the pillar opposite to the square niche, was for something tall, with several sides. The Gold! Vivian thought. From the tiny grooves in that niche and the large oval one, she could see that two of the Caskets were beautifully ornamented.

"What are these spaces for?" she asked the Patroller, to make quite sure.

He looked a little embarrassed. "Well," he said, "the story goes that those are for Faber John's polarities. They're supposed to come back to the pillar at the end of time. That's only a story, of course—but we keep them empty that way in case."

"You should have known that," Vivian said to Jonathan.

He went pink and took on his most lordly look. "If you live in this place," he said, "you leave the Gnomon for tourists. Let's go. The procession's nearly got here."

"You get the best view in the city from this window here," the Patroller said, thinking that Jonathan was in a hurry to see the ceremony. "You're welcome to watch from here with me."

"Oh good!" said Sam. He slid between the case with the hat in it and the case with the glove and pressed his face to the window beyond. Vivian slid in beside him. Jonathan sighed and leaned on the case with the hat.

They were looking straight down the hill at the zigzag steps. The procession had just reached the bottom of them, and the elderly Annuate Guard who walked in front carrying a huge golden spear was starting to climb up. Behind him came Jonathan's father, stiff and tall in his pleated coat and high headdress, and behind that a mass of people in robes of all colors, with banners, standards, pots streaming red smoke, and large feather fans. As the Sempitern put his foot on the lowest step, there came a tremendous noise. It burred through the room and through their heads. The museum cases vibrated.

"There goes the clock," said the Patroller, leaning beside Jonathan. "I must say the Sempitern does know how to time his ceremonies. That's perfect!"

The Sempitern started to climb. Beside him a figure in green was suddenly trying to struggle up the steps too.

"Only the Endless ghost," the Patroller said soothingly.

Vivian was having trouble with the vibrations from the clock. She nodded, then shook her head to clear it. She had scarcely got her head comfortable when the noise came again. It seemed to set the whole tower quaking. Below, Sempitern Walker climbed past the Endless ghost without looking at it. The rest of the stately colorful procession followed, ignoring the desperate green man, sweeping around and beside and through him. The clock struck again. And one person in the procession noticed the struggling green ghost. Vivian had glimpses of him, a gray figure among the colored robes, bending to stretch a helping hand out to the ghost. He seemed puzzled when his hand went through the ghost, and he tried again and again, more pleadingly each time. The

Endless ghost simply went on struggling up the steps, and the procession ignored both of them. The clock struck four, five, six, while stately people climbed past.

"Iron Guardian," Sam whispered, making the window misty with his breath.

"Poor thing," Vivian murmured. She felt sorrier than ever for the Iron Guardian. He seemed quite unable to tell that it was only a ghost he was trying to touch. She knew why he kept trying. The struggling man was the ghost of the Watcher of the Gold. And he's going to try to bring the Gold to the tower, and something's going to stop him! Vivian thought. She turned to look at Jonathan. He had recognized the Watcher too. He was pale with alarm.

But the clock went on striking and the procession went on climbing. They lost sight of the Endless ghost and the Iron Guardian, when Sempitern Walker's beautiful timing brought him to the top of the steps exactly on the stroke of twelve, and their view of the steps was blocked by real people in colorful regalia.

"I'm afraid we have to leave now," Jonathan said politely.

"I'm staying," said Sam.

"All right. But V.S. and I have to get something to eat before we go to Dr. Wilander," Jonathan said. He and Vivian thanked the Patroller and left the museum room by the steps on the outside of the tower. That way, they came out near the back and avoided the ceremony.

Vivian was still troubled by the vibrations from the bell. Her legs shook. Down on the ground, she felt as if the solid earth of Endless Hill was quivering. "The sound does that to some people," Jonathan said. "It'll go. Well, what do you think? It was so obvious that the Casket wasn't there that I think it *may* be."

"You're being too clever," Vivian said, and only just stopped herself from adding, "As usual!" She said patiently, "Whoever arranged that tower was trying to show people the Casket was somewhere else. Sam said so. That's the kind of thing he's usually right about."

"Then he's being too clever, and so are you," Jonathan said. "We haven't a clue where else to look. You'll have to ask Dr. Wilander this afternoon."

"*You* ask him," said Vivian.

"No, you do it," said Jonathan. "You got him going beautifully last time, and it looks better if you do it. I'm supposed to know about the city."

"But you know how to get around him best," said Vivian.

They argued about it all the while they were eating seaweed shrimp sundae in Aeon Square, and the whole time, Vivian went on feeling as if the ground was shaking. It can't be the clock *still*! she thought. "Jonathan, can't you honestly feel something like the earth trembling?"

The look Jonathan shot at her told her that he could. "I was hoping it was the bell," he said.

"Then the city's got to the end of time," Vivian said. "This is it."

"Yes, but which *it*?" Jonathan said. "Is it shaking because it's slowing down, or because it's breaking up?" They got up and crossed the square among crowds of people drifting away from the ceremony. "You *must* ask Wilander," Jonathan said. "Cunningly. It's urgent."

"Why me?" Vivian demanded.

This brought on the argument again, and the argument went on all the way up the stairs of Perpetuum, where the stairs seemed to be shaking worse the higher they went. "You have to do it," Jonathan said, as they turned into Herodotium, "because he likes you."

"What makes you think *that*?" said Vivian. The dark wood around them was creaking and shifting. "All he does is glare and growl and make fun of me!"

"He only makes fun of people he likes," Jonathan said, and that won the argument. As they knocked at the door of Seldom End, Vivian agreed to do the asking.

Her nerve failed as soon as they were inside. There, among the warm smell of wood and books, Dr. Wilander sat in his hairy coat, lighting his pipe and looking at them through the smoke with his small, clever eyes, as if he had never moved since they saw him last. Only the shabby purple gown flung over a pile of record cubes showed that Dr. Wilander must have moved to take part in the ceremony.

"I'm doing the Mind Wars with you today," he snarled through the cloud of smoke. "Start attending. It's the most unpleasant episode there ever was in any Fixed Era. Its effects are felt all through the following Unstable Era and go on to give rise to the Icelandic Empire. Consult your chart, Vivian, and tell me the main facts about the Mind Wars."

Vivian looked at her chart. She supposed she should start asking by saying innocently, Dr. Wilander, why is the ground shaking? But she could not seem to feel it in here. It was impossible to think of anything except that Dr. Wilander showed no signs of liking either of them. *Hate* and *contempt* seemed better words for the way he was glaring at her.

"Before she does," Jonathan said, seeing that Vivian was in trouble, "she wants to ask you something."

Beast! thought Vivian.

"Then she had better speak for herself," Dr. Wilander growled. "Go ahead, Vivian. You can use deaf-and-dumb language if it's more comfortable."

Making fun of me, Vivian thought. Does that *really* mean he likes me? She gulped. "It's—it's about that paper you gave me to translate. Why does it tell you where to find three of the Caskets but not the Lead one?"

"I assume because the lesser Caskets are attracted to the Lead Casket and will find it for you," Dr. Wilander grunted. "There is no point looking for the Mind Wars in the Stone Age. You will find them in Fifty-seven Century."

"Yes, but suppose that went wrong and someone *had* to find the Lead Casket," Vivian said. "Have you any idea where Faber John put it?"

"We're not going to waste the afternoon playing Hunt-the-Slipper for legendary objects," Dr. Wilander retorted. "But while we're at it, tell me the meaning of Faber John's name."

Vivian sighed. Each time they tried to ask Dr. Wilander something, he went off on another tack. It did not seem worth trying anymore. She was so annoyed that she quite forgot for the moment that she was supposed to be Vivian Lee. "Smith," she said. "It means boring old John Smith."

This produced quite a lecture from Dr. Wilander. "Boring?" he said. "Our founder's name *boring*! It's the most honorable name there is! In the days when names began, the name Smith had to be earned, and you earned it by being the most gifted man in the area. The first Smith was a genius who found out how to work metal. People came to him for science and for magic. He wasn't just strong, if that's what you mean. He made things. And he knew how to put virtue in those things so that they would do their proper job. He dared to find out about such matters and to use his knowledge. But if you simply mean that Smith is a common name, you are saying that there are remarkably many gifted people in the human race, and that is not boring either. And now consider the Mind Wars, please."

And they did. Vivian thought they were sickening. She had not realized such cruel things could be done to people's minds. Under attacks from various mind weapons, all the nations she knew about disappeared for good, which upset her as much as the weapons. She had never been so glad to get away from the hot, wood-scented den in Seldom End.

Jonathan, however, had clearly been thinking about something else the whole time. As they went down the quivering stairs, he said, "If he's right about the other Caskets' attracting the Lead one, then we've *got* to get the Silver in order to find it."

Vivian said queasily, "But the Silver Age is just after the Mind Wars."

"Yes, I know," Jonathan said, dismissing this in his most lordly manner. "But we're not going to get anywhere without it—unless Elio's managed to find out more than we have, of course."

E lio and Sam were waiting for them by the fountain in Time
Close, where the water was all in crisscross ripples from the
shaking of the ground. Elio looked displeased. There was a frown
on his smooth forehead, but it had nothing to do with the quaking
of the earth.

"I have ransacked the records," he said, "and there is no sign
of the things Leon Hardy knew. I wish I had not been so hasty
in banishing him to Italy. Furthermore, the being who watches
the Gold Casket is a complete fool!"

"You mean you've been to the Age of Gold? Today?" Jonathan
said.

"I wish we'd seen you first," said Vivian. "The time ghost
that climbs the steps to the Gnomon is the Watcher of the Gold."

"That is another thing I did not know," Elio said, frowning
harder. "So he is bound to come here whatever I said." He seemed
so upset that Vivian daringly patted his arm. It was nothing at all
like touching the Iron Guardian. Elio's arm felt like an ordinary
human arm.

"I think we'd better find the Silver Casket quickly," Jonathan
said anxiously.

"Yes," Elio agreed. "We will go now." They walked toward
the palace, past a time ghost in ceremonial robes, who must have
been a former Sempitern. "My visit to the Age of Gold was a
great waste of energy," Elio said. "There were wild persons in
the trees, who made considerable efforts to kill me, and then an
armed person on a horse, who seemed to feel it his business to
kill all of us. And when I gave them the slip and made my way
to Laununsun, the Watcher stood chewing a piece of grass and

refused to respond to any of my arguments. I had to leave hastily anyway, for the person on the horse came back." He sighed. As they went into the hall of the palace, he said, "I hope we have better luck in the Age of Silver." Nobody said anything. Vivian thought that if her own feelings were anything to go by, Jonathan and Sam must be hoping that something would stop them from going there. "Master Jonathan," said Elio, "you have not yet revealed whereabouts in the Third Unstable Era Master Hardy told you to look for the Silver Casket."

Jonathan went lordly. "Oh, haven't I?" he said carelessly.

They turned the corner into the gallery, where the strong light made it plain that Jonathan was rather red. "You rat!" Sam cried out. "You went without me again!"

"*That* was where you disappeared to this morning!" Vivian said.

"Master Jonathan, you took a grave risk," Elio said reprovingly. "There is constant war in that era. Furthermore, you must have used the worn-out control, for I had the functional one with me all day."

"Yes, but I put it back in the hat," Jonathan said. "And there's no need to glare at me, Sam. I didn't find a thing. It was all salt desert with not a soul in sight. I thought I'd go to a hundred years before the thief got there, you see, to make quite sure. But there wasn't a sign of any Guardian, even when I shouted, and no way of telling where the Casket was. It was a dead loss."

"And did the egg work properly?" Vivian asked.

"No," said Jonathan. "When I tried to get back, it landed me in the Golden Age, quite near Laununsun. And it *was* you I saw there, Elio. I thought it was, but you were running across the meadow so fast that I wasn't sure."

"But it did take you back in the end?" Vivian said.

"Obviously," said Jonathan, "or I wouldn't be here. But it took ages, and I only got back just before my parents left for the ceremony. I was quite scared."

"Rightly," said Elio. "This time we will use my control. And we will go to five minutes before the thief reaches the Casket, since it is clear that he has information which we have not and can lead us to the place. That is, Master Jonathan, if you will now be generous enough to tell us where to go."

"It's in the Baltic Sea," Jonathan admitted. "Leon said Sixty-four Century was the best time, because the sea's dry for a hundred years on both sides of then." And he told them a map reference that meant nothing to Vivian.

Elio seemed to understand. He looked dubious. "I hope Master Hardy told you right," he said. "That is certainly a war zone in that century, however history runs, and as I told you, I found that era very disturbed. However," he added, looking more cheerful, "I shall be there to make sure you are safe, and I have taken care to provide us all with protective clothing. This way."

He led the way toward the display cases at the far end of the gallery. Vivian stopped in front of the one that held her own luggage. It looked dusty and foreign to her now, and not at all useful. "Elio," she said, "if we do get the Silver Casket and Time City's all right, I'm going to need this for when I go home."

Elio stopped with his head twisted around, staring at the luggage with obvious regret. "I have never had anything from Twenty Century before," he said. "But of course, you must have it when you need it." Vivian could tell that it cost him a real wrench to say it.

But it *is* mine! she thought as Elio went on to the case that had held the Martian boots. There were now four flat silver packets in it instead. The label said TWENTY-FOUR CENTURY NYLON STOCKINGS (FOR MEN). Elio opened the case, took the packets out, and turned the label over. That side read DISPLAY REMOVED FOR REPAIRS. He handed them a packet each as he led the way to the chained door.

Vivian's stomach wobbled, and seemed to wobble worse every

step of the way down to the underground room. Her fingers shook when she opened her packet by Elio's belt light. Odd-shaped filmy silver cloth spilled out.

"These are mind-shield suits from Fifty-six Century," Elio told them. "I procured them from then because Mind War suits have never been bettered. Put them on over your heads and faces, and let the rest spill down to your feet."

"Why does it have to go all over?" asked Sam. "*My* mind's in my head."

"Ah, but there are nerves all over your body that lead to your head. A mind warrior only has to find an unprotected nerve," Elio explained. "These suits will stop that. They will also stop other weapons to some extent, provided you are not at close range."

This made Vivian feel more wobbly than ever. It did not help to feel the ground still gently shaking, even down here. She pulled the strange cloth over her head. It was easy to breathe through, and it fell across her shoulders and down over the rest of her with the gentlest of touches. She spread her arms to look down at herself all covered in flowing silvery folds. We're not going to be able to walk far, trailing around in this stuff! she thought. But after a pause, in which the cloth must have been adjusting to her, it suddenly shrank around her.

"Lift your feet, one after the other," Elio said.

Vivian did so, and the silvery stuff promptly shrank itself around the underside of each of her shoes. And she was wearing an all-over suit of filmy silver. The others were silver all over too. Sam's face and Jonathan's looked at her through the film, squashed and whitish.

"I can't see too well," Jonathan said. "It seems to be cancel-ing out my optical function."

"Then keep close to me," said Elio. The belt light coming from under his suit made him look like a luminous ghost. "You must all keep close to me. I shall do my utmost to ensure our safety, and as you are aware, my utmost is more than twice that of a born-human.'' He raised his hand with the red egg-shaped control in it, filmy under the suit, and pointed it at the flickering slate.

The slate vanished into a door opening on dazzling brightness. White, white sand stretched away to a distant pale blue sky. They stepped through it, and their suited feet crunched and slipped on what felt like frost. Probably it's salt from the dried-up sea, Vivian thought. But the place felt cold, too. Her suit did not do much to stop a keen, icy wind. She turned her head away from the wind and the white glare and realized that the white land was not a level desert at all. Blue shadows showed that it was a mass of hummocks and holes. Some of them were regular-looking ditches that reminded Vivian of the trenches in World War One.

Jonathan's eye function had darkened in the glare. He turned his face rather blindly from side to side. "What's happened? It was flat when I came here this morning."

"Someone's dug a lot of holes," Sam told him.

A voice spoke. It rapped out words in a foreign language from overhead.

"Down!" said Elio, and threw himself flat on the white ground.

They all threw themselves down beside him. The whiteness was icy cold. The place where Vivian fell turned out to be on a slope, so that she rolled as she went down, and then slid. She ended flat on her back some way from the others, staring into the cloudless sky. The sky almost above her was filled by a half-transparent thing like a raft, which was floating in the air about fifty feet up. Leon Hardy told us wrong! she thought. He meant us to get killed! She did not dare move. The raft was bluish, and she could see the bottoms of people's feet through it. The faces of the people were peering down through paler bubbles at the edges of the raft. They were blank, squashed faces, covered in something yellowish, which must have been mind suits rather like her own.

The voice rapped out again, and the raft fired on them. Whatever it was came down in whitish ripples. Vivian screamed. For just an instant, before her suit canceled the weapon out, something seemed to tearing the inside of her head away. Then she just lay and watched the white ripples and hoped that the others' suits were working properly too.

The firing stopped, but not because the people in the raft had finished. Another raft, a slightly greenish one, was coming in from higher up to attack the first one, moving very fast with a small whistle of wind. The first raft rose another fifty feet and sheered away sideways. As soon as it moved, Vivian saw a third raft, different again, with a mauve tinge, plummeting out of the high sky at the first two. Both the lower rafts shot away sideways, and then shot back again to attack the mauve one. They circled the sky, all three, up and down and around one another, fighting furiously without any sound except the thin whistling of the wind. Vivian had never imagined this kind of warfare. Since it was not aimed at her, her suit did not block very much of it out. Ripples sped sideways across her, bringing calm voices of madness, giggles of rage, hymns of nastiness, screams of exhaustion, tinkles of death, whistles of despair, and loud songs of horror. And none of it made a sound. Vivian had to lie on the cold ground and bear it, in all its back-to-front wrongness.

Then, in the part of the sky that she could see between her own silvery feet, Vivian noticed a cloud of blue-gray smoke. It drifted nearer, fast and high, streaming this way and that and groping about as if it were looking for something, until it located the three fighting rafts. Then it came snaking in, grabbing for them like some enormous grayish glove. All three rafts tried frantically to get out of its way. One hurtled straight up into the air, and a man fell off it. Vivian heard him give a real scream as he crashed to the ground. The second raft went low and hurtled past a few feet above Vivian, wobbling and weaving and spraying out ripples as if something was wrong with it. The last raft put on speed and raced away in the opposite direction. The cloud dived around and went after it. Two seconds later, the blue sky and the glittering white desert were completely empty.

Sam rolled over on the slope above Vivian. "How many sides *are* there in this war?" he said.

"Time alone knows!" said Jonathan, crawling to his hands and knees. "That was nasty!" He stood up, shivering.

Vivian got up, with her teeth chattering, and helped Sam to his feet. Elio was the last to stand up. He raised himself slowly and painfully and, to their horror, most of the suit under his right arm had gone blue and melted-looking.

"It is nothing," he said. "Just something from that low-flying raft. I am all right. I was made to withstand adversity. Let us find that Casket before any more warriors appear." He tore open his suit on the side opposite to the melted blueness and fetched out a small gleaming gadget. The suit sealed itself up behind it.

Sam forgot his fright. "Hey!" he said. "That's a Hundred-and-ten-Century metal detector! My dad's got one. He says you can't get one for love nor money these days. How did you get hold of it? Can I work it?"

Sam got his way because Elio was limping and swaying and Jonathan was stumbling about with his hands out like a sleep-walker. With his eye function dark in the glare and the veil of the suit in front of it, he could barely see at all. He switched it off disgustedly in the end.

Sam confidently turned the metal detector to detect silver and went stumping off in widening circles. "My dad says there's nothing to beat these," he called out. "You can find needles in haystacks. Keep close. It's showing something already!"

They tried to keep up with Sam as he tramped off in the direction the cloud had come from, but it was hard going. The salty sand was a mass of holes and frozen hummocks, ditches and mounds. One moment they would be sliding down a glittering slope, and the next, they would be having to jump a deep blue trench. Vivian had to help Jonathan most of the time. She tried to help Elio too, but he waved her away.

"I am fine," he panted. "My efficiency is in no way impaired."

Vivian did not believe him. Elio's face, mistily showing through the suit, seemed to be twisted with pain. What will Sempitern Walker do if Elio's badly hurt? she was wondering, when Sam pointed the detector at the side of a tall white mound ahead and it gave out a strong, clear cheeping sound.

"*Got it!*" Sam bawled. "It's here! Did you bring something to dig with, Elio?"

"You won't need to do any digging," said a soft voice from the top of the mound.

Their heads all jerked up to look at the silvery person standing there. It was a woman, as far as they could see. She was not easy to see because she seemed to be made of masses and masses of trailing silvery whiteness. All in silver, Vivian thought, which befits an Age where men create and kill in marvelous ways. She's made of layers of mind suit! Under the silvery layers, Vivian could just pick out what seemed to be a lovely face.

"Are you the Guardian of the Silver Casket?" Sam asked.

"That is right," said the woman. Her voice had a lilt to it, or a trace of a foreign accent. Vivian could just see very red lips move, smilingly, as the Guardian said, "And why do you come seeking me and my Casket two days before the proper time?"

"A thief is trying to steal it, madam," Elio said. His voice sounded forced and scratchy. Vivian was sure he was in a lot of pain. "This will bring about the destruction of Time City and possibly also render all history violently unstable. We therefore think you should take the Casket to the safety of Time City at once, where it will enable us to discover the mechanism of all the other Caskets, particularly the Lead."

Jonathan was shading his eyes with both hands in an effort to see the Guardian. "We need it urgently," he said. "You see, we think the Caskets attract one another, and if they do, the Silver will help us find the Lead before it's too late to do any good.''

"You do not have the Lead Casket?'' said the Guardian. She sounded quite surprised.

"Not yet, madam, but we know it is in Time City,'' Elio said.

"The Lead Casket is in Time City,'' the Guardian declared. Her voice rang out, strong and comforting. "It can be found by using the Silver to attract it. Very well. As you need the Silver so badly, I will break the injunctions that were laid on me and give you the Casket now.'' And to their great relief and surprise, her hand came forward among the floating draperies around her, a long silvery hand, holding a large, shiny, egg-shaped thing. As Elio hobbled awkwardly up the mound and took the Casket, Vivian saw that it was wonderfully ornamented, in lacy shapes. She was rather ashamed that it reminded her so much of an Easter egg.

But she forgot that the next moment. A white flash of movement caught the corner of her eye. She looked around just in time to see a small silvery figure slide along the blue shadow of a nearby ditch and scramble among the hummocks beyond. *"The thief!''* she yelled, and dashed off after him.

As she raced along the ditch and leaped among the hummocks, someone screamed, *"Vivian!''* after her. She took no notice. She had the silver figure in sight now, with the sun glinting off it. The boy was running for his life across the uneven ground, and she knew she could run faster than he could. She had nearly caught him last time. He had somehow got himself a mind suit, but he was not carrying the Iron Casket, and Vivian was sure that this meant he would not be able to escape by time-traveling this time. It's the Caskets that time-travel! she thought, in a surge of understanding. Her frozen feet warmed up, and the cold air hurt in her chest. She shut her mouth and pelted joyfully across the jumbled, pitted ground. The thief glanced around, saw she was gaining, and swerved away desperately.

Then the ground gave way under Vivian. Something the same

color as the white sand tore under her running feet, and then came apart all around her with a soggy ripping noise. She was pitching down into a deep hole. Much to her own surprise, her finger went to the low-weight stud on the belt under the mind suit and pressed it in time to save her from breaking a bone. She went light as she hit the gray rocks at the bottom of the hole, and bounced, and came down again; where she lay staring up at a torn shape of blue sky high above.

"Oh, bother and *damn*!" she said. The thief had tricked her and got away again.

"Are you badly hurt?" someone asked. It was a man's voice, but it was high and quavering and nervous.

Vivian lay quite still and turned her eyes carefully sideways. There was a mind warrior in a silver suit like her own huddled at the other side of the hole. She remembered the man who had fallen screaming out of the raft. I shall pretend to be dead, she decided. Perhaps he'll climb out and go away.

"I ask because I had some skill in healing once," the warrior said in his nervous, fluting voice. When Vivian did not answer, he sighed loudly. "You may not believe this, but I am quite peaceful," he said. "I was a lover of all the arts before these terrible wars began. I painted pictures and made music. I even wrote an epic once."

Vivian went on lying still and tried to let her eyes fall gently shut. I'm dead, she thought. My last word was *damn*!

The warrior sighed again. "Perhaps it will convince you that I am harmless," he said, "if I were to recite you my poem. It is in twelve parts, in the ancient manner, and its title is 'The Silver Sea.' The opening line is 'Mind and the men I sing'—this because it celebrates the great civilizations that once flourished around the shores of this sea. Do you follow me? Shall I recite?"

No! Just go away! Vivian thought.

Rasping footsteps sounded overhead. Elio's veiled face looked down at her through the torn slit overhead. "Miss Vivian?" he said. His voice sounded thick and wobbly.

Vivian sat up with a jerk. And far from trying to kill her, the warrior cringed away against the wall of the hole. "Oh, Elio!" Vivian called. "You've hurt yourself trying to run after me!"

"Are you all right?" Elio called down.

"Yes," she called back. "There's a mind soldier down here, but I think his brain's been hurt in the fight."

This was the wrong thing to say. Elio instantly came floating down on his low-weight function. Even that hurt him. He gasped as he landed and turned to the warrior crouching by the wall. "If you have harmed this young lady, you shall pay," he croaked.

The warrior shook his head and held up both shiny hands. "Not I," he said. "I am an artist and a man of peace. My mind is indeed hurt, but not in any fight."

Elio simply grunted at this and sank down to sit beside Vivian, panting. This seemed to interest the mind warrior. To Vivian's alarm, he left the side of the hole and came crawling cautiously toward Elio. She was very relieved when Sam's voice boomed out overhead. "They're in here." The warrior at once darted back to cringe against the wall again. "Hold on to me," Sam boomed. "Then press the stud and jump."

The slit above went dark. Vivian realized what was happening and scrambled up in time to give Jonathan and Sam a shove as they both came heavily down on Jonathan's overweighted low-weight function. That way they missed Elio and landed in the other side of the pit from the mind warrior.

"Ow!" said Jonathan. "What's *this* now?"

"It's a shelter," Sam told him, "with a warrior in it."

Jonathan made an exasperated noise and pressed his eye function stud. He tried to peer around the pit in spite of its flicker being crisscrossed by an opposite flicker from the mind suit. "I think Elio's much worse than he says," he whispered to Vivian. "Is that warrior fellow safe?"

"He's balmy," Vivian whispered back. "He's the one that fell out of that raft, and I think they got him with their ripples."

"No. I am not that one," said the warrior. He was kneeling halfway across the pit, with his hands spread out in a helpless sort of way. Now he was under the light from the split covering and she could see him clearly, Vivian thought she had never in her life seen a face that was so much like a skull. It was the warrior's real face, too. He did not have a veil to his suit. "That man fell some meters away from here," he said, "and I fear he is dead." His skull of a face turned to Elio. "Forgive me, friend, but you seem badly hurt too. Will you allow me to help you? I was once quite good at healing."

Elio drew himself up proudly against the wall. "Thank you— no," he said. "It is the merest scratch. I shall just catch my breath, and then we shall leave. We have an important errand elsewhere."

The warrior bowed his head politely. "Of course. Forgive me— how big is the scratch?"

"No more than a foot long, and probably only six inches wide," Elio said dismissively. "I cannot think why I allow it to inconvenience me."

Long before he had finished saying this, Sam, Jonathan, and Vivian were shouting, "Oh, *Elio*! That's *serious*!"

"It is?" Elio asked, looked questioningly from them to the warrior.

"Most people would consider that a serious wound," the warrior agreed.

"I did not know!" Elio said. "I have never had my flesh injured before. Perhaps then I have been after all functioning quite well in adversity. Can you repair me, sir?"

"I can try," said the warrior. He crawled forward and stretched a bony silver-covered hand toward the crumpled blue part of Elio's suit. Long before his hand came anywhere near, Elio made a noise that was almost a scream and threw himself away sideways. The warrior crawled after him, reaching out again. As far as Vivian could tell, he never did actually touch Elio. Elio went on making the noise, and she and Jonathan and Sam all rushed to stop the warrior.

"Stop it! You're hurting him!" Vivian cried.

"He's killing him!" Jonathan said.

"He's an enemy! Stop him!" Sam shouted.

Then they all fell quiet and stood still when Elio stood up with the silver egg under one arm. He ran his hand rather wonderingly down his crumpled blue side. He did not look well. His face was shiny with sweat. "That must have been pain," he said. "Thank you, sir. You have given me another experience I have never had before. And the scratch appears to be mended."

"I am afraid I am not able to mend your suit," the warrior said apologetically. He had gone back to his side of the pit, but he was standing up too. They looked at him nervously. He was very tall and almost as thin as a skeleton. "What are you?" he asked Elio. "You are not easy to mend either."

"I am an android," Elio said. He said it as proudly as Jonathan said he was a Lee. "Are you one also? You do not strike me as normal for a human."

"I am not sure," said the warrior. "I think, like you, I was specially made." His skull face turned up toward the torn cover of the pit. He sighed. "It is over," he said. "The woman has gone, and I should go back to my task, the one I was made for. I was designed to be Keeper of Faber John's Silver Casket, if that means anything to you. But I think I have been a poor Keeper."

"You can't be!" Jonathan exclaimed.

"He *is* balmy!" Sam whispered loudly to Vivian.

"I fear," Elio said politely, "that you are under a misapprehension, sir. The Guardian of the Casket is female, and she gave the Casket to me just now. This is it." He took the silver egg from under his arm and showed it to the warrior.

The warrior smiled, a sad grin that made him look more like a skull than ever. He shook his silver head. "That is not the

Casket," he said. "It is not even silver." He came forward and stretched a long, bonelike finger toward the egg. He did not touch it. But one end of it melted and dripped like wax between Elio's fingers. "See?" he said. "Primitive plastic."

Elio peeled silver stuff off his hand and looked at it dubiously. "Are you sure?"

"Open the thing," said the warrior.

Elio took hold of the egg in both hands and pulled it into two halves. He held the halves dumbly out to the rest of them. "What does it say?" Jonathan asked, peering at them.

"On one half," Elio said disgustedly, "there is the legend 'A Present from Easter Island.' On the other there is written 'Made in Korea 2339,' which I take to be the place and date of its origin. We must go back to that female and show her we are aware she has tricked us."

"She has gone," the warrior said desolately.

"We will see about that," Elio said. "I do not like to be tricked. And, if you are in truth the Keeper of the Silver, sir, then this female must be a born-human. Would you say she was?"

"I think so," said the warrior. "But she wore many mind veils to make me the more helpless against her, and it was hard to tell."

"That's the one!" said Jonathan. "Of course, they were layers of mind suit, now that I'm thinking straight!"

It looked as if Elio were having another new experience and getting angry. "I have my honor as an android to consider," he said. "We are not *supposed* to be fooled by ordinary humans! Let us get out of this hole." He threw the two halves of the plastic egg down and leaped for the edge of the pit without bothering to turn on his low-weight function. There was much flabby rending of the stuff that covered the hole. They were dazzled by daylight. "One of you catch hold of my hand," Elio called down from the glare.

Vivian boosted Sam up the wall of the pit. Elio caught hold of one of Sam's waving arms and pulled him out with no trouble at all. Vivian and Jonathan turned on their low-weight functions, and Elio pulled them out just as easily. Vivian could hardly see at first. Elio set off across the glaring ground so fast that she had trouble catching him up. As for Jonathan, his eye function went dark again, and he floundered about, trying to turn it off and keep up with the rest of them while he did.

"We're going wrong," Sam was puffing, as Vivian came panting up beside Elio. "The mound was over there."

Vivian could see by then. She looked around the jumble of blue shadows until she saw one she thought she recognized. "No, it's over there," she said pointing the opposite way to Sam. "I remember that ditch—oh, no, that's not right! Maybe it was that one."

They stared around the confusing desert. It all looked the same. Elio cried out, "We are lost! I got turned around in my weakness! I have no memory of the spot at all!" He banged his own head violently with the time control. "I am a failure!"

"You were hurt," Vivian pointed out.

"What use is an android who cannot function when hurt?" Elio demanded, and hit his head again.

Luckily, since they were beginning to find Elio quite alarming, the warrior came up behind them just then, courteously helping Jonathan along. At least, he seemed to be helping Jonathan, but Vivian noticed that whenever he put out his long, glistening hand to help Jonathan over a hummock or across a ditch, that hand did not really touch Jonathan. Yet Jonathan behaved as if someone was firmly supporting his elbow. He kept saying, "Thanks," and "That's kind of you," and "You needn't!" in the bothered way you do when someone is giving you help you wish you didn't need.

This made Vivian sure all of a sudden that the warrior really was the Keeper of the Silver. The sunlight flashed gently off his long silver body, making it hard to see whether or not he had the same spread-thin look as the Iron Guardian. He seemed as solid as the Watcher of the Gold. But the silver body was not a mind suit. His bare, skull-like face was silvery too.

As the two came up, Vivian could see Jonathan was as upset as Elio. "The place is over here," the Keeper said in his gentle, fluting voice. "Come quickly and quietly. The era was very disturbed for some time before that woman arrived. It will certainly have gone critical now. There will be enemies about."

At this, Elio pulled himself together enough to look carefully around the empty blue sky. Vivian and Sam turned to stare nervously over their shoulders at almost every step. Those rafts flew so quietly.

"Who *was* that woman?" Jonathan burst out as the Keeper urged him along.

"I have no idea," said the Keeper. "All I know is that she had the aura of time travel about her, as you four do, and she knew about the Caskets. When she and the child appeared, I therefore greeted them politely, just as I greeted you. I told you I am civilized. My ways are peaceful. But she rudely demanded the Silver Casket. 'We need it,' she said, 'to take possession of Time City.' Of course, I refused. I pointed out that I would be bringing the Casket to Time City shortly in the natural course of things and she might have it then. She laughed. 'But we want it now,' she said. 'We want to be ready when the city is standing still with its defenses down.' And when I refused to let her have it, she took the Iron Casket from under her veiling."

"I bet she was the thief's mother," Sam said.

"Whoever she was, she knew the properties of the Caskets," the Keeper said sadly. "They respond to the will of the one who holds them. Iron is weaker than my Silver, but she was protected by veiling, and she turned her will on me before I was aware. 'Go and crouch in a hole over there,' she said, 'and don't dare come out until we've gone!' And that I was forced to do. I told you I was hurt in my mind. Here is the mound."

The mound looked like any of the others, although Vivian thought she recognized the wide blue ditch beyond it for the ditch where the boy had hidden. The Keeper led them swiftly around the other side of it.

They all stood and stared miserably. A hole had been hacked in the white side of the mound. In deep bluish shadow inside the hole there was a square space beautifully lined with shiny, feathery stuff. In the middle of the feathery stuff was a large egg-shaped hollow, quite empty. Another wad of the feathery stuff was blowing around the side of the mound where the thieves had thrown it. The Silver Keeper sadly picked the wad up and floated it between his hands back into the hole. "They have taken the Casket," he said.

"The green *rats*!" said Sam. "I found that Casket for them with the metal detector!"

"They were waiting for us to find it for them!" Jonathan said bitterly. "It's all my fault for telling Leon Hardy so much!"

At that, Elio had another burst of despair. "I have been most horribly unintelligent!" he cried out. "I am like a goose, given a china egg to sit upon! I deserve to be recycled!"

Vivian looked at the tall Silver Keeper drooping desolately beside her. "I'm sorry," she said. She knew she had made the worst mistake of all when she let the boy decoy her away from the mound. He had been waiting in the ditch, listening for the right moment to show himself.

"There is no further use for me," the Keeper said.

Sam was angry, and being the kind of boy he was, he expressed his anger in a perfect roar. "I WANT TO GET BACK AT THEM!" he bellowed.

"Oh, hush!" Elio said distractedly. "That could fetch mind warriors."

But it already had. The booming echoes of Sam's voice were mixed almost at once with the thud and crunch of boots. Warriors in filmy mind suits sprang out of trenches on two sides of them.

More came leaping across the top of the mound. Before the echoes of Sam's roar had finished rolling out across the glaring plain, the warriors had them surrounded. Shiny boots covered with film trampled the ground on all sides, and things that were certainly guns pointed at them.

"This is it," one of the warriors said. "We've got the disturbance all right. Take them in."

Elio looked around and saw there were too many warriors to fight. He put his hands in the air.

"That's right. That's sensible," a warrior said in a woman's voice. "Hands in the air, all of you."

The filmy warriors closed in. Vivian's upheld arms were seized. She lost sight of the others as she was hustled toward one of the trenches. But she had three separate glimpses of warriors grabbing for the Silver Keeper, and then grabbing again, and each time the Silver Keeper, in his untouchable way, went sliding out from between the grabbing hands.

"Something queer about that one!" Vivian heard a warrior say breathlessly as she was hurried along among a mass of filmy bodies. "Can't keep hold of it, have to let it go!"

"It seems to be coming along anyway," another warrior said. "Don't take your eyes off it."

Something was queer, Vivian thought, being dragged headlong toward a trench. Something queer about those boots. I've seen something like those boots before! Then the boots jumped with her into the trench, and she had a moment of sheer terror when the trench was suddenly not there anymore.

V ivian's feet and the boots around her landed with a *clang* on metal floor. She was pulled briskly forward onto a floor which was a hard grayish white, into light that was much easier on the eyes than the glare of the Age of Silver. The floor seemed to be marble, and it was shaking. But she could not see much more because her eyes were burning and watering from the brightness of the Baltic Plain. Mostly she noticed the warmth. Sweat broke out on her, and then she started to shiver, as if her body had only just noticed how cold it had been.

"Expedition Three reporting back from Sixty-four Century Baltic, sir," said one of the mind-suited people ahead of her. "We found the disturbance. I'm afraid you're not going to like this, sir."

A hand expertly twitched at the film over Vivian's face. She blinked hard as her suit there ripped away. The blurry place around her cleared into the great front hall of Time Patrol Building. There were the stone stairs softly rumbling up and down. There was the circular kiosk in the middle, with a curving row of busy time booths beyond. There was an identical curve of shiny booths behind her too, and a row of men and women dressed in Golden Age armor were filing into one over to the left. Through the great glass doors she could see Aeon Square and a rank of brightly robed people carrying banners. Evidently there was a ceremony going on, in what looked like early-morning light. And as if that was not enough to make Vivian's heart go thumping down into her stomach, Mr. Donegal was standing in front of her, looking very grim indeed.

"I don't know what you lot thought you were doing," he said, looking from her, to Elio, to Jonathan and on to Sam. "You realize you've broken half the laws there are *and* sent history into convulsions, do you? It won't be only a hiding this time!" he said to Sam. Sam stared at his father out of red-rimmed, runny eyes and plainly could not think of a word to say. Mr. Donegal turned to Elio. "I'm not only surprised at you," he said. "I'm astonished, Elio! I thought you had more sense than the rest of Time City put together, and now here you are gadding about in an Unstable Era and leading a parcel of children astray with you."

Elio's eyes were red from the Baltic glare too. He was pale with his despair. "I beg your forgiveness," he said stiffly. "We had evidence that thieves were stealing the city's polarities and we were trying to prevent them. We failed. This is the reason for convulsions in history. Two polarities are now missing."

Mr. Donegal did not believe a word of this. "Then why didn't you report it to Time Patrol?" he said over his shoulder as he turned to Jonathan. "As for you, Jonathan," he said, "I don't know what your father's going to say to you! Do you *know* you've been missing since yesterday afternoon? Jenny and Ramona have been worried sick!"

"No, I didn't know!" Jonathan said, blinking under his eye flicker. His eyes were not as red as Sam's or Elio's, which made him look much calmer than he really was. "If we *have* been missing, then it's Time Patrol's fault. Your people brought us back to *now*. If they'd left us alone, we'd have been back yesterday."

"That's enough!" Mr. Donegal said. "You don't stand there and cheek me, son, not after all the trouble you've caused!" He turned to one of the Patrollers who had brought them back. "Go and tell the Sempitern we've found them," he said. To the rest of the squad he said, "You two take this lot over by the kiosk out of the way. Make sure they don't stir a foot until I've time to deal with them. All the rest of you get out of mind suits and into Thirty-eight Century gas coats. We've six Observers stuck in a war in Paris then." He turned and glared at Elio. "I'm having to recall every single Observer because of you! The whole of history's gone critical overnight, thanks to this caper of yours! I hope Chronologue orders you all shot!" With that, he swung away and went off toward the moving stairs at a rolling run.

"Come along," said a Patroller next to Vivian. She and Elio were pushed through the busy crowd to the kiosk. Jonathan and Sam were brought there by another Patroller. The others, in a great clatter of boots, raced off toward the back of the building.

Ow! Vivian thought. We *are* in trouble! She watched the shiny mind suit of the Patroller who had been sent to tell the Sempitern. He was forcing his way among other Patrollers in every imaginable kind of costume, and he was almost at the door. Vivian just could not think what Sempitern Walker was going to say. And I've caused Jenny such worry, and now she's going to find out I'm not even her niece! she thought.

As the mind-suited messenger reached the glass door, it wafted open in front of him. The messenger dodged. A long-legged figure in a floppy hat pranced past him into the building.

"Not again!" said one of the Patrollers guarding them. "That thing's been in and out of here half the night!"

"And all this morning," said the other Patroller. "It's only some student's idea of a joke. Take no notice."

The two of them turned their backs and watched Elio sternly. Vivian, Sam, and Jonathan watched the Iron Guardian. He went prancing questingly this way and that among people who were all firmly ignoring him, until he suddenly halted and seemed to listen. A huge smile spread on his face, and he bounded unerringly for a clear space near the doors. The Silver Keeper appeared there out of nowhere. The two flung their arms around each other. Then they stepped back and stared at each other. The Iron Guardian shook his head sadly. The Silver Keeper, even more sadly, shook his. And both of them slowly faded out of sight, leaving two long, thin eye blots in the space near the door.

"Poor things," said Vivian. "Neither of them knows what to do."

"They aren't the only ones," said Jonathan.

Outside, the ceremony was still going on. It was clear that Sempitern Walker was not going to arrive until it was over. There was no sign of Mr. Donegal either. They stood for some time, deserted and guilty, with the two Patrollers looming beside them, watching time locks open and shut almost continuously and listening to the operators in the kiosk handle emergency after emergency.

"Ten-oh-two morning, Time Patrol here," said the lady operator nearest to Vivian. "I have you located, Observer, in A.D. 79. Volcano in violent eruption above Pompeii. Use breathing apparatus and insulated clothing, Observer, and I'll get someone to you as soon as possible."

Almost at the same time, the man next to her was saying, "Yes, I locate you, Observer. Year 9892. Woman crossing forest with child in Sixty Century clothing. Can you hold the bandits off long enough to make a further report? This could be serious. No? Then I'll reroute the squad in Ninety-three to come to your aid right away."

Meanwhile, Patrollers streamed down the stairs wearing wetsuits, kilts, loose robes, ponchos, trousers with hoops in the legs, in brief shorts or in so many clothes they could hardly be seen, and in a hundred other costumes. They hurried to time booths, went in, and seemed to come back the next second looking tired out, helping other people in the same kind of clothes. Some of the people they helped were in a bad way. They were muddy, their clothes were torn, some had a wild look, and others were bleeding. A man in hooped trousers was streaming blood from a cut on his head. These people were handed over to a medical squad waiting to take care of them, while the Patrollers joined a draggled line of costumed figures going up the ascending half of the stone stairs.

"They really are recalling all the Observers," Sam said,

watching the man with the bleeding head being helped onto a floating stretcher.

"Dug in beside the French rocket station," the lady in the kiosk was now saying. "Patrol is on its way, Observer. Use ultraviolet flares to identify yourself."

"Have you a cell to yourself in the prison?" asked an operator on the other side of her.

"Unforeseen revolution in Canada," said another. "Control yourself, Observer. Someone can still get to you even if the time booth in Montreal *is* being bombed."

"Ship on fire attacked by Dutch aircraft," said another voice.

"Posing as a refugee," said the nearest man. "That should enable you to get through the Icelandic battle line, Observer, and someone will meet you outside Tübingen."

"Patrol Medical now thinks the plague is being carried by horses," said someone farther off, and her voice was drowned by a nearer one saying loudly, "Yes, Observer, but all history has gone critical. If the riots have not yet reached Cardiff, you will have to wait an hour or so."

Elio hung his head wretchedly. "This is all my fault," he said, "for allowing that woman to dupe me."

"It's my fault just as much," said Jonathan. "I messed things up twice in Twenty Century. If only I could go back and put things *right*!"

"I wish you could too," Vivian said. "I might have a chance of going home then."

They stood for a while in silence except for Sam's breathing, listening to the Patrollers in the kiosk dealing with a rescue team attacked by germ bombs in Forty-two Century, a flood in Eighty Century Africa, wars in every era, and an Observer trapped on a hijacked spaceship in 12648. This Observer caught the attention of the two Patrollers guarding them. He or she was obviously a friend of theirs. Both of them put their elbows on the ledge of the kiosk to listen to what the lady inside was saying.

"It's not so easy to get a team into space," one said.

"Too right," said the other. "Kim Yo may be stuck there."

Sam's eyes swiveled toward them. When he saw they were not paying attention to him, he whispered breathily to Jonathan, "We *could* put it right. If we went back to that station, we can catch the thief when he goes up to that warty woman. Then we could bring him back here and show my dad."

"You know, we *could*!" Vivian whispered.

Elio ripped back the mind suit from his hand and slipped the egg control into Jonathan's. "This works in a modern time lock," he murmured. "Get into one that is open and use it, while I make a diversion."

"You come too, V.S.," Jonathan whispered. "It'll take two to hold him."

"*And* ME!" Sam said, in such a fierce, breathy whisper that both Patrollers turned around to look at him. "I'm hungry, too," Sam said hastily.

They were not quite fooled. "Too bad, son," one of them said, and neither of them turned back to the kiosk. Everyone stood helplessly. Jonathan tried to hold the egg control out of sight beside his leg.

"Observer Kim Yo," the lady said in the kiosk, "are you receiving us? Good. Operations has come up with a plan for you to overpower the hijackers." The Patrollers heard her. Both of them turned eagerly back to the kiosk.

Elio instantly went berserk.

One moment he was standing beside the kiosk. The next, he was a blur in a mind suit, zigzagging among the people in the hall. *"Shoot me!"* his voice rang out. *"Shoot me! I am a failure!"* He was going so fast that his voice seemed to come from several places at once. As Vivian raced for the semicircle of time booths, she could see at least two Patrollers with raised guns, uncertainly trying to aim where they thought Elio was going to be next. *"I deserve to be shot!"* Elio shouted. He leaped onto the moving stairs and raced up the half that was moving downward, weaving around startled people in costumes, who were all far too surprised even to try to stop him. *"Shoot me!"* he yelled.

"Elio, don't be a fool!" Mr. Donegal shouted from somewhere in the middle of the hall. "You're much too valuable to shoot!"

This was the last Vivian saw of the diversion, because someone behind her shouted too, and she had a glimpse of a crowd of Patrollers running after her, hard. By this time Jonathan had nearly reached the time booths. Vivian set her teeth and pelted to catch him up. Home! she thought. If they don't catch me, I shall be home!

Sam was somehow keeping up with her, though his face was purple and he was puffing like a train. A time booth chanced to open just as Jonathan reached the semicircle. They charged into it. The three Observers who were in it hastily bundled themselves and their baggage clear. Vivian supposed that they bundled themselves out of the booth, since they did not get carried into 1939 when Jonathan used the control. Jonathan just kept running and shouted to the time egg as he ran. And all three of them were suddenly running along an empty platform in a station that seemed to be deserted.

Vivian's first thought was, How dingy and dirty it is—and how it smells! Then, as she slowed down, her second thought was, Where *is* everybody? Beside her, Sam crouched down, coughing for breath, and Jonathan stood and stared. There were no adults waiting to meet the train, no sign of Cousin Marty, no evacuees, and no train either.

"What's wrong?" said Vivian.

"History's gone critical," said Jonathan. "We ought to have thought. It's all changed. But my father and the other people from Chronologue must be here somewhere, because they *did* come here. And I told the egg to get us here a moment before the train comes in, so there's got to be a train, too."

"Let's ask," said Vivian.

So, quite forgetting the way they were all dressed, they hauled Sam to his feet and hurried up the platform to the exit. A surprised porter stood there, staring at them through a transparent face piece under his peaked hood. Vivian could tell he was a porter because his uniform was navy blue, but it was a strange bulky allover suit with navy blue gloves to it. "Please, is there going to be an evacuee train?" Vivian asked breathlessly.

"Due any moment," said the porter. His voice came out of a transparent grid on the front of his mask. Behind the mask, his eyes wonderingly looked at Jonathan's pigtail embalmed in Jonathan's mind suit and then went to the flicker over Jonathan's eyes. "Is this the new issue protective clothing then?" he said.

"The very latest Government issue," Vivian said hastily. "Where are all the other people meeting the train?"

"Down in the bunker in the forecourt, of course," said the porter, "where you should be too. But you might as well stay as you're all suited up. Stand well back. Over there." While they were obediently backing toward the waiting room, he looked sideways at them. A chuckle came out of his mask. "What will the Government dream up next?" he said. "That rig makes you look as if you come from heaven. Could have put in a halo or so while they were at it, though!"

Bunkers? Vivian thought. Protective clothing? This war has gotten very strange! But the railway lines still looked like railway lines. And a train *was* coming. She could hear the metal rails thrumming with the train moving on them.

"Just coming!" the porter called over to them.

Almost as soon as he said it, the train was there. It came in a sort of yelling thunder that had Vivian covering her ears. It was no steam train, and there was no smell and no smoke. It was a huge dark green pointed monster. As the engine howled past and stopped some way down the platform, Vivian caught sight of red letters on it against a white background: RADIOACTIVE FUEL KEEP CLEAR. She stared bemusedly at rows of hooded windows rattling by.

"Oh no!" said Jonathan, and pointed down the platform.

Time Patrol had traced them. The Patrollers who had chased them to the time booths were appearing near the engine in twos and threes. Most of them had been in too much haste to put on Twenty Century costume. Probably history was changing so fast now that they had not had time. Two of them were in mind suits and two more in hooped skirts. Vivian saw short kilts, gauzy robes, Patrol uniforms, and a person in red feathers. But there was no time to do anything about it. A recorded voice spoke overhead, and all the train's hooded doors opened at once as if they were mechanically controlled. Evacuees came pouring out, hundreds of them.

Sam, Jonathan, and Vivian were instantly surrounded in a horde of milling children. The world seemed nothing but gray shorts, school blazers, plastic boxes labeled RADIATION SUIT WAR OFFICE ISSUE, striped caps, gym tunics, pale faces, straw hats, labels, thin legs, and shrill London voices. At the other end of the platform, the Patrollers were fighting through the throng toward them. But more and more evacuees kept coming off the train, pushing them backward. The green monster must have held twice as many children as the train Vivian remembered.

Don't we all look sickly! Vivian thought, as she searched frantically in the swelling crowd for the face of the boy thief. She caught a glimpse of her own face in the distance under a blue felt hat, looking pale and worried, and she supposed Jonathan's former self must have been there too, but she did not see him. And nowhere could she see the thin, ratlike face of the thief. "We're never going to find him in all these!" she shouted to Jonathan.

"We *must*!" Jonathan shouted back. "Keep looki— Great Time! What's *that*?"

It was a noise like the sky tearing apart. It made the thunder of the train sound puny. Vivian looked up to see where it was coming from and saw a great dark thing diving from the sky toward the train. She never saw it clearly. All she knew was that it came down at the train and then screamed up over the station out of sight, tearing the sky open as it went. It left the train on fire. Flames leaped high, instantly and fiercely. The glass in the hooded windows went *spung* and fell out onto the platform, and clouds of dark yellow smoke rolled over everything, smelling sharp and choking. There was a lot of screaming. A siren started off somewhere and yowled up and down the scale like a hoarse and seasick cat. The porter was bellowing too.

"Get back! Get clear! Everybody get clear before the engine blows!"

"Back to the city!" Jonathan screamed. "We'll have to get back!" He seized Sam by the arm and dragged him down the platform among the murk and flames and milling children, coughing and shouting instructions to the time egg as he went. But it was clear that the egg was only going to work somewhere near the place where they had arrived. Vivian got behind Sam and pushed. They fought their way down the platform for a nightmare age, and like a nightmare, Vivian saw another set of their former selves calmly walking the other way: Sam in a striped cap and huge boots, herself with a shrunk navy cardigan not quite hiding violet and yellow stripes, and Jonathan loftily stepping out with a thing like a gas mask box on his shoulder. But they'll get killed! she thought, as the three people vanished into the yellow smoke.

"Come on! This way!" Jonathan shouted while she was trying to see where the three went.

Ahead of them, the Patrollers were shouting too. "This way! This way! Get back before that thing blows!"

Most of the evacuees began to run toward the Patrollers' shouts. They thought they were being told to go that way. This made it much easier for Jonathan to drag Sam along and for Vivian to push him. For a long moment, they were all running and running, part of a gray mob in the thick smoke. Then the time egg worked. They were rushing forward into the hall of Time Patrol, coughing, frightened, their mind suits dingy from the smoke, with the sound of some kind of explosion hammering in their ears.

"Come here, you three!" Mr. Donegal shouted at them. His

voice seemed thin and far away compared with the sounds they had just been hearing. He was beckoning angrily from beside the kiosk. Elio was standing there between two Patrollers. His head was hanging, and he looked so dejected that Vivian was fairly sure that the diversion had been a demonstration of Elio's true feelings.

"We've made things worse again," Sam said as they trudged toward the kiosk.

"Cor!" said a high London voice from behind them. "I didn't know it looked like *this* out in the country! Take a look at that dirty great escalator!"

All three of them jumped and turned around. An evacuee boy had come out of the booth behind them and was staring at the moving stairs. Beside him, his smaller sister was pointing at Sam. "Are you sure we ain't in Hevving?" she said doubtfully. "Them lot look like angels." As she said it, she was pushed aside by a crowd of other evacuees who were fighting to get out of the booth behind her. More evacuees were pushing out of the next booth along. In fact, now they looked, every single time booth in the semicircle was open, and evacuees were flooding out of them all, pausing to gape at the hall, and then being pushed forward by others crowding out behind.

"I think we've only made things about a hundred times worse," Jonathan said, as the Patroller in red feathers struggled out of a booth in the distance among a mob of little girls in blazers.

By now a klaxon was sounding from the kiosk—a sort of gentle *crake-crake* that sounded very mild after the siren at the station. "Time booth misfunction," announced a mechanical voice. "Time booth misfunction. Everyone stand clear except for armed personnel and medical teams."

Mr. Donegal came striding over. "Look what you've done *now*!" he shouted. "I shall larrup the lot of you for this!"

"That's not fair," said Sam. "Those children would be dead if we hadn't been there. Their train blew up."

"What's that got to do with it? These children are *history*!"

Mr. Donegal shouted, waving his arm around the crowding evacuees. All of them heard him. They stood and looked at him wonderingly.

"Is he an Air Raid Warden?" one of them asked.

Vivian found herself shouting back at Mr. Donegal, "They are *not* history! They're real people! You people in Time City make me *sick* the way you sit here studying things. You never raise a finger to *help* anyone! This is all Time City's fault anyway! It was *you* that tinkered with history. And now it's gone critical, and people like these kids are getting hurt all over time, and all *you* think about is getting your beastly Observers out!"

"What do you expect me to do about that?" Mr. Donegal roared back. "There must be over five hundred damn children here!"

The evacuees were now in a ring all around them, staring and listening, but Vivian was too angry to feel shy. "Then look *after* them!" she screamed in Mr. Donegal's face. "You've got things in Time City to help the whole human race! It won't hurt you to help just these few. There are far too few children in this city anyway. It's a disgrace!"

Mr. Donegal's hand went up to hit her. Vivian winced and waited. But before his hand came down, a great voice shouted, "Bravo!" Mr. Donegal stepped back, looking rather deflated, and Vivian looked up to find Dr. Wilander towering over her in his shabby purple gown. His clever little eyes were laughing at her as usual, but she could tell that he was on her side.

"He must be the vicar," one of the evacuees told a friend. "And the others must be bishops and things," he added, as Sempitern Walker came up beside Dr. Wilander and gave Vivian a truly agonized stare from under a flat silver hat. She could see they had both come straight from the ceremony.

The Patroller in red feathers pushed up beside Mr. Donegal. "Sir, I'm sorry about all this. An explosion in history seems to have blown all the time booths open, and now they've stopped working—"

"Then we can take it that Time City has gone critical like the rest of history," Dr. Wilander said. "Come with me and help organize something for these children." He took hold of the Patroller by one feathered shoulder and pushed her in front of him as he limped away, booming, "Come with me. All you children, come with me." Most of the evacuees obediently followed, so that Dr. Wilander and the Patroller departed in a crowd of children, like two ill-assorted Pied Pipers. But a number of evacuees remained, staring.

"Some people are lucky, having their mums to meet them," one of them said wistfully.

This was because Jenny and Ramona, both in robes from the ceremony, had arrived with the Sempitern. Ramona was hugging Sam, then shaking him, then hugging him again. Jenny had her arms wrapped around Jonathan. "We've been so worried!" she kept saying. Vivian looked up to find Jonathan giving her a shamed look over Jenny's shoulder. She thought it was because he was being hugged, until he said, "You were quite right about Time City. We never help anyone."

Then the blow fell. Mr. Donegal pushed his way through to them in quite a different mood, smiling widely. "Ramona! Jenny! Look who's here!" He brought with him three smiling people. They were the three Observers who had been in the time booth when Jonathan had rushed through it to 1939. The man was tall, with the same eyefolds as Jonathan, Jenny, and Sam, and he wore a baggy tweed suit and carried a fedora. The woman was in a square-shouldered dress. Her lipstick was a very bright red, and she had her fair hair in a contraption that was not unlike Vivian's string bag. Vivian knew it was very fashionable, and she found it quite hideous—though not as hideous as the girl's short, puffed sleeves and shiny, ankle-strap shoes. "Viv and Inga Lee!" Mr. Donegal said. "They got here at last! Sam, this is your cousin Vivian."

Vivian backed quietly away, through the watching evacuees,

hoping they would hide her. She did not know what to do. The circle of time booths was standing empty and open on both sides of the hall, and she could see they had stopped working, just as the Patroller with red feathers had said. She thought Dr. Wilander might have helped her, but she could not see him anywhere in the hall. She looked for Elio and saw him being led away by two Patrollers. The Lees were laughing and being embraced and welcomed by the rest of their family, but it was only going to be moments before someone turned toward Vivian and asked, "Then who is *she*?"

But it was worse than that. She knew the face of the man whom Jenny was hugging so delightedly. It had looked out at her from a helmet when he had tried to kill Jonathan in the Golden Age. Sempitern Walker was clasping the woman's hand, and Vivian knew it was the same hand that had passed them the plastic egg in the Age of Silver. She remembered that color lipstick under the layers of mind suit. As for the girl Ramona was kissing, Vivian thought she would know that face anywhere. Though it was wreathed in smiles, with a big baby blue bow in the hair above it, she could remember it vividly, glaring like a cornered rat, when Jonathan tried to rescue the Iron Casket. She wondered what the Lees had been doing since they got out of that time booth so hurriedly. Getting their bearings and waiting for the right moment, she supposed.

Jonathan and Sam had recognized the thieves too. Sam, being the smallest, ducked out of the hugging and hand clasping almost at once and edged through to Vivian. They stared at each other. There seemed nothing to say. A moment later, Jonathan slithered away from beside his uncle. He was white. "I don't believe this!" he whispered. "Do you think perhaps they did it for the sake of Time City after all?"

"No!" Vivian and Sam said together.

As they said it, the whole group—Mr. Donegal, Sempitern Walker, Jenny, Ramona, and all three Lees—turned and came smilingly toward them. Vivian braced herself. Sam and Jonathan took deep breaths.

"You three," said Jenny. "Can you take the Lees for a walk around the City? They want to get used to it all again, and we've all got such a lot to do."

Nobody seemed to wonder who Vivian was. She stared at Jenny and at the smiling Lees. It was like not getting smacked when you richly deserved it, she thought—or worse. It was all wrong. "What? Now?" Jonathan said.

"Yes, but be sure to bring them to the palace for lunch," Jenny said.

"I'm not going," said Sam.

"Oh, come on. Of course you are," Mr. Lee said, smilingly waving his fedora at Sam.

And there they all were, not quite knowing how, walking with the Lees across the busy hall and out through the glass doors, while Sam's parents and Jonathan's cheerfully waved them off from beside the kiosk.

As they stepped out into Aeon Square, Mr. Lee laughed. "That was easy!" he said. "I hadn't realized the Silver Casket was so powerful. They were eating out of my hand in seconds!" He gestured with his hat again, and silver flashed from inside it.

Inga Lee patted her square white handbag. "The Iron Casket helps it, I think." She had the slightly foreign accent Vivian remembered from the Age of Silver. "You should have seen that Silver Keeper react when I turned it on him!"

"Wasn't that fun!" Cousin Vivian said, skipping along beside them. "I do think I was clever, finding that silver egg to trick them with! And you did it beautifully, Mummy! I loved the way you got them to tell you all the things we wanted to know!" She stopped skipping. "The ground *is* shaking, isn't it?" she said. "Let's go and see how Faber John's Stone's getting on. I want to see if the Lee Documents were right about that too."

The ground was indeed shaking, much harder than it had been before, making Aeon Square strange to walk on. There was a grinding feeling coming from below somewhere. But this did not bother Vivian nearly so much as the way the three Lees behaved as if she and Jonathan and Sam were not there at all. As they crossed the square, walking briskly toward Faber John's Stone, Vivian tried to call out to a group of tourists who were hurrying past quite near. She found she could not. She could not seem to do anything but walk after the Lees. It was frightening.

There were very few people about in the square anyway, which was odd, considering that a ceremony had just been held there. There was only a scattering of tourists, and all of them were hurrying in the same direction, toward the Avenue of the Four Ages.

Vivian could see a few people in robes or city pajamas in the distance, but they were all hurrying away too. Almost the only people who were not hurrying were some little groups of evacuees who had somehow escaped Dr. Wilander's efforts to organize them. The Lees walked past more than one bunch of dingy little figures carrying plastic boxes labeled WAR OFFICE.

"This looks just like Hollywood!" Vivian heard one say.

The next group was arguing. "I tell you this ain't the country!" Vivian heard. "There ain't no bleeding cows!"

"Don't be stupid!" another said scornfully. "We're still in the bleeding station. It's the trains what's shaking the ground!"

"A big posh station then," a third said dubiously.

Even if Vivian had been able to call out to them, she did not think they would have been much help. By the time the Lees reached Faber John's Stone, she was very scared indeed. Sam was biting his lip, and Jonathan was whiter than ever.

The stone was a mass of tiny pieces. It was like some of the graves Vivian remembered in Lewisham churchyard, neatly spread with little chips of marble. The Lees looked at it with great satisfaction.

"It really has broken up!" Cousin Vivian said delightedly. "The Lee Documents were quite right, Daddy!"

"Yes," said Mr. Lee. "This has to mean that the city's only an hour or so from the end. We timed it right in spite of the muddles."

"We timed it perfectly, my love," said Inga Lee. "You weren't to know that they'd go to the Age of Gold first. Time travel is so confusing."

"I love time traveling!" Cousin Vivian said, skipping around Faber John's Stone. "It was fun fooling that po-faced Iron Guardian by hopping in and out of the Lee time lock with Leon Hardy. Then, when he caught on to it, I went there by train instead! You should have seen that terrible warty woman's face when I told her what I thought of her!"

"Let's get to the Gnomon," said Mr. Lee.

They set off briskly again, toward Continuum, and Vivian, Sam, and Jonathan were forced to trudge through the loose chippings of the stone and follow. Inga Lee glanced back at Time Patrol Building a little nervously. "No one following," she said. "We took a risk, coming through a Patrol lock."

"It was worth it," said Mr. Lee. "We needed our hostage."

Aeon Square was almost deserted when they came to Continuum. Mr. Lee looked up at its towers with what seemed to be real affection and then across to the twin domes of Science. Cousin Vivian came skipping back.

"There's funny lopsided old Perpetuum!" she said excitedly. "I remember it ever so well!"

Her father looked up at Perpetuum with the grim look he had had in the Age of Gold. "The most useful place in Time City," he said. "I intended to keep all that knowledge under lock and key. The Fixed Eras are going to have to pay a realistic price for anything they want to know from now on. And I'm going to throw that fool Enkian out into history. I'll keep Wilander and put him in charge. I want Wilander to suffer. He was the one who gave me that lousy low report and got me stuck in history as an Observer."

"You told me, my love," said Inga Lee. "Just hand him over to me."

"And me," said their daughter. "I hate him too. He told me I was a silly little girl."

She was skipping ahead to the steps that led to the Avenue of the Four Ages, where she began pointing excitedly to the right. When Vivian came up behind Mr. Lee, obedient to the Silver Casket in his hat, she found the Avenue crowded. Tourists and Time City people were hastening from both ends toward the arches that led to the river. Long lines of city people were waiting at the arches where you could hire boats, and all of these were carrying bundles and bags. Out in the country, where the River Time wound through the fields, Vivian could see the footpaths along its banks dotted with hurrying figures, all going the same way, toward the time locks up the river. It was not exactly a panic. But Vivian thought of the time ghosts they had seen beating at the locks, and she knew it soon would be. Most of those people were going to arrive to find that the locks had stopped working.

Cousin Vivian was pointing over the heads of the crowds. "What's that beautiful place with the blue glass dome?" she said.

"Millennium, dear," said her mother.

"Oh, do let's live in it when we've got the city!" Cousin Vivian said.

Her father looked rather taken aback. "I'll think about it," he said.

"Oh, *please* let's, Daddy!" his daughter said, snuggling up to him as they all went down the steps. "After all, Mummy's an Icelandic Emperor's daughter, and *we're* both Lees. The Annuate isn't really grand at all."

"We haven't taken over the city yet," Mr. Lee said, laughing, as he turned left toward the Gnomon. "But I'll see."

The walk along the Avenue was hard going. Everybody else was hurrying the opposite way. The Lees threaded their way through them easily enough, but they did not bother to find a path that gave room for Jonathan, Vivian, and Sam. They were continually bumped and jostled, and often there was no way they could dodge the people hurrying toward them. And the shaking of the ground seemed worse here. The lacy metal arches were vibrating, giving an unpleasant blurred feeling when they had to walk under them. Inga Lee kept glancing over her shoulder at something that seemed to be behind Vivian. She was so obviously nervous that Vivian began to feel hopeful. By bumping sideways into a fat woman hurrying the other way, Vivian managed to get herself turned half around, before the power of the Silver Casket pulled her straight again.

The Iron Guardian and the Silver Keeper were gliding among

the people side by side, a few yards behind her. The Iron Guardian's long face was sober. The Silver Keeper's skull face looked grim and sad. Vivian did not wonder that Inga Lee was nervous of them, but she did not think they were going to be any more help than the evacuees.

"Take no notice," Mr. Lee said soothingly. "They're probably forced to follow wherever the Caskets go."

They came to Endless Hill and climbed the steps, to and fro, between the ornate balustrades. Every time the steps turned, Vivian caught a glimpse of a silver figure and a drab one, following behind on long, silent feet. Oh, please let them do something to stop the Lees! she prayed.

But whey they turned into the last flight, with the tower straight above, the two Guardians simply stopped on the landing below the stairs. Vivian saw them standing there, side by side, by imitating Sam, who had found a way of looking behind under his own arm. Her heart sank.

Mr. Lee gave a loud, joyous laugh which showed he had been as nervous as his wife. "You see?"he said. "They're quite helpless!" He looked irritably up at the Gnomon, standing like a lighthouse, with sky showing through the windows and sunlight dazzling off the midday bell in the pagoda at the top. "Where's Leon?" he said. "I told him to meet us here."

"That young man is a born double-crosser," Inga Lee said. "I warned you."

"I know," said Mr. Lee. "But we had to have someone to keep watch in Time City in case anyone got suspicious. And you must admit he did a good job enticing the children to find you the Silver. And he did set the boy Jonathan up for me to kill when we knew he was getting dangerous."

Again they were talking as if Jonathan was not there, trudging up the steps behind them. Inga Lee said, "Maybe—but he didn't warn us they were going for the Gold *first,* Viv. Don't trust him."

"I won't," said Mr. Lee. "We'll get rid of him as soon as he shows up."

They went up the last flight of steps, across the platform in the front of the tower, and in through its nearest open door. There was an Annuate Guard on duty there. He came toward them, beaming all over his wrinkled face. "Mr. Lee, isn't it? Welcome back. I thought no one was going to come to the Gno—"

That was all he said. Mr. Lee waved his hat like someone swatting a fly. The Guard fell over on his back and lay there, still smiling. None of the Lees took any more notice of him. Mr. Lee stepped to the spiral pillar and went riding up it. His daughter followed him. Inga Lee waved her handbag, and Jonathan was compelled to follow his cousin. After him, Vivian found herself stepping onto the mysterious spiral ledge. Up she went and, to her surprise, found herself stepping out into the bright sunlight of the museum room, through what looked like the solid glass of the pillar. As she did so, Jonathan fell heavily in front of her. Vivian could not stop her own feet from going on walking and she fell over on top of him. From where they lay in a heap, she could see that there had been a Patroller up here, looking after the museum. She was lying against a display case, and her head did not seem to be on straight.

Sam was emerging from the pillar. "I don't know—" he began, and stopped when he saw the Patroller.

Inga Lee came out of the pillar behind Sam. She must have stopped using the Iron Casket, because Vivian and Jonathan both found they could move as they wanted. They started to get up. Cousin Vivian dodged out from behind the pillar and kicked them both, hard. "I've been longing to do that!" she said. "That's for interfering!"

"Stop it, Vivvie," Mr. Lee said, not very seriously. He was carrying a suitcase and he seemed very pleased about it. "Look at this, Inga! The Silver Casket sent all our stuff through, right on time. It appeared just as I came up here. Put those three upstairs. I don't want them in the way while we set things up."

Vivian was no sooner back on her feet than she was forced to walk, past the first-ever automat, through the archway in the wall and up the stairs. When she reached the tall archway leading to the next floor, she found herself turning smartly through it, into the bright, bright tinkling space beside the works of the great clock. There, nothing seemed to stop her from turning around to look at the archway. Sam came through it behind her, puffing hard, with that look a person has who is trying not to cry. Jonathan came after him, and his face was a dull red. Vivian heard Inga Lee's high heels clattering on the stairs and expected her to come in behind Jonathan. Instead, there was a slight swishing noise. A panel of yellowish stone began sliding across the archway. Jonathan whipped around and tried to put his foot in the gap before it slid home. But he was too late. He clawed at the panel and kicked it, but it was firmly in place, filling the arch, and he could not budge it.

He turned back again. His eyes were staring and strange behind the darkening flicker of his eye function. He said, in a queer, strangled voice, "He *killed* that Patroller! Himself! She wasn't dead when I came out of the pillar. He knocked her over with the Casket and then kicked her head. I tried to stop him, but he just knocked me down with the Casket too!" He put his hands over his face, even though his flicker was now black, and turned his back on Sam and Vivian.

Sam sat down on the glassy floor. "He's not my uncle anymore," he said thickly. "And she's not my cousin. I disinherit them."

Vivian stood uncertainly between them until she saw a tear trickle down Sam's cheek. She sat down beside him and patted his shoulder under the slithery mind suit. The mind suits had not done much to help them against the two Caskets, she thought, but then look at the layers and layers Inga Lee had worn to protect herself from the Silver Keeper!

Sam did not say anything, but he did not shake Vivian's hand off either. Vivian sat there, staring into the twinkling, turning glass heart of the clock, listening to the faint chime and jangle and chinking as it moved, wondering if there was anything they could do now. She did not seem to be able to cry like Sam. Things were too bad for that. She tried not to think of home, or to wonder what had happened to Mum and Dad now that the Twentieth Century had changed so queerly. She tried not to think what would happen to Time City. That was not easy. She could feel the tower shaking, smoothly and constantly, so that she felt almost as if she was riding on a train. And she could see a big dark blot rising slowly up the glass pillar in the middle, turning, turning, and becoming strange shapes as she saw it through different pieces of the glass works. It took her a moment to realize it was the dead Patroller. Then she tried not to follow it up with her eyes. She was glad that Jonathan and Sam were not looking.

Time City is going to be a terrible place with someone like Mr. Lee in charge, she thought, looking firmly at her own knees. That brought her to the thing she wanted most of all not to think of. Suppose Mr. Lee meant them to stay here while the clock struck and be deaf for the rest of their lives? Try as she would, Vivian kept thinking of that. The myriad glass cogs in front of her kept reminding her of it. The shaking of the tower was causing all sorts of extra glassy noises, jingles and tinks and squeaks, which cut across the regular chiming hum of the works in a way that was urgent and irritating. It got on Vivian's nerves so, that she just had to switch on her clock function to see how near it was to midday.

Her wrist lit up and of course it said ten past six. Their journeys to the Silver Age and then to Twenty Century had put it completely out of step with Time City. There was no knowing how soon the great clock would strike. "Oh *blast*!" Vivian muttered.

As she said it, the glass works dimmed to a yellowish twilight. All three of them looked up. The windows were now covered by panels of the same yellowish, translucent stone as the walls. They could hardly tell which was window and which was wall.

"Sealing the tower," Jonathan said. "I'd heard there were shutters for all the doors and windows, but I don't think they've ever been used. Do you think that means there's someone outside and the Lees don't want them to get in?"

They looked at one another with a great deal more hope.

"If you can get in and out of the pillar in the museum room," Jonathan said, "mightn't it work the same here? Do you think there's a way to get through the works of the clock?"

Sam jumped up. "I'll try. I'm smallest."

"But—" said Vivian, thinking of the dead Patroller. Then she decided not to say anything. Sam was already crawling nimbly among the nearest huge saw-edged cogs. He looked as if he would be cut to pieces any second. "Come back!" she said feebly.

"Let him go. He might have a chance," Jonathan said. "It's the one good thing left." He looked up at the high ceiling and more or less howled, "This is all my *fault*! Every time I get an idea I make a complete mess of it! I found them the Silver Casket—and on top of that I went and told Inga Lee where the Lead Casket is!"

"Shut up!" Vivian snapped. She had to look away from Sam among the glimmering machinery. He was trying to squeeze under a glass rod that kept coming downward at him, while an enormous disk edged up on him from behind. She turned on Jonathan instead. "You're being as bad as Elio!" she said. "It is *not* your fault! It's the Lees who've done all this! And *no one's* got the Lead Casket yet! You ought to be thinking where it is, instead of doing a song and dance like a—like a raving android!"

"And the same to you!" Jonathan said. He snatched a look at Sam, who was now edging under a giant elbow of glass, dimly going up and down like a bent piston. In order not to see Sam crushed, he turned to Vivian and said reasonably, "The Lead Casket—all we know is that it must be the small egg shape, because the Silver one's big. You could see the size from its packing. And we think we know it's attracted to the other Caskets."

Here he and Vivian both had to look at Sam again. He was back-ing away from a cog like a circular saw, and another, even big-ger, was coming sideways at him. The sight angered Jonathan. "But if you know anything that size that gets attracted to the Caskets," he snapped, "do please tell me, because *I've* never seen it!"

Sam lay down flat on the glass floor, and both cogs missed him.

"But we *have*!" Vivian cried out, in a burst of relief. "We all have! The time egg! The one Elio thought was a dud! It took us after the Iron Casket a whole hundred years—and it didn't want to take us back to the city."

Jonathan stared at her an instant. Then he called out, "Sam! Lie there for a moment—it's important. Can you hear us?"

"Only just," Sam called back. "It sort of hums. What do you want?"

"An egg-shaped thing," Jonathan called back clearly and pre-cisely. "Dark gray, about the size to fit in my hand, that gets attracted by the Caskets."

Sam's voice boomed among the chiming machinery. "You mean that old time lock control? The one that took Elio after the Silver and landed him among the bare ladies?"

Jonathan and Vivian clutched each other. "It *is*!" said Vivian.

"Sam," Jonathan called carefully, "that egg is the *Lead Casket*. Got that?"

"I can't hear!" Sam said petulantly. "I thought you said that egg was the Lead Casket."

"It *is*!" Jonathan and Vivian both called.

There was a short humming, tinkling silence. Then Sam called, "Who do I tell?"

"If you can get out, tell Dr. Wilander," Jonathan called. He said to Vivian, "It sounds as if he had an idea what my uncle's like. Who else, if Sam can't find him?"

"He oughtn't to tell anyone Mr. Lee used the Silver on, just in case,'' Vivian said. And being unable to think of anyone else, she called, "Mr. Enkian.''

"Mr. Enkian,'' Sam called back. "All right.'' He began wriggling on toward the glass pillar, still lying on his back. After about a foot, his way was blocked by a nest of glass rods, where he had to stand up and sidle around them. Beyond that was a flurry of glass shapes, all working very fast, and beyond those was the pillar. Just as Sam sidled behind the nest of rods and his pale mind suit became very hard to see, the shutter in the archway slid aside. Cousin Vivian came in, holding the Patroller's gun.

"They want you all downstairs now,'' she said. Her skinny arm with its little puffed sleeve looked ridiculous holding the gun, but Vivian and Jonathan had no doubt that she would shoot with it, far more rapidly and ruthlessly than Leon Hardy. They went slowly toward her. Vivian Lee backed against the side of the arch, so that she could hold the gun steady with both hands and still see the rest of the dim, tinkling room. "Where's the other one?'' she said sharply. "The sticky baby with red hair.''

"Sam's hiding in the works,'' Jonathan said. "If you shoot him, he'll stop the clock.''

"It's a suicide mission,'' Vivian said, hoping that this was not true.

"Stupid thing!'' Cousin Vivian said. "Nothing can stop that clock! Come *out*!'' she shouted. "You'll only get squished!''

Neither Vivian nor Jonathan could help looking at the place where Sam had last been. And Sam had made it. They saw the faint glimmer of his mind suit slowly rising through the middle of the pillar.

"Then you can stay there and go deaf when the clock strikes. It's ten to twelve now!'' Cousin Vivian called. She waited a moment in case Sam decided to come out. Vivian and Jonathan looked down at the glass floor in order not to follow the glimmer upward with their eyes. "Very well. Stay there!'' said Cousin Vivian.

She beckoned with the gun. "I've got the safety off," she said warningly.

They had to go past her and down the stairs without another look at the pillar. There are stairs all the way down outside, Vivian thought. He can be out long before the clock strikes.

The museum room was almost as dim and yellowish as the room above. All the windows were shuttered except for the one that looked directly out over the Avenue of the Four Ages. There, the museum cases had been pulled aside, and Cousin Vivian's parents were setting up some kind of apparatus in the space. The two Caskets had been put in the niches. Vivian could see them, first dark and distorted by the glass and then clear and in plain view, as the pillar went slowly around—one flattish iron box, a little rusty, and one large silver egg on which pearls and red stones gleamed from whorled settings.

"I only got two," Cousin Vivian said. "The other one got in the clock."

Inga Lee turned around. "The small one—he could be small enough to get to the pillar," she said nervously.

Without bothering to turn, Mr. Lee said, "It won't make any difference if he does. I put the shutters down in the bell pagoda. All he'll get is a bad attack of deafness. Nobody's going in or out of the tower, and we won't need Sam until later. Bring those two over here, Vivvie. I need them now."

"Why do you need us?" said Jonathan.

"Shut up," said Mr. Lee. He said it as if he meant it. Vivian and Jonathan went over to the window without daring to say anything else. "Stand there," Mr. Lee said, shoving them to one side of it. "And remember—the only use you are to me is as hostages. So keep quiet until the clock strikes and the Gold Casket gets here. I may let you go then."

"Why do you need Sam later?" Jonathan said.

Mr. Lee laughed. "To continue the Lee line," he said. "You won't mind a deaf husband, will you, Vivvie?"

Vivian could not see Cousin Vivian's face from where she stood backed against the bay of the window, so there was no way of telling what she thought. Beside her, Jonathan was chewing the end of his pigtail. Vivian was sure he was thinking about Sam, waiting beside a dead Patroller to be deafened. There was no way out of the pagoda except by the outside stairs, and from what Mr. Lee said, it seemed as if there was a shutter between Sam and the stairs.

"Ah! Here they come!" said Mr. Lee. "The fools have smelled a rat at last."

Vivian craned across Jonathan. A group of Patrollers and other people were hurrying up the zigzag steps to the Gnomon. Mr. Donegal was bounding up in front. Vivian saw Sempitern Walker near the back beside Dr. Leonov, the High Scientist, and the great purple figure of Dr. Wilander towering in the middle. Scattered people were hurrying behind, trying to catch up, Patrollers and Annuate Guards mostly, but one of them was Petula, and another looked like Ramona. And a long way in the rear, rushing down the middle of the Avenue of the Four Ages, was Mr. Enkian with his robes flying.

"That android's with them—beside Wilander," Inga Lee said. "I thought we'd made them lock it up."

"It must have got loose and alerted the rest," said Mr. Lee. "Well, they're not much of a threat. I must say, I expected them to be better organized than this!"

Vivian suspected that Mr. Donegal was better organized than Mr. Lee thought. There were movements in among the bushes beyond the stairs that looked like more people keeping out of sight while they got Endless Hill surrounded. While she was trying to see if they were indeed Patroller uniforms creeping through the shrubs, she heard a faint scuttering. It was outside the tower, from above somewhere. Jonathan's head moved slightly and then stopped, stiffly, showing he had heard it too. It *couldn't* be a trailing shoelace! Vivian thought. Sam's feet had been enclosed in that mind suit. But it did sound very much like one. And the scuttering was coming around the wall and getting lower, where the Lees might hear it at any moment.

She looked at Mr. Lee. He was smiling and holding a small round piece of metal to his mouth. He spoke into it. *"Stop!"* his voice blared from outside the tower. *"None of you come any nearer. This is Viv Lee speaking, Abdul."*

The people coming up the stairs faltered. Their faces turned up to the window, but none of them quite stopped climbing.

"I told you to stop," Mr. Lee's voice blared. *"We have taken possession of the Gnomon, and we have two of the so-called polarities of Time City up here with us. We will not hesitate to turn the force of the polarities on anyone who comes any n*·*arer. Get off the steps!"*

The group on the stairs stopped. They did not seem to be quite as well organized as Vivian hoped. They were turning to one another, asking one another for something. She listened hard in the silence, but she could not hear the scuttering anymore. Then a Patroller climbed over the stone balustrade beside Mr. Donegal and put something into his hand. They heard his voice, as if he were speaking from right beside them.

"Viv, you're mad! What are you trying to do up there?"

"I'm taking over Time City," Mr. Lee blared. *"It will come to a halt at the end of time in six minutes from now. When it does, the Gold Casket and the Lead Casket will be brought to the Gnomon. I warn you not to interfere with those Caskets in any way. Get off the steps."*

"Viv, I think we should talk about this," Mr. Donegal's voice suggested quietly from beside Mr. Lee's shoulder.

"Do as I tell you!" Mr. Lee blared. *"I have hostages here. I shall start by shooting one of them to show I mean business."* He nodded to his daughter. She prodded the gun into Vivian's arm and then Jonathan's and pushed them out in front of the window, where the group of upturned faces could clearly see them.

Mr. Lee took the gun from his daughter and waved it so that they could see that too. Vivian felt unreal. It was like that first night in Patrol Building. She felt as if she were in a film. And perhaps that's merciful, she thought. *"Do you see them?"* Mr. Lee blared. *"Do I shoot one?"*

There was more confusion among the group. Heads turned. Arms waved, beckoning to the stragglers hurrying up the flight of steps below. Mr. Donegal's voice said irritably, "I *know* he's violent! And that wife of his—" and this was followed by a click as he turned his loudspeaker off and waved everyone toward the side of the steps. In an untidy sort of stampede, everyone hurried to the balustrade and bundled themselves and one another over it into the bushes. Jonathan's teeth crunched on his pigtail. Elio was still standing there, a small pale figure in his mind suit. The two Guardians were advancing down the steps toward him, one a long silver glitter and the other tall and dull brown, casting dim, not-quite-real shadows across Elio and dwarfing him completely.

"Inga!" snapped Mr. Lee. "Get what those things are saying to one another. Quickly!" He held the gun against Jonathan's head, and neither Jonathan nor Vivian dared to move. Their eyes turned sideways to watch Inga Lee fiddling with knobs on top of her apparatus.

There was a noise like an army marching through tinfoil. Out of it, Elio's voice said faintly, "The Lead Casket." As soon as he said it, Elio turned and leaped over the side of the steps into the bushes. The two Guardians glimmered out of sight, leaving two long faint eye blots on the stairs.

"I think those creatures set up some kind of interference," Inga Lee said irritably. "I can't pick up what they're saying in the bushes at all."

"At least the steps are clear for the other two Guardians," Mr. Lee said. He passed his daughter the gun and turned to help his wife. There was more tinfoil crunching from the machine. A voice that might have been Elio's said, "We could not discover . . . ."

"Where will the other Guardians come from?" Cousin Vivian asked.

"A time lock at the bottom of the steps—don't interrupt," said her father.

At that point Mr. Enkian, who was clearly not much of a runner, reached the bottom of the steps. He leaned on the balustrade to pant before taking the climb. And Vivian saw a small figure come toward him around the hill at a tired, rolling trot. It was Sam. She recognized him mostly by the trot, because most of him was a fluttering, shapeless bundle. His mind suit seemed to have got shredded into a thousand trailing strips.

Jonathan's elbow went into her side. They both did what they could to distract the Lees. "I'm hungry," Jonathan said. "That automat over there still works."

"Does it?" Vivian cried with loud, artificial delight. "I'd *love* a butter-pie!"

"Can I work the automat, Daddy?" Cousin Vivian asked.

Mr. Enkian was not listening to Sam, Vivian saw with one eye. He was waving him angrily away.

"Give your mother the gun first, Vivvie," Mr. Lee said, still bending over the crunching apparatus.

From one eye, Vivian saw Cousin Vivian's skinny arm stretching out to pass the gun to Inga Lee. From the other, she saw Dr. Wilander rise out of the bushes like a purple whale and go crashing down Endless Hill toward Sam. When the stairs zigged the right way, he jumped the balustrade in a whirl of robe and went down them three at a time in huge, limping leaps. When they zagged at the landings, he jumped the balustrade again and tore his way through the shrubbery. He reached the bottom while Mr. Enkian was still waving Sam off. Mr. Enkian whirled around angrily, and the two of them began shouting at each other.

What a time to start another quarrel! Vivian thought, as her other eye watched Cousin Vivian fetch the little pot with a stick in it out of the antique automat. "One butter-pie," Cousin

Vivian announced. She laughed jeeringly and began to eat it herself.

Elio went tearing down the hill, following the broken path Dr. Wilander had made. As soon as he reached the bottom, Sam grabbed his arm and seemed to be explaining.

"Mean beast!"Vivian said, desperate to distract the Lees. "I'm starving!"

"She always was," Jonathan joined in, shaking with nerves. "When I got a new automat, she poured quick-set plastic into it, and I had to make do with the old one."

"Served you right for being so snooty!" said Cousin Vivian. She closed her eyes in bliss. "Oh, I'd forgotten the beautiful taste of these things!"

When Vivian looked away from her out of the window, there was no one at all at the bottom of the steps. Even Mr. Enkian had disappeared.

Mr. Lee gave up on the amplifier and turned it off. "There's not much anyone can do now anyway," he said, looking tensely at the watch on his wrist. "It's one minute to twelve."

They waited, and the minute seemed endless. Jonathan switched on his time function. It said twenty-nine minutes past six. They watched the green-lit second hand creep around to half past. It had got two-thirds of the way when Vivian caught sight of a blur in the distance down the Avenue of the Four Ages. It came closer and larger with astonishing speed, and she saw it was Elio—Elio running faster than she could have believed possible. He was getting bigger and nearer as if there was a zoom lens on him. She could see his legs pounding, his arms beating and his head rolling from side to side, and she knew he was running flat-out. But fast as Elio was coming, the second hand on Jonathan's arm seemed to move faster still. It was nearly at half past now. She could hear chinks and slidings overhead where the works of the endless clock were adjusting to the shaking of the tower and getting ready to strike.

Elio is bringing the time egg, Vivian thought, but what if it's *not* the Lead Casket? Or what if it *is,* but this just helps the Lees to get their hands on it?

BOING went the great clock, burring everything around them.

And as soon as it did, a tall young man in green strode to the steps and began jauntily and confidently to climb them.

This young man was not the time ghost, but the Watcher himself, bringing the Gold Casket. He cast a solid shadow that folded across the steps. Everything about him was solid and confident. Elio was still running, off to one side. The Watcher was going up briskly, sure of his duty, and he was halfway up the first flight of steps already.

BOING went the clock, a second time, and again everything burred. Vivian looked for Elio, but he must have reached the bushes. The only person in sight was the briskly climbing Watcher. "Here comes our Gold Casket!" Mr. Lee said triumphantly through the burring.

BOING came the third stroke. And the Watcher was suddenly struggling. He labored to put each foot on the next step as if his boots weighed a ton apiece. BOING went the fourth stroke. He staggered onto the first landing and dragged himself across it by holding on to the balustrade. Doggedly he began to climb the next flight, foot by weighty foot.

"Now we know what's stopping him," Mr. Lee said, as the fifth stroke rolled out. "It's those two damned Guardians."

The Iron Guardian and the Silver Keeper had materialized at the bottom of the last flight before the tower. They were standing, waiting. As Vivian looked at them, her eye caught something purple and a glimmer of mind suit down the hill beyond them, at the edge of the path Dr. Wilander had torn through the bushes. Then she knew what was really stopping the Watcher. The time egg. It *was* the Lead Casket. They had been right. Elio was using it as a kind of magnet to pull the Gold Casket back. But he did not dare be seen in case the Lees shot one of their hostages. When the steps zigzagged away from him, he could only come to the edge of the broken bushes.

In proof of this, the Watcher dragged himself up that flight while the next mighty BOING was ringing out. But Elio was waiting in the bushes at the second landing. The Watcher lurched and almost fell to his knees. Vivian could see the Gold Casket, distantly, tall and heavy and glinting. The Watcher held it proudly in front of him, which only left him one hand to drag himself across the landing with.

"He never does get to the top," Inga Lee said anxiously.

"We don't know that. He disappears on the twelfth stroke," Mr. Lee contradicted her. "Vivvie, fetch me the Silver Casket. I'll give him some help."

BOING rang the great clock. Vivian had lost count by then. Cousin Vivian went to the pillar, licking her butter-pie slowly to make it last. By the time she came back with the huge pearl-embossed egg, the Watcher was on his knees, crawling near the top of the third flight. From the swirling of the bushes, Vivian thought that there were a lot of people with Elio, pulling one another in a line, to help hold the Watcher back. She prayed that Mr. Lee would not notice as he took the pearly egg and bent over it. Funny! she thought. I *wanted* the Watcher to get up the steps when he was a time ghost. Now I hope and hope he doesn't! Beside her, Jonathan had most of his pigtail in his mouth.

The steps zagged away from the Lead Casket. With Mr. Lee's help, the Watcher doggedly plugged up that flight during the next great stroke of the bell. But he almost stuck on that landing. It seemed that the three Caskets might balance out and pin him to the spot.

"Get me the Iron Casket, quickly!" Inga Lee said. Cousin Vivian ran this time and got back as the great clock went BOING again.

"We *are* going to win, aren't we?" she asked plaintively as she handed the square, rusty box to her mother.

"Of course. We're intended to," Inga Lee said. She put the gun down on the amplifier and bent over the Iron Casket.

Now, by looking sideways at the struggling green climber, Vivian could see the force that was being used. It was roiling and streaking the air with nearly invisible whorls, so that when the clock rang out yet again, burring everything, Vivian could hardly see the Watcher. He was a green smear, still creeping upward. As the burring went off a little, she saw the whorling force bellying upward to cover the two waiting Guardians, then down to eddy across the Watcher as he rounded another landing and toiled on to the next flight.

BOING went the clock. Jonathan murmured through his pigtail, "Eleven." The Guardians were moving, walking slowly down to join the Watcher. The Watcher, still holding the Casket carefully to his chest, seemed to look up at them.

"We're winning," said Mr. Lee. "They've had to go to meet him. Obstinate, isn't he?"

BOING went the clock for the last time. The burring died to silence except for the shaking and chinking of the tower. The whorls of force died away too, fading and curling gently to nothing.

The Watcher stood up, near enough for Vivian to see he was smiling, and climbed briskly to meet the two Guardians. They turned and came up the steps on either side of him. Up they came and up, to the very foot of the Gnomon. Elio and the other people in the bushes, who seemed to be on both sides of the stairs, kept pace with them, but it was clear that the Lead Casket now had no effect at all.

"We've won!" said Mr. Lee. The Lees stood and laughed at one another.

"Open the door for him," said Inga Lee.

"In a second," said Mr. Lee. "I'll get rid of the hostages first. We don't want another Lee around to claim the city, and both of them know too much." He leaned over and picked the gun off the amplifier.

Vivian could not feel as if she was in a film then, though she wanted to very much. The gun was horribly real as it came up to point at her. And it seemed to be true that all your life came flooding into your mind in your last moments. She thought of Mum and Dad and London and the War and Time City, and she wanted to shout to Mr. Lee, Wait, I haven't thought of everything yet! Beside her, Jonathan let his pigtail fall out of his mouth and stood straight and lordly-looking.

But it seemed as if the Guardians were already coming. There was the sound of shutters and doors sliding all over the tower, above and below. The yellow panels over the windows swept sideways into the walls, flooding the museum room with sunlight. Vivian's eyes watered, but she could just see the pillar in the middle go suddenly dark as a person rose up inside it. Mr. Lee turned and peered to see who it was, pointing the gun uncertainly.

Dr. Wilander stepped out of the pillar, bulging the strange material of it wide with the size of him. He was holding the time egg in one huge hand. It looked no bigger than a pigeon's egg.

Mr. Lee fired the gun at him, twice, two blunt, coughing sounds.

All that happened was that Dr. Wilander gathered his shabby gown around him with his other huge hand and cleared his throat. "Hrrrhm." The gun clattered to the floor. "I apologize," Dr. Wilander grunted to Jonathan and Vivian. "I should never have let you get into this mess." There was embarrassment all over his big bear's face. "The truth is that I have to have this artifact in my hand before I recollect what I am. Oh no," he growled. Mr. Lee was reaching for the Silver Casket. "Oh no. You drained that one and the Iron one trying to fight this." He held up the little leaden egg on the palm of his huge hand. The air was in transparent whorls and shimmers over it. "All the force went back into this one, where it belongs," he said. "Elio's idea. But you Lees couldn't have won anyway, not with Lead and Gold both outside the tower. We just didn't want anybody to get shot. Now I'm afraid I'll have to get rid of you."

Cousin Vivian took the butter-pie away from her mouth. "You can't get rid of us," she said. "We're Lees!"

"What does that mean?" growled Dr. Wilander. "You descend from a very nice young man who happened to wander into Time City from China a very long time ago and ended up marrying the ruler's daughter. But that doesn't entitle you to anything, you know. I told you that when you were six. Now what shall I do with you all?" He frowned at the little gray egg, considering. "I can't have you anywhere where you can get at that time lock in Lee House, and it'll have to be somewhere stable, because you're all three thoroughly disruptive. Let's see. I think young Vivian had better go to Ancient China—"

"Over my dead body!" Inga Lee exclaimed. "My daughter descends from the Icelandic Emperor!"

"Then I'd better remove you first before you do anything silly," grunted Dr. Wilander.

The rippling in the air from the time egg surged out to surround Inga Lee. Just for an instant, she seemed to be standing on rather soggy grass beside a low house made of rough bits of stone. There was sea edged with ice in front of her and a sheer and frosty-looking mountain behind. Then the rippling edges of the air surged together and there was nothing but a cold draft and a writhing swirl in the air where Inga Lee had been.

"What have you done?" Mr. Lee said chokily.

"Sent her to Iceland, at the time it was first settled," growled Dr. Wilander. "It should suit her. Her kind used to be known as 'a stirring woman' there. For you, Viv, I'm afraid it'll have to be the last days of the Depopulation of Earth. I can't have you getting together with her again. She pushes you into things. I'll put you near the last spaceship, and if you ask them nicely, they may take you aboard. But I don't promise you they will."

The ripples surged from the egg again. Mr. Lee was surrounded by a hot-looking concrete field with pieces of broken brick wall sticking up here and there. He cried out, "No! I'll reform!"

"You said that before, several times," Dr. Wilander grunted as the ripples came together again, leaving a hot wind and a chemical smell where Mr. Lee had been. Dr. Wilander turned to Cousin Vivian.

Cousin Vivian tipped her head sideways and held her butter-pie as if it were a posy of flowers. A tear trickled prettily down her nose. "You won't do that to me, will you, Uncle Hakon?" she said in a little lisping voice. "I'm only just eleven."

As Dr. Wilander opened his mouth to reply, Vivian said quickly, "Would you mind waiting a second, Dr. Wilander?" The little eyes looked at her and looked amused. The big face nodded. "*Thank* you!" said Vivian. And she flew at Cousin Vivian. She seized the hand that was holding the butter-pie and made Cousin Vivian stick the butter-pie into her own eye. Then she snatched it away and forced it down the neck of Cousin Vivian's frilly blue frock. Cousin Vivian shrieked and kicked and fought harder than Sam, but Vivian Smith was something of an expert by now, and she held that butter-pie inside Cousin Vivian's frilly collar until the cold part melted and the hot ran out.

"*Ow!*" screamed Cousin Vivian.

Vivian let her go. "I've been wanting to do that all day!" she said.

"I can't go to China like *this*!" Cousin Vivian screamed.

But she had to. The ripples expanded while she was still screaming. Vivian and Jonathan looked with great interest at an instant of rainy street and a house with tipped-up ends to its roof. A person in stiff robes under a large umbrella halted and stared at Cousin Vivian across his long mustache, looking haughtily unable to believe his folded eyes.

"And that's that," grunted Dr. Wilander as the scene disappeared. "Pity I didn't realize what they were up to before this. I knew Time City was bound to go critical when it got back to the beginning. That blinded me, I'm afraid. Let's go down. Would each of you take one of those Caskets?"

Jonathan rather nervously picked up the jeweled silver egg.

Vivian took the heavy iron box quite gladly. After all, it belonged to her own era. Dr. Wilander stepped to the glass pillar again. They realized that it was no longer turning. "Has the clock stopped?" Jonathan asked.

"For the moment," Dr. Wilander answered, bulging the pillar as he went in. He vanished smoothly downward. Jonathan followed, then Vivian. It was just the same as going up, just as mysterious. When Vivian stepped out into the ground floor of the Gnomon, all twelve doors were open and the Annuate Guard was sitting on the floor, looking dizzy and puzzled. Dr. Wilander patted his shoulder as he limped past. "Feeling better now?" he asked, and went out through the front door onto the platform at the top of the steps.

Mr. Donegal was standing at one side with a group of Patrollers. Elio was standing at the other side, panting rather, with Sempitern Walker, Mr. Enkian, Ramona, and a number of other people. Sam was sitting on the ground near his mother's feet. He looked tired, and his mind suit was indeed a mass of fluttering strips. Everyone called out gladly when Vivian and Jonathan came through the door behind Dr. Wilander, but they did not move. It was clear none of them liked to get in the way of the three Guardians. The Guardians were standing in a row in front of the door like Patrollers on duty, except that they looked a great deal more powerful than any Patroller ever did.

The Watcher of the Gold came slowly forward, smiling all over his blunt face, and held the Gold Casket out to Dr. Wilander. It was beautiful, a miniature golden model of the Gnomon. The golden bell tinkled in the top as the Watcher presented it.

"One moment," Dr. Wilander said to him, and he asked Vivian and Jonathan, "Would you mind giving the other two their property back?"

Jonathan carefully put the Silver Casket into the long, shiny hands of the Silver Keeper, who bowed courteously as he took it. Vivian gave the Iron Casket into the eager, cloudy hand of the

Iron Guardian. He rewarded her with a great smile, wide and sly, but she felt the same jolt of fear when he touched the Casket that she had felt from him before. She realized now that she had had the same jolt off Dr. Wilander more than once.

"Thank you," the Iron Guardian said softly. He joined the other two Guardians, and they all stood holding their Caskets out expectantly to Dr. Wilander.

Dr. Wilander sighed a little. "Very well," he said. "Now, I suppose." He held out the time egg, and the three Guardians brought their Caskets forward to meet it. Vivian noticed that they were all exactly the same height as Dr. Wilander, no taller, no shorter, different as they were. The four Caskets came together at the center of their four outstretched arms, where they wavered for a moment and then dissolved into the small egg shape of the Lead Casket. As they did, three of the Guardians shimmered also and faded forward and inward to overlay Dr. Wilander. For an instant, he had the long, mad face of the Iron Guardian. Then that gave way to the sad, polite skull of the Silver Keeper; and that, in turn, became the countryman's face of the Watcher of the Gold.

Dr. Wilander did not seem to find this at all comfortable. He worked his elbows and stamped his feet and a scowl of what might have been pain came across the four blending faces. But finally he shivered and harrumphed and took a look at the Lead Casket. It was paler now, with silvery and brown and gold streaks, and the air around it played in tighter and stronger whorls, shivering the front of Dr. Wilander's purple robe. He nodded in a satisfied way. He was still Dr. Wilander, but with a difference. His face was more shapely, with a long twitch to the mouth, which was like the Iron Guardian's, except that it had the nervous politeness of the Silver Keeper. His chin was the blunt and obstinate chin of the Watcher of the Gold. When he looked suddenly and sharply over at Vivian, his eyes were not so small, but they were still bearishly shrewd, and they still laughed at Vivian.

"Know who I am?" he asked her. His voice was less of a

grunt. It blared like the Watcher of the Gold's and was lightened by the voices of the Iron Guardian and the Silver Keeper.

"Still making fun of me," Vivian said. "Well, you seem to be all sorts of people. Perhaps everyone is. But I think you *might* be Faber John."

Everyone else gasped. "Correct!" shouted Dr. Wilander. "She got the right answer for once in her life! But then she *has* met all the other parts of me that were out in history trying to hold the city in place."

Elio hurried forward and went down on one knee. "Faber John," he said. "My lord. You ordered me to be made—"

"Oh, get up, man!" said Faber John. "So I did order you, but don't start my-lording me for that. I'm in a hurry to get to Aeon Square." He strode past Elio and away down the steps. He still limped a little, Vivian saw as they all hurried after him, wondering what he was going to do in Aeon Square.

Time City was in upheaval all around them as they went down the steps. Vivian had grown used to the ground shaking, the way you get used to riding in a train, and she had not noticed that it had been getting worse all the time. Now it was really bad. The steps heaved under them with long shudders, and cracks appeared under their feet. In the distance, people were running across the Avenue of the Four Ages, in order to get to the river and escape, and Vivian did not blame them. A particularly grinding shudder produced a long crashing, over to her right. She looked in time to see the golden Dome of The Years slide away sideways and disappear in a great billow of dust. One of the metal arches in the Avenue tipped crooked, and beyond that, with a mighty tinkling, the blue glass dome of Millennium crumbled down on itself and poured blue shards into the River Time.

Faber John simply limped on as if none of it were happening. Vivian found she trusted him. When they reached the bottom of the steps, she ran as well as she could over the heaving road, and caught him up. Jonathan was beside him, and so was Elio, who was carrying Sam. Sam was leaning on Elio's shoulder with a smug and heroic look. He gave Vivian a two-toothed grin as she came up.

"A lot of rebuilding to do," Faber John remarked to her. "Most of it shoddy stuff put up after I divided." Something had happened to whatever made the streamers of light on the arches. They were producing wild, misty scribbles and making popping noises, although the first arch seemed to revive a little as Faber John limped under it with the time egg.

"Did you know what was going to happen?" Vivian asked as they left it behind.

"I guessed most of it," said Faber John. "Stupid of me to leave it all written down in Lee House where that trigger-happy failure could get hold of it. But I thought my descendants ought to have a few clues in case something went wrong. I didn't want the Caskets lost forever. So I left some documents describing more or less what I'd done with them. I made the Iron Casket quite easy to find, because that was the weakest and it didn't matter if it fell into the wrong hands. I said where the Silver was too, but I took care to put it in such a confusing site that it needed advanced technology out of late history to find. And I gave three different locations for the Gold to muddle anyone who tried to steal that. Luckily I didn't say a word about the Lead. I hoped part of me would be here and in the city to look after that."

"And did you know about me?" Vivian asked.

"How could I? I didn't know about myself," he grunted. "I spotted you were a sham, of course, straight away. And I knew you were one of those time ghosts. So I figured that the safest thing to do was to take you as a pupil and make sure you knew the important facts. But don't ask *me* to decide what to do about you now. That's the Time Lady's department."

This sounded alarming. Vivian trotted beside his huge figure in silence after that, under arch after arch, each of which sputtered back to life as they went under it, until they were near the end of the Avenue. There were only a few scattered people running away by then. As Faber John got near them, a house fell down and poured rubble across the road in a long sliding heap, almost at his feet. Mr. Enkian jumped nervously sideways from it.

"If you want to run away, Enkian," Faber John said, pointing to the fleeing people, "feel free to follow those."

Mr. Enkian cast a tempted look at the river and then drew up his chin in a very dignified way. "I am proud and pleased to stay and serve the city," he replied.

"What a damned lie!" said Faber John. "Seriously, Enkian, I won't hold it against you if you want to go."

"I—er—" said Mr. Enkian. "If you must know, the wide-open spaces of history frighten me more than anything else."

Just like Jonathan! Vivian thought. It made her feel kinder toward Mr. Enkian. Perhaps Faber John felt the same. As they climbed across the rubble of the house, he said to Jonathan, "Keep reminding me not to bait that man in the future, will you?"

They went up the steps and between Perpetuum and Science. The twin domes of Ongoing and Erstwhile were standing quite unmoved. Faber John squinted up at them and seemed pleased. Perpetuum was tottering, shaking in every lopsided honeycomb part, but it seemed to be holding together, almost as if it had been made to take just such a strain. "Good," said Faber John. "Built all these myself." And he swept on into Aeon Square.

Here the buildings were shaking too, though most of them were whole, except for Time Patrol Building, which had lost large pieces off its white front. There were a lot of people out in the middle of Aeon Square, because that was clearly one of the safest places to be. Most of them were city people, but there were quite a few stranded tourists and a large crowd of evacuees, who were staring rather nervously at the falling domes and shaking towers.

"It's bombs," Vivian heard an evacuee say as Faber John swept up to the crowd. "We didn't ought to be here. We ought to be in an air raid shelter." But around that, Vivian could not quite tell how, a murmur was spreading among the city people and the tourists.

"It's Faber John!"

By the time Faber John reached the stone in the middle, he was in a ring of awestruck spectators, who all seemed to know who he was. Here Jenny gave up trying to organize the evacuees and rushed up to Jonathan. "Oh, you're safe! But what is happening? What *is* happening, and *where* is Viv?" She looked at Sempitern Walker and then at Ramona and the way they looked back told her about the Lees. Jenny's face then made Vivian think soberly, You can't put something like that right. Not really. It isn't all right, and it never will be.

Faber John took up a position a little way from the broken chippings of the stone, where he folded his arms and stood looking at it. "I seem to have timed it about right," he remarked. "Nothing yet, but should be any moment now."

Almost at once, there was the most violent bucking of the ground yet. In the distance, Vivian saw the tall finger of Whilom Tower sway to and fro. She watched it anxiously, thinking of all the films stored inside it, and she almost missed the moment when the rubble of the stone blew away into fine dust. Dust stung her face like a sandstorm. She put her arm over her face and looked back to see it showering away sideways in clouds, leaving a dark, oblong hole.

"There's the air raid shelter!" an evacuee cried out in great relief.

But next moment, the evacuees were backing away with everyone else. Something was moving in the hole, something huge and slow and rather clumsy. There were heavy, heaving footsteps. Vivian's back prickled as she realized that whatever had been sleeping under Time City was awake and about to come out.

The footsteps slithered and seemed to find a purchase. Pound—slide—bang. The face of a huge horse appeared in the hole. It pricked its ears and blinked at the sight of Aeon Square and the ring of staring faces. Then it gave a mighty scramble and climbed out onto the flagstones, putting each enormous hoof with great care. There was a woman on its back, dressed in homemade clothes—a fair, untidy woman with her hair in a bun and worried lines on her face.

Faber John's face broke into a great smile at the sight of her. "Time Lady, my wife," he said, "why the horse?"

The Time Lady smiled slightly too. "Why not?" she said. "I found him going begging in the Age of Gold while I was wandering in spirit. And I brought him because I was fairly sure there wouldn't be enough animals here when I woke."

"There aren't any," said Faber John. "People didn't like the mess."

"How stupid!" said the Time Lady. "I must get more at once." She swung her leg across the vast back of the horse as if she were going to dismount, but she stayed there, looking around at Aeon Square. Jonathan and Vivian exchanged incredulous looks. They knew that horse, rather too well for comfort, and they knew the Lady, too. She was the one who had cured Jonathan. But she was not quite the same as the woman in the Age of Gold. She was paler, and she seemed a more complicated person, as if it was a very important part of her that had been asleep under the city. How silly of me! Vivian thought. When I saw that sleeper, I thought of Mum first thing, but I never realized it was a woman even then! But she's not big enough! I don't understand.

"I see you've brought in some new blood," the Time Lady said, nodding at the evacuees.

"Well, not exactly," said Faber John. "They came of their own accord. But I had an idea that some children would arrive somehow in time for the renewal."

The Time Lady laughed. Then she did dismount, sliding to the ground and running to meet Faber John, both of them looking wonderfully glad to see each other. "So you brought it off, you old genius!'' she said. ''I thought you'd never manage a renewal.''

As soon as she was off it, the horse came clopping over to Jonathan and Vivian and thrust its great pulpy nose into Vivian's face. Clearly it remembered them too. Vivian did not know what to do about it, but Sam did. He slid down from Elio's arms and came trotting over with a thousand strips of mind suit fluttering all over him. ''Here. I've got a peppermint,'' he said, and gave it to the horse.

''What happened to that suit? Did you get caught in the clock?'' Jonathan asked.

''No, it was the shutters at the top of the Gnomon,'' Sam said. ''They were spiky at the bottom, but there was just room for me to squeeze underneath if I wriggled and wriggled. *You* couldn't have got out. What happened to you?''

''Well,'' said Jonathan, ''the best part was when V.S. stuffed a butter-pie down V.L.'s neck.''

Sam grinned, a huge two-toothed grin that suddenly faded to wistfulness. ''A butter-pie,'' he said. ''That's what I need.''

''You!'' said Vivian. ''I thought I'd cured you of butter-pies!''

''You did,'' said Sam. ''But it's come on again.''

The last important event took place in the Chronologue later that day. Vivian was very alarmed by it. For one thing, it was an Enquiry and Court of Law, and she was one of the ones on trial. For another, the Chronologue by daylight was even more rich and decorated than she had realized. It awed her. Every scrap of it was painted, or gilded, or jeweled, from the mosaic of semiprecious stones on the floor to the starry sky painted on the ceiling.

The carved seats were crowded. Jonathan told her that this was most unusual, which made another alarming thing. Everyone Vivian knew was there, from Petula and her helpers to the Patrollers who had arrested her in the Age of Silver. Though at least half the population of Time City had run away into history when houses started falling down, there were enough rescued Observers and tourists, who had been stranded when the locks down the river stopped working at midday, to force Annuate Guards, Patrollers, and important people in robes to stand at the back. There was quite a sprinkling of evacuee children, too. They had now been shared out to people who had not left the city and had been brought along by foster parents who were too interested to stay away. They sat looking wide-eyed and sleepy and fingering their Time City pajamas in a surprised way. Most of them seemed to be getting thoroughly pampered by their new parents. Those who were not clutching new toys were secretly being fed sweets.

Another unusual and alarming thing was that Sempitern Walker, sitting in the Sempitern's Chair, down to one side, was not wearing ceremonial robes. He was in simple black, which made him look very severe and earnest. Rumor had it that Faber John had said that no one was to wear robes. And Faber John, of course, was the most alarming thing of all. The two great thrones under the canopy at the end, with animal heads on the arms and winged suns blazing on the high backs, which Jonathan said had been left empty for uncounted thousands of years, were now occupied by Faber John and the Time Lady. And whatever Faber John had said about robes, the Time Lady had somehow managed to get him into a new purple gown. She herself was wearing a dress of deep night blue.

Sempitern Walker opened the Court by knocking for attention. Then he took up the winged sun with the Koh-i-noor diamond in it and solemnly walked over to give it to Faber John.

"What's this?" Faber John rumbled. "Am I expected to fan myself with this thing? Or what?"

The Time Lady nudged him. "You know what it is," she said.

"The standard of office," said Sempitern Walker. "I assume that you are now ruling as Sempitern of Time City."

"Not as Sempitern," Faber John declared. "You're better at parading in ceremonies and greeting Ambassadors and making speeches than I shall ever be. I need a Sempitern to do that for me. You're stuck with it, Ranjit. Take your standard away.''

"But you will, of course, be wanting to move into the Annuate Palace," Sempitern Walker said. "If you will give me a day—"

"Not that either," said Faber John. "The Time Lady and I have always lived in what is known as Lee House. Now it's empty, we shall go back there. But since you're all obviously expecting me to do something kingly, I shall make a short speech.''

Sempitern Walker went back to his seat, looking anguished in a way that Vivian could not decide was relieved or disappointed. When he was sitting down, Faber John began.

"Sorry about the inconvenience," he said. "The time locks are going to be shut for three days while Time City shakes itself on to a new piece of time. After that, it will start a new circuit of history. By then history should have shaken itself down too, into new Fixed Eras and new Unstable ones, and we can take a look at the best places to plant the Caskets out when that time comes. But the city will move for quite a while on the full power of the Lead Casket, so I shall be with you for many centuries before I have to divide and go out again—"

The Time Lady said, "Next time it's my turn to go out and yours to sleep. We're not going to have another quarrel about that.''

"We'll talk about that later," said Faber John. "It's no fun being divided. What I want to say to everyone is that next time around we're going to do better. Time City has traded so long with the Fixed Eras that it thought it was fixed itself. We had got very selfish and far too safe. It took someone quite young and from an Unstable Era to point that out. In future, we're going to be of use to the whole of history. Chronologue is going to study what we can do, and Patrol is going to think of ways to do it. Have you got that, Abdul? You can start your Enquiry now.''

Sam's father stood up. He cleared his throat. He fidgeted. It was clear that he was far happier giving orders than speaking in public. "Two months ago, Ongoing Science drew the attention of Time Patrol to massive anomalies in the First Unstable Era," he began. "Look, you know all this. You were there when I reported to Chronologue."

"Yes, but my Time Lady wasn't," said Faber John. "She wants to know."

"Well, Chronologue referred to Ongoing for a full analysis," said Mr. Donegal. "Dr. Leonov will tell you." He sat down thankfully.

Dr. Leonov stood up, between an evacuee and a tourist, looking a little strange because he had obviously not been able to decide whether to wear his robes or not. He had settled for a high white Science hat and black pajamas. "We made a thorough analysis," he said. "The Time Lady will appreciate that we have a whole new range of delicate and precise instruments since her day." The Time Lady gave him a smile and an impatient nod. This was probably intended to make Dr. Leonov speak plainly and quickly. It did not. Dr. Leonov discoursed of temporons and chronons, of socio-economic graphology and day sampling, of lode-hours and chrono-nexus effects until most of the evacuees fell asleep. Vivian had not been so bored since Sempitern Walker last soothed Mr. Enkian.

"What does all this mean?" the Time Lady asked at last. "In plain words."

"It means there were two kinds of disturbance, madam," said Dr. Leonov. "Both contained chronons, which meant they could threaten the city. But one was local, in 1939, and the other spread through the entire era and was far more massively weighted. Chronons of the same massive type were detected in two other Unstable Eras and in Time City itself. The source was eventually pinpointed to September 1939 as a young girl by the name of Vivian Smith."

Vivian sat up and stared.

Dr. Leonov sat down. Mr. Donegal reluctantly got up. "They gave us the report," he said, "but of course, I had to put it

before Chronologue—you were there. I asked permission for Time
Patrol to meet the train the source of trouble was on and remove
her to a Fixed Era where her chronon load might be neutralized.''

Mr. Enkian rose from a bench somewhere near the back and
coughed for attention. "I must point out that this scheme struck
me as barbarous," he said. "I argued against it but was voted
down, though I was happy to find that, for once, Sempitern Walker
agreed with me. We therefore insisted that we be allowed to in-
spect the foster home Patrol had found the child in Forty-two
Century. Which I did, at some personal cost, and when I found
it inadequate, I personally selected another. After which, the
Sempitern and I demanded to be among the party meeting the
train so that we could explain properly to the child, who would
certainly be frightened and confused, why it was we had to take
this step. The rest, in a manner of speaking, is history. We failed
to find the girl.''

Jonathan's face had been growing redder and redder while Mr.
Enkian spoke. As Mr. Enkian sat down, Jonathan slouched right
down in his seat, hoping to escape notice.

"It seems to me," said Faber John, "that we'd better hear
Jonathan Walker's story now.''

Looking as anguished as his father, Jonathan slowly stood up.
"I made a mistake," he said. "I mean, I got the right girl by
mistake.''

The Time Lady laughed. "Tell it in order," she said.

"It began as an adventure," Jonathan confessed. But he told
the story quite clearly and sensibly without trying to excuse himself or blame himself too much. Vivian was impressed.
Jonathan's learning! she thought. I wonder if I am, too. She looked
to see what the Time Lady thought. She had her elbows on her
knees and her chin in her hands, and she was frowning. Faber
John was frowning too. When Jonathan got to the part where Elio
rescued them from Leon Hardy, he said, "Sit down for now. Elio
can tell the next part.''

Elio sprang up. He came into the space in front of the thrones and once more fell on one knee. "Forgive me, my lord!" he cried. "My lady! I behaved, as I thought, with great cleverness, but I was very unintelligent indeed. I deserve to be punished!"

"Elio," said Faber John, "if you can't stop groveling, I'll send you back to that factory. I ordered you to be delivered in time for the renewal partly because I thought you might stop things going wrong, but mostly because I was hoping for intelligent company for the next few hundred years. If you can't be rational, I'll get them to send you to Mars as soon as the locks open. Stand up and pretend to be a man at least!"

Elio climbed hastily to his feet. "But I failed to recognize the Lead Casket!" he said.

"It was meant to be hard to recognize," said Faber John. "We couldn't have every Tom, Dick, or Harry waving it around. Get on and tell your part in the business."

So Elio told it, up to when Time Patrol brought them back to the city that morning. Faber John stopped him there. "Does Sam want to say anything?" he asked.

"No!" Sam said fervently.

"Right," said Faber John. "Then, Time Lady, my wife, regardless of the fact that history was coming apart around their ears, Jonathan led Vivian Smith on another dash to Twenty Century in hopes of catching his cousin disguised as a boy. That, of course, failed, because history had gone critical and his cousin had already returned to Time City. The only good thing is that they didn't take the Lead Casket with them that time. What do you think?"

The Time Lady considered, with her chin in her hands. This was the judgment on the Enquiry. Vivian watched the Time Lady frown and felt much as she had when Mr. Lee pointed the gun at her.

"I think," the Time Lady said slowly, "that I'll take Jonathan first, because I see you're going to raise an outcry if I don't leave you to deal with Elio yourself. Jonathan has broken the law. But he's a citizen of Time City, which means that he doesn't carry

what Mr. Leonov would call chronons, so he's going to have to
go on trial before Chronologue when it gets back together again.''

Jonathan went white. Vivian stood up, without knowing she
had. ''That's not fair!'' she found herself saying. ''Jonathan was
the only one who was really bothered about Time City! And he
even started caring about history in the end!''

''It's perfectly fair,'' the Time Lady said in her irritable way.
''And I've no doubt that Chronologue will take Jonathan's mo-
tives into account. Now I'll take Sam—''

''Hey!'' Sam's voice boomed out. ''You can't! I'm a hero. I
saved Time City.''

''But you broke the law, too,'' the Time Lady said. ''I'm going
to ask Chronologue to postpone your trial until you're older, on
condition that you don't break any more laws until then.'' Sam
subsided against Ramona, looking stunned. ''Now Vivian Smith,''
said the Time Lady. ''She is in bad trouble.''

''I didn't do anything wrong,'' Vivian said.

''You mean you didn't mean to,'' the Time Lady said tartly.
''You still don't understand, do you? My girl, you came from
history, which means you carry what talkative Mr. Leonov calls
temporons anyway, and then you were three times in the same
place at the same exact moment. And the second time you took
the Lead Casket with you. On top of that, you jumped about
history with it. No wonder Ongoing Science spotted you! No
wonder Patrol nabbed you quick out of the Age of Silver! You're
absolutely loaded with what Mr. Leonov calls chronons. The way
I say it is that you're going to disturb every bit of history you
touch for a long time to come. You can't go home. Twenty
Century would just blow up around you. I think we'll have to
send you out to the stars. Would you like that?''

Vivian did not know. She was not really sure a person *could*
go to the stars. She stood there thinking of home. But home was
a strange place now with bunkers and radioactive trains. She felt
lost. There was nowhere to go.

She was only vaguely aware that Sempitern Walker was standing up too, saying something about "invaluable adjunct to palace life." And now Jenny jumped up. Vivian had carefully not looked at Jenny before this, because Jenny had been crying quietly about her brother Viv. But she looked with everyone else when Jenny kicked the carved seat and shouted.

"Great Time, woman! I say *blast* you and Faber John! Who *cares* how many beastly chronons the child's got? I don't!"

There was a great and deadly silence. Jenny went brick red, and tears came out from under her eye function. She sat down with a thump. But Sempitern Walker still stood there. He waited until people started to shuffle and then he said loudly, "My wife and I demand that Vivian Smith stays in Time City and lives with us in the palace. If our demand is not met, I resign from office." He once more took up the standard and walked with it to the thrones. "Here it is," he said. "And one of you will have to do the job, because you won't find anyone else in the city who's fool enough to try."

There was another strong silence. Then Faber John said in a soft but deadly voice, "How would you and Jenny like to live in the Stone Age?"

"I wouldn't like it," said the Sempitern, "but I could bear it. So could Jenny. I would ask you to take charge of Jonathan—"

"No you wouldn't," said Jonathan. "I'll go with you. You're right."

Elio stood up too. "If that is your plan," he said, "I shall go with them also. They need my help. And Miss Vivian is a particular favorite of mine."

At this, Faber John put back his head and gave a great laugh. "Well," he said, "Time City has just about stood up to Vivian so far. We can always keep building it up again. What do you say, my Time Lady?"

She smiled too. "It's a risk, but I agree. How do you feel about it, Vivian?"

Vivian was pleased, but she felt sad, too. "I—I'd *love* it— but—but—I do miss Mum and Dad quite a lot."

"That might be arranged. You came from a war, and people do disappear in wars," Faber John said. He looked inquiringly at the Time Lady. She nodded. "Very well," he said to Vivian. "We can't do anything until the time locks open, but I'll tell you if it's possible when you come for your next lesson."

This, Vivian had not expected. "You're going to go on teaching me?"

"I never give up anything once I've started," said Faber John. "Once I persuade you to use your brain, you might even be a good pupil. Come to me with Jonathan in three days' time, in Seldom End as usual."